KATHERINE HEINY is thnd *Single, Carefree, Mellow* and h ed in the *New Yorker, Ploughsha* nd many other places. She lives i band and children.

Praise for *Early Morning Riser*:

'Gorgeous. Very, very funny, but so tender, so beautiful. I loved all the characters, I cared deeply'   MARIAN KEYES, author of *Grown Ups*

'Glorious. I love how it evokes the rhythm of life in all its joy and ordinariness and chaos. I loved the dialogue, the relationships. I love the one-liners, the humour, the gorgeous detail, the food, the innermost thoughts, and the love'

NINA STIBBE, author of *Reasons to Be Cheerful*

'Charming and tender, an offbeat and original gem that cracks your heart wide open'

PANDORA SYKES, author of *How Do We Know We're Doing It Right?*

'Wise, sad and barkingly funny. Katherine Heiny writes brilliantly about what we mean by the word 'family' and her novel is loving without being soppy and warm, without being cosy – I didn't want it to end'   LISSA EVANS, author of *V for Victory*

'Warm, witty, touching – and frequently hilarious'

DAVID NICHOLLS, author of *Sweet Sorrow*

'Heaven. Everything I have ever craved in a novel'

DAISY BUCHANNAN, author of *Insatiable*

ALSO BY KATHERINE HEINY

Single, Carefree, Mellow

Standard Deviation

Early Morning Riser

Katherine Heiny

4th ESTATE • London

4th Estate
An imprint of HarperCollins*Publishers*
1 London Bridge Street
London SE1 9GF

www.4thEstate.co.uk

HarperCollins*Publishers*
1st Floor, Watermarque Building, Ringsend Road
Dublin 4, Ireland

First published in Great Britain in 2021 by 4th Estate
First published in the United States by Alfred K. Knopf,
a division of Penguin Random House LLC, New York in 2021
This 4th Estate paperback edition published in 2022

1

Grateful acknowledgement is made to the following for permission to reprint previously
published material: Kobalt Music Publishing: excerpt from 'Gold in the Air', words and
music by Jesse Tyler Woods, copyright © 2013 by Songs from Defend. Administered by
Songs of Kobalt Music Publishing. All rights reserved. Reprinted by permission of Kobalt
Music Publishing. Warner Chappell Music Scandinavia AB: Excerpt from 'Tangerine', music
and lyrics by Klara Söderberg, copyright © Warner Chappell Music Scandinavia AB.
Reprinted by permission of Warner Chappell Music Scandinavia AB

Portions of this work originally appeared, in different form, as 'If You've All Done Like You
Said You'd Be' in the *Alaska Quarterly Review* (Fall/Winter 2014) and 'Sweet Violets'
in the *Southwest Review* (2015)

ISBN 978-0-00-839513-1

Set in Bulmer
Designed by Anna B. Knighton

Printed and bound in the UK using 100% renewable electricity at CPI Group (UK) Ltd

MIX
**Paper from
responsible sources**
FSC™ C007454

This book is produced from independently certified FSC™ paper
to ensure responsible forest management.

For more information visit: www.harpercollins.co.uk/green

For my father

I see gold in the air
And promises in our streams.
I see love in our hearts
And futures in our dreams.

—JESSE WOODS, "Gold in the Air"

I like it in the light, but the world is different
Than it was last night

—THE WEEPIES, "Early Morning Riser"

2002

JANE MET DUNCAN less than a month after she moved to Boyne City. She had locked herself out of her house and had had to ask a neighbor to call a locksmith. She was sitting on her front steps in the early twilight wearing her pajamas—she taught second grade and it was Pajama Day—when Duncan drove up in a rust-spotted white van.

"Whoa," he said when he saw her. "Exactly how long have you been waiting?"

He was in his early forties, with slightly shaggy auburn hair and a full moustache. His eyes were brown with amber flecks, and his features were so symmetrical that his face looked as though it could have been cut from a piece of paper folded in half. He was of medium height, medium build, wearing nothing more distinctive than jeans and a denim shirt, yet he seemed to stand out vividly, like the subject of a photo with a blurred background. To Jane he looked like the Brawny paper towel man, and no less handsome.

"Only about twenty minutes," she said. She stood up and gestured at her front door. "I'm afraid you may have to drill the lock out."

"Oh, I doubt that," Duncan said. "I bet we can find another way in. Folks always think their houses are totally safe because they have a couple locks on the front door, and then they call me and it turns out they've been sleeping with a bedroom window open for half a year. Let's take a walk around."

They circled the house slowly. It was a pretty little one-story house, white with black shutters. Duncan kept stopping to look in the flower beds. "It's also possible the previous owners left a key in a false rock or some such."

At the back of the house, Duncan pointed to the bathroom window. "Here's what I'm talking about. I could pop the screen off there and climb right in if the window's not locked."

"Okay," Jane said meekly.

He slid the end of a screwdriver under the edge of the screen, and it popped loose with alarming ease. Duncan caught it with one hand. "Not much crime around here," he said to Jane, "but last year Shirlene Talbot woke up to find a man making himself a ham sandwich in her kitchen. He was pretty harmless—turned out he was the Masseys' houseguest and was too drunk to remember which house they lived in. Still, I'd hate for that to happen to you."

He dragged Jane's garbage can over, climbed on top of it, and pushed the window open. He ducked inside, and a minute later, he opened the front door and called out to her.

Jane thanked him and asked him to stay for supper. She had never spontaneously invited a man to stay for supper before but she was grateful he hadn't charged her anything. Also, she hadn't had a real conversation with a man since she'd moved here, unless you counted the elderly man at Glen's Market who had asked her to help him find his car.

She was twenty-six years old, tall and slender, with dark blond hair that looked good in a ponytail, and she didn't need much makeup. That last part was fortunate because she rarely wore any. Her eyebrows and eyelashes were naturally dark despite the light color of her hair, and her pale blue eyes were almond-shaped, with slightly hooded lids that made eyeshadow pointless and hard to apply. (This had baffled Jane in her teen years when she followed step-by-step eyeshadow tutorials in magazines—wait, where was the crease of her eyelid? Why did she look exactly the same afterward?) She had a straight nose and a generous mouth. She was very pretty when she remembered to sit up straight, and pretty enough when she slouched.

During supper—Jane made an omelet and a salad—Duncan told her that he was really a woodworker and specialized in custom-made tables and chairs, but since someone wanted one of those only every once in a while, he also did antique furniture restoration and locksmithing, and that he'd grown up in a small town in the Upper Peninsula, and that he used to be married to a real estate agent named Aggie who could not tell the difference between a smallmouth and a largemouth bass. (Jane wasn't sure if that was just some descriptive detail about Aggie or Duncan's reason for divorcing her.)

"Where is Aggie now?" she asked.

"Where?" Duncan looked puzzled "This time of night, she's probably home over on Alice Street, I guess."

"Oh," Jane said. "I didn't realize she lived around here."

"Yeah, nice little house. I mow her lawn still."

Jane folded her napkin into smaller rectangles. "You must be very close."

"I don't know about *close*." Duncan took a bite of his omelet. "We're friendly enough, I guess, seeing as she up and left me for Gary Polnichik at State Farm, and they've been married almost ten years now."

"Why doesn't Gary mow the lawn?" Jane asked.

"He doesn't like it, and I don't mind," Duncan said. "Plus, he helps me with my taxes."

Duncan talked a lot. He told Jane that she should buy eggs from the farmers' market, and that she should never order the clam chowder at Robert's Restaurant, and that the dentist had a drinking problem but morning appointments were generally okay, and that Bradley Reed up on the corner had a tendency to watch folks with his binoculars if they left their window shades up, and that the olive burger at the Boyne River Inn couldn't be beat, and later he said, "I'm the luckiest man in Boyne City," as he pulled Jane's pajama pants off while she lay back on her sofa.

"But Boyne City is only about two hundred people!" Jane protested.

Duncan looked thoughtful. "Actually, more like three thousand."

"Still, you're supposed to say *in the universe*," she said.

"How about Northern Michigan?" Duncan ran his hands up the insides of her thighs. "Will that do? I'm the luckiest man in Northern Michigan."

That was on a Friday, and neither Jane nor Duncan left the house until Monday morning, when Jane had to go to school.

THIS WAS ONLY Jane's third year of teaching. You could say she was still getting the kinks out.

During her first two years of teaching—one in Grand Rapids, one in Battle Creek—she had made the first day of school as fun-filled and exciting as possible: extensive school tour, scavenger hunt, time capsule, extra recess, dance party, LEGOs, working with clay. The result had been that both Jane and her students were hollow-eyed and slack-jawed with fatigue by three thirty, and no one remembered where the bathroom was the next day anyway.

She had eventually realized that although second graders were officially entering the third year of schooling (more if they'd gone to preschool), they had clearly wiped all previous school experience from their hard drives over the summer. They had to relearn everything, like stroke patients: how to find their desks, how to form a line, how to walk quietly in the hall, how to keep their hands to themselves, how to grip a pencil, how to hold scissors safely, how to take off and put on their coats, how to flush the toilet—how to *aim* for the toilet, in some cases—and to wash their hands afterward.

They had to relearn the rhythm of the school day, too. Some children were still on a summer rock-star schedule and would arrive at school still half-asleep, only to become suddenly alert about ten in the morning and look around in a slightly startled fashion, as though their minds had just caught up with their bodies. Others for whom naps were a very recent memory (for instance, the day before school started) would grow wobbly-headed and slow-blinking right after lunch and remain that way for at least an hour. Always on the first day, at least three students would turn their heads to the clock at 3:25 and slowly count down the remaining seconds. (Probably more would have done it, but hardly any of them remembered how to tell time.)

This year, Jane had kept the first day of school extremely simple. The only writing materials were chubby three-sided pencils and soft dashed-line writing paper with one-inch lines. The bulletin boards were bare, and she'd turned most of the displays toward the wall or covered them with plain brown paper. (Her classroom looked like the background in a proof-of-life hostage photograph.) She put only plain wooden blocks in the toy chest, no cars or trucks, not the farm animals or the pretend grocery items. The art table was covered in butcher paper and only primary-color crayons were available for drawing. The Library Corner held only board books, nothing longer or more challenging or less familiar than *The Very Hungry Caterpillar*.

They had begun the day by making nametags (a boy named Tad Berman had raised his hand and asked Jane how to spell his own first name) and storing their gym shoes under their desks. They counted to one hundred by tens, and discussed "greater than" and "less than." They reviewed the days of the week and the months of the year. ("Just twelve of them?" Tad Berman asked. "Are you sure?") They read sight words that Jane printed one at a time on the whiteboard, and then Jane read *The Gruffalo* aloud. After lunch they made "All About Me" posters and sat in a circle to play Jingle Bell Pass, and by the end of the day, her students had emerged from the first day with some semblance of sanity and awareness.

The second day, she uncovered the bulletin boards and added wooden cylinders and triangles to the toy box. (A girl named Alicia Sweet had stared at one of the triangles, frowning, for at least thirty seconds before asking Jane what that shape was called.) Jane unrolled the Peter Rabbit rug in the Library Corner and put the Dr. Seuss books on the shelves. They measured lengths of string and practiced adding ten to any number. They discussed word families and phonetics.

On the third day, Jane turned all the displays so they faced the room and added glue and glitter and ribbon to the Art Table. She hung the "All About Me" posters on the walls and left work folders on everyone's desk. Tad Berman was able to identify her by name (two out of three times anyway), and Paul Blankenship, who was the first week's Attendance Messenger, was gone for only twenty minutes or so when he took the attendance sheet to the school office three doors down (the day before, it had taken him almost an hour). Jane passed out math workbooks and had the students open to the first page. The school year had begun.

And now, only three weeks later, Jane was suffering from such massive sleep deprivation after her weekend with Duncan that she had to show a video during Science while she sat at her desk, trying not to doze off in the darkened room. She showed videos during Health and Social Studies, too. At the end of the day, Kenny Rutledge said that was more screen time than he was allowed in a whole month and that he would need a note to take home to his mother.

JANE DID HAVE one friend in Boyne City, Freida Fitzgerald.

Jane and Freida had met at the teachers' ice cream social at the very beginning of the year (the fact that Jane went showed how desperate she was to meet people). The social was held in the high school media center, which meant everyone had to worry about tripping over electrical cords. Or everyone would have had to worry if anyone had come besides Jane and the other second-grade teacher, Mr. Robicheaux, and the school custodian, who said he was just waiting for everyone to go home so he could lock up.

An ice cream sundae bar had been set up on one of the printer tables: two cartons of vanilla ice cream, a can of Hershey's syrup, plastic cups of sprinkles and graham cracker crumbs, peanuts lying loose on the tabletop. It was possibly the most depressing sight Jane had ever seen. The only sign that the school had put any thought or effort into the event was that they'd hired live entertainment. A woman was playing a mandolin in the corner, plucking out "Man of Constant Sorrow" with deceptive ease.

The woman had a round, friendly face, and her hair was like a hundred brown notebook spirals—that thick, that dense. Each lock was a tightly coiled individual ringlet, yet Jane had the impression that the curls were all interlocked, that a comb could never be drawn through them. The mandolin player wore a striped cotton dress that flared across her wide, flat hips and showed lovely girlish legs without a single varicose vein. When she saw Mr. Robicheaux drink directly out of the Hershey's syrup container, she abruptly started a new song and sang out: *"I'll let you drink that can of lard, but when you throw up in the yard—"*

Jane laughed and went over to introduce herself. The woman turned out not to be hired entertainment after all, but the high school music teacher. She told Jane that her name was Freida Fitzgerald and suggested they leave the ice cream social and go to the Sportsman Bar instead, and they had been friends ever since.

The word—according to Boyne City in general, and Mr. Spriggs at the hardware store in particular—was that Freida had never been married, never been engaged, never had a boyfriend, never even been kissed. (Mr. Spriggs also told Jane that Freida couldn't be a lesbian, either, because she didn't own any cats.) Jane's own theory was that Freida was married to music, but she was still curious about these rumors. Surely someone as sweet and friendly as Freida didn't get all the way to thirty-eight without being kissed? Kissed and then some?

Every Thursday night, Jane and Freida went to the Sportsman and drank vodka martinis until Freida got out her mandolin and the Sportsman asked them to leave. On the Thursday after she met Duncan, Jane told Freida about him.

"Duncan Ryfield?" Freida asked immediately.

"Yes," Jane said, loving the sound of his name.

"Oh."

"Do you know him?"

"Oh, yes." Freida cleared her throat and then paused for a long moment. When she spoke again, her speech took on a slow, hiccupping rhythm. "He's very . . . nice. He's quite . . . kind. And extremely . . . social."

Jane narrowed her eyes. "But there's something you're not telling me?"

Freida sighed. "It's just that he's had an awful lot of girlfriends."

"Isn't that to be expected, though?" Jane asked. "He's forty-two, after all."

"I think he's had enough girlfriends for, like, a lot of forty-two-year-olds," Freida said. "Maybe even for a lot of eighty-four-year-olds."

Jane flipped rapidly through her mental files of the past few days. It *had* seemed to her that every woman they came in contact with had known Duncan by name. Waitresses and cashiers and shopkeepers and receptionists. She had thought it was just living in a small town.

"Are you saying he won't be monogamous?" she asked Freida.

Freida took a long sip of her martini, considering. "No, it's not that," she said at last. "Actually, some women have told me he makes a very good boyfriend. I mean, not Cathy Guthrie, she only says bad things about how he was always going over to his ex-wife's house to fix stuff, and Karen Vickers complains about the times he asked her to call customers and tell them their furniture wasn't ready. Most people, though, say he's just set on being single but doesn't like to sleep alone. Oh, but don't listen to me, Jane! What do I know? He really is very kind to Jimmy Jellico, the man who works in his shop. I don't think anyone else in Boyne City would have the patience."

Jane stirred her drink thoughtfully, and they moved on to other subjects.

This was not the night Jane got drunk enough to ask Freida if it was true she hadn't ever had sex with anyone, not even a drunk migrant worker, but Jane felt strongly that such a night was in her future. It was as inevitable as sunrise.

PEOPLE HAD WARNED Jane about how hard winters were in Northern Michigan, but she hadn't paid much attention. (It had been April when she interviewed; the air had smelled fresh and warm and full of promise.) And even now, as the days shortened rapidly and the trees shook their branches free of leaves, she scarcely paid attention. She was too busy.

Duncan slept at her house every night and drove her to school every morning in his rusty white furniture-delivery van. Jane kissed him good-bye and tumbled out the passenger side, laughing—half the time, her skirt would catch on a wire poking through the uphol-stery and the schoolyard would get a view of her long legs in black tights—and then she'd be on the sidewalk, waving after him.

She was getting to know her students. Tad Berman had turned out to be something of a math whiz, although he still didn't know the months of the year. Scott Stafford, who struggled with reading and writing and spelling—changing his answers so many times there were holes in the paper—lost all his awkwardness at recess and swung through the bars of the climbing structure like a boy made of molten steel. Sierra Sawicki permitted Mariah Visser to sit next to her during lunch, an act akin to Yitzhak Rabin shaking hands with Yasser Arafat. Jenna Leblanc, whose father was a veterinarian, correctly diagnosed Gregory Dorsey's hand, foot, and mouth disease.

Jane moved among them, smiling and serene, amazed that no one could see that her lips were slightly swollen from Duncan's kisses, that she functioned on five hours of sleep, that her sweet and generous nature sprang from her own happiness.

Afternoon would come, and Duncan would be waiting in his van at the curb. She ran out of her classroom in a hurry, always trailing a scarf or a cardigan sleeve, and climbed in beside him.

Hard winter? Who could worry about such a thing?

JANE HAD FALLEN IN LOVE with the thrift store. Of course, it wasn't perfect—love never is—and you had to close your eyes to the dusty baby bottles and the used Tupperware and the awful paperbacks swollen from someone else's trip to the beach. But Jane loved the other things—the intricate dessert glasses and chunky cookie jars and patchwork quilts and out-of-date leather jackets and sweatshirts so soft and faded that looking at them made you crave sherbet.

She took Duncan to the thrift store because it seemed like a place he would like, full of potential. But Duncan spent the whole time sitting on a flea-ridden chair near the front of the store, talking to the man behind the cash register about spin fishing, and paging through a big cardboard box of *Playboy*s dating back at least fifteen years. The *Playboy*s weren't for sale, they were just there to be looked at—it was another thing you had to close your eyes to.

"I don't understand the purpose of all those *Playboy*s," Jane said when they were back on the street.

"What's not to understand?" Duncan asked.

"Well, isn't it something you like to look at alone, in your bedroom, with the curtains shut, at midnight?" she asked. "Not out in public at the thrift store?"

"Oh, either way is pretty nice," Duncan said, and took her hand.

NOW THAT JANE had a boyfriend, she wanted to have a dinner party. She imagined that she would wear something vintage—velvet lounging pajamas if she could find them—and later everyone would say, *That Jane is such a good match for Duncan, so poised and sophisticated.* She would serve pot roast with carrots and mashed potatoes, and later everyone would say, *Such a simple meal, but Jane made it seem so elegant.* She would light dozens of votive candles and drape red scarves over the lamps so the house would have a warm, cozy atmosphere, and later everyone would say, *Jane was glowing and has the loveliest home.* It did eventually occur to her that the only part of the dinner party she was looking forward to was one that happened after everyone had gone home, and that she wouldn't, in fact, be around for it, but by then the invitations had gone out.

In addition to Duncan, she invited Freida, the Marshalls from next door, and her ophthalmologist, Dr. Elgin, and his wife, who lived in Petoskey. She also told Duncan to invite Jimmy Jellico—the man who helped him out at his workshop.

Duncan was the first person to arrive, having been there since the night before. He put out the chips and dip and a bowl of nuts in the living room while Jane made Bellinis in the kitchen. She wanted to serve her own signature cocktail so that later everyone would say—would say—well, they'd say something Jane could no longer remember wanting them to say as she struggled to puree canned peaches without spattering juice all over her outfit. She had been unable to find lounging pajamas. Instead, she wore a lace blouse and a long patchwork skirt from the thrift store. Duncan had told her she looked like a pretty farmer, which wasn't quite what she'd had in mind.

The Marshalls were the first to arrive—Jane actually heard them leave their own house next door a moment before they rang the bell. They were a look-alike couple in their late forties, both with short brown gray-flecked hair and eyeglasses.

Almost as soon as they were seated, with Bellinis in hand, Mr. Marshall said to Jane, "I see you bought new patio furniture."

"Yes," Jane said, smiling, "I—"

"And a new coffee table." His look was easy to read: she was spending too much.

"I got them both from the thrift store," Jane said uncomfortably. "I buy basically everything at the thrift store now."

Mr. Marshall looked startled. "What? Even underwear?"

"No," Jane said. "But I did buy sheets there, so I suppose I'm only one step away from buying underwear."

"Me, I buy underwear new." Mr. Marshall turned to his wife. "Imagine buying used underwear."

Mrs. Marshall seemed more interested in talking to Duncan. "Might I inquire as to when you're planning to refinish my dining room chairs?" she asked him. "You've had six of them for four months now."

"I've had *four* of them for *six* months—that would be an accurate statement," Duncan said, leaning forward from his place on the couch for more onion dip.

"Well, see, you've had them for so long I've forgotten how many

I even had," Mrs. Marshall said, and Duncan gave an admiring grunt, the kind of sound he made when someone sank a free throw during a basketball game.

The doorbell rang again, and Jane leapt from her chair so eagerly that she nearly tripped on the hem of her long skirt.

It was Freida, her mandolin bag over her shoulder, and she had brought Jimmy Jellico.

Jimmy was a slight young man with rumpled brown hair and a faintly clumsy gait. He looked to be about twenty, although Jane knew from Duncan that he was in his late thirties. He had been described to Jane by various people as "slow learning," and she could see immediately what they meant. His expression was slightly vacant, even when he was smiling. She doubted that he was significantly intellectually disabled—more likely he had an IQ below eighty, and growing up in such a small town, he hadn't received the early intervention that might have helped him compensate. He was fresh-faced and lightly freckled, and the skin between his eyebrows was utterly smooth, as though he'd never had a worried thought in his life. He came close to being handsome, but he lacked the intellectual maturity that would have made him attractively boyish; he had stalled out at sweetly childish instead.

She shook Jimmy's hand, and gave Freida a hug, and then Dr. Elgin and his wife arrived. Dr. Elgin was talkative and outgoing—which was why Jane had invited him—but his wife had the politely bewildered air of someone who has not quite figured out the evening's agenda. Jane introduced everyone and excused herself to the kitchen to make fresh Bellinis.

She carried the tray of drinks into the living room just as Dr. Elgin said, "Jane, I believe your lamp is about to catch on fire."

Jane had to set down the tray in a hurry and rush over to yank the red silk scarf off the table lamp where it was, indeed, beginning to smolder. She opened the windows so the smoke detector wouldn't go off and fanned the air with the scarf. "Please go ahead and enjoy your drinks," she said to her guests, and tried to throw the ruined scarf out the window without anyone noticing.

She turned back to the room just as Jimmy gave a startled yelp. She had put cute little candy-striped glass cocktail stirrers in everyone's drinks, and Jimmy had thought they were real candy canes and bitten his in half.

"Goodness, I feel dreadful," Jane said to everyone while Jimmy was in the bathroom, spitting out blood and shards of glass. "Should we take him to the ER?"

"Oh, he'll be fine," Duncan assured her. "He didn't go to the ER that time he accidentally locked himself in the finishing room and inhaled varnish fumes all night."

That didn't seem like the soundest piece of logic to Jane, but Jimmy came back into the room at that moment and said, "I'm okay, really, Jane. I'll just keep this napkin in there to stop the bleeding."

So Jimmy spent the rest of the evening with a white cloth napkin poking out of his mouth, and looked vaguely like a trout.

The pot roast was delicious, but the platter Jane served the carrots on was slightly too small and every time someone picked it up carrots rolled all over the place. The mashed potatoes were too thick and people had trouble even getting the serving spoon out of the dish. She had made raisin bread rolls but evidently she hadn't mixed the dough thoroughly enough and some of the rolls had only two raisins, giving them the disturbing appearance of staring mice.

It had seemed even before dinner that Mrs. Elgin had wanted to say something, and finally she laid down her fork and said to Duncan, "I'm sorry, but how is it possible that you don't remember having sex with me after a Grateful Dead concert in nineteen ninety-four?"

Dr. Elgin was struggling to open a bottle of prosecco, and at that moment his thumb slipped and the cork popped off with a surprised-sounding *ping.*

Duncan looked up from his plate. "I went to thirteen Grateful Dead concerts in nineteen ninety-four. Can you be more specific?"

There was a little pause, and then Mr. Marshall commented that you can always tell the economy is bad when people serve pot roast at dinner parties. Mrs. Marshall told Dr. Elgin about her mother's cataract surgery. Jimmy choked on his napkin.

By the time Freida drank another two glasses of prosecco and got out her mandolin and made everyone sing "I'm Gonna Eat at the Welcome Table," Jane was actually grateful.

JANE AND DUNCAN were sitting in Duncan's van outside Kilwins ice cream store one day the next week when a large woman knocked on the driver's-side window. Duncan rolled it down, and the woman said, "I believe your left taillight is broken."

"I know that," Duncan replied, unperturbed. "I let Jimmy back the van around the lumberyard."

"Oh, for heaven's sake," said the woman, as though anyone with any sense would know better than to let Jimmy drive anywhere. (Which was sort of true, Jane supposed.)

The woman glanced across at Jane, and it seemed her look was disapproving. Jane was eating a chocolate ice cream cone, and she felt like a child who'd knowingly gotten into the van of a pedophile.

"You could get a ticket driving around like that," the woman said to Duncan.

Duncan sighed and rubbed the back of his neck. "I'll take care of it, Aggie."

Aggie! This was Aggie! Jane looked more closely at the woman and saw that it wasn't accurate to say she was large. She had a wide face, which automatically made you assume she had a wide body, too, but in fact, her figure was exceptional, lush and buxom, and even more distressing, she had a hearty, healthy, milkmaid sexiness about her. Her hair was pale and wavy and pulled back casually, and the neckline of her peasant blouse showed a good deal of creamy-skinned cleavage.

"Perhaps you could introduce me to your friend, Duncan," Aggie said pointedly.

"Aggie, this is Jane," Duncan said. "Jane, this is Aggie."

"Hello," Jane said.

"Hello." Aggie shaded her eyes. "You must be the girl who bought the Kellers' place."

Jane nodded. "Yes—"

"It's such a shame they got divorced and moved downstate," Aggie said.

"I didn't actually know them." Jane fought the urge to sink lower in her seat. "I only bought their house."

Aggie made a noncommittal sound. Jane remembered then that Aggie was a real estate agent, and she wondered if that accounted for her piercing, evaluating look—all that assessing of people and their houses.

"Is there something else we can help you with, Aggie?" Duncan asked.

Aggie looked away from Jane and said to Duncan, "It seems the motor on our leaf blower has frozen up, and I wondered if you could come take a look at it."

"Have you been running it on straight gasoline?" Duncan asked. "Because you're supposed to use a gas-and-oil mixture. Have Gary check the spark plugs."

Aggie frowned. "You know Gary doesn't hold with leaf blowers."

What did that mean? That Gary didn't approve of leaf blowers, or didn't believe in them, or somehow didn't get along with them?

Jane wanted to ask, but her ice cream cone was melting, so she had to keep licking it. She felt like a dog drinking from a water bowl while its owners talked over her head.

"I can stop by your place on Tuesday, I guess," Duncan said. "Now, you better get back to Gary before he gets any more horizontal over there."

They all glanced toward the sidewalk, where a man sitting on a bench was indeed getting more horizontal by the minute—his legs were stretched out before him, and he'd slumped down until his head rested against the back of the bench. He was a thin, balding man with a slightly concave chest. Jane could only stare in disbelief: Aggie had left Duncan for *him*?

Aggie made an annoyed sound and marched off toward the bench.

Jane bit a chunk off her cone. "So that was Aggie."

"Yup," Duncan said. Then he added unnecessarily, "She has some control issues."

"I think she's still in love with you," Jane said. She could not have explained why she said that, why she half thought it. Except that maybe Aggie wasn't the only one with sharp instincts.

Duncan shook his head. "Oh, no. The last time we slept together was at least five or six years ago."

"The last time?" Jane stared at him. "You mean you've slept with Aggie since she remarried?"

Duncan looked uncomfortable. "Yes, but it didn't mean anything."

"It always means something," Jane said. And that was true. It might not mean the same thing to both people, but it always meant something.

"We don't do it anymore," Duncan said. "Now I really do just mow the lawn when I go over there."

Jane knew it shouldn't matter—it was history now. It had all happened before Jane had met Duncan, before she had even moved to town. But still her heart felt like a sponge you find forgotten under the sink: wrinkled and stiff and squeezed dry.

"Your ice cream cone is melting all over your hand," Duncan said gently.

IN MID-NOVEMBER, Jane had parent-teacher conferences, and even though most of the parents of her students were concerned and loving and valued education, she was still anxious. All parents want to hear good things about their children, but sometimes you had to say bad things. If you said the bad things too subtly, the parents didn't believe you. If you said the bad things too baldly, the parents got upset. Actually, they often didn't believe you anyway and then they got upset, too. It was like having an intervention for an alcoholic every twenty minutes for an entire working day.

Duncan spent the whole of that day at school with Jane. Oh, Jane knew that he talked a little fly-fishing with the assistant principal, and that he tortured Freida by calling and pretending to be someone interested in private mandolin lessons, but mainly he was there for her.

He came to Jane's classroom between every conference and massaged her shoulders. For lunch he brought her a sandwich with sliced turkey two inches thick, and a bunch of daisies. He fixed the squeak on her swivel chair, and reattached the whiteboard tray to the wall, and stood on Jane's desk and used the pointer to retrieve a banana from on top of the fluorescent lights where someone had thrown it.

Another stressful element of parent-teacher conferences was that sometimes Jane got a little insight into her students' lives that she'd rather not have.

Like when Crystal Orr's father asked what grade this was, and when Jane told him second grade, he said, "Wow, Crystal's in second already?"

Or when Seth Dorsey's mother asked what would happen if, hypothetically, a parent did a student's math homework. Jane told her that parents who did their children's homework were preventing their children from learning. "What would happen, though?" Seth's mother asked. Jane said if it became a regular thing, she would have to involve the principal. "What if you couldn't *prove* it, though?" Seth's mother continued. "What if the child denied it?"

Lindsey Mercado's father told Jane that Lindsey had told him that the moonlight is actually reflected sunlight and wanted to know why Jane was spreading falsehoods.

Brianna Wooten's mother let the class hamster out of its cage without asking and spent almost the entire conference dashing around the classroom calling, "Cuthbert! Cuthbert! I need you to listen!" Jane had only a minute there at the end to tell her that she thought Brianna might have some attention deficit issues.

And Kenny Parish's father told her indignantly that Kenny could *definitely* read at a second-grade level because he could tell the difference between Foster's Lager and Foster's Special Bitter when asked to fetch one from the fridge.

After the last conference, Duncan brought Jane her own beer from a cooler in his van and held her feet on his lap and gave her a foot rub—massaging her insteps with hard, smooth strokes. It was actually better than sex, in a way, because really, how often do you sit around thinking, *I'm so tired, I wish someone would have sex with me*?

"All the time," Duncan said when she told him this. "I literally think that all the time."

And so they did that, too, right there in the classroom, with the door shut and the lights off. For weeks after, Jane felt horribly guilty whenever she looked at the Peter Rabbit rug.

JANE HAD HOPED that Duncan would want to spend Thanksgiving alone with her—a romantic long weekend by the fire. But he told her that he always spent Thanksgiving in the Upper Peninsula at a friend's cabin, fall fishing for steelhead.

(It seemed to Jane that people who lived downstate had cabins in Northern Michigan, and people who lived in Northern Michigan had cabins in the Upper Peninsula, but where did people who lived in the Upper Peninsula have cabins? Canada? And where did *Canadian* people have cabins? At what point did there cease to be an appeal in going north and people gave up and bought time-shares in Florida?)

So Jane drove down to Grand Rapids to spend Thanksgiving with her mother. Her mother worked as a receptionist in a dental office, and they always had Thanksgiving dinner with the dentist and his family. Every year, Dr. Wimberly told Jane that her mother kept his practice afloat singlehandedly. Jane had no doubt that was true.

Her mother was a stout woman with a slight bullfrog neck, a broad, leonine face, and an imposing manner. Jane took after her father—he'd had the blondness and the slighter build. Her mother had darker hair and darker eyes. She wore her bifocals on a chain around her neck, and when she put them on and tilted her head back to examine you, you knew she was going to find you wanting, and you weren't wrong. Jane had heard her mother on the phone, confirming dental appointments: "We expect to see you tomorrow at nine, regardless of the weather." "You're not going to waste our time like you did last week, are you?" "I do hope you'll manage to be prompt and not inconvenience everyone."

It was even worse in the dentist's waiting room, where Jane had spent many afternoons as a child, coloring or reading. "Put the magazines back on the rack when you're done reading them," her mother would say sternly to patients, "and don't go taking one just because it has a recipe you fancy trying." And, "If you've brushed and flossed like you're supposed to, I'm sure you have nothing to worry about."

You would think patients would leave the practice in droves, but maybe they were afraid Jane's mother would hunt them down. Dr. Wimberly either didn't know or didn't care about her mother's scare tactics. He always got emotional on Thanksgiving, patting her mother's arm and saying, "I would be lost without Phyllis, completely lost."

"Nonsense," Jane's mother would say, looking pleased.

This year, Jane suspected Dr. Wimberly had had some predinner drinks because he gave her a hug that was at least thirty seconds too long. "Jane, little Jane!" he said. "Look at you, so grown up! Phyllis tells me you love it up north."

"Yes, I do," Jane said, retreating a step.

"Phyllis also says you have a boyfriend," Dr. Wimberly continued. "Some sort of day laborer? Or is he a tinker?"

Jane gave her mother an annoyed look. "He's a woodworker," she said to Dr. Wimberly.

"Ah!" Dr. Wimberly smiled condescendingly, as though Jane had just told him that Duncan was a bard, or maybe president. "Are you two serious?"

"Yes, very," Jane said firmly. (Dr. Wimberly was looking like he might start hugging her again.)

"Not serious enough for him to come here for Thanksgiving," her mother said to no one in particular.

On Saturday, Jane drove back up to her house. She hadn't heard from Duncan because the fishing cabin had no phone and neither Jane nor Duncan had cell phones. (No one in Boyne City did—the reception was almost nonexistent because Boyne City rested in a slight hollow. The only person Jane knew who had a cell phone was Dr. Haven, the local family doctor, and he had to hike up Avalanche Mountain on Sunday nights to check his messages.)

She drove past Duncan's apartment on her way into town, hoping that maybe he, too, had returned early, but it was dark and shuttered-looking.

Yet there was his van in Jane's driveway, and there was Duncan sitting on her front porch steps. He was wearing a denim jacket with a shearling collar that shone faintly in the darkness.

She parked her car and got out, carrying her overnight bag. "Oh, hey," she said softly. "What are you doing here?"

"I called your mother and she said you'd left a couple hours ago, so I thought I'd come see you."

Jane stood for a moment, her bag bouncing lightly against her legs. "Weren't the fish biting?" she asked.

"They were biting," Duncan said. "I just missed you."

The moon glowed (with reflected sunlight, remember) through the bare trees like a heavy silver ball resting on elegant black fingers, and Jane thought she had never seen anything so beautiful.

THE FIRST SNOW came in early December. Jane awoke to the rumble of machinery and peeked out her window to see Duncan clearing her driveway with a snowblower. The world was soft and white and crystalline; the red of the snowblower and the green of Duncan's jacket were the only splashes of color.

It snowed again the next week, and twice more before Christmas. Each time, Jane could stay in bed, secure and cozy and cared for, knowing that Duncan or Jimmy would come to clear her driveway and sidewalk before she had to leave for work. Of course, she knew that one of them was also over clearing Aggie's driveway because

Gary was apparently not in harmony with snowblowers either. Actually, it might have been more than just Jane's and Aggie's driveways. Maybe Duncan did the driveways of *all* his former lovers, though Jane didn't suppose he had that much time.

If Duncan cleared her drive, he would let himself in quietly afterward and get in bed with Jane, pulling up her nightshirt, his body warm from exercise, only the tips of his fingers cold on her spine. (If Jimmy cleared the drive, that part didn't happen.)

JANE BOUGHT a too-short tuxedo jacket at the thrift store and trimmed it with a three-inch ribbon of satin and added white silk piping to the pockets and lapels. She was not much of a tailor, and all this took her many days, and she wound up with bruised fingers and a tuxedo jacket that looked almost exactly like one she'd bought at a Detroit flea market two years earlier, only not as nice.

When she showed it to Duncan, he stroked his moustache for a full minute. "Winters are long here," he said. "That's a fact."

CHRISTMAS CAME, as it always does, bringing a rising anxiety about gift giving and gift receiving. Always there's the worry that you will undergift someone who will overgift you, or that you will give a gift to someone who looks at you blankly in return, or that you will receive an unexpected gift that requires the impromptu gifting of one of your own (hastily wrapped and sometimes beloved) possessions in return. Jane also lived with the fear that a student's family would give her some horribly intimate gift—like a nightgown or massage oil—and she would have to write a thank-you note for it, or that Duncan would give her a horribly nonintimate gift—like a wastebasket—and she would have to pretend to love it. The run-up to Christmas was sort of like the Cuban Missile Crisis in terms of escalating tension.

But in the end it was okay. Jane's students gave her small, thoughtful, easily thankable gifts: gift cards and coffee mugs and scented candles. Jane gave Freida a Bob Dylan biography, and Freida gave Jane a CD of Christmas carols she'd recorded herself. Jane gave Duncan a blue button-down shirt made of Egyptian cotton. It had thin amber stripes that exactly matched his eyes, and the cloth was as soft as water. Duncan gave Jane a delicate silver necklace with a leaf-shaped pendant. It would have made Jane completely happy except that she'd seen an identical necklace on one of Duncan's former girlfriends—a waitress at Robert's Restaurant—and it brought to mind the image of Duncan having bought these necklaces in bulk years ago. But it made her mostly happy even so.

IN JANUARY, Freida invited Jane to play in her all-female jug band, who called themselves the Jug Bandits.

"It's a good way to meet people," Freida said. "The other players are all very nice. Well, mostly. Monica Daniels won't shake hands with anyone because she says it stresses her bowing hand. I know all violists think they're bullied, but sometimes it almost seems called for."

Jane didn't want to say that now that she'd met Duncan, she had no interest in meeting anyone else, so she agreed.

The Jug Bandits had gotten their first paying gig—the Association of Women Radiologists had hired them to play at their annual meeting at the library—and Jane wore a black pantsuit with a thin black velvet ribbon tied around her neck. (Some of her thrift-store outfits were more successful than others; she looked vaguely like an undertaker in this one.)

Jane didn't experience anything you might call a performer's high, but it wasn't so bad, beating on a saucepan with a pair of wooden spoons while Freida played the mandolin and the band worked their way through "Happy Feet" and a number of other songs made famous by the Muppets. Freida wore a fringed leather headband that made looking at or speaking to her very difficult, and the band outnumbered the audience, but otherwise it was a good night.

Duncan was one of the five audience members, which made Jane happy, and the assistant children's librarian went home with the band's washtub player afterward, so it might have been a night of sexual awakening.

"Not unless there've been big changes," Duncan said on the walk back to Jane's house. "Because I slept with both of them, back in the early nineties."

"At the same time?" Jane asked. Her face was flushed, and the cold painted her cheeks in a way that made her feel every brush stroke.

"No, a couple of years apart," he said.

"Is there anyone in Boyne City you haven't had sex with?" she asked irritably.

"Oh, sure," Duncan said. "Freida Fitzgerald, for one."

JANE AND DUNCAN were invited over for dinner at Aggie and Gary's.

"Aggie said she wants to get to know you better," Duncan told her, and Jane felt a little thrill of competition. She wore jeans and a T-shirt, so it wouldn't seem she was trying too hard, with her new tuxedo jacket, so she would seem stylish and unique, under a vintage embroidered beige dress coat that was sure to be prettier than any coat Aggie owned. The coat was also far too thin for the fifteen-degree weather, and Jane hopped lightly from foot to foot as she stood shivering on Aggie's front porch. Duncan, carrying a bottle of merlot, rang the doorbell.

Inside they heard Aggie say, "Who do you suppose is at the door?" and Gary say, "No idea. Are you expecting someone?"

Jane rolled her eyes at Duncan.

He looked thoughtful. "Could be she meant *next* Friday."

Just then Aggie opened the door. "Oh, for heaven's sake," she said. She was wearing a denim skirt and pink ruffled blouse, and as always, her milk-fed, creamy-skinned appearance made Jane feel like a gym teacher, or maybe a greyhound.

"Hi there, Aggie," Duncan said, as if everything were going according to plan. "Thank you so much for inviting us over."

"Honestly." Aggie shook her head. "You are just hopeless."

Duncan walked past her into the house, and Jane trailed along timidly. "Sorry if I might have gotten the day wrong," he said, "but we're here now. Hey, Gary. How are you?"

"Okay, I guess," Gary said slowly. He was sprawled on the couch in front of the TV wearing a gray sweat suit. Jane sent up a brief prayer of thanks that he wasn't wearing just his underpants.

"Gary, this is Jane." Duncan gestured vaguely. "Jane, this is Gary."

"It's nice to meet you," Jane said formally.

Gary squinted at her through his bifocals. "What's your opinion of three-way lightbulbs?"

"Three-way lightbulbs?" Jane blinked. "Um, I think they're okay."

Gary frowned. "You're saying you're fine with having to make a *decision* every time you turn on a lamp?"

"Duncan, I don't have a thing for dinner," Aggie interrupted. "We were going to have sandwiches."

"They're not open-faced sandwiches, are they?" Gary asked.

"No, dear," Aggie said.

"I don't like open-faced sandwiches," Gary said to Jane. "Too much like toast."

"Well, luckily, Jane and I like any kind of sandwich." Duncan held up the bottle of merlot. "Shall I open the wine?"

Apparently they were staying. Aggie took Jane's coat, saying, "Aren't you terribly cold in such a thin wrap?"

"No, not at all," Jane said, trying to keep her teeth from chattering.

The worst part of the evening was not that the sandwiches— grilled tomato, chèvre, and thyme on baguettes—were easily the best sandwiches Jane had ever eaten, or the fact that Aggie served *homemade* potato chips to "round out" the meal, or that she "happened" to have made apple dumplings the day before, so dessert was taken care of. (Fucking show-off.) The worst part was that it began to feel to Jane like a blind double date where she and Gary were struggling and Duncan and Aggie were hitting it off.

Jane had tried several times to speak to Gary, asking him how he liked working at State Farm and how long he'd lived in Boyne City, but he had ignored her, watching the news over her shoulder.

She tried to talk to Duncan and Aggie, but they were talking to each other.

"Did you hear Clive and Michelle Parsons are getting divorced?" Aggie asked.

Duncan speared a potato chip with his fork. "Is it because of Clive sleeping with that woman who runs the produce stand in Mancelona?"

"You knew about that?" Aggie said, looking startled.

Duncan shrugged. "Everybody knew about it but Michelle, and I guess she found out."

Aggie sighed. "It seems like everyone we know is divorced. I think it's so sad, like a decline in civilized living."

"You didn't think it was so sad when you divorced me," Duncan said. "Back then you said it was the smartest thing you ever did."

"Did I say that?" Aggie looked fondly nostalgic.

"Many, many times," Duncan said without rancor. "And you've been saying for *years* that the way shops put a tip jar by the cash registers is the cause of decline in civilized living, not divorce."

Their conversation was like the apple dumplings, perfectly crimped around the edges and sealed off. Jane couldn't get in.

"What is an Alsatian?" Gary asked her abruptly.

Jane was pleased he was at least trying. "Well," she said, thinking, "it's kind of like a German shepherd—"

Gary interrupted, "Who is Jules Verne?"

Jane could see a blue screen reflected in Gary's glasses. Understanding came to her like a sip of ice water: *Jeopardy!* was on mute on the television behind her.

At seven thirty, Gary leapt to his feet and there was a mad scrabbling around for the TV remote because apparently he strongly disapproved of *Wheel of Fortune,* which was on next. Once he'd turned off the TV, it seemed like time for Duncan and Jane to go.

"Thanks, Aggie," Duncan said on their way out. "I'll come over and fix that toaster oven for you later this week."

Jane smiled and waved as she shivered in her embroidered coat. She was suddenly cheerful again as she took Duncan's hand. Let Aggie have her moment with Duncan, let Aggie have her memories, let Aggie have her toaster oven fixed. Who was Duncan going home with? Jane—that's who.

"WELL, he wasn't *drunk,* particularly," Freida said thoughtfully, stirring her drink. "And he wasn't a migrant worker, though he was in town for the Cherry Festival. And when I woke up the next morning, he'd up and left with my best tuning whistle."

And that was February, pretty much.

———

WINTERS WERE LONG HERE. It was a fact.

IN MARCH, Duncan called Jane and said, "We have a crisis."

"What?" Jane asked happily. If you were having a joint crisis, it must mean you were also having a relationship.

"Aggie's pipes froze and her house is flooded."

"Oh," said Jane.

"She and Gary went to Livonia for four days, and their heat went out, and Gary hadn't even thought to leave the tap dripping," Duncan continued. "So along comes that cold spell last week, and the pipes froze and the waterline burst above their bedroom and soaked everything all the way down to the kitchen. They might have mildew in the drywall."

This seemed to call for some sort of response, so Jane said, "Goodness."

"They have to move out for at least a week," Duncan said, "and they can't stay at a hotel because hotel heating is bad for Aggie's sinuses."

This was a crisis? Jane wanted to laugh. She dealt with crises greater than this every day. A true crisis was when all the second-grade girls except Mariah Visser clustered under the slide on the playground, whispering, and Mariah sat on a swing and pushed herself back and forth with the tip of one white sneaker.

"Aggie and Gary can stay here," she said. "And I'll stay with you."

JANE STOOD at the door on the morning Aggie moved in, striving for an expression of warm and loving welcome, but the first thing

Aggie did was gesture at the bowl of dried flowers on the kitchen table and say, "I believe that's my soup tureen."

"No, it's mine," Jane said. "I bought it at the thrift store."

"I'm sure you did." Aggie put her hands on her hips. "But it used to be mine. Duncan and I got it as a wedding present from the Mitfords. I recognize the chip on the handle. How much did you pay for it?"

"Ninety-nine cents," said Jane. (It had actually been twelve dollars.)

"Now, wait a minute," Duncan interrupted calmly. "Who are the Mitfords and what's a soup tureen? How's it different from a bowl?"

"Oh, for heaven's sake," Aggie said. "The Mitfords are my *godparents*. You only went over to their house for Sunday dinner a hundred times."

Duncan looked thoughtful. "Are they the people with the Doberman who tried to attack you when you wore the coat with the squirrel-fur collar?"

"No, that was the Masons," Aggie said. Her eyes were flickering over the soup tureen and over Duncan, who was examining it. She looked proprietary of both.

"Why did you give our wedding present to the thrift store?" Duncan asked.

"Well, the chip on the handle." Aggie shrugged. "Besides, Gary doesn't really approve of soup."

Jane excused herself and went to get her overnight bag from the bedroom. The overnight bag was from the thrift store, too, but suddenly the leather looked old and scuffed, not classic and well loved, as she had previously thought. Of course, that was the bad thing about the thrift store. You knew everything was there for a reason, like a chipped handle. You brought other people's things home— soup tureens, suitcases, husbands—and tried to love them as best you could, but it didn't always work.

LIVING IN DUNCAN'S APARTMENT was a lot like living in Duncan's furniture repair van: a small rectangular space, smelling strongly of paint thinner, and filled with dust and wooden spindles and empty beer cans. Really the only difference was that Jimmy had a key to the apartment, and twice he walked in while Jane and Duncan were having sex.

The first time, Jimmy merely grabbed a putty knife and then stepped tactfully back out. The second time, he and Duncan had a short conversation about someone's grandma's chifforobe.

"Christ." Duncan spoke to Jimmy over his shoulder. "Is it that woman from Boyne Falls?"

"Sure is." Jimmy nodded. "Said she's coming in today to see how much progress you've made."

"Well, put the chifforobe in the middle of the workroom and scatter some sawdust around it," Duncan said. "I'll be there soon."

"Okay," Jimmy said cheerfully.

Duncan turned back to Jane, who lay beneath him, and said, "Sorry about that," in exactly the same way the teller at the bank said it when the line was longer than two people.

Duncan had a single bed (Jane suspected it was to discourage women from sleeping over), and every night, Jane slept with her bare shoulder blades pressed up against the wall like a child's hands against a pane of glass.

During the ten days she lived there, she had a constant low-level headache from the varnish fumes, she stubbed her toe repeatedly on a piece of cast-iron fence propped behind the bathroom door, and she discovered there wasn't a single article—not one!—that she wanted to read in *Field & Stream*. She had never been so happy.

JANE HAD INVITED her mother to visit the last weekend in April, or rather, Jane's mother had invited herself.

"Dr. Wimberly is renovating the office, so I have a long weekend," she told Jane on the phone. "Thought I'd come on up and have a look-see at your house and this Duncan I've heard so much about."

Jane was nervous about her mother meeting Duncan—conversations with her mother were often thorny and barbed.

But Duncan wasn't nervous. "Oh, it'll be fine," he said. "I've met more women's parents than you've had hot dinners. She'll like me."

Of course, that made sense. Meeting your lover's parents got easier the more you did it, just like tying your shoes or boiling an egg or looking interested when people talked about their pets. It was just that you didn't necessarily want your lover to have had all that practice.

But apparently if you were good with women—and certainly Duncan was good with women, the way other people are good with cars or numbers—you were good with *all* women. Seeming to sense that Jane's mother would be suspicious of a compliment on her appearance, Duncan complimented her instead on her Ford Fiesta and her wisdom in buying an American-made car. He debated the weather with her politely before agreeing that a heat index was nothing more than a meaningless number manufactured by the Weather Channel—it was as though he knew she wouldn't respect someone who agreed with her right away. When Jane's mother told a very pointed story about a handyman who had overcharged her, Duncan replied that Jane didn't need a handyman—that she could change the batteries in a smoke detector faster than a mongoose could kill a snake—and it just went to show how well she'd been raised.

On the way out to dinner, her mother held on to Duncan's arm and looked up at him with a shiny sort of expression that Jane had never seen before.

On the second night of Jane's mother's visit, Freida invited them all over to her house for a combination barbecue and recital. Jane wore a dark green maxi dress with yellow and maroon flowers—her mother said it made her think of three-bean salad, the kind with garbanzos—and Duncan escorted both of them over to Freida's.

Freida lived in a tiny brick house, almost anonymous until you got inside and saw the baby grand piano sitting proudly in the middle of the living room and glimpsed the lush and shady backyard with its tall oaks. Jane and Duncan and her mother let themselves in the front door and walked through the house to the backyard. Freida crossed the grass to greet them. She was wearing black pants and a white blouse with neck ruffles and looked oddly like Mozart.

Jane introduced her mother, and Freida pointed out the teenage students who would be performing—two boys and three girls— and their parents. It was warm for April and most people were in shirtsleeves.

Aggie was there, Jane saw, and so was Gary, looking bewildered. Jane introduced her mother to both of them.

"It's a pleasure to meet you, Phyllis. We've been getting to know Jane quite well," Aggie said, in the way people say they've finally caught up on their ironing. "How was your drive up from Grand Rapids?"

"I ran into terrible roadwork outside Cadillac." Jane's mother shook her head. "I honestly think road construction should be outlawed for all but two weeks of the year."

"That's exactly how I feel about carrot peelers," Gary said so unexpectedly that Jane spilled a little wine down the front of her dress.

"Duncan," Aggie said, her eyes taking on a slight possessive sheen, "it looks like you and I will have to be in charge of barbecuing. I believe Freida thinks the food is going to cook itself."

Jane glanced over and saw that Freida had a grill set up, and the table next to it was stacked with hamburgers and sausages still in the supermarket packs and with unopened plastic bins of coleslaw and potato salad. A new-looking bag of charcoal was propped against the grill, which looked almost new itself.

"We're going to have to thin those burger patties right down." Aggie's voice throbbed with bossy satisfaction. "Duncan, light the fire and see if there are any small oak branches lying in the yard. I doubt Freida has mesquite chips."

"Maybe she has plans you don't know about," Duncan said, but he went off good-naturedly. Aggie marched off toward the house, Gary following obediently.

Jane's mother stepped closer to her. "That Gary fellow," she whispered, "is he an alcoholic?"

"Gary?" Jane was surprised. "No, I don't think so."

Her mother frowned. "Then what exactly is wrong with him?"

"No one really knows," Jane said. Duncan had told her once that Gary had been slightly higher-functioning before he married Aggie but that he had regressed somewhat since. He thought it was because Aggie never allowed Gary to make a single decision on his own. ("But then that's why she married him," Duncan had said. "Because he does what she says so." It was an odd turn of phrase, but Jane found it very fitting.)

"Hello, Mrs. Wilkes," a shy voice said. It was Jimmy Jellico. "It's awful nice to meet you."

"My pleasure, young man." Jane's mother shook his hand. "You work with Duncan at his shop, don't you?"

"Sure do," Jimmy agreed, smiling.

"And I believe Jane said you were a Boyne City native," her mother said. "Were you born here?"

"Oh, no." Jimmy shook his head. "I was born at the hospital over in Charlevoix."

Jane's mother paused, looking at Jimmy thoughtfully. "Tell me where you live now, Jimmy, and what your house is like."

"I live with my ma over on Pearl Street." Jimmy looked pleased. "It's a green house with brown shutters, and it has a sleeping porch."

"A sleeping porch sounds perfectly lovely," Jane's mother said. "Do you sleep out there every night in the summer?"

"No, mainly I take naps back there," Jimmy answered. "I like naps."

"I do, too," Jane's mother said. "Now, tell me some other things you like. What are your favorite TV shows?"

Jane didn't realize she was holding her breath until she let it out. Sometimes she thought being with her mother was like crossing a desert: long, hard stretches of burning sand that exhausted you, but every once in a while, you happened on a little oasis of kindness.

For dinner, Aggie performed some sort of minor miracle with canned pineapple, grilling it with honey and red pepper sauce, transforming the most basic fare into something memorable. Duncan said it reminded him of a chicken casserole Aggie had made once without a single fresh ingredient. He said it was the best thing he'd ever tasted.

Freida had set up her back deck as a stage, with two barstools and a music stand. After dinner, she had everyone drag their lawn chairs over. "Thank you all so much for coming tonight," she said, her voice tremulous with gratitude. "I have five of my most promising students here to perform for you and I'll be accompanying them on the mandolin."

Jonathan Floyd was first, playing "Take Me Home, Country Roads" on the clarinet to moderate applause. Next, Chloe Jensen played "Amazing Grace" on the violin. Her short lavender lace dress was too tight in the armholes, and the hemline rose perilously when she reached for the high notes. The Myers sisters sang "Poor Wayfaring Stranger" while Freida strummed along and sang out in places where she obviously thought the girls would be unable to hit the notes, making the lyrics oddly emphasized: *"There is no sickness, no*

TOIL, nor danger, in that BRIGHT land to which I go!" Sexy Nicky Burdine played "Afternoon Delight" on the guitar and sang, while looking directly at the younger Myers sister, who was thirteen:

> *Please be waiting for me, baby, when I come around.*
> *We could make a lot of lovin' 'fore the sun goes down . . .*

Mr. Myers grew murderous-looking and muscles bunched in his jaw.

The last notes of Nicky's guitar faded away, and Jane's mother said, "Imagine the *less* promising students!" in a loud whisper.

Jane sighed. They were back in the desert.

SUMMER FINALLY CAME, all at once. Grass turned green, flowers burst into bloom, birds were everywhere, and temperatures zoomed up into the eighties, as though the weather wanted to catch people unawares and make them complain about the heat.

To celebrate, Jane took her class to the park for the day. She brought a laundry basket full of water bottles and a big cooler of popsicles. They played Mother May I, and Red Rover, and Red Light, Green Light—all the old standards that are still fresh to seven-year-olds.

Duncan and Jimmy came at lunchtime with pizzas, and afterward, they chased the children through the playground until the children screamed with laughter. Jimmy pushed Corey Navarro around and around on the tire swing until Corey got dizzy and threw up, and Alicia Sweet accidentally locked herself in the park restroom and had to be rescued.

Freida joined them in the late afternoon with her mandolin and led the children through "The Old Gray Mare" and "I'll Tell My

Ma" and "Kookaburra" while Jane sat on a nearby bench with Duncan's arm around her. Duncan sang, too, and his voice was so deep compared to the light, golden voices of the children that it was less a voice than a rumble beneath the words.

When the children grew too sleepy to sing along—Scott Stafford was actually asleep on one of the picnic tables, covered with Duncan's sweatshirt—Freida switched to more sophisticated songs and sang by herself. "Red Dirt Girl" and "I Ain't Marching Anymore" and "Sweet Old World" and a song Jane didn't know:

> *Well, I could've loved you better, didn't mean to be unkind.*
> *You know that was the last thing on my mind . . .*

The afternoon sunlight hit the trees, making the leaves shine like a million tiny shifting mirrors. Jane leaned her head on Duncan's shoulder, wondering how she could have gone so long without realizing that mandolin music was the most beautiful music in all the world.

THE NEXT DAY was a Saturday, and Jane rode with Duncan to Alpena to deliver a pair of beautiful French rococo chairs with blue-and-white upholstery to a client. Jane wore jeans with the cuffs rolled up and an old flannel shirt of Duncan's. They drove with the windows down, Jane's outstretched hand cupping the wind and letting it go, cupping the wind and letting it go.

Once they got to Alpena, they drove through a residential area where the homes grew progressively larger, making it look as though the houses were stalking them, creeping toward the street. Duncan parked in the driveway of a big white Colonial-style house, and Jane followed him up the porch steps.

The woman who answered the door looked as if she'd just been called off a photoshoot. Green-eyed and red-lipped, she had glossy blond hair that hung over one shoulder in a shining banner. She wore a white-on-white embroidered caftan that stopped above her knees to reveal shapely legs. She looked at Duncan with such sleepy bedroom eyes that Jane was surprised the woman could see anything at all.

"Hi, Duncan," the woman said. Her accent was Midwestern, but her voice was husky and smooth. She looked past him to Jane, and her expression didn't change; Jane got the bedroom eyes, too. Maybe the woman had just woken up.

"Hey, Amanda," Duncan said easily. "How are you?"

"Good," Amanda breathed. The word was like a puff of smoke. "Thank you for bringing the chairs."

"No problem." Duncan sounded cheerful. "I can bring them in right now if you tell me where you'd like them."

"I made space in the bedroom." Amanda gestured vaguely. (Of *course* the bedroom, thought Jane.) "Would you and your friend like some iced tea?"

"That would be great," Duncan said. "Amanda, this is Jane. Jane, Amanda."

Amanda stepped aside. "Come on with me," she said to Jane. "Duncan will bring the chairs."

She led the way languidly to an ordinary kitchen—Jane had expected something more exotic. When Amanda reached into a cupboard for glasses, Jane saw a wide gold band and big diamond sparkler on Amanda's left hand. She felt a little better. Amanda took so long pouring three glasses of iced tea that Duncan—who seemed to know where the bedroom was without being told—had carried the chairs in and joined Jane at the kitchen table before she was done.

Amanda set the glasses down and seemed to drift into her own chair.

Duncan took a drink. "So how do you like living here?"

Amanda gazed around as though she had just discovered where she was. She shrugged. "It's not bad," she said. "More to do in the winter. More to keep me . . . busy."

Everything she said sounded like sexual innuendo. Jane thought Amanda could say *How is Boyne City?* and it would sound rich with erotic promise.

"How is Boyne City?" Amanda asked.

"Same as ever." Duncan nodded. "And how's married life?"

Amanda smiled lazily. "I like it. How about you? Are you and"— she frowned minutely—"Jane tempted?"

"No, ma'am," Duncan said immediately. "I'm never getting married again."

Suddenly there was nothing slow and languid about Amanda's eyes—they flicked straight to Jane, and something like triumph showed in them.

Jane kept her face completely neutral. She forced the muscles in her cheeks to relax so it wouldn't look like she was clenching her teeth. Her eyelid was threatening to twitch, and she focused all her attention on not letting it.

Amanda asked Duncan how business was, and he shrugged. He said if Amanda wanted a loveseat to match those chairs, he'd keep an eye out. Amanda said she didn't know, that she didn't like the bedroom to be (she paused and made a vague gesture) cluttered.

Jane took a sip of her tea. It was bitter—Amanda had oversteeped it. Jane wanted to add sugar from the pretty little white bowl Amanda had set out, but she was afraid her hands would shake too much and she'd scatter grains of sugar all over the table. Besides, bitter tea seemed appropriate. Bitter was how she felt.

————

JANE WAS QUIET on the ride home. She rolled her window up, and after a while, Duncan asked if she'd like him to roll his window up, too.

"Yes, please," Jane said.

He glanced over at her. "Are you hungry? Should we stop for something to eat?"

Jane shook her head. "No, thank you."

"I have to go to Traverse City tomorrow," Duncan said. "Want to come along? We could visit some wineries."

"I'm sorry," Jane said. "I didn't hear what you said."

In the back of her classroom, Jane had a Good Manners Wall—a green felt board with a number of laminated cards Velcroed to it. The cards had polite phrases printed on them, everything from *Yes, please* and *No, thank you* and *May I have the bathroom pass?* to *I'd like to use the scissors* and *I'm ready to listen* and *I'm sorry I hurt your feelings.* The children were supposed to consult the board when they didn't know how to say something politely. (It didn't always work—Shawn Vandenberg had figured out right away that he could abuse it by saying things like, "I'm sorry I hurt your feelings, Lizard Face.") But right now it was working for Jane. She felt as though she were plucking the cards off one by one and handing them to Duncan.

Duncan didn't repeat his invitation. He said, "You're being awfully quiet. Is it what I said to Amanda about not wanting to get married? Because you knew that, right?"

Jane sighed and looked out the window at the trees flashing by. "I know it now."

"I guess I thought we understood each other," Duncan said.

Jane said nothing.

Duncan cleared his throat. "You being so young and all, and new in town—I thought you wanted an interim type of relationship.

I figured when you wanted to get married, you'd look around for someone else."

Jane reached for the Good Manners Wall in her mind again. "Yes, I think you're right."

After a moment, Duncan took her hand and squeezed it. She squeezed back.

When they got to her house, dusk was settling in like a giant had shaken out a lavender blanket and left it to drift down. Duncan came inside, and they both wandered around aimlessly, opening and shutting the refrigerator, turning on and off the TV.

"Maybe I should go," Duncan said finally. "I have to get up early to leave for Traverse City."

Jane wanted to ask Duncan to hold her, but she suspected he'd get tired of holding her after about five minutes, and she knew she could make sex last a lot longer, so she took him by the hand and led him upstairs.

They made love quietly in her bedroom. The lights were off, but the window shades were up. The sheets glowed faintly silver in the darkness, and shadows lay like spiderwebs in the corners. The love they made was ghostly, insubstantial. If Duncan noticed that Jane used only phrases from the Good Manners Wall—"Yes, I would like that" and "Is this okay?"—he didn't say so.

AFTERWARD, Jane stood on her porch steps and watched Duncan drive away in his van. He honked lightly from the street, and she waved. She was wearing her robe, the silk one with all the embroidered daisies that were beginning to come unstitched. The wind had freshened and ran cool fingers through her hair, chilling her scalp.

Jane knew then that she couldn't go on seeing Duncan. Of course she would still *see* him, because it was impossible to live in Boyne City and not see someone else who lived there, but she wouldn't go on trying to have a relationship with him. She wouldn't keep trying to make him something he wasn't.

She stood on the porch with her chin down and her arms crossed, hugging herself slightly. She thought that the worst part was not that Duncan had taken her heart as surely as Freida's long-ago lover had taken her tuning whistle. The worst part was that she'd given it to him. Yes, that was always the worst part. You gave it to him. You carved out a crucial little part of yourself, and you not only gave it to him, you begged him to take it. You pushed it on him, the way you might press food on a hungry traveler or money on a less fortunate relative. You were sure at that moment that you would always have an endless supply, or at least more than enough, because you were one of the lucky ones. So you gave it to him. You did it—you did—you stupid, reckless fool.

2005

S URELY NOT ALL BRIDES woke up so bad-tempered on the day before the wedding. At least, Jane didn't think they did. But then probably not all brides put off everything until the last possible moment, the way she had. She lay in bed, her to-do list beating a pulse in her temples. Caterer—cake—flowers—

The phone beside her bed rang. "Hello?"

"I take it your mother's in town," Duncan said, "seeing as how she just nearly ran me over in the Glen's parking lot."

"Of course she's in town," Jane said. "She's here for the wedding."

Duncan continued in a cheerful, headlong way. "Then I saw her at the gas station getting coffee, *then* she's at Johan's getting croissants, *then* she goes back toward Glen's. All this before nine in the morning, mind you."

Jane squinted at her bedside clock. "It's nine already?"

Duncan was still talking about her mother. "She's like a CIA agent," he said. "Always doubling back and randomly turning down side streets."

"She probably went back to Glen's because she leaves her credit card behind a lot," Jane said. "And I think she turns down side streets because she sort of forgets where she is sometimes."

"Then she's *worse* than a CIA agent," Duncan said. "She's like a CIA agent who's had a nervous breakdown and can't remember why she does these things. She's going to kill someone one of these days."

"Look, I should probably go," Jane said. "I have a million things to do."

"I'm sure you do," Duncan agreed. "It's like that for brides. The night before Aggie and I got married, she *ironed* a whole bunch of five-dollar bills to use as tips on our honeymoon—"

"Was there a reason you called?" Jane asked.

"Actually, yes," Duncan said. "Darcy wanted me to ask you if it's okay for her to leave right after the dinner tonight or if you want any post-rehearsal photos."

Darcy was the wedding photographer, and Duncan's girlfriend.

"No, that's fine," Jane said.

"Then I'll see you at the rehearsal," Duncan said cheerfully. "Just think, tomorrow you'll be Mrs. Lance Armstrong!"

"Good-bye," Jane said, and hung up.

Obviously, Jane wasn't marrying Lance Armstrong. She was marrying *Luke* Armstrong, a very nice financial analyst who lived in Petoskey, although he spent most nights at Jane's house and would move in after the honeymoon. He had a shock of reddish-blond hair and a long, interesting face, and a slanting smile. He was smart and ambitious and kind and loyal. He valued family and education, he volunteered at the Humane Society, he overtipped in restaurants, he truly thought Jane looked good in high-waisted jeans, and he didn't slide his hand down her shirt in a bored way during *ER*. He had a million sterling qualities! But Duncan and Freida and all Jane's Boyne City friends couldn't resist calling him Lance Armstrong. Ironically, Luke liked to cycle, and sometimes he would bike all the way from Petoskey to Jane's house, and if she happened to be in her yard, he would join her there wearing his black cycling shorts and a yellow polyester jersey. Then Jane would hope that no one would see him, because it would make them all happy in a way she didn't care for.

Jane got up and looked out the window. Hot and cloudless. A July bride could ask no more.

She walked toward the kitchen in her nightgown, glancing into the tiny guest bedroom as she went. The single bed was made with a sort of aggressive neatness, signaling that her mother was definitely up and about.

Was there anything more dispiriting than your house the day after a big craft project? No, was Jane's opinion as she surveyed her kitchen, which was littered with bits of ribbon and paper and sticky puddles of glue. She and her mother had been up late making the wedding centerpieces: two dozen mason jars transformed with burlap and rough yarn and vintage lace into lovely rustic centerpieces that would be filled with wildflowers and add charm and individuality to her reception (as a catalogue might put it) and yet—Jane thought they still looked an awful lot like mason jars.

She cleared the trash off the table and began scraping at a glue puddle with a butcher knife.

Outside, a car door slammed and a moment later Jane's mother hoisted herself up the porch steps, looking sturdy and vital, her eyeglasses glinting in the sunshine. She was carrying at least a half-dozen plastic bags, which hung from the fingers of her right hand like shiny tan wisteria bunches. She used her left hand to yank up the skirt of the gaily colored two-piece knit dress she was wearing. Jane knew that dress well. Jane's mother believed that this dress never went out of fashion, and that it flattered her figure, and that the colorful chevron pattern hid stains well. None of these statements were true. Its only redeeming feature was that whenever it got baggy, Jane's mother could wear it front-to-back for a while and it would regain its former shape (such as it was).

She came in and dumped her plastic bags on the table.

"I can't believe you don't get the newspaper delivered," she said to Jane by way of greeting.

"I never have time to read it in the mornings," Jane said.

"You should make time." Her mother spoke vigorously. "It's part of your responsibility as an educator. What happens when some child in your class asks who the Kurds are? Do you say, 'Darned if I know! I was too busy hitting the snooze button'?"

"Mom, I teach second grade—"

Her mother was rummaging through her purchases. "Oh, here, I brought you a jelly doughnut."

This was the paradox of Jane's mother. For every ten—possibly twenty—irritating things she said or did, she did one sort of perfect thing, like producing a jelly doughnut right when you needed one, or having a wet wipe in her purse when your hands were sticky, or massaging your temples with her strong, capable fingers when you had a headache.

So Jane ate her jelly doughnut and drank a glass of milk while her mother read aloud to her from a *Detroit Free Press* article about the dwindling supply of anthrax vaccine in Southwest Asia. The doughnut didn't help, though. The day refused to brighten.

AFTER BREAKFAST, Jane and her mother loaded all the centerpieces into the trunk of Jane's Honda Civic and drove to Petoskey to pick up Luke's mother, Edith-Louise, from her hotel and go to the bridal salon for Jane's final dress fitting. They were a little late starting, and Edith-Louise was already sitting on a stone bench in front of the hotel entrance when Jane drove up. At her feet was a shiny white shopping bag, which presumably contained the dress she planned to wear to the rehearsal dinner.

God help us, Jane thought miserably. She's planning a whole day of togetherness.

Edith-Louise was one of those women who aged into perfection. It wasn't that she didn't appear to get older, but that she looked so lovely now that you suspected (at least, Jane suspected) that she looked better in her fifties than she had in her twenties or thirties. Edith-Louise's short, thick, dark hair was shot with strands of silver and her pale blue eyes were edged with sexy crow's-feet. She was tall and slender, wearing a crisp white blouse and dark blue linen pants. A row of delicate silver bangles on her wrist caught the morning sun.

Jane sighed as she put the car in park. She herself was wearing black jeans and a faded pink T-shirt and pale pink high heels. (She was trying to break her wedding shoes in but it seemed as though her feet might break first; the shoes had not one molecule of give.) Jane feared that on some personal elegance spectrum, she was much closer to her mother's end than Edith-Louise's.

Both Jane and her mother got out of the car and Jane made introductions. "Mom, this is Luke's mother, Edith-Louise—"

"Just call me Phyllis," Jane's mother interrupted. "I'm not one who goes in for fancy names."

Was she implying that a hyphenated name was unnecessarily fancy? Jane struggled to find an alternate interpretation but failed.

"I'm so pleased to meet you." Edith-Louise had a quiet voice.

"Now, I hope you don't mind if I ride in the front," Jane's mother said. "I'm prone to motion sickness."

"Not at all," Edith-Louise said softly. She was smiling at Jane's mother, but already—less than a minute after they'd been introduced—the smile had taken on a slightly fixed look.

Once they were back in the car, Jane's mother began firing off questions. How had Edith-Louise slept? How was the hotel? When had they arrived? How was their journey? Where were they from?

"Deerfield, Massachusetts—" Edith-Louise started.

"Oh, my husband and I drove through Deerfield once on our way to Boston years ago," Jane's mother interrupted. Then she questioned herself. "Was it Deerfield or some other place? Anyway, we stopped for lunch, and there was a dead moth in the clam chowder."

"I'm . . . awfully sorry to hear that," Edith-Louise said. Her smile now appeared to be set in concrete.

"Here we are at the bridal store!" Jane interjected in a bright, desperate voice. She pulled into the parking lot with a flourish. They all got out of the car, and Jane's mother hitched up her skirt again.

The interior of the bridal shop seemed shadowed and gloomy after the bright sunshine, and Jane's mother, who was wearing eyeglasses with transition lenses, stumbled and grasped Jane's arm. The floor of the shop was dark wood and the walls were mirrored, reflecting the dozens of wedding gowns hung in garment bags on the racks that lined the length of the shop. The shop reminded Jane of a spider's lair, the gowns dead silk-wrapped insects to be eaten later.

"Oh, hi, Jane," said the girl behind the counter. Her name was Natalie, and Jane knew her fairly well because Natalie also worked as a waitress at the barbecue restaurant in Boyne City. She was young and freckled, wearing jeans and a plaid cowboy shirt. She looked like she'd shown up for work at the wrong place.

"Hi, Natalie," Jane said. "This is my mother, and Luke's mother."

Edith-Louise smiled. "Hello, Natalie."

"I can hear you, but I can't see you," Jane's mother said. "I won't be able to see you until my glasses lighten up."

"Goodness!" Natalie looked alarmed. She probably thought Jane's mother was vision-impaired. "Let me help you to the seating area."

She grasped Jane's mother's elbow and led her slowly toward a scrolled white loveseat with matching end tables. Jane and Edith-Louise followed.

"There you go," Natalie said as Jane's mother sat down with a small grunt. Edith-Louise sank gracefully beside her. "Now you come with me, Jane. I have your dress in the fitting room."

Jane followed Natalie into the small curtained room at the back of the store. Natalie swung the curtain shut. Jane's dress was hanging from a hook in a pearl-colored garment bag. "Just one minute and we'll have you set," Natalie said, unzipping the bag. "You go ahead and get undressed."

Obediently, Jane took off her jeans and T-shirt. She held up her arms as Natalie took the dress out of the bag and slipped its soft billowing folds over Jane's head.

Jane looked at her reflection in the mirror.

Something strange seemed to have happened to her wedding dress. For one thing, it had changed color since the fitting two weeks ago. At that time, the dress had appeared to be a delicate shell pink, but now Jane thought it looked distinctly flesh-colored. Also, the princess bodice seemed to have stretched and was now too large in the bust. The silky woven fabric of the overskirt had looked glossy and rich then, but now it glittered like cheap nylon.

"Oh, Jane, you look lovely!" Natalie said, rapidly fastening the covered buttons up the back of the dress. But Jane had sat in Natalie's section at the barbecue restaurant many times; she knew that was Natalie's cheery waitress voice. *Hello, I'll be your server! What a good choice! You have a good night now!*

Jane looked in the mirror, biting her lower lip. "Prom dress" were the words that came to mind.

"Let's go show your family," Natalie said. She held back the heavy white curtain.

Jane left the dressing room and walked into the showroom. Her mother and Edith-Louise were sitting side by side on the loveseat. Edith-Louise seemed gracefully posed there, long legs crossed at the ankles, one slim hand draped on the armrest. Jane's mother's eyeglasses had returned to normal, and she was sprawled comfortably next to Edith-Louise, holding a small bag of potato chips and saying, "At first I thought it was Lyme disease, but it turned out to be a rash from wearing wool socks."

"Here she is, ladies!" Natalie chirped. "Our beautiful bride."

They turned to look at Jane. Edith-Louise blinked rapidly as though a fan were blowing in her face, and Jane's mother paused with a potato chip raised halfway to her mouth.

"It's *pink*," Jane's mother announced, and took a bite of her chip.

"The color is called blush," Jane said, stepping onto the little circular platform in front of the mirrors. The platform was covered in tufted white velvet and stained with the sweat of a thousand anxious bridal feet. She looked at her reflection in the mirrored walls. She turned slightly from side to side, but the view did not improve. The ruffled straps on her shoulders stood out like epaulets.

"I think it's lovely," Edith-Louise said softly. "So—so distinctive and fanciful."

Jane's mother rustled her chip bag. "It looks like you put it through the wash with a red sock."

"Oh, no," Natalie protested, kneeling to fuss with the hem of the dress. "Blush is one of our most popular colors. Hardly anyone goes for plain old white anymore."

"Actually, it's a very Victorian, old-fashioned notion that brides must wear white," Edith-Louise said in her gentle voice. "Modern brides can choose to wear any color."

Jane knew that Edith-Louise meant this as only the most general comment on fashion and nothing whatsoever to do with virginity, but Jane's mother cackled and poked Edith-Louise with her elbow. "Listen to you, you dirty bird!"

A small silence descended then, like an invisible cloth dropping down from the ceiling.

Edith-Louise gazed at her lap, seemingly suddenly absorbed by the slender taper of her own fingers. She examined her cuticles.

Jane knew with certainty that Edith-Louise was thinking ahead, that she was looking down a long dim corridor at all the future meals and holidays that might include Jane's mother, and feeling a black, despairing sort of dread.

FROM THE BRIDAL STORE, they drove to meet Luke and his father, Raymond, for lunch at the golf course. The inside of the Civic had heated up like a toaster oven, and the air conditioner warbled noisily, making conversation difficult and Jane very relieved.

Evidently, Luke and Raymond had both forgotten to bring sport coats because they were standing in the lobby of the restaurant wearing bright plaid blazers that must have come from the club's community closet. They looked like a pair of sweaty used-car salesmen, and yet Jane and Edith-Louise both greeted them with glad cries and soft kisses—Jane suspected she and Edith-Louise were both just so happy to see someone who wasn't Jane's mother.

Raymond leaned forward to kiss Jane's cheek, and she introduced him to her mother.

Jane had tried very hard to feel fond of Luke's father, but two things made this difficult. The first was that Raymond looked so much like an older, dissipated, bloated, sun-blotched version of Luke. It took no imagination to see—less than no imagination! You had to actively *suppress* your imagination to avoid it—how Luke's lean face would spread and become jowly, how his strawberry-blond hair would fade and recede, how his pale blue eyes would grow watery under crepey lids, how his freckles would multiply and run together until his skin looked like sandblasted granite. Jane found it difficult to look at Raymond without feeling as though the Ghost of Christmas Yet to Come was standing beside him, smirking.

Still, she took his arm as they followed the hostess to their table. "How was your morning, Raymond?"

"Not bad at all," he said. "I'm pleased that greens fees have only risen by seven percent since last year. I honestly believe the current economy will force the industry to provide affordable golf for everyone."

This was the second thing that made it hard to love Raymond: he talked about finance all the time.

"Dad, I'm not sure Jane cares about that," Luke said, forcing Jane to say, "Oh, no, I'm very interested."

The hostess led them to a round table near a window overlooking the golf course. Beyond the careful green fairways, Lake Michigan heaved like a large blue dinosaur. What would it be like to run across the golf course and throw yourself into the waves? Just to keep swimming and not come back?

Jane sat between Luke and Raymond. Luke draped his arm over the back of her chair, and Jane looked over at him gratefully.

"How was your morning?" he asked quietly.

She smiled. "Let's just say I'm glad it's over. Although I'm starting to wish we'd eloped."

"Tomorrow it will all be worth it," Luke said, squeezing her shoulder. He smiled at Jane's mother. "Now, Phyllis, tell me, what are you going to order?"

"I'm not sure." Jane's mother was holding the menu at arm's length. "I do believe I've grown lactose intolerant. If I so much as look at a piece of quiche these days, I get the most terrible upset stomach."

Jane sighed. She turned to speak to Raymond and found him eyeing her in the manner of someone wondering what he could possibly find to talk about. (That made two of them.)

"Oh, hey," he said suddenly, looking relieved. He must have thought of something. "Where are you two going on your honeymoon?"

Jane smiled. "We're going to Banff," she said. "I've never been—"

"Excellent choice!" Raymond said. "The Canadian dollar is so weak now. Do you know why that is?"

"No," Jane said. "I'm afraid I don't."

"Terrible national deficit." Raymond shook his head. "Also, oil prices are low."

"Oh," Jane said. She made herself start again. "Oh, well, that's lucky for us, I guess."

"Edith-Louise and I went to Corinth on our honeymoon." Raymond's voice had taken on an expansive tone. "Of course, the Greek economy is hopeless, always has been and always will be. The Greeks' problem is that they don't produce anything except olives. They just have no place in the world market. But I think it's also a cultural thing, like our neighbors—honey, what's the name of those people down the block? The Greeks?"

"The Korbas," Edith-Louise said with the slightly weary voice of a longtime detail supplier.

"Yes, the Korbas," Raymond said to Jane. "Now, these people have lived in Massachusetts for twenty years, and yet they plant strawberries in late July! Total insanity. They *have* to know the growing season is less than a hundred and fifty days, and yet there they are every July, sometimes August, planting strawberries way past the time most people have their strawberries picked and eaten. I said to Edith-Louise, 'That right there is indicative of what's wrong with the Greek economy.'"

"That's a remarkable story," Jane said, but now it was she who thought of the future, the lunches and dinners and drinks, and she who despaired.

AS THE DAY WORE ON, Jane's every thought seemed to start with *Oh, why.*

Oh, why hadn't she packed for the honeymoon? Oh, why hadn't she gotten a manicure? Oh, why hadn't she broken in these stupid shoes? (Her toes were pinched cruelly, and her heels were rubbed raw. It felt as though her feet were no longer feet but fleshy bags filled with gravel.) Oh, why hadn't she written a check for the caterer? Oh, why hadn't she finalized the seating chart? Oh, why, oh, *why* couldn't she have a different mother?

And why, she thought as the Civic bounced along the dirt road—the air conditioner now spitting water and wheezing heavily—hadn't she chosen to have the reception at the country club or a restaurant where the staff would do everything for her? Why choose this stupid barn in the countryside?

The answer was a sentimental one: Jane and Luke had gotten engaged there. They had come one October night to see a five-piece string band called the Soulful Mittens, and they had brought Freida with them because Freida tended to get jealous and bothered if Jane went to concerts without her. In the middle of the band's last number, Luke had taken Jane's hand and kissed her palm. Then he slipped something cool and smooth onto her finger: an engagement ring.

Jane remembered so clearly walking out the barn's double doors into the moonlit dooryard, marveling that she'd entered the same doors earlier as a single person and now she was exiting them as an engaged woman. Her new ring had sparkled when she held out her hand, and Luke smiled at her. "Will you?" he asked.

Jane laughed. "It seems I will."

Freida was so excited and happy for them that she bounced slightly up and down on the back seat of the car all the way home. Jane loved that Luke had included Freida in their engagement. She loved the ring, with its lacy gold filigree and rough diamond. She loved the Soulful Mittens. She loved Luke. But she couldn't shake the feeling that she'd never been properly proposed to, that she'd been somehow . . . gotten around. But surely it was uncharitable to think that.

Now Jane turned the car into the small gravel parking lot outside the barn and bumped over a pothole. The car rocked wildly, and Jane's mother spat a breath mint onto the dashboard with a startled woofing sound.

"Sorry," Jane said for Edith-Louise's benefit.

"Whoa." Jane's mother leaned forward to retrieve the mint. "Nearly jolted my spine right through my head."

Jane put the car in park and switched off the ignition. It seemed to her, for a long moment, that she couldn't speak.

"Here we are," she said at last. Her voice sounded faint and small.

They climbed out of the car, and Jane unstuck her shirt from her back. The wind puffed a breath of hot air at them.

Like her wedding dress, the barn seemed to have undergone some changes since Jane had last seen it, and not for the better. Or maybe Jane had seen it before only at night. Then it had been starlit and pastoral, the open barn doorway glowing like a golden rectangle. Here, now, soaked in the bright afternoon sunlight, the barn had a dilapidated look, the red paint faded clean away in places to reveal weathered gray planks. The double doors were propped open on sagging hinges. The ground was baked hardpan with only forlorn tufts of grass scattered here and there like spiky green hedgehogs.

Jane's mother moved the breath mint from one side of her mouth to the other. "Looks like there ought to be diseased chickens running around," she said finally.

Jane waited for Edith-Louise to politely disagree, to say the barn was lovely and rustic and charming, but Edith-Louise remained silent. Perhaps she agreed with Jane's mother's assessment, or perhaps she was too tired to take up the lance and shield of her gracious commentary. Jane couldn't blame her.

"Let's go to the office," Jane said. "And ask where we should put the centerpieces."

They walked across the hard dirt yard to a small clapboard building the size and shape of a tollbooth. A handwritten note on the door read: *Concert in progress! Please join us in the barn!*

Jane's mother squinted at the sign. "'Concert in—'"

"We can all read, Mom," Jane said impatiently. She sighed and lifted her hair off her neck with one hand. "I guess we'd better go to the barn. It's too hot to wait in the car."

They crossed the yard again and entered the shadowy, stuffy barn. Inside, Jane was relieved to see that fairy lights and paper lanterns had been hung from the rafters. Pushed against the back wall were trestle tables and wooden folding chairs and white linen still in the plastic laundry packaging. Apparently, her wedding reception really was going to happen.

At the front of the barn, more wooden chairs had been set up in a semicircle around the wooden platform stage where the concert was taking place, although Jane could not help thinking that "concert" may have been overstating things. Five sleepy-looking audience members—one of whom was presumably the office manager—were fanning themselves with folded-up programs while onstage a bearded man played a steel drum and a woman strummed a decrepit-looking lute and sang. The woman was in her fifties, with a waterfall of long black hair pulled back in a high ponytail, and overplucked eyebrows that gave her a startled expression. She looked like an insane flamenco dancer. Jane knew her, by sight at least, because the woman also worked at the dollar store, and she knew the man, too, because he sometimes worked shifts as a cashier at Glen's. (Was every resident of Boyne City moonlighting? It was like living on the set of some underfunded community theater that didn't have the budget for enough actors.)

Jane and her mother and Edith-Louise slipped into three empty seats in the second row just as the insane flamenco woman was winding down the final chorus of "If I Had a Hammer."

"It's a song about—love!" she sang out choppily, strumming. "Between—my brothers and my sisters—and my sisters—and my other sisters—and these—new people! Hello!"

Jane looked up, startled at the change in the lyrics, and realized that the flamenco woman was actually singing directly at them. (Evidently the bearded man was startled, too; he hit the steel pan with his drumstick and then had to silence it with his hand.)

Jane smiled self-consciously, but her mother waved like someone hailing a taxi in a rainstorm. "Hello yourself!" she called.

"Welcome, friends!" the flamenco dancer said. She shielded her eyes to look at them, which Jane thought was pretentious considering there wasn't actually a spotlight. "Do you have any requests?"

"Oooh, yes!" Jane's mother said happily. "Do you know 'The Ballad of Eskimo Nell'?" (She had a love of bawdy songs.)

The bearded man frowned. "I'm not sure that's appropriate."

Jane's mother was unembarrassed. Jane had, in fact, never known her mother to be embarrassed about anything. Jane had gone through life having to feel it for both of them. "What about something by Jimmy Buffett?"

"Any particular song?" the man asked.

"I'm flexible," Jane's mother answered magnanimously. "Whatever you two decide on is fine by me."

The man and the flamenco dancer consulted briefly and then started playing "Come Monday."

Jane settled back in her chair and started making a mental checklist. She needed to figure out that something-old-something-new business. Her dress was new, so that was okay, and she had some pretty vintage opal earrings, so old was taken care of, too. She supposed she could borrow a blue mandolin pick from Freida and slip it into her shoe, although wasn't it supposed to be a penny you slipped into your shoe? And what if Freida didn't have a blue pick, or more likely, wouldn't let Jane borrow it? (Freida was fussy about other people handling her musical instruments.) What about blue flowers? Maybe they would have cornflowers at the farmers' market. God, why hadn't she planned all this months ago? You would almost think she didn't want to get married.

Familiar chords caught Jane's attention and she stared up at the stage.

"Patsy Cline!" Jane's mother exclaimed.

Jane's mother had always loved Patsy Cline. Jane had done her homework at the kitchen table most nights while her mother made dinner and played Patsy Cline cassettes on the tape deck that rested on the kitchen shelf. To this day, Jane could not look at the periodic table without hearing piano chords and careful phrasing.

The bearded man beat the drums, and the flamenco woman strummed. She smiled widely while she sang, which made her look even crazier. She sang so slowly that it made Jane's throat ache.

> *He loves me, too, his love is true.*
> *Why can't he be you?*

"'Youuuuu?'" Jane's mother sang along joyfully. Glancing at Jane, she broke off abruptly. "Goodness, what ails you? You look like you're about to cry."

"Nothing," Jane said irritably. She stood up. "I think the concert's over. Wake Edith-Louise and let's get the centerpieces. I'll meet you at the car."

BACK AT JANE'S HOUSE, the sun beat down on their shoulders like the blows of soft, hot hammers as they crossed the driveway. Jane's feet felt almost too heavy to lift as she trudged slowly up the porch stairs to her house, with her mother and Edith-Louise behind her.

"That lunch was delicious but now my skirt feels too tight," her mother said.

Jane paused with her key in the lock. She suddenly felt she might start screaming if she had to endure another minute—another second—of conversation. She needed some quiet time or she couldn't survive. It was as simple as that.

When she felt this way in the classroom, she clapped her hands and said, "One, two, three! Eyes on me!" and ordered all the students to fold their hands together on top of their desks. Then she would play *Healing Sounds of Nature* on the portable CD player until everyone's heads began swaying in time to the ocean waves. (When Mr. Robicheaux in the classroom next door wanted quiet time, he just turned up the thermostat, forcing all his students into a state of helpless lethargy. It was very effective, though frowned upon by the principal.)

Sadly, Jane didn't feel she could use either method on her mother and Edith-Louise, so she did the next best thing. As soon as she unlocked the door, she waved them both toward the living room. "Please have a seat," she said. "I'll be right back."

She went into the kitchen and poured two glasses of iced tea. She sliced an elderly lemon and arranged the wedges on a saucer. She emptied a whole sleeve of Oreos into a cereal bowl, balanced everything on a tray, and carried it into the living room.

"Now, I noticed Luke had the grilled vegetable ciabatta for lunch," her mother was saying. "He's not one of those vegetarian idiots, is he?"

"Here you go, ladies," Jane said breezily, setting the tray down on the coffee table. Edith-Louise was sitting in the recliner, and Jane's mother had settled down on the couch. Jane was pleased—the couch was very deep and her mother had trouble getting out of it unassisted. "You two just relax."

"You're not joining us?" Edith-Louise looked alarmed by that prospect, and who could possibly blame her?

"I'll be back in a minute," Jane said. "I have to pack for the honeymoon."

She walked quickly from the room. She knew she should stay, be kind and gracious. Have cups of peppermint tea and lemon snaps, maybe. Ask Edith-Louise what Luke had been like as a little boy. Practice calligraphy. Press some flowers. (What *did* people do with their mothers-in-law all day? She would have to figure that out.)

Instead, Jane walked into her bedroom and sat down on her bed. She pried off her shoes and winced at the sight of the red, chafed skin on her feet. She had a blister on the knuckle of each of her big toes, and more on her little toes, more on her heels. They glowed like hot wires under her skin, fires she couldn't put out. She flopped back, her feet still touching the floor, and watched the ceiling fan rotate.

In the other room, she heard her mother say to Edith-Louise, "Now, I myself have never seen the point of organic food."

Edith-Louise said something too faint to hear.

Jane would get up in a second and pack. She had a new pale green nightgown, still in the lingerie-store box, and she should take a cardigan in case the restaurants were chilly, and her camera, and her passport, and—

Jane fell asleep.

SHE WOKE UP—unrefreshed, unrestored, decidedly unfriendly—in a sweaty confusion. She sat up. The doorbell chimed, and she realized it was ringing for the second time—the first ring must have woken her.

She walked out of her bedroom and into the living room, where her mother and Edith-Louise were still sitting. Evidently, they'd been discussing families.

"Now, tell me about your brother," her mother was saying. "Isn't he sort of a ne'er-do-well?"

"Gene's on the board of the Red Cross!" Edith-Louise's voice was delicately edged with exasperation.

"I wonder where I got the idea he was such a layabout?" Jane's mother said idly. "Has he had any run-ins with law enforcement?"

Jane pattered past them and down the short hall to the front door. Her blistered feet were stinging, and the inside of her mouth was dry and clothlike. She yanked open the door, knowing her face had a hostile, Thor-like expression and yet was helpless to change it.

It was Jimmy and his mother.

Mrs. Jellico was a heavyset woman, with the kind of white, wooly curls that seem absolute and inevitable, as though her hair might have gone white when she was a toddler. Every single time Jane had met her, Mrs. Jellico was wearing the same awful lace-collared polyester blue dress sprigged with small green leaves. (Was it actually possible she owned only one dress? Maybe she just had a bunch that looked alike.) Worse, she had fearful blue eyes, a constant self-conscious smile, and a whispery voice. And then there was Jimmy himself, who didn't get jokes and found even the simplest idiom confusing. Jane considered them the most high-maintenance pair in all Boyne City, and here they were showing up at her house uninvited!

Except they *were* invited; Jane had invited them herself. Back in some previous lifetime when she was planning this day and thought what a pleasant, gracious touch it would be to have everyone over to the house before the rehearsal.

"Come in," she forced herself to say, aware that her tone was neither pleasant nor gracious.

"Sorry we're early, Jane," Jimmy said.

"I gave them a ride," Freida said, coming up behind them. She was wearing a floral-patterned dress and a flower crown made of roses, daisies, and what looked like Italian parsley. (Freida took her maid-of-honor role seriously.) Her cheeks were flushed, and her burnished curls were amplified from the humidity. She looked so fresh and cool that Jane envied her unbearably.

Over Freida's shoulder, she saw a blue Buick edge its way into the driveway. It was Luke and Raymond, straight from picking up Uncle Gene at the Traverse City airport. When they got out, Jane saw that they were all wearing suits and ties. Uncle Gene was going to be the best man. He was another older, sunburnt version of Luke, and Jane knew from previous meetings that he liked to talk about falconry.

"Hi, Lance!" Freida called, and Jane poked her sharply.

"Hey!" Luke called, holding up two shopping bags from the party store. "We brought a cheeseball and some crackers, and chips and salsa, and olives and almonds."

Thank God! This alone seemed reason enough to marry him. Although, obviously, there were other reasons. Love and whatnot.

Everyone came into the house, and Jane did a round of introductions while Luke unpacked the food. "You go on and get ready," he said when she came into the kitchen. "I can handle this."

Jane hurried into the bathroom and sat on the edge of the tub, putting Band-Aids on her blisters. She splashed water on her face, and then swiftly applied mascara and a swipe of rosy-red lipstick, examining her reflection critically. She looked pale and washed-out, ghostly, like an overexposed photo found in a drawer.

She crossed the hall to her bedroom. She could hear her mother saying, "Now, Gene, tell me—" but she closed the bedroom door before she heard the rest.

She stripped off her clothes and threw them in the hamper. She pulled on a narrow pale blue skirt and a beige cotton Victorian blouse. The blouse was high-necked with puffed sleeves and corset-style lacing at the waist. Duncan had told her once that she looked like a sexy schoolmarm in this outfit. She drew her hair into a lady-like knot at the nape of her neck. She slipped on ballet flats—*Thank you!* she imagined her feet crying. *We'll do whatever you ask, but please don't put on those other shoes again!*—and surveyed herself in the mirror. How much better this thrift-store outfit suited her than that awful pink wedding dress, which was—oh, *shit*—still lying in the trunk of her car like a murder victim waiting to be dumped in the dark of night.

She put on dangly seed-pearl earrings and then opened the bedroom door a crack. She could hear the rumble of voices and the clinking of glasses, and smelled the smell that is particular to cocktail parties and not altogether pleasant: stale peanuts and aftershave. She steeled herself to go out and join them. She was the bride. This was her special day, and these people were waiting to help her celebrate. They were good people, all of them—*such* good people. It should not matter that they wanted to talk about the difference between true hawks and booted eagles, or the cost-benefit analysis of mushroom farming, or the water spot on the living room ceiling, which Jane's mother was convinced was black mold.

It should not matter, yet it did.

THEY COULD HAVE all walked to the church, which was only six blocks away, but instead they divided up into foursomes, like bridge players, and drove there in a small caravan. Jane and Luke rode in Freida's car and when they pulled into the parking lot, she could see that Duncan and Darcy were sitting on the church steps, talking to the church handyman.

"Welcome, Jane!" the handyman exclaimed as Jane and the others made their way up the walk. He gestured to include everyone. "Welcome, friends and family!"

Jane realized the handyman was actually Reverend Palumbo, wearing paint-spattered coveralls. (Evidently the minister moonlighted, too.)

"Hi, Reverend," Jane said.

"I don't believe I've had the pleasure of making your acquaintance, young man," Reverend Palumbo said to Luke.

"This is my fiancé," Jane said. "La— Luke Armstrong."

Dear God! She had almost called him Lance. She flushed deeply and stared at the ground. She had the sense that Duncan was smiling, but when she glanced at him, his face was pleasantly neutral.

"Pleased to meet you," Reverend Palumbo said, shaking Luke's hand.

"You, too," Luke said. "These are my parents, Raymond and Edith-Louise, and my uncle—"

Jane sighed. Would the introductions never stop? This whole day had been like singing "John Jacob Jingleheimer Schmidt" endlessly. (This comparison was not idle speculation on Jane's part; her classes had always loved that song.) Luke already knew Duncan, and knew about him, had agreed to have him at the wedding. He liked Duncan. He said that if you weren't trying to date Duncan, you didn't have a problem with him. He liked Jimmy, too. It had been his idea to have Jimmy serve as their usher. Luke really was the nicest man.

As always, when she hadn't seen him for a while, Jane was struck by how handsome Duncan was. His features were so regular that his face should have been boring to look at, but its symmetry caught people's attention, made their gazes linger. It made them think, *Is he famous—? Is that the guy from—? Did he used to be the front man for—?* Even his slightly weathered skin looked like the result of too much Hollywood high life, though Jane knew perfectly well it was from plain old lack of sunscreen.

Reverend Palumbo pulled a large ring of keys from his pocket and unlocked the church's red wooden doors. They all followed him in and stood clustered in the foyer, and those who hadn't met began another round of John Jingleheimer-ing. Freida introduced Duncan to Luke's parents and uncle, but she obviously feared saying, *This is Duncan, who used to be Jane's lover,* so she kept saying "This is Duncan—" in a foreshortened way.

Duncan himself seemed at ease. "I'm here with Darcy, the photographer," he said, shaking hands.

"You must be so excited about tomorrow, Jane," Darcy said. She was in her twenties, and very pretty in a monochromatic way: hazel eyes, chestnut hair, coffee-colored skin. In addition to being a wedding photographer, she worked at the health-food store. Jane liked her. Honest, she did.

"More nervous than excited," she said.

"Totally normal." Darcy hitched the strap of her camera bag up on her shoulder. "All brides feel that way. But don't worry about a thing—it will all come together tomorrow."

Jane smiled. "I hope so."

Darcy squeezed her arm. "I'm going to go set up now." She slipped by Reverend Palumbo and walked down the aisle to a pew about halfway to the front. She began unpacking her camera bag, her long hair falling forward. Jane tried to remember why they had ever ordered the photo package that included rehearsal pictures.

Reverend Palumbo looked around. "Now, which one of you is the wedding coordinator?"

"We don't have one," Jane said.

Reverend Palumbo's look became severe. Jane thought he might quote a Bible verse about wedding coordinators, but all he said was, "Well, who is going to cue the processional?"

Jane glanced at Luke. "We—we hadn't really thought in terms of a formal processional. Jimmy's just going to seat people as they arrive."

"Well, all right," Reverend Palumbo said. "Jimmy, come over here."

Everyone rustled around and looked for Jimmy, but they found only Jimmy's mother, sitting on the foyer bench, hands clasped over the hill of her stomach.

She gave her usual scared rictus smile. "Jimmy had a salsa stain on his shirt, so he went over to the gas station to get some wet paper towels, and if that doesn't work he's going to wash the shirt in the bathroom sink and blow it dry with the hand dryer."

This story was so typically Jimmy that Jane actually wondered for a second whether Mrs. Jellico was joking. But no, she looked serious. Jane wondered if Mrs. Jellico could be pressed into service as a wedding gatekeeper, but she had settled onto the bench in the deeply rooted way of someone who was glad to be off her feet and who intended to stay that way for as long as possible.

"I can cue the processional," Duncan said. "And I'll go over it later with Jim."

"That will have to do," Reverend Palumbo said. He rubbed his hands together briskly, like a football coach in a huddle. "Now, here's what happens. I'll enter from a side door and stand at the front when we're ready to begin. Once you"—he pointed at Duncan— "see me up there, start sending them out. Leave at least two minutes between each one so we don't get a bottleneck up there by the altar. Usually we have a wedding coordinator"—he shot Jane a disapproving look—"and they often recommend reciting the Lord's Prayer between each member of the processional as a way of marking time."

Good God, there was no way Jimmy could handle that! (If he was even here tomorrow. Jane felt there was a strong possibility Jimmy would spend the night in the gas station, wetting and drying his shirt endlessly.) It would have to be Duncan.

Reverend Palumbo was still talking. "Then it goes mother of the bride, parents of the groom, best man, maid of honor, bride and groom."

"Wait," Jane's mother said. "Isn't the groom supposed to be waiting at the front?"

Honestly. Had Jane's mother ever just accepted anything? Ever chosen silence as an option? Ever thought, *Well, that's unusual, but perhaps I'd be better not saying anything*? No. Jane could not remember a single such episode.

"This is the order that Jane specified," Reverend Palumbo said. It was true. Jane had liked the idea of walking down the aisle with Luke.

"But traditionally, the groom—"

Luke put his arm around Jane's mother's shoulders. "I tell you what, Phyllis," he said. "Why don't I walk down the aisle with you and escort you to your seat?"

"Well," Jane's mother looked pleasantly flustered. "I guess maybe—"

Luke gave her a squeeze. "And then I can walk to the front of the church and we'll watch Jane walk down together. Would you like that?"

"Yes, I think—" Jane's mother began.

"Perfect," Luke said. He winked at Jane and then looked at Duncan. "So now it goes Phyllis and me, my parents, Uncle Gene, Freida, Jane."

Imagine how much Luke must love Jane. Just imagine.

Right then, the church door opened, and a petite lady with short salt-and-pepper hair stepped briskly inside. "Hello, everyone!" she called. "Sorry to be late!"

Instantly, the air was electric with jealousy, and from this Jane knew that the lady must be Beatrice Mooney, the church organist.

Last spring, when Jane had called Freida to tell her that she and Luke had set a wedding date, Freida had interrupted happily, "And you want me to play the organ!"

"No," Jane had said. "I want you to be my maid of honor."

"Oh." Freida went quiet for a moment. "Who *is* going to play the organ?"

"I don't know," Jane said. "The church organist, I guess."

"Which church?"

"Mercy Fellowship."

"Beatrice Mooney is the organist there," Freida said in a foreboding way. "She rushes the processional every time."

"Well, anyway—"

"Normally I would suggest you call the church and request me by name," Freida had said, "but not if it's Mercy Fellowship. Beatrice Mooney would never stand for it. I hate to speak out against a sister musician, but that woman is like a viper when it comes to sharing her organ time."

A little pause followed, during which Jane sensed strongly that Freida was hoping she'd say, *To hell with Mercy Fellowship, in that case!* But instead Jane had said, "Will you be my maid of honor, though?" and Freida had said, "Oh, sure."

It had been a most unsatisfactory conversation.

Now here was Beatrice Mooney, not looking at all viperlike, although when she saw Freida, she tucked the corners of her mouth up in a smug way. Freida gave her a slit-eyed look.

"Okay, shall we begin?" Reverend Palumbo asked. "Beatrice, you go ahead and get set up."

Beatrice gave Freida a final smirk and then sashayed down the aisle toward the organ loft, which was behind the pulpit, concealed by a half wall and some ferns.

"Now I'm going to go around and come in through the side

entrance," Reverend Palumbo said to Duncan. "It may take me a minute because sometimes the lock sticks on the side door. But as soon as I'm up there, Beatrice will start playing and you can send folks down."

He went out the double doors, and moments later, they heard him rattling the side door. The rattling seemed to go on for a while. "Horse pucky!" he said quite distinctly, and the side door banged open. Reverend Palumbo crossed in front of the pews and stood on the low steps at the front of the church. Unseen, Beatrice played the first chords of Pachelbel's Canon in D.

Luke offered his arm to Jane's mother, and together they began walking down the aisle. Darcy raised her camera.

Duncan made no attempt to recite the Lord's Prayer or even look at his watch. "Okay, your turn," he said to Luke's parents. Raymond took Edith-Louise's arm, and for the first time, Jane noticed that Edith-Louise had changed into a gently flowing black dress with tiny white polka dots. Maybe someday Edith-Louise could teach Jane how to dress. They walked down the aisle.

"Beatrice is rushing the processional," Freida whispered to Jane. "She's going to have to repeat the song at this rate."

"All, right, Uncle Gene, you can go," Duncan said.

Uncle Gene walked down the aisle in a stiff, self-conscious way that reminded Jane of how some of her shyer students crossed the room to use the pencil sharpener.

Freida took a breath to whisper to Jane again, but Duncan said, "Now, Freida, you stop bad-mouthing Beatrice and get on up here."

Freida moved to stand by Duncan. "That woman has no innate sense of rhythm," she said to him. He patted her shoulder reassuringly, but she just made a *tsk*ing sound. She went down the aisle, the hem of her flowered dress fluttering indignantly.

Jane stepped up next to Duncan.

"You make a gorgeous bride, kiddo," he said.

"Thank you." She didn't feel gorgeous. She felt hot and flustered. But she smiled anyway. "Maybe you and Darcy will be next."

"Oh, I expect Darcy will be moving along one of these days," Duncan said cheerfully. "You know I don't want to get married again."

Yes, Jane knew that. Better than anyone.

"I didn't want to get married the first time," Duncan continued, "but I slammed Aggie's mama's hand in my truck door by accident when we were all going out to dinner. Mrs. Fontaine was a good sport about it, but *Mr.* Fontaine—he looked like he wanted to go home and get his deer-hunting rifle, and Aggie was crying and carrying on right there in the restaurant parking lot, and so I proposed."

"But why?" Jane asked, fascinated that she'd never known this. It was the closest she'd felt to happy all day. "What does one thing have to do with the other?"

"I've asked myself that a time or two, believe me," Duncan said, stroking his moustache. "It just seemed like a quick way to make everyone happy, and it did. Aggie and Mrs. Fontaine planned the whole wedding in the ER waiting room, and eight weeks later, we was man and wife. Of course, Mrs. Fontaine still had the cast on her hand in all the wedding pictures. I think you'd better go."

It took Jane a second to realize that he meant it was her time to walk down the aisle.

"Oh, yes, of course," she murmured. She took a deep breath and began walking. Luke smiled at her from the front of the church. Jane smiled back—

"Beatrice!" Reverend Palumbo shouted. "You're rushing the processional!"

The music cut off. Freida gave Jane a look of such scorching vindication that Jane thought all the church hymnals might burst into flames.

Beatrice poked her head through the ferns like a soldier emerging from a foxhole. "I'm playing the same as I always do," she said to Reverend Palumbo.

"And you always rush it," he shot back. "These folks look like they're marching to a polka."

"Myself, I always play Pachelbel's Canon in eight/four time," Freida said in a loud, reflective voice to no one in particular. "But of course, not everyone agrees."

"They certainly don't!" Beatrice Mooney snapped, and ducked back into her foxhole.

"Let's try it all again," Reverend Palumbo said, and his shoulders slumped sadly.

AFTER THE REHEARSAL, they bid farewell to Reverend Palumbo and Beatrice Mooney (who gave Freida a final hot-eyed look through the ferns) and walked the three blocks down to the restaurant. Jimmy came running up to them on the street, his shirttail untucked and flapping. A wet patch with a red-dotted center covered the left breast pocket of his shirt—it looked like he had been stilettoed in the heart.

"I sure am sorry, Jane!" he said, panting. "I kept scrubbing and scrubbing, but it only seemed to make it worse."

"Don't worry," Jane said, putting her hand through his arm. "Duncan will tell you what to do. And now you're here to walk me to the restaurant."

Jimmy ducked his head in a pleased way. It was so easy to make Jimmy happy. It was actually so easy to make almost anyone happy. Why didn't she do more of it?

The rehearsal dinner was alcohol-free because Luke's father was a recovering alcoholic. Apparently he'd been a moderate drinker up until about fifteen years earlier, when he began drinking more and more heavily, and finally hit bottom when he lost $350,000 on the pork belly futures market and had to go to rehab. (Jane suspected this had contributed to Edith-Louise's sexy crow's-feet.) He said he was more than happy for alcohol to flow at the wedding, and, well, amen to that, in Jane's opinion. But tonight the waiters around the big round table at the restaurant offered only ginger ale, iced tea, or sparkling water. A few people raised their eyebrows, but no one said anything, not even Jane's mother. (But, then, she was a teetotaler.)

The menu had been arranged in advance by Luke's parents, and the appetizer was shrimp cocktail and the entrée was chicken or fish. Or maybe it was goat or spaniel. Maybe it was Styrofoam. Later, Jane could never remember. She just knew it was rectangular and covered with tan gravy, and she used her knife to cut a small piece off it, speared the piece with her fork, put the piece in her mouth, chewed, swallowed, took a sip of water, used her knife to cut another small piece, speared it with her fork, put it in her mouth, chewed, swallowed, took a sip of water. And again.

Around her, conversation went on. The flowers in Freida's hair were drooping slightly, and now when she turned her head to talk to someone, the flowers all turned their faces, too, as though she were a floral sort of Medusa. She was nodding, and saying, "I see . . . I see . . ." in an uncertain way to Raymond, who was explaining the importance of the voluntary investment component of her pension plan.

Duncan was giving Mrs. Jellico an estimate on the probable worth of her great-aunt's cuckoo clock. "Now, in general, would you say you've wound the clock regularly for the past fifty years?" he asked, and Mrs. Jellico furrowed her brow in concentration.

Jane's mother was sitting next to Uncle Gene and saying, "I don't think anyone truly *likes* children," while Jimmy told Edith-Louise about the time he knocked a bowl of potpourri into the toilet.

Darcy and Luke were talking about the healing power of essential oils, in particular tea-tree oil and whether it might help Luke's foot fungus. "It's a toss-up between tea-tree oil and eucalyptus oil, really," Darcy said, and Luke told her he'd also tried soaking his feet in apple cider vinegar, but that just made him smell like a pickle and wasn't all that helpful.

Jane looked out the window. The lake was a flat silver disk, the waning sunset a ripple of orange cream. She could see the deserted beach and knew how the sand would feel at this time of day: warm on top and cool where your toes dug in.

Across the table from her, Darcy was wearing a buff-colored sheath dress. Duncan had his arm around her; from time to time, he stroked her bare shoulder with his thumb.

Everyone smiled, and smiled, and smiled.

AFTER DINNER, on the sidewalk outside the restaurant, they all had a long logistical discussion, like generals making a not-very-important battle plan. Luke's parents wanted to return to their hotel in Petoskey. (Edith-Louise had the hollow, defeated look of someone who needed alcohol badly and had failed to receive it.) Freida said she needed to go to choir practice—Jane gathered that some of the lesser singers were having difficulty with the fourth and fifth intervals—and would take Mrs. Jellico home on her way. Darcy had promised to go take some sunset photos for a tourism brochure. Luke, Uncle Gene, Duncan, and Jimmy were going to walk back to the church parking lot, where they'd left their cars, and then go out for an unofficial bachelor party. Jane and her mother would walk home, where Jane would—please, God!—be allowed to collapse in a heap.

While everyone was sorting out the details, Luke took Jane's arm and pulled her gently to a deserted stretch of sidewalk. "Are you sure you don't mind me going out?" he asked, holding both her hands.

"Not at all," she answered.

"See you tomorrow, then," Luke said. His blue eyes glowed down at her, and Jane squeezed his hands.

"Tomorrow," she said softly.

Luke brushed her lips with his, and Jane had a sudden image of how staged they must look, holding hands and kissing chastely in the soft white circle cast by the streetlight. She felt embarrassed—fraudulent, somehow—and stepped away quickly.

"Make sure Jimmy gives his wallet to Duncan," she said, "and tell the bartender to water his drinks down."

She didn't really need to say that. Here in Boyne City, the bartenders would already know.

JANE AND HER MOTHER started walking back toward Jane's house. They'd gotten almost to the corner when Jane became aware of a nervous panting behind them. She turned, and there was Mrs. Jellico puffing slowly up to them. What was she doing here?

Jane's mother was saying, "Do you ever feel you have spinach stuck in your teeth and then—" and Jane made a shushing motion.

"Is there something we can help you with, Mrs. Jellico?" she asked.

It took a few seconds for Mrs. Jellico to catch her breath. "I'm afraid I left my pocketbook at your place."

"Why, that's all right," Jane said, in exactly the way she might have said, *Oh, for fuck's sake.* Mrs. Jellico looked startled. Jane forced her voice into a gentler tone. "Come with us."

They all began walking, Jane ahead of her mother and Mrs. Jellico. She felt like a sled dog pulling a very heavy toboggan toward the lodge at the end of the day.

"Jimmy is a charming young man," Jane's mother said to Mrs. Jellico. "It's a shame he's a bit simpleminded."

"Mom!" Jane snapped impatiently.

"Don't be so sensitive, dear," her mother said. "We've all been there." She turned to Mrs. Jellico. "I was forty-two when Jane was born, and I was terribly afraid she'd be an imbecile. She was a very red, wrinkly newborn, and that certainly didn't help matters—she just didn't *look* intelligent. Then she rolled off the changing table when she was four months old, and I thought, 'Brain damage on top of mental defect! We might as well just put her in a home right now!'"

"Oh my!" Mrs. Jellico breathed in a startled voice. She goggled at Jane slightly.

"And, look—she turned out just fine," Jane's mother said. "And I'm sure Jimmy will, too. Although we went through a rough patch when Jane was in the third grade and couldn't memorize the times tables. Just absolutely could not learn them, not for love nor money! And I thought, 'Well, now I surely am paying the price for taking aspirin in my fifth month.'"

They were on Jane's street now, and as they approached her house, Jane put on a little burst of speed, like a marathoner approaching the finish line, and raced up the porch stairs, leaving her mother and Mrs. Jellico behind. She threw open the door and glanced wildly around the living room. Mrs. Jellico's old-lady purse was perched on the loveseat like a black vinyl beetle.

Jane snatched it up—it weighed nothing at all, and she was suddenly sure that it contained only Kleenex and a lipstick, no money or valuables, not one single item that couldn't have waited until tomorrow—and turned back toward the door. Her mother's car keys were on the hall table, and Jane grabbed them by the fringed leather keychain.

She stepped back out onto the porch just as her mother and Mrs. Jellico were reaching the steps.

"Good Lord, Jane," her mother said. "You ran off without a word! Left us both standing on the sidewalk! I said to Mrs. Jellico here, 'I do believe she's got cold feet and is rushing off to call the church and cancel. Either that, or the shrimp cocktail disagreed with her.'"

Jane smiled, slightly out of breath. "I just wanted to find Mrs. Jellico's pocketbook," she said. "I know it's such a horrible feeling, not knowing where your purse is."

It was easy to be gracious now that she knew her mother and Mrs. Jellico were not going to get inside and settle in for coffee and conversation. She handed Mrs. Jellico's purse to her and gave her a little pat on the arm. "My mother will drop you off at home now, and we'll see you tomorrow."

Jane's mother looked startled. "You want me to drive her home?"

"Yes, if you will be so kind," Jane said. She took her mother's hand and pressed the keychain into it, then closed her mother's fingers over it. This was a trick of the classroom: Jane did this every time she handed a child the wooden hall pass, or the magnifying glass, or the whiteboard pointer. *This is yours now; hold it tight.* It worked with everything but the class hamster, who didn't take kindly to squeezing.

"Well, all right," her mother said. She turned to Mrs. Jellico. "My car is right over there."

The two crossed the driveway toward Jane's mother's elderly Ford Fiesta, Mrs. Jellico tottering, Jane's mother stalking in her usual purposeful gait. The sight of them leaving was physically, bodily delicious, like seeing a glass full of cold Chardonnay resting on a white-clothed tabletop. And speaking of! Jane went inside, pulling the door shut behind her, and hurried into the kitchen.

She pulled a half-full bottle of Chardonnay out of the fridge. She poured some into a glass—the wine as sweetly yellow as a buttercup—and drank half of it right there, standing in the cool swirl of air from the open refrigerator. She refilled the glass, shut the fridge, and went into the bathroom, shedding her skirt and blouse along the way. To be alone was heavenly; she felt it was all she could ever want.

She started the shower and rested her wineglass on the bathroom counter. When the water was hot enough, she peeled off her bra and underpants and stepped into the tub, her blistered feet stinging. She stood under the spray for a long time, shampooing and soaping and then just letting the water beat down on her face.

Jane turned off the taps and pressed the water out of her hair with her hands. She stepped out of the shower and stood dripping on the bath mat while she reached for her wine. The cold glass felt as smooth and cool as a polished river stone in her hand.

In the corner of the fogged-over bathroom mirror, written in the steam, were the words *milk English muffins orange juice*. Her mother must have written that after her own shower this morning. It was a leftover habit from Jane's childhood, when she and her mother had kept the grocery list on the bathroom mirror, adding to it every day. Jane smiled, wondering why it was only possible to feel fond of her mother when she was not actually in her mother's presence.

Jane pulled on her robe and walked down the hall, picking up her discarded clothing.

"Mom?" she called toward the living room. No answer.

She threw her clothes into the hamper and went into the kitchen to refill her wineglass.

The sight of the living room—half-filled glasses and plates with cracker crumbs everywhere, the cheeseball looking like someone had run a Tonka truck through it—was so depressing that instead of sitting there, she carried her glass outside.

The sky was lavender-colored now. The sun had set, but the light lingered, like a child reluctant to go to bed. Jane crossed the lawn, wincing as the grass poked at her sore feet, and sat at the round little wrought-iron table under the pergola.

Where was her mother? Perhaps she was having cocoa with Mrs. Jellico. (If so, she was a better woman than Jane.) Perhaps she'd gone to Glen's for English muffins. Perhaps she'd gone to put gas in her car, or to the ATM, or to do some other last-minute errand. Did it really matter, as long as Jane had this peaceful alone time?

Jane took a sip of Chardonnay. She stretched her legs out and rested her bare feet on the other patio chair. She still had wedding-related things to do, but they no longer weighed so heavily upon her. Instead, she reached for the mantra of her college days: *In twenty-four hours, this will all be over.* She used to apply it to exams and doctor appointments, but she could apply it here, too. In twenty-four hours, she would be married, the wedding over and done with, the processional rushed or not rushed, the food eaten, the drinks drunk. She and Luke would be at the bed-and-breakfast in Traverse City, ready to fly out to Chicago and on to Calgary the next day. They would order room service and—

The sound of sirens whooping in the distance startled her, and looking up, Jane realized that the last light had slipped away. Night had fallen. She should go inside and try to get some sleep.

The sirens grew louder. Fire truck or ambulance—whichever it was, they were on Lake Street now, heading to some emergency, some accident.

Knowledge bloomed in her mind like a black flower opening, and Jane jumped to her feet, then had to hold on to the back of the chair, swaying. She knew then that her mother was not having cocoa with Mrs. Jellico, or buying English muffins, or searching for an ATM.

She knew those sirens were racing toward her mother, but something else was racing toward Jane. Something shadowy, and bullet-shaped, and almost sentient was hurtling through the night. It was looking for her, and she knew that she must let it find her. She must take ownership of it. She must close her fingers over it and never let it go. This terrible thing. It belonged to her now.

2006

I T WAS JULY AGAIN, and sunny. The weather was warm, sultry, almost literally seductive—the kind of day when even locals who hadn't dipped a toe in the lake for years gazed yearningly in the direction of the beach. Jane sat at her kitchen table, picking the raisins out of a piece of raisin toast. The phone on the counter rang, and when Jane stood up to answer, she saw that the number on the caller ID screen belonged to her mother. She sighed and picked up the receiver. "Hi, Mom."

"Hello, Jane. It's your mother."

Jane didn't point out that she'd obviously known that, and that her mother would have *known* she'd known from the way she answered the phone. Conversations with her mother tended to get a little circular these days, and Jane didn't want to start off that way.

Instead, she said, "How are you, Mom?"

"Not too bad," her mother said. "I had a little indigestion after breakfast, but that's to be expected at my age, I suppose. Anyway, I just wanted to read you an article."

Jane heard the rustling of newspaper. Phone calls with her mother were full-body experiences. Jane heard whatever her mother was saying, obviously, but lots of times, her mother was eating and Jane heard that, too. Her mother had a particular fondness for root-beer barrels and butterscotch disks, and the suck of saliva and crunch of candy as she polished one off could make Jane's own mouth feel sticky. Her mother also had a habit of settling into her recliner as soon as she got someone on the line, and the whistling clunk as she put up the footrest was enough to whizz Jane straight back to childhood and the feel of the deep, soft leather of the recliner holding her like a giant's hand. Invariably, her mother said, "Now, don't let me forget I have carrot cake in the oven." Or blueberry muffins. Or chocolate chip cookies. Jane could smell them for hours after she hung up. Her mother also kept up a running commentary—"I'm looking at the Penney's catalogue. Now, what do you call that shade of yellow?"—which provided a visual component as well. (Deep down, Jane was unsure whether her mother knew that the telephone was a two-way communication device and not a radio she could switch on and off at random.)

"This is from *The New York Times*," her mother said. "It's about adequate calcium intake for women your age."

"I take a multivitamin—" Jane started.

"'Intakes of five hundred milligrams of calcium per day in women with high osteoporosis rates help to reduce fracture risk, as does increased physical activity to strengthen bones and muscles,'" her mother read in a fulsome, newscaster sort of tone. Then she broke off and said in her regular voice, "Now, I know Luke soured you on marriage and children, dear, but you need to think of your own health."

"Luke did not sour me on marriage!" Jane protested. "I'm the one who called off the wedding!"

"I'm sure that's true," her mother said. "Or partly true. But he has certainly seemed to give you a moment's pause, if you don't mind my saying so. And even if you choose to be single, you don't want to end up a hunchback."

"Kyphosis has nothing to do with lack of calcium," Jane said.

"Well, I'm not talking about kyphosis, I'm talking about hunchbacks."

"It's the same thing."

They had arrived at the circular part of the conversation. They went back and forth over the definition of kyphosis and how that differed from scoliosis and how Jane's mother thought they were both just excuses for poor posture and how Jane's own posture was certainly going to have health ramifications in later life. Then Jane's mother remembered she had some gingerbread in the oven, and they said good-bye.

IT WAS SATURDAY, and as usual, Jane drove over to Jimmy's house to check on him. She knew Saturdays were long when you lived alone. She lived alone, too—sometimes her book club on Sunday nights was her only weekend outing. She drove absently, her mother's comment still gnawing at her thoughts. It was true, Jane told herself, she *had* been the one to call off the wedding.

Jane's memory of the night of the accident was patchy. She remembered Luke driving her to the hospital in Petoskey to see her mother in the ER. The sight of her mother sitting on a gurney with her left arm in a sling, her large, leonine face looking so slack and old, had caused Jane to burst into tears.

Her mother had turned to her and held out her good hand. "Don't cry, dearheart," she said. "I'm okay."

"Oh, Mom." Jane took her mother's hand. "I'm so glad you're not hurt."

"I'll be fine," her mother said. Then her face had contorted, twisted with sorrow. "And, Jane, I am so, so sorry."

In the hospital hallway afterward, Luke had put his arms around Jane and said that of course they must postpone the wedding, and she agreed, nodding wordlessly against his chest. They had driven to Jimmy's house, where Duncan and Darcy and Uncle Gene (who

Jane had totally forgotten about) were clustered around Jimmy as he sat crying on the low plaid sofa with the broken spring.

Luke left to take Uncle Gene back to his hotel room and to begin making all the necessary calls to Reverend Palumbo and Freida and the barn venue people and the caterer and all their guests. Darcy had made coffee in the dingy yellow kitchen while Duncan sorted through Mrs. Jellico's papers and called the funeral home.

And Jane? What did Jane do? She sat down next to Jimmy and put her arm around his shoulders.

Jimmy's eyes were red-rimmed, and the skin around them was blotchy and pink. His lips were raw-looking, and Jane noticed for the first time that there were faint lines on his forehead.

"But what happened, Jane?" he asked. "Ma doesn't drive. She doesn't even know how to drive. Why was she driving?"

"She wasn't driving," Jane said slowly. "My mother was driving."

"Your ma?" Jimmy frowned. "Why was she driving my ma home?"

"Because I asked her to," Jane said.

"And what happened?" Jimmy asked. "Folks keep telling me, but I just don't understand."

"Well," Jane began hesitantly, "apparently, they were driving along East Street, and my mother—my mother was supposed to turn right onto Water Street, but she went straight instead. And then she tried to—to back up, and she backed into the intersection and another car hit them."

"Hit them where?"

"Right there on the corner of East and Water."

"But where on the car?"

"On the, um, the right side." Jane did not want to say *passenger side.*

"And Ma just—she just—?"

"Yes," Jane said as gently as she knew how. "She died."

"Oh." Jimmy's voice was almost too soft to hear. Then suddenly, "Is your ma okay?"

Jane hesitated. "She broke her arm, but she's going to be fine."

"That's good," Jimmy said, nodding. "That's good."

Was it good, though? Was it good that right this minute her mother was sitting in a hospital bed, while Mrs. Jellico lay in the morgue? Was it good that by next week, Jane's mother would be back in Grand Rapids, terrorizing dental patients and hitching up the waistband of her skirt, while Jimmy staggered around with an emotional hole blown in him like the cyborg in *Terminator 2*? Jane wasn't sure.

Over and over, Jimmy and Jane had this conversation, or some variant of it. His mother's death seemed too much for Jimmy to process. It was like a game of *Chutes and Ladders,* and Jimmy kept hitting the longest chute and sliding back to the beginning: Why was his mother driving? Why was Jane's mother driving? What exactly had happened? His mother was dead, actually dead? He would seem to accept this for a few days, and then he'd hit the chute again. Eventually he stopped asking, but Jane wasn't sure that meant he'd stopped sliding down the chute.

Three months after the accident, Luke had suggested they pick a new date for the wedding, and Jane had told him truthfully (or truthfully as far as it went) that she was too overwhelmed with straightening out Mrs. Jellico's affairs to even think about it. And then three months later, he brought it up again.

They had been in the kitchen at her house, with Jane measuring out spaghetti to add to the pot of boiling water on the stovetop. She was in a distinctly unreceptive mood. It was National Law Enforcement Day, and Jane had dressed the part for school: black polyester pants and a tan polyester button-down shirt with black pocket flaps, a cowboy hat with a tin star glued to the hatband, and mirrored sunglasses. Her students had loved it, but the hat was too small and squeezed her temples, and she had broken out in a rash from all that polyester and had to change into sweats and an old T-shirt borrowed from Coach Gillis during recess. She had arranged for an actual policeman to join the class for lunch, and he had squeezed a juice box too hard and sprayed lemonade all over the Peter Rabbit rug.

"I just can't begin to wrap my mind around planning a wedding," she said. "Not tonight."

Luke stood behind her and rubbed her shoulders. "No wedding, then," he said. "Just you and me at the courthouse."

"Oh, Luke." Jane sighed. "I don't know."

He stopped rubbing. "You don't know about what?"

"Just getting married," Jane said. "I don't know if I want to."

This didn't seem to her, at that second, any more momentous than saying she didn't want to grade papers or load the dishwasher. I don't know if I want to go to a movie tonight. I don't know if I want to have the Marshalls over. I don't know if I want pizza again. I don't know if I want to drive all the way to Petoskey. I don't know if I want to go hiking today. I don't know if I want to get married. What was the difference, really?

Luke's hands closed hard on her shoulders for the briefest of moments, then released. "Thanks for letting me know," he said. "Finally."

Why had Jane imagined he would take this news cheerfully? Just because he was, overall, a cheerful person? He was not her personal support system, not some professional caregiver she had hired. He was a man she had failed to love, or at least failed to love in the way he deserved, and now he knew that.

Luke left that very night, even before the spaghetti was done cooking. Jane stood at the stove, swirling the spaghetti around the pot with a wooden spoon while Luke walked silently through the house, stuffing his clothes and CDs and paperbacks into a single duffel bag. She had never before realized how few possessions he had at her house.

The worst part of it was that Jane knew she had the power to take it all back, to say she didn't mean it, to say it was just the stress of Law Enforcement Day, that the courthouse suited her just fine. But she didn't want to say that. What she really wanted to say—what she dared not turn around for fear that she would say—was, *You aren't really leaving me alone, are you? You aren't leaving me alone to take care of Jimmy?*

OTHER PEOPLE HELPED with Jimmy, of course. Aggie was very generous about delivering food. She brought Jimmy dishes of baked ziti and chicken cordon bleu and her special Polish meatballs, along with bossy notes about how to warm and serve them, but Jimmy never ate them. Jane knew because she was the one who scraped the pans out when the food grew hard and moldy; she was the one who washed and dried those pans, for Jimmy's house had no dishwasher. Duncan packed a lunch for Jimmy along with his own every day now, after Jimmy had shown up for work three days in a row with no lunch. (Only then had it occurred to them: Mrs. Jellico had packed Jimmy's lunches. Of course she had.) Mr. Estes from across the street raked and mowed Jimmy's lawn along with his own, and another neighbor cleaned the gutters once a year. The Lymans took out Jimmy's trash and recycling, and put the bins back afterward. The Holcombes took him to church with them on major holidays, and Mrs. Morse took him to bingo night once a month. The Deatons had him over for dinner whenever they made ham with pineapple rings.

But almost everything else—paying bills, cleaning the house, shopping for food, making doctor appointments, the endless process of keeping Jimmy *alive*—fell to Jane, because the accident was her fault. Jane's mother had been the one driving, but the accident had been Jane's fault.

Jane, who had been shown a million kindnesses that day and who had refused to show any in return. Jane, who had been too sullen and selfish to take five minutes and drive a nice old lady home safely. Jane, who had insisted that her mother—someone whose driving she *knew* to be unsafe—drive instead. Jane, who could not be bothered to give her mother directions, so that her mother missed the turn and reversed back onto Water Street just in time for a man driving a lavender Saab to hit their car broadside. Jane, who had not even taken the time to help Mrs. Jellico put her seatbelt on, which meant that when the Saab struck the car, Mrs. Jellico's head swung forward like a thrown bowling ball and struck the windshield. It was Jane's fault that Mrs. Jellico had sustained head injuries that would almost certainly have killed her except the crush injuries to her chest and abdomen killed her first. It was Jane's fault that Mrs. Jellico had died on a dark street in a pool of broken glass. It was Jane's fault that Jimmy no longer had his mother. It was *all* Jane's fault—can't you see that?

Everyone else could.

JANE PARKED HER CAR in front of Jimmy's house and sighed.

She was never sure why Jimmy's house looked so much like it was trembling on the verge of an abrupt slide into decrepitude. The lawn was no shaggier than many of the other lawns on the street. The green paint on the house was no flakier than the paint on some other houses; the roof was missing no more shingles. Other houses had off-kilter shutters, and sagging porch steps, and neglected flower beds. But no other house had *all* these deficits, she realized. No other house had quite so many signs of inattention, which, though small, together seemed to be a banner proclaiming AN UNLOVED SINGLE PERSON LIVES HERE.

She knocked on the front door, and Jimmy answered it, wearing his pajamas and carrying a plastic bowl of cereal.

"Hi, Jane!" he said. "Come in."

"What are you up to, Jimmy?" Jane asked, although she knew it was a pointless question. When left to his own devices, Jimmy never did anything but eat and watch television.

"Just watching TV," Jimmy said, as though to prove her point.

Jane stepped into the dim house and then closed the door on the beautiful day outside, on the trees that shook their emerald leaves like cheerleaders shaking pompoms. She and Jimmy should buy sandwiches and sit on a bench at Peninsula Beach and look at the lake and let the wind cool their faces. But the idea of getting Jimmy dressed and out the door, of figuring out what kind of sandwich he wanted, of answering his million questions about why they were doing whatever it was they were doing—it all seemed like too much effort. Way too much. Jane felt exhausted just considering it.

"Want some Lucky Charms?" Jimmy asked.

"No, thank you," Jane said. "You go back to your show, and I'll just check a few things in the kitchen."

"Okay," Jimmy said agreeably, and walked back down the shadowy hallway.

They couldn't go to the beach, anyway, Jane told herself. So many things here needed her attention. She should change the sheets on Jimmy's bed and run the vacuum, wipe down the bathroom and sort through the mail. She went into the kitchen, which looked like the morning-after scene of a lame frat party: empty pizza boxes, sticky soda cans, smudged glasses, crusted cereal bowls, overflowing trash can.

Jane sighed. She washed the glasses and bowls and left them to dry in the dish drainer. She bagged up the trash and recycling and carried the bags out to the bins by the garage, making another trip for the pizza boxes. Five pizzas in a week.

Back in the kitchen, she opened the Humpty Dumpty ceramic cookie jar—it was so ugly it almost defied description—where Jimmy insisted on keeping his money. The worn envelope inside contained three singles. Jane added four tens from her wallet. This was Jimmy's weekly spending money.

The road to Jimmy's fiscal independence was a long one—possibly endless, Jane sometimes thought. Luke had been the one to sort through Mrs. Jellico's finances after the accident, had crunched the numbers of Jimmy's income and expenses. They were very small and extremely crunchable numbers, like pounding a bag of graham crackers to make an undersized pie crust. Mrs. Jellico had owned the house, but she had no other income besides her social security benefits and Jimmy's long-dead father's pension. She'd owned no other assets or investments besides a small savings account and an even smaller college fund set up for Jimmy in the distant past. (The hopefulness of that college fund had made Jane's heart clench painfully.) Luke had consolidated these accounts into one owned jointly by Jane and Jimmy, transferred the bills into Jane's name, set up automated payments, and outlined a budget for Jimmy that would cover property taxes, utility bills, insurance premiums, food, and clothing. The budget Luke had created was a tight one, with no room for extras. Jane had gone over it diligently with Jimmy, although she could see he paid little attention. She kept meaning to work with him, to teach him the basics of accounting, but she never seemed to get around to it. It was just easier for her to handle the money and dole out this weekly allowance.

She went into the living room, where Jimmy was watching the Lifetime Movie Network. It was almost all he watched. This had seemed a strange choice to Jane, and she asked him about it once, and he said he liked it because the shows were all two hours long. "Sometimes, on other channels," Jimmy said, "the shows are only half an hour, and I finish watching and look at the clock and realize there's three more hours before I can go to bed."

Since then Jane had learned not to ask so many questions.

"You want to come watch with me?" Jimmy asked.

She didn't, of course. The Lifetime Movie Network depressed her, as did people who watched the Lifetime Movie Network. And she really should do some laundry. But she knew that Jimmy would rather have company watching television than all the clean clothes in the world, so she sat down next to him. On the screen, a doctor was talking about a double-blind study.

"*Double-blind* means that neither the doctor nor the patient knows whether the medicine is real or fake," Jane said automatically, knowing that Jimmy would need this explained.

It had surprised Jane at first, the things Jimmy didn't know. Jimmy didn't know how to cook anything but ramen noodles, or how to tell if fruit and vegetables were fresh. He didn't know how to read food labels for nutritional information or check expiration dates, and he was a little sketchy on which items needed to be kept in the fridge or the freezer.

Jimmy knew his name, address, and telephone number (Jane was heartily relieved), but he didn't know where his social security card and birth certificate were, or where his mother kept her important papers, or whether they had a mortgage.

He didn't know the name of his doctor. (Jane was able to figure out that it was Dr. Haven after a form of Twenty Questions: Is it a man or woman? Is he old? Does he have a beard? Does he wear glasses?) Jimmy didn't know what kind of insurance he had, nor did he understand the concept of a co-pay. He had a vague idea of which over-the-counter medications were for pain, diarrhea, or cold and allergy symptoms, but Jane didn't trust him to follow the directions for using them.

He knew to call 911 in an emergency (Jane checked with him just to be sure) but had no idea how to treat cuts, burns, insect bites, or splinters. He didn't know how to check the batteries in a smoke detector, nor was he aware of the dangers of frayed electrical cords, unattended candles, overloaded power strips, or using a knife to get bread out of a toaster.

He knew how to shower and shave and dress himself, and to wash his hands after using the bathroom. But he didn't know that even though you *get* clean in the shower, you still have to *clean* the shower. And the rest of the bathroom. And the kitchen. And the floors. And, well, forget about dusting, Jane had decided.

He knew how to use the washer and dryer, but no longer did so after he shrunk all of his shirts down to the size of infant sweaters by using the hottest possible setting on the dryer, which was some very old model that dried with the heat of a thousand suns and was probably a fire hazard.

He knew how to change a lightbulb but not what kind of lightbulbs to buy. He didn't know how to replace a vacuum cleaner bag, or stop a toilet from running, or reset a circuit breaker, or change a fuse. He didn't even know where the fuse box *was*.

He didn't know how to balance a checkbook or read a bank statement; he didn't know there were fees for using ATMs, or what being overdrawn meant. He didn't understand how credit cards worked or that not paying the electric bill meant your electricity got cut off. He didn't know how to file a tax return (of course he didn't—Jane was just tossing out wild ideas here) or read a pay slip or understand the difference between gross pay and net pay. Or the difference between gas and electric, or colors and whites. Or between broiling and baking, or the furnace and the hot water heater. Or between rum and whiskey, prime rib and ribeye, or Land Rover and Range Rover. Or free market and command economies, allegory and parable, India and Bangladesh, radon and radium, politics and partisanship, classical and baroque, light conversation and true communication, lust and infatuation, love and sex, and all the rest of it.

AFTER THE MOVIE WAS OVER, Jane left Jimmy's house and went to Glen's to buy groceries for both of them. Buying Jimmy's food—Pop-Tarts, boxed macaroni and cheese, potato chips, peanut butter, saltines—was like shopping for someone who lived in a fallout shelter. Her own list was equally depressing: a packet of chicken breasts, six eggs, a half gallon of milk, one bag of salad, the smallest container of yogurt, the smallest bottle of syrup. A single person's groceries.

She was in the frozen foods aisle, buying a mere pint of strawberry ice cream, when a shopping cart blocked her path. She looked up in annoyance. It was Duncan.

"You were lost in thought," he said. "Anything interesting?"

"Not really," Jane said. "I haven't seen—seen you around much."

She flushed. She knew she hadn't seen him around much because he was dating a Charlevoix woman named Tabitha who worked in a bakery that, according to Freida, sold overpriced croissants. But Jane didn't want Duncan to know she still kept track of his romantic life.

"Tabitha and I broke up," Duncan said, apparently not at all deceived. "She was moving downstate, and I don't do so well with long-distance relationships."

"Oh," Jane said. "That's a shame."

"Well, I don't know about that." Duncan sounded cheerful, as he always did about breakups. "Her herb garden bothered my hay fever no end."

Jane nodded; she'd known relationships that hinged on less.

He was wearing a dark gold-colored shirt that matched the golden glints in his auburn hair. Jane noticed that he had new lines around his mouth. Just imagine: lines carved by experiences that Jane knew nothing about.

They regarded each other for a moment that was really only a regular moment but that seemed as endless as a river, as open as a mountain vista. Duncan looked at her and his amber-flecked brown eyes seemed to Jane, as they always had, to fix her in a warm spotlight.

Duncan rocked his shopping cart back and forth so it nudged hers gently. Nudge. Nudge. Finally, he said, "I see you've bleached the hair on your upper lip."

Jane sighed. "Yes, but I didn't know it was going to make me look like Colonel Sanders."

"More like a very pretty Mark Twain," Duncan said.

And just like that, they were a couple again.

WELL, *almost* just like that. First, they had to pay for their groceries, and there was a little flurry of embarrassment over which checkout line to choose. The first lane was problematic because Duncan had had the cashier's grandmother's painted satinwood cabinet in his workshop for about a year now, and the cashier was likely to bring it up and be unpleasant about it. The cashier in the other lane was a woman Duncan had slept with a number of years ago after a car show in Manistee, and while she would (probably) not be unpleasant, Jane would just as soon not talk to someone Duncan had had sex with right before she herself was planning to have sex with him. But luckily, Mr. Fairmont came out from behind the customer service desk and opened a third lane, and he and Duncan had a small discussion about walleye fishing.

"Walleye are just so darned *smart*," Mr. Fairmont said.

"They're smart, but they're lazy," Duncan said. "I find if you can just get the worm in front of them—"

"That's all well and good if you're using a worm harness," Mr. Fairmont said, somewhat critically. "If not, just forget it."

Afterward, Jane loaded her groceries into her car, and Duncan loaded his groceries into his rust-spotted white van. They drove in a caravan straight to Jane's house and made love on the old leather sofa without even unpacking the groceries, and Jane's strawberry ice cream melted right down to a puddle.

JANE WAS ASLEEP in Duncan's arms when the phone rang the next morning at seven thirty. She answered drowsily.

"Hello, Jane, dear," Aggie said. "Now that you and Duncan are back together, I feel I can ask—"

"Wait—how did you know about that?" Jane asked. She and Duncan had been back together for about eighteen hours.

"Well, last night I was watching the coverage of the California wildfires on CNN," Aggie said, "and Gary got upset."

"Gary cares about the wildfires?" Jane asked. Up until this point, she hadn't known Gary cared about anything but himself.

"No, no, he disapproves of CNN," Aggie said. "He says the news ticker makes him nervous. Often a little drive and a piece of pie calm him down, so we drove over to the pie shop in Petoskey, and on the way, we saw Duncan's van parked down the street from your house. I said to Gary, 'Why, I believe Duncan's taken up with Jane again. Either that, or Mary Winslow is being unfaithful to her husband.'"

"Oh," Jane said.

"Anyway," Aggie continued, "we brought Jimmy a piece of coconut cream pie, and when we dropped it off at his house, I couldn't help noticing that the porch railing is loose, and I wonder if you might ask Duncan to tighten it down."

Jane glanced over at Duncan. He was still asleep. His eyelashes made golden crescents on his cheeks. Look at that, Duncan asleep in her bed.

"I'd be happy to do that, Aggie," Jane said in a strange, upbeat voice she didn't recognize as her own. "I'll take Duncan over there with me today. Thank you *so* much for letting me know. And thank you for *all* you do for Jimmy. You really are so *very* kind."

The world was as bright and shiny as a fishing lure.

IF AGGIE KNEW Jane and Duncan were back together, then it was just a matter of days—perhaps hours or even minutes—before everyone else in Boyne City knew, too. So Jane called Freida and told her right away.

"Why, that's—wonderful," Freida said in the uncertain tone people use when setting up Wi-Fi networks. "Do you know that he still clears my driveway every single time it snows?"

"He does?" Jane didn't mind that Duncan did that; she only minded that she didn't know about it. That was how Boyne City she'd become.

"Oh, yes," Freida said. "And once, my car got stuck in the school parking lot, and he came over right away and pulled my car out with his van. He really is much nicer than most people think."

Jane even told her mother, who said, "Duncan again? I thought he was over you."

"Well, it turns out he wasn't," Jane said cheerfully. She was too happy to take offense.

Everyone seemed baffled, even if (unlike her mother) they were too polite to say so, and Jane couldn't blame them. They all knew she and Duncan had broken up the first time because he didn't want to commit, and he showed no signs of having changed his mind about that. It was Jane who'd changed. She understood now that time was too valuable to deny yourself things that gave you plea-sure. There had to be more to life than teaching second grade, and taking care of Jimmy, and drinking a whole bottle of red wine while you watched *The Bachelor* (though that last part was pretty nice). She wanted Duncan—she had never stopped wanting him—and now she was willing to take him on his terms.

Jimmy's reaction was much better. Jane and Duncan told him together when they went over to drop off his groceries later the next day.

Jimmy smiled broadly—the smile that made you realize how handsome he would have been if he'd been born just a little smarter—and shook Duncan's hand over and over, saying, "Good for you, buddy! Good for you!"

Then he turned to Jane and said, "Now we can have Duncan and Aggie and Gary over for Taco Tuesday!"

Taco Tuesday was a tradition Jane had started with Jimmy. It had originally been Pizza Night, but that was before Jane discov-ered how often Jimmy ordered pizza on his own. So they'd switched to tacos, and now on Tuesday nights, Jane brought the ingredients and made tacos and they watched a video Jimmy had chosen. Last week, they'd watched *Ernest Scared Stupid,* and of all the prices Jane had paid for her mother's accident, she thought watching that movie might have been the highest.

Now she felt insulted, too. Wasn't her presence alone enough to make Taco Tuesday successful? Now they had to have Aggie and Gary, too? *Gary?*

But this time around, Jane was determined to do everything right. She wouldn't be jealous, not of Aggie, not of Duncan's legion of ex-girlfriends, not of the new waitress at Robert's with the long, dark eyelashes, not of the girl at the video store who carried her breasts in front of her as though they were a couple of large cup-cakes. She would not be demanding, not of Duncan's time, not of his attention, not of his commitment, not of his money. (He didn't have any, so that part would be easy.) She would be all the things she had always meant to be in their relationship and somehow never managed to be: wise and cool and levelheaded and regal and hopelessly alluring, like a single ball bearing gleaming on a black velvet background, or maybe a Swedish nanny. If that meant inviting Aggie and Gary to Taco Tuesday, so be it.

She smiled. "Of course, we can include them. We can invite Freida, too."

Jane called them later that night. Freida said she would be delighted, and Aggie said that Gary had some issue with tacos— apparently he'd found a stone in a street taco in 1980 and been off them ever since—but she would bring enchiladas.

AGGIE AND GARY were already on the porch of Jimmy's house on Tuesday when Jane and Duncan arrived. Jane and Duncan had made love less than an hour before, and Jane's mind was pleasantly slowed, like her classroom's Newton's cradle when someone had set it going very slowly: *tick . . . tick . . . tick.*

Aggie was wearing a dark purple sheath dress with an apple-green cardigan, and by all that was good and holy, Jane thought, she should have looked like Barney the dinosaur, but she didn't. As always, Aggie's wide-faced, rosy-lipped, flaxen-haired prettiness took Jane by surprise.

"Oh, hello," Aggie said, ringing the doorbell. "Now, Gary, I'm sure you remember Duncan's girlfriend, Jane."

Gary peered at Jane. "You're not the one with the fondness for Grape-Nuts, are you?"

"No," Jane said, sighing. "That must've been someone else."

Jimmy answered the door wearing the chinos and yellow polo

shirt that Jane knew he considered his best outfit. (Honestly, Jimmy could break your heart without half trying.) The shirt was tight across Jimmy's stomach. All that pizza, Jane supposed.

Before they could go inside, Freida's car pulled up to the curb, and Freida got out. "Hey, everyone!" she called.

"Who's that?" Gary asked.

Aggie *tsk*ed in an annoyed way, but Jimmy said helpfully, "That's Freida Fitzgerald."

Gary looked doubtful. "Is she new in town?"

"Gary," Duncan said patiently, "she's taught music at the high school going on twenty years now."

Freida came up the porch steps, carrying her mandolin case. She was slightly out of breath and had ringlets of brown hair pressed flat against her forehead from the heat.

"Hi, Freida!" Jimmy said. "Are you going to play the mandolin?"

"You bet I am," she answered cheerfully. She noticed Gary staring at her. "Hey, how are you, Gary?"

"She knows me," Gary said to Aggie.

"Of course I know you!" Freida exclaimed. "We've known each other for *years*. I've been to your house, you've been to my house. You handle my homeowner's insurance."

Gary frowned. "Broad form or comprehensive?"

"Maybe we should all go inside now," Duncan suggested.

"Yes, please," Aggie said. "I've been holding this dish of enchiladas so long my fingers are numb."

They all went into the kitchen to help themselves to drinks. Jane was relieved at this self-service. If they waited for Jimmy to serve drinks, they'd be here all night. Normally, Jane would stay in the kitchen to make dinner, but tonight Aggie was doing that, so Jane was free to sit in the living room with everyone else.

Jimmy seemed very excited to have guests and told a long, confusing story about how some lady was threatening Duncan with legal action if he didn't refinish her grandfather's trestle table, which he'd had for at least a year and for which he'd already accepted payment.

"People," Duncan said, shaking his head.

Freida settled herself on the couch next to Jane and took out her mandolin. Part of being friends with Freida meant getting used to her playing the mandolin all the time—softly if people were talking, louder if they weren't. If the conversation got heated, she would strum faster; if they were all tired, she would play something soothing. It was like having a constant soundtrack to your life, or maybe a mandolin-playing Greek chorus, because sometimes she sang, too—little snatches of lyrics that always seemed to fit the occasion. When Aggie called to Duncan from the kitchen to please adjust the air conditioning, Freida sang, "'You can fill my pipe and then go fetch my slippers,'" and when Gary got up to look for the bathroom, Freida sang, "'I can't help but wonder where I'm bound.'"

"Dinner is ready!" Aggie called.

Everything Aggie ever made was delicious, and the enchiladas were no exception. After dinner, Jane cleared the table and ran water in the sink for the dishes.

Aggie came in to help her. "Now, if you'll wash the dishes, I'll clean out the fridge," Aggie said, which was annoying because Jane was *already* washing the dishes. She didn't need to be told.

Aggie began unscrewing the lids of jars from the fridge and sniffing them. "Gah!" she said each time, and threw the jar in the recycling bin. There was no *particular* reason that this should make Jane feel like swatting Aggie with her own pie server, but it did. Aggie dumped the last jar and began wiping down the inside of the refrigerator. Jane moved on to washing the glasses.

They cleaned in silence for a minute or two. Then Aggie said, "How are things with Duncan? He seems very happy."

Jane had noticed that Aggie often asked a question, then answered it herself. She supposed that was a real estate agent habit—*How do you like this place? I love that third bedroom!*—but it also might be the result of living with Gary.

"What makes you say that?" she asked.

"Oh, well, he and I were in the hardware store buying hinges for my kitchen cupboard yesterday, and I asked how you were, and he looked all sort of pleased. Normally, when I ask about some girl he's seeing, he looks, I don't know, sort of *belligerent*."

Duncan and Aggie had gone to the hardware store together? To buy hinges? Jane's mind raced like a beagle down that alley, and then she made it stop. She didn't do that anymore.

"I think you're good for Duncan," Aggie continued. "He needs someone who isn't so concerned with being glamorous all the time, someone who isn't outrageously pretty—"

Funny how this conversation was making Jane feel, well, belligerent. They finished cleaning the kitchen in that tiresome way that you clean someone else's kitchen, when you know you won't be there to enjoy the fruits of your labor. Jane rinsed out the sink and wandered into the living room where the others were gathered around the television.

"I don't understand this movie," Gary said suddenly. "Not one bit. It's almost like the baby is talking."

"The baby *is* talking," Jimmy told him. "I mean, not really, because babies can't talk. Some actor is talking. You're just supposed to think it's the baby."

"But the baby's lips aren't moving." Gary pushed his glasses up his nose and stared at Jimmy accusingly.

"Well, maybe not talking," Jimmy said patiently. "More, like, those are supposed to be the baby's thoughts."

"Then it should be called *Look Who's Thinking*," Gary said.

Jane had sometimes thought that Jimmy and Gary could be combined into a whole functioning person, but now she decided she was wrong about that. They would need a third person, maybe even a fourth.

She sat on the arm of Duncan's chair. He smiled and put his arm around her. "Hello, darlin'."

Freida strummed her mandolin and sang:

> *You don't have to call me darlin', darlin',*
> *You never even called me by my name.*

Jane gave her an annoyed look, and Freida immediately glanced up at the ceiling in a show of innocence.

Always, the worst part of visiting Jimmy was saying good-bye, knowing that you were abandoning him to the Lifetime Movie Network and gray bedsheets and cold pizza. (Now he didn't even have cold pizza—Aggie had thrown it all out.) But it was better than usual tonight because Jane was not alone. Jimmy walked them to the door, and they went out into a summer night as soft and deep as raven feathers.

"Oh, Jimmy, I nearly forgot," Aggie called. "I left you some enchiladas in the fridge—just cover them with foil and bake at three-fifty until they're warmed through, and add the sauce at the last minute."

"I sure will," Jimmy said, although Jane knew the chances of him doing that were less than zero, literally less than zero—negative chances.

Freida had put her mandolin in its striped cotton bag, but she sang, "'Good night, ladies, we're going to leave you now!'" softly as she walked to her car.

"Now, Gary," Aggie said as she followed Jane and Duncan down the sidewalk, "I need to stop at Glen's on the way home for flaked coconut so I can make Swedish coffee cake tomorrow. It won't take but a minute, and you can wait in the car."

"Now, that's something I don't miss," Duncan said to Jane in a low voice.

"What is?"

"Being told to wait in the car."

That did seem to sum up what married life with Aggie must be like, but part of Jane was now longing for coffee cake with flaked coconut in it.

"Good night, everybody!" Jimmy called from the front porch. "Good night! Good night!"

The ancient porch light threw a buttery spotlight down on him, burnishing his hair and gilding his yellow shirt, and moths swarmed around him like confetti. He waved goodbye, smiling, and Jane could almost believe he was happy.

JANE DECIDED to have the hair on her upper lip waxed. Freida recommended one of her clarinet students, a woman named Nancy in Petoskey who did a little beauty work out of her basement and would give Jane a discount. Yes, it would have been far simpler and more sensible just to book an appointment in a salon, but that's how things were done in Boyne City.

Duncan went with Jane to the appointment because Duncan liked to go on any sort of errand. It was one of the very nicest things about him.

It turned out that Nancy knew Duncan, not because he'd slept with her, but, she said, because he'd stood her up at a pancake supper ten years ago.

"I find that hard to believe," Duncan said. Jane did, too. Duncan really liked pancakes.

"Well, it's true." Nancy looked at him sternly. She was a petite blonde in her late forties. "I'm not likely to forget. I was awful excited since you said you were a navy doctor."

Duncan nodded slowly, as though Nancy had suddenly begun speaking a language he could understand. "That was something I told women 'round about that time."

This seemed to indicate the end of the social niceties. "Well, come on downstairs," Nancy said to Jane. They followed her down to her basement where an old pink beautician's chair was bolted to the floor. Jane sat down and leaned back in the chair. Nancy spread warm wax on Jane's upper lip and then ripped the wax off with a practiced flick of her wrist, like a heavy drinker throwing back a shot of bourbon.

Jane gave a little yip of pain.

"Ah, a whole new girl," Duncan said when she stood up. He put a finger under her chin and examined her face. "Is it going to grow back all thick and brown?" he asked Nancy.

"No, that's only with shaving," Nancy said.

Duncan paid, making Jane feel like they were on a date. No mention was made of a discount, but that was probably understandable.

Afterward, Duncan said he wanted to go to IHOP for lunch—Jane assumed the mention of the pancake supper had made him hungry. The hostess led them to a table, Jane trailing along with her head down, worrying that the skin above her upper lip was still pink.

Their waitress was a broad-hipped woman with faded red hair and a stubborn chin.

"Now, what do you recommend?" Duncan asked her. "Sweet pancakes, or savory?"

"Depends," she said.

"On what?"

Her voice was impatient. "On whether you're in the mood for something sweet or something savory."

She was clearly impervious to Duncan's charm. There were others like her, Jane had noticed. Disturbingly, they tended to be women in career fields that required the ability to assess people's characters: social worker, law enforcement, human resources. Office managers in particular seemed to dislike him. And teachers, except for Jane.

Finally, Duncan settled on the apple pancakes, and Jane had the French toast, and then felt guilty because Jimmy loved French toast, and here she and Duncan were having lunch on a weekday while poor Jimmy slaved away at Duncan's workshop. At least Jane assumed he was slaving away.

"I can't believe I've never asked you this before," she said, tearing the paper off a straw. "But what does Jimmy actually do at work?"

"Do?"

"Yes, what are his, you know, job responsibilities?"

"Not the jigsaw," Duncan said firmly. "Not ever. Not the handsaws either. Actually, no saws of any kind. Or drills. Sometimes he sands and uses the stapler. Sometimes he helps me varnish. Sometimes I let him tighten up screws."

The waitress set their plates down wordlessly and stalked off.

"That's it?" Jane asked. "That's all he does?"

"He sweeps and runs errands, too," Duncan said, pouring syrup over his pancakes. "And he answers the phone when I don't want—would rather not."

That meant when some woman was trying to get ahold of him. Jane herself had been a victim of the force field of frustration that was Jimmy answering Duncan's phone: *Gosh, no, Jane, he's not here. No, he didn't tell me when he'd be back. I mean, I think he'll be back to lock up, which is around six. Usually he is, unless he has to go somewhere to buy something, like to Traverse City for router bits. But that's just an example, he hasn't actually gone to Traverse City. Sometimes he just goes fishing. He's never not been here to lock up, but—* It was an extremely effective repellent.

"I can't believe that's all he does," Jane said.

Duncan looked at her. "What did you think he did?"

"I don't know," she said miserably. "I guess I hoped he was more—more *with it* at work than he is at home."

"Not really," Duncan said. "A lot of times he just watches TV in the back."

"And you keep him on full-time?" Jane asked. "Can you afford that?"

"Where else would he work?" Duncan asked. "They'd never hire him again at the feedstore, not after what happened with the parakeet seed. Besides, I like Jim. He's nice to have around."

They finished eating, and Duncan ordered coffee and then changed it to tea, which seemed to irritate their waitress disproportionately.

"Duncan Ryfield?" she said when Duncan handed her his credit card. "Why, I believe you slept with my sister Lisa after you installed her closet organizer."

Duncan looked startled. "Lisa Gladden?"

"No, Lisa Strickland."

"I don't recognize that name," Duncan said thoughtfully. "Would that have been Lisa over in Elk Rapids?"

"Nope." The waitress crossed her arms.

"Kalkaska?"

"Guess again, Sunny Jim."

"Would it be possible to give me a time frame?" Duncan asked. "Or else some details about the closet?"

"Well, this would have been, oh, about—" The waitress broke off, looking at Jane. "You okay, honey? What're you laughing about?" She frowned at Duncan. "What's wrong with your girlfriend? She's going to make herself sick if she doesn't stop."

—————

JANE THOUGHT that nobody had ever loved her body the way Duncan loved her body. He loved it deeply and simply and entirely, the same way he loved a winter sunset or fresh banana bread. He seemed happy to stroke her endlessly—the curve of her hip seemed to fascinate him, the smell of her hair to intoxicate him, the taste of her skin to transport him.

He did not seem to see any of her body's imperfections. It was not that he ignored them—he truly didn't see them. His eyes grew dreamy-looking with desire when she leaned down to get something from under the sink and her shirt rode up, or when she pulled on a pair of underpants and let the elastic snap against her hip.

That night he lay for hours—what seemed like hours—between her legs, licking, caressing, murmuring, "I love this so much, this makes me so happy." (Which was exactly what he said about banana bread, come to think of it.)

Suddenly, Jane stiffened.

"What's wrong?" Duncan asked, lifting his head.

"Nothing," Jane whispered. "Don't stop."

The idea that some people—Jimmy, Freida—might never know sex like this, love like this, it broke Jane's heart.

ON A SATURDAY in early August, Duncan and Jane drove to Grand Rapids. Duncan was going to the fishing expo, and Jane was going to visit her mother. (Jane felt she might honestly prefer the fishing expo.)

They got to her mother's little brick house in the late morning, and Jane was relieved to see a neighbor kid was mowing the lawn. Jane's mother had mowed the lawn herself when Jane was growing up, pushing the roaring lawn mower up and down in crooked rows while the flesh on her upper arms wobbled and her face grew shiny with sweat. Even as a child, Jane had always begged her mother to hire someone to mow it for her. "It's honest labor," her mother had always said. "You shouldn't be embarrassed about it." Jane had never been embarrassed—she didn't know how to explain that watching her mother struggle to mow the lawn made her feel an overwhelming sort of sorrow. She had taken over the lawn mowing as soon as she turned twelve.

Now she waved politely to the neighbor kid as she and Duncan walked up the porch steps and rang her mother's doorbell.

"Hello!" her mother said heartily, opening the door. "Welcome!" Then she leaned past them, squinting, and shouted, "Timmy, you mind my rhododendrons!" loud enough to make Jane's eardrum flex.

They followed her mother inside. She was wearing black polyester pants and a black-and-white print blouse and a twinkly black beaded necklace and matching bracelets. Jane realized her mother had dressed up for the visit, and was pleased.

"Now, I have a pot of coffee on," her mother said. "Duncan, would you like some before you start?"

Jane frowned. "Start what?"

"Don't look so worried, dear," her mother said. "I just have a few handyman chores that I was hoping Duncan could take care of."

"He came to visit!" Jane protested. "It's not like you hired him for the day."

"I don't mind," Duncan said. "I will take that cup of coffee, Phyllis, and while you're seeing to that, I'll get my toolbox from the van."

When he came back, he drank his coffee quickly and said, "Now, why don't you show me where we should start?"

He seemed to know instinctively that Jane's mother would want to supervise the chores, not just assign them. Jane sat at the kitchen table with her own cup of coffee and listened as her mother and Duncan moved from room to room. "Okay, right there, not so much!" her mother cried out. "Just give it a little tap or the whole thing is likely to fall down!" And, "Wait, I think that's the wrong type of screwdriver!"

To everything, Duncan only replied equably, "You're the boss."

Jane sighed. Her mother had made Luke do her taxes and Jane's college boyfriends change the oil in her car. Honestly, it was amazing anyone wanted to date Jane at all.

Duncan left to go to the fishing expo—lucky him—while Jane and her mother had lunch outside at the picnic table. Timmy had finished mowing the lawn, and now the yard was quiet, filled with the peaceful, somnolent heat of late summer. Jane's mother had prepared a lunch she'd often made in Jane's childhood—tuna salad sandwiches with pickles and Fritos—and she served it on the same brown-and-yellow earthenware plates she'd had for an eternity. Jane hoped she'd still be here when Duncan came back to pick her up, that she wouldn't be stuck in some 1985 time warp.

Their conversation was as desultory as the weather. Jane said that after lunch, they should go downtown for some pie. Her mother admired Jane's blouse and said not many women would be brave enough to wear that shade of yellow, given how it muddied the complexion.

And then her mother said, "And how is Jimmy doing?"

Jane swallowed a Frito with difficulty. "He's okay, considering."

"Considering what?"

Considering that his mother died! Jane thought. Considering that when she died, some vital part of Jimmy died, too. Considering that he measures time by television, that he sometimes doesn't speak to a living soul for twenty-four hours, that he invites the pizza delivery guy to stay and eat with him! Considering that I have to make sure there are never more than four Tylenol in the bottle for fear Jimmy might overdose by accident, or worse, on purpose! Considering that every day when he walks to work, he passes the corner where his mother died in *your* car because of *your* reckless driving!

But she didn't say any of these things because her mother might say, *Well, dear, you're the one who asked me to drive his mother home.*

"Goodness, Jane!" her mother exclaimed. "Do you know that you just had the most remarkable series of facial expressions? First you looked very sad and shook your head a little bit, and then you looked sort of scared and, I don't know, almost haunted, and then you got an extremely angry glint in your eyes."

Jane had forgotten how randomly perceptive her mother could be. "I was just thinking about Jimmy," she said shortly. "He's had a hard time."

Her mother reached across the table, bracelets jangling, and put her hand over Jane's. "I know he has, dear." Her voice was soft. "And, please, you must know how sorry I am that Jimmy is mother-less now."

Well, that wasn't quite true, was it? Jimmy was without *his* mother, yes, but he had *a* mother. Of course he did. Jane was Jimmy's mother now.

OH, THE JOY OF A SHARED LIFE! The joy is not—as many people believe—building a future with someone, or opening your heart to another human being, or even the ability to gift each other money with limited tax consequences. The joy is in the *dailiness*. The joy is having someone who will stop you from hitting the snooze button on the alarm endlessly. The joy is the smell of someone else's cooking. The joy is knowing that you can call someone and ask him to pick up a gallon of milk on his way over. The joy is having someone to watch *Kitchen Nightmares* with, because it is really no good when you watch it by yourself. The joy is hoping (however unrealistically) that someone else will unload the dishwasher. The joy is having someone listen to the weird cough your car has developed and reassure you that it doesn't sound expensive. The joy is saying how much you want a glass of wine and having someone tell you, "Go ahead, you deserve it!" (Although it's possible to achieve the last one with a pet and a little imagination.)

And all these joys were Jane's that summer. Duncan had moved even fewer possessions into Jane's house than Luke had, but his stuff seemed to take up more space, seemed more permanent, seemed to *belong* more. Jane realized that was just foolishness: a toothbrush is a toothbrush is a toothbrush. It was Duncan himself who belonged, who made her feel perpetually on the edge of some exciting discovery, who stroked her upper lip lightly and said, "I miss your moustache."

Duncan was there to get up with her at four thirty in the morning when Jimmy called to tell her there was a scary tapping sound coming from his living room.

"It's not like them other times, Jane," Jimmy whispered hoarsely. "There's really someone there!"

Jane tried not to sigh. "Okay, Jimmy. I'll be right over."

She hung up the phone and saw that Duncan was already out of bed and pulling on his jeans.

"Jimmy's hearing scary noises," she said. "I think it's branches scratching at the window or maybe just his imagination."

"Easy enough to go take a look," Duncan said, and Jane saw suddenly that he was right. It *was* easy, now that she had Duncan to go with her. It was easy to get up and dressed with him to keep her company, easy not to resent the lost sleep knowing that he would be tired, too, easy to follow him out to his van.

They arrived at Jimmy's house, and Duncan used Jane's key to unlock the front door, calling, "Jim! Cavalry is here!"

It had obviously never occurred to Duncan, as it had to Jane on other nights, that maybe it *wasn't* just the wind or Jimmy's imagination, that maybe there was an actual intruder who would attack anyone who disturbed him.

"Jim!" Duncan called again.

At the end of the long, narrow hall, the door to Jimmy's bedroom cracked open. "Duncan?"

"Come on out," Duncan called. "I've got Jane here with me."

Jimmy stuck his head out the door and looked at them. "Oh, it *is* you guys."

"Of course it's us," Duncan said. "Now let's investigate this mystery sound. Where is it the loudest?"

"In my bedroom," Jimmy said. "But generally it stops when other people are around."

This was true. Jane had never once heard it. In the past, whenever Jimmy called her in the middle of the night, she and Jimmy had huddled together, whispering, in the living room until dawn, when they fell asleep in armchairs.

"Well, let's try and see if we can lure it out," Duncan said. He led Jane down the hall to Jimmy's grubby bedroom with its narrow twin bed and wooden dresser. Jane and Jimmy sat on the edge of the bed, but Duncan stood, his head tilted.

"Jimmy, have you—" Jane began to ask, but Duncan motioned her to be quiet.

They waited. Silence.

Jane started again, "Jimmy—" but again Duncan shushed her.

It seemed like even the house was holding its breath, but at last they heard the sounds: a staccato rapping as though unseen fists were knocking on the walls. Jimmy clutched Jane's hand, but Duncan said calmly, "That's your water heater, Jim. Dirt in the bottom makes that popping. We'll flush it out this afternoon. It's nothing to worry about."

Jimmy smiled at him worshipfully, and Jane felt the kind of gratitude usually associated with rescued kittens. She realized that there were two types of people: those you called in the middle of the night and those you didn't. And Duncan was the kind you called. How lucky, how insanely lucky, she was.

"You know what?" Duncan said. "Now that we're all up, we ought to go see the sunrise at the beach."

"Oh, I don't know." Jane bit her lip. "Maybe we should try to get some sleep. We'll all be so tired later."

"That's what coffee is for," Duncan said.

Jimmy frowned worriedly. "Last time I drank coffee, I accidentally stapled my shirtsleeve to the workbench."

"That's because you drank the whole pot," Duncan told him. "I'll watch you more closely this time."

"Okay, let's do it," Jane said. Or perhaps it wasn't Jane who said that but the carefree new person she'd become. She could take a nap later.

As soon as Jimmy got dressed, they all rode in the front seat of Duncan's van—Jimmy in the middle—to the gas station. Jane and Duncan went in and bought two large coffees and a hot chocolate from the hot-beverage machine.

"I've rethought the coffee thing," Duncan said to Jane about the cocoa.

Then they drove to Whiting Beach and sat on the playground swings, the rubber seat cold against Jane's legs even through her sweatpants. She sipped her coffee and wrapped one hand around the chain.

They were just in time. The sky was striped with every flavor of sherbet—raspberry, orange, peach, lemon—and every stripe was reflected in the lake. The sun peeked over the horizon slowly, slowly, growing to a shimmering gold oval that trembled for a moment, heavy, gravid—like a giant egg yolk that would fall forward and fry itself on the silver pan of Lake Charlevoix. And then it rose higher, a perfect yellow circle.

Nants ingonyama bagithi Baba! sang a part of Jane's brain that seemed to have been given over permanently to *The Lion King*.

The sun inched up in the sky until it was just the sun again, that plain old heavenly body everyone takes for granted. But the wondrous feeling continued. Maybe it was the false euphoria of caffeine, but it seemed to Jane as though she and Duncan and Jimmy were the only people awake in Boyne City. No, more than that—the only people *alive* in Boyne City. It felt as though some apocalypse had roared through town, and they were the only survivors. And right then, just after dawn on that summer morning, Jane felt she could never want for anything more.

"That sunrise was so beautiful," Jimmy said, and his voice was both awe-filled and matter-of-fact. Jane knew exactly how he felt.

2008

FOR MANY YEARS TO COME—for the rest of her life, in fact—Jane would associate the arrival of Willard Williams in their lives with the "People in Our Community" learning unit at school. She always taught this unit during the month of October, and near the end of the unit, she took her class on a field trip to the farmers' market and they bought caramel apples, resulting in a mass loss of baby teeth.

This year Jane had decided to invite a series of guest speakers to talk about their roles in the community. She convinced the other second-grade teacher, Mr. Robicheaux, that it would be better if they combined the classes during the speaker visits.

Mr. Robicheaux was an underfed man in his fifties with a scraggly white beard, a plume of white hair, and slightly pinched features. Two years ago, on the first day of school, a little girl named Jordan Chandler had looked at him and whispered "Bird!" in a fearful voice. Jane knew exactly what Jordan meant. She even knew what kind of bird—a cockatoo.

Jane understood that most parents hoped to look back on their children's succession of elementary school teachers as a perfect string of flawless pearls, and she suspected that Mr. Robicheaux was more like a dark, misshapen dud. He was famous—or, more accurately, infamous—for arriving after the last bell, calling students "Boy" and "Girl" well into the first quarter, being unable to correctly add up the class milk money, misplacing his bifocals (he usually borrowed a student's eyeglasses), accidentally shredding completed worksheets, and carrying a whiskey flask on field trips. There was a widespread belief that he didn't understand the metric system because his students often entered third grade unaware that it existed, and he had been passing out a spelling list with *joyful* spelled with two *l*s for at least twenty years. Jane found working with him strangely rewarding; even on her worst days, she knew she was a better teacher than Mr. Robicheaux.

"What's the point of guest speakers?" Mr. Robicheaux had asked.

"It's an opportunity for the children to hear from people who contribute to the community," Jane had said. "And to learn about how we all work together to make Boyne City a better place."

Mr. Robicheaux looked unconvinced.

"When the guest speakers are here, you won't actually have to teach," Jane said.

Mr. Robicheaux shrugged. "Well, in that case, okay."

Honestly, why did she even bother?

Jane had extended invitations to more than thirty local people, and had managed to secure visits from the mayor, a doctor, a volunteer firefighter, and a yoga teacher. Mr. Robicheaux had invited the bartender from the Sportsman, and Mrs. Robicheaux, who was a seasonal tax preparer for an accounting firm.

"The thing is," Jane said delicately, in regard to Mrs. Robicheaux, "in general, I think the children will respond more to people whose jobs they understand."

"Aw, Georgina will take care of that," Mr. Robicheaux said. "She'll explain it."

It seemed rude to argue further, so Jane put Mrs. Robicheaux on the schedule and decided to kick things off with the bartender. The bartender's name was Albert Jackson, but everyone called him Banjo, and he was, perhaps not surprisingly, a very popular guest.

Jane had asked him to come at eight thirty—speakers were always best first thing in the morning, when the children were still digesting breakfast and moving slowly—and Banjo arrived right on time, wheeling a hand trolley loaded with cardboard boxes of supplies.

Jane and Mr. Robicheaux pushed back the heavy vinyl accordion divider between their classrooms, and all the children sat on the floor in a semicircle around the table set up at the front. Banjo showed them how to make a classic gin fizz with gin, lemon juice, and egg white. "This is actually the most difficult drink to make," Banjo said over the knocking sound of the cocktail shaker. "Most people don't shake it long enough."

He gave the completed gin fizz to Mr. Robicheaux and then delivered a short lecture on bartending, during which he said, among other things: "If you hold your finger over the air hole on the pour spout, you can slow the flow right down to a trickle while making mixed drinks and most people never even notice."

He ended by mixing a Shirley Temple and adding a maraschino cherry.

"Now, I've brought all sorts of ingredients," Banjo said, gesturing to his cart. "You kids can invent your own drinks and give 'em a special name, like Shirley Temple."

"Who's Shirley Temple?" Matthew Harvey asked.

"A famous actress," Banjo said. "Like Johnny Depp or Nicole Kidman."

"Who are they?"

Jane often thought that seven was the last age at which you were immune to Hollywood celebrities. Or at least until you reached your eighties and just didn't care about them anymore.

"You could also name your drink after a superhero or movie character," she said tactfully. Immediately a happy babble of conversation broke out among the children: "Spider-Man!" "Buzz Lightyear!" "Princess Fiona!"

Jane had cleared off the counters that ran along the back of both classrooms, and while the children tied on their science aprons, she helped Banjo set out the bottles of juice and soda and seltzer, the plastic bowls of lemon slices and cherries, and the shot glasses. Jane was moved by Banjo's thoughtfulness. If no parents called to complain, she planned to have him back next year.

The children mixed drinks happily, needing only minimal supervision. Banjo ranged among them, making suggestions, and Jane leaned against her desk. The gin fizz had apparently hit Mr. Robicheaux hard; he was asleep at his desk with his eyes open and his chin cupped in one hand. Jane was just wondering if she should wake him before or after recess, when Banjo approached her.

"Banjo, you did a wonderful job today," she said. "I really appreciate it."

"Oh, it was my pleasure," Banjo said. He paused and said more slowly, "Listen, I've been meaning to talk to you about Jimmy's bar tab, but last night his friend paid it all off, so I guess that's okay."

"Jimmy?" Jane asked. "My Jimmy?" Bar tab? What was Banjo talking about?

"Oh, yeah, him and his friend." Banjo nodded. "They don't ever drink anything except pitchers of light beer, but still, it was beginning to add up, and I thought you should know."

"You're saying Jimmy goes to the Sportsman," Jane said slowly. This information was so startling that she felt the need to repeat it, like some form of teach-back learning. "And drinks pitchers of beer with someone."

"Yeah, that new fellow, just moved to town to work as a cook over at the mountain for the winter season," Banjo said. "The mountain" meant Boyne Mountain, the resort. "He's staying at the City Motel until the ski season starts, I guess, and then he'll move to employee housing—"

"How long has Jimmy been going to the Sportsman?" Jane

asked. She had not thought it possible that Jimmy did anything that was unknown to her.

"He used to show up once in a while, usually on a Sunday. He just sits at the bar and has a beer, and I talk to him if we're not busy. I know he's been lonely ever since his ma— since she passed." Banjo bit his lip in embarrassment—everyone was embarrassed to talk to Jane directly about the accident—and then hurried on. "But now that he's made friends with this other guy, he's been coming pretty much every night. I guess I thought you knew."

"What's this friend's name?"

"Willard," Banjo said. "I don't recall his last name, if I ever even knew it."

"That's all right," Jane said. "I'll ask Jimmy."

JANE DROVE OVER to Jimmy's house that very afternoon. Right away, she saw that things were out of place. A car—a boxy maroon Buick, gray showing through thin spots in the paint—was parked in the driveway, and Jimmy couldn't drive. The side door to the house was ajar, with just the glass storm door closed, and Jimmy never left the door unlocked (at least, not since he'd started watching *Unsolved Mysteries*). The radio was playing in the living room, and Jimmy never listened to the radio. Cooking smells were coming from the kitchen, and Jimmy never cooked.

A large man was also coming out from the kitchen, and the man wasn't Jimmy.

"Hello!" the man said. "Looks like we have a visitor."

Jimmy emerged behind the man, wiping his hands on a towel. "Hey, Jane," he said, smiling. "What are you doing here?"

"Oh, I just thought I'd stop by and meet your friend," Jane said. "Will you introduce us?"

"Okay." Jimmy turned to the man obediently. "Willard, this is Jane. Jane, this is my friend Willard."

My friend Willard. Jimmy's voice was stuffed with pride.

"It's nice to meet you, Willard," Jane said.

"And you, too." Willard shook her hand. "I have heard so much about you from Jimmy. Won't you come on in the kitchen? Can I offer you a drink? Soda? Beer?"

"I'd love a beer," Jane said, hiding her surprise. Since when did Jimmy keep beer in the house?

She followed both men back into the kitchen and sat at the table. Jimmy began drying plates from the dish drainer and putting them into the cupboard. Willard fetched a Bud Light from the refrigerator and opened it with an old-fashioned can punch. Jane would have bet that Mrs. Jellico had never used that can punch to open anything stronger than ginger ale.

"There you go, ma'am," he said. "I hope you don't mind if I keep going with dinner prep here?"

"Not at all," Jane said.

Willard's appearance was full of incongruities, as though he were still discovering himself, even though he looked to be in his fifties. He was very tall and had the sort of belly that Jane's mother had always called a "front porch." Willard's front porch wasn't the wraparound kind, at least not yet; it was more of a stoop, dense and jutting proudly forward. Yet he moved gracefully, almost daintily. His hair was black and tightly curled on top, straight on the sides— the hairstyle of a man who had reached maturity long before the days of styling gel and blow-dryers—and his eyes were cobalt blue, vital, alert. His voice was deep and cultured, but his shirt was cheap yellow polyester, and his shoes had run-down heels. His heavy face was seamed and ruddy, but open and relaxed, kind. He seemed to be smiling even when he wasn't actually smiling.

He took another dish towel from the counter and draped it over his shoulder like a burping cloth.

"We're having coq au vin," Jimmy told Jane. "That's French for 'rooster with wine.'"

"It sounds delicious," Jane said, although, last she knew, coq au vin had dark-meat chicken in it, and garlic, and button mushrooms, and red wine, which were all things Jimmy didn't like. "I heard you were a chef, Willard."

"More like a line cook." Willard turned the burner on under a frying pan of bacon. "But I do have one or two specialties. Jimmy, I think I'm ready for you to chop the onions."

"I better get my snow goggles, then," Jimmy said cheerfully. "I used to wear them when my ma made me help her can spaghetti sauce. Onions make my eyes water something terrible."

"I think your goggles are in the basement," Jane told him. "There're a few cartons down there with winter clothes in them."

Jimmy went off, and Jane could hear him clumping down the basement stairs. She knew it would take him at least ten minutes to find the goggles—it took Jimmy at least ten minutes to find anything—and she was glad.

"Willard," she began, speaking slowly and choosing her words carefully, "I'm very pleased that you and Jimmy have become friends"—odd that she spoke to a man who was at least twenty years her senior like this, but Jane's life was full of oddness—"but Jimmy's not like other people. He needs a lot of support."

"Oh, yes, I could see that right away," Willard said agreeably, turning the bacon with a spatula. "But he's a good guy. I think he's capable of more than you think." He glanced up at her suddenly, contrite. "Not that I'm criticizing. Jimmy's told me how well you take care of him."

Jane smiled, but she kept her voice serious. "Jimmy needs a lot of guidance. A lot of assistance. He doesn't—he doesn't always make sensible decisions."

"That's why I told him we ought to stop going to the Sportsman every night," Willard said. "It didn't feel right, him becoming a regular."

Jane was silent; she couldn't argue with that.

"I had a little brother with developmental delays," Willard said. "He passed away many years ago, but we were close when I was growing up. Right from the start, Jimmy reminded me of my brother. Sweet and funny, completely genuine, completely open. Needing guidance, like you say, but just a pleasure to be around."

A pleasure to be around? Someone else had said almost the same thing about Jimmy recently. Jane frowned, trying to remember. Duncan. Just last week, Duncan had taken Jimmy with him on a run to Traverse City. "Does him good to get out of town, and I can use the company," Duncan had said. "Jim keeps it simple, and I like that." Talking to Jimmy made Jane feel like flying into a million pieces, but apparently other people were much nicer than she was.

"Well," she said now, drinking the last of her beer, "I should be going."

"You're welcome to stay for dinner," Willard said.

"Thank you, but I need to get home." Jane picked up her purse. "It was good to meet you, Willard."

"I'm sure we'll be seeing each other again," said Willard, who had begun to perspire in the heat from the frying pan. His eyes were the bright, hot blue of a summer sky. "And don't you worry, I'll take care of Jimmy."

Jane passed by the basement stairs just as Jimmy was coming up with the goggles in his hand.

"Jimmy," Willard called from the kitchen, "be sure you walk Jane out to her car."

Jane's car was in the driveway behind the maroon Buick, and it was still daylight, so it didn't seem especially dangerous for her to walk to her car alone, and she couldn't imagine what help Jimmy would be if some danger did happen to present itself, but she smiled and said that would be lovely.

"What did you think of Willard?" Jimmy asked as soon as they were outside. "Isn't he nice?"

"Yes, he's very nice," Jane said. Jimmy looked so pleased that Jane felt suddenly ashamed, disloyal. Why had she doubted him? Did she truly think Jimmy was incapable of making a genuine friend? She reached out and put a hand on his arm. "He's wonderful, Jimmy."

Jimmy smiled. "Willard would love to meet Duncan, I know, and Aggie and Gary and all them guys."

"I'm sure he would," Jane said.

She got in her car and backed out of the driveway. Then she paused for just a moment and looked at Jimmy as he stood there, the mild October breeze ruffling his hair and stirring the golden leaves piled at his feet.

DARKNESS FELL as she drove home, and when she pulled into her own driveway, the lighted windows of her house glowed like promises to all the world's weary travelers. Winter would be long, and Jane didn't look forward to it, but that glowy-window thing was awfully nice. As she walked up the porch steps, she could see Duncan standing at the kitchen sink, cleaning the grease from his hands with a pumice stone.

"Hey, Janey," he called over the sound of running water as she came in.

"Hey," she said, smiling as she hung her blazer over a chairback.

Duncan lived at Jane's house full-time now, but Jane felt it was an unsatisfactory, impermanent kind of full-time. He paid for groceries and contributed to the utilities and did a hundred home repairs, and yet to Jane their lives remained maddeningly untangled, frustratingly separate. Duncan didn't even rent out the apartment above his workshop. Jane doubted he could find a renter, given how strongly the apartment smelled of spar varnish, but she wished he would try. It seemed too much like he was keeping the apartment as an escape hatch.

Often in the mornings, Duncan would sing as he shaved in the bathroom, and while the fact of Duncan shaving in her bathroom pleased her greatly, the song he chose did not. And he always sang the same one, the lyrics floating out to Jane on the steam from his shower.

> *Would you care to stay till sunrise?*
> *It's completely your decision.*

Now Duncan nodded his head toward a foil-covered dish on the counter. "Aggie brought us some stuffed peppers," he said. "All we have to do is bake them for thirty minutes."

Really, if there was one thing Jane could do with less of, it was Aggie. But one thing she could always do with more of was Aggie's stuffed peppers. That was the Aggie conundrum. "How nice of her," she said.

Duncan turned off the water and dried his hands on a dish towel. "She stopped by to tell me Jim has been drinking beer with someone at the Sportsman."

"I was going to tell you the same thing!" Jane said. She sat at the kitchen table and told him about Willard, and the coq au vin, and all the rest. "Did *you* know Jimmy went to the Sportsman?"

"I'd heard that," Duncan said. "But I thought it was only once in a while, when the walls were closing in on him."

Did the walls ever close in on Duncan? Jane wondered.

"Anyway, today, I began work on the Wheelers' dining table," Duncan said. He was never happier than when he was commissioned to custom-build a piece of furniture, although it meant he fell even further behind in his refinishing business.

"I thought you began work on that yesterday," Jane said.

"Well, technically, yes," Duncan said. "But today was the first day the boards came in, and I got to feel them with my hands. Pure elm planks with hollows for resin."

Sometimes when Duncan talked all evening about lumber, or table legs, or the art of modern woodworking in general, Jane told herself that if they were married, she would feel like killing her own husband, and wouldn't that be terrible? But the thought wasn't that comforting because she already felt like killing him and they weren't even engaged.

Marriage was not something they discussed, and yet, it was not something they avoided discussing either. Duncan was always interested in hearing about other people's engagements and weddings, and he didn't grow restive or frightened-looking when they watched a movie where the characters got married. They made future plans together without hesitating—a trip to Chicago for Easter, Mackinac Island next summer, a hammock for the backyard. They never spoke of breaking up. It was totally possible, Jane thought sometimes, that Duncan had changed his mind about marriage. And yet—and yet— she couldn't bring herself to ask him if he would like to marry her, or even if he thought about it, which was strange, because it was usually so easy to talk to Duncan about anything. Really, she should ask him. He might say, "I've been thinking about the same thing!" Or he might say, "That's definitely where I see us heading." He might even say, "How about December next year?" Or he might say, "Marriage isn't for me—you know that, Janey." So she said nothing.

MISS HEATHER, the yoga teacher, was the next guest speaker. She looked like a time traveler from the eighties with her puffy blond bangs and blue eyeliner and shiny leggings, but she was young and enthusiastic, and the children seemed excited to see her. Mr. Robicheaux went out back and had a cigarette, but Jane helped Miss Heather push the desks out of the way so everyone had enough space to lie down, and she joined the students in following the poses. Cat Pose was first.

"Stretch just like a kitty cat," Miss Heather told the class, getting down on all fours and arching her back. "*Feel* the stretch in your lower spine. Stretch, stretch, stretch. You can even meow."

"Our cat sharpens her claws on the furniture," Zachary Walton said. "Can we do that, too?"

"No, you're all *well-behaved* kitty cats," Miss Heather chanted rapidly, folding her legs beneath her. "And now we're going to be lions in Lion Pose. Kneel on the floor and cross the front of the right ankle over the back of the left—"

"Just watch Miss Heather and do what she does," Jane said quickly. Many students were still struggling with right and left.

"Can we roar?" Zachary asked.

"Yes!" Miss Heather said. "Let's hear those roars!"

"Very soft roars," Jane added. The third-grade class next door was doing MEAP testing, and she didn't want to be responsible for someone failing to get into college ten years from now.

Miss Heather led them through Cobra Pose, Swan Pose, Butterfly Pose, and Tortoise Pose—Jane was thankful that these were all silent animals—and they ended with mindful breathing, during which most of the class fell asleep.

"It's like that in the first quarter," Jane said, turning her head to talk to Miss Heather as they lay on the floor. "They're still young enough for naps."

"Oh, that's all right," Miss Heather said. Her bangs fluffed up from her forehead like a cresting wave. "But, Jane, mindful breathing is so beneficial, truly, even for children. It's a way to connect the mind and body, to renew energy and sharpen focus, to eliminate negative feelings and refresh compassion."

"That does sound valuable," Jane said. She didn't add that all that could be accomplished by morning recess, too.

TACO TUESDAY was going to be different this week. Special. Jimmy had called Jane to tell her not to bring any food.

"Me and Willard are going to do everything," he said. "You guys don't need to bring anything but yourselves."

Jimmy never said that kind of thing. Just like he never thought to say "Thank you for thinking of me" or "I look forward to hearing from you." It wasn't that Jimmy was ever impolite or unappreciative—he had just never learned gracious phrasing. It was one of the infinite number of deficits that marked Jimmy as different. Jane was touched by the effort he must be making.

"Duncan and I can't wait," she said, and just like that, she and Jimmy had a normal phone conversation. (Although Jimmy set the receiver down without saying good-bye or hanging up, and Jane could hear him in the background asking Willard if it was possible to barbecue spaghetti, so maybe it wasn't as normal as all that.)

When Jane and Duncan got to Jimmy's house the next night, Aggie and Gary were just getting out of their car. Aggie was wearing a chocolate-brown skirt and a low-cut apricot-colored silk blouse. It seemed to Jane that every item of clothing Aggie owned was the color of some delicious food: melon, honey, peach, salmon, butterscotch, raspberry, lemon. Perhaps because she was such a good cook. But also those colors suited her, emphasized the creaminess of her complexion and made her pale hair gleam.

"Look at *that*," Duncan said, and for an awful moment, Jane thought he was referring to Aggie's cleavage.

"What?" she asked.

"Someone's raked the leaves," Duncan said.

Someone had, Jane saw now, looking at the greenish-brown combed-looking grass of Jimmy's yard, although it was nothing she'd have noticed on her own.

"And they bagged all the leaves," Duncan said in a pleased voice. Mr. Estes used to rake Jimmy's yard, but he'd developed heart problems the previous winter and Duncan had taken over. Except that now he didn't have to rake it, because it was already done.

Freida pulled up to the curb behind them as they got out of the car, and there was the usual flurry of greetings. Gary even addressed Freida by name. (He seemed to recognize her now, although one time last year she had come to Taco Tuesday after getting a haircut and he'd stared at her suspiciously all evening.)

"I feel absolutely boorish arriving empty-handed," Aggie said. "I kept saying to Jimmy, 'Why don't I bring dessert? I could whip up a lemon meringue pie in two shakes!' But he insisted that he and Willard would handle everything."

"Who's Willard?" Gary asked.

"Gary, we went over that on the way here," Aggie said impatiently.

Jane wondered, not for the first time, if Gary was actually as unobservant as he appeared, or if he was just trying to drive Aggie slowly insane.

The front door opened, and Jimmy stepped out onto the front porch, calling, "Why are you all standing outside? Come in!"

By the time they all got through the front door, Willard was coming out of the kitchen balancing a tray with three frosty glasses on it.

Each glass was filled with pink liquid and garnished with a black-berry and a mint leaf.

"These are my world-famous blackberry vodka tonics," he said. "Made especially for you girls." He was wearing chinos and a powder-blue polyester shirt that floated gracefully over his belly. His full cheeks were freshly barbered, and he smelled of aftershave. He set the tray on the coffee table. "Now, Jimmy has told me about how much you ladies have done for him since his mother died, so tonight, you three just rest easy and let the menfolk do the cooking."

"We're going to have steaks and home fries and all sorts of stuff," Jimmy said happily. "I been peeling potatoes all afternoon."

Willard gestured toward the kitchen. "Come on in, gentlemen."

"Gary doesn't like kitchens," Aggie said. "He has a thing about linoleum."

"Well, life is all about adventure." Willard clapped Gary on the back. "Come on with us now."

Gary tilted his head back and looked at Willard through his bifocals, but he went in the kitchen. Duncan went, too, saying, "I can't tell you how much I appreciate you raking the lawn," and Willard said, "Oh, it was nothing. An hour's work at most."

Jane and Aggie and Freida sat down and sipped their vodka tonics. Freida took out her mandolin and strummed it quietly. Usually at this point on Taco Tuesdays, Freida played the mandolin and Gary requested songs, which Jane privately found fascinating. Little insights into the murky liquid that sloshed around in the fishbowl of Gary's mind! She was actually surprised that he knew the titles of *any* songs. He seemed to request songs exclusively from the 1960s: "Barbara Allen," "Little Boxes," "The Water Is Wide." Did that mean he thought it *was* still the sixties? Jane wondered. Once, he had requested "Blue Moon of Kentucky," and Freida had played it in a somewhat rollicking style (she loved Bill Monroe), and color had come to Gary's thin cheeks and he'd clapped along, and afterward he had tried to tip Freida five dollars. It was very embarrassing, and no one spoke of it again.

But tonight, Freida just plucked the strings idly. "I hear you're having guest speakers," she said to Jane.

"Oh, yes." Jane sipped her drink. "The mayor and Dr. Haven and Banjo."

"Any musicians?" Freida asked in a slightly aggressive way.

"The only musician I'd want is you, and you're coming to the farmers' market with us at the end of the month," Jane said.

Freida seemed mollified.

Aggie was sitting up very straight and clenching her drink glass tightly. Every few seconds, she twitched slightly and cleared her throat. Jane realized that relinquishing control of the kitchen was causing Aggie actual physical discomfort. Finally, Aggie seemed to reach her breaking point and called, "Yoo-hoo! You men in the kitchen! Remember, Gary has an aversion to Yukon Gold potatoes!"

Willard stuck his head out of the kitchen. "Now, you just relax, missus," he said kindly to Aggie. "Gary can speak for himself, can't he?"

Aggie frowned. "No, not really."

Dinner was exactly what you'd expect a line cook to serve—sirloin steaks, braised short ribs, grilled scallops, an enormous platter of crunchy golden French fries. It even appeared on the table very rapidly, with all four men rushing out of the kitchen carrying Jimmy's mother's best Corelleware heaped with food.

"What movie are we watching tonight, Jimmy?" Jane asked when everyone began passing the dishes.

"We're not going to watch a movie," Jimmy said. "Willard says when you have friends over, you should talk to them. He says TV gets in the way of conversation."

Duncan looked up, startled. "But that's what television is *for*," he said, holding a short rib above his plate with a pair of tongs. "That's probably why it was invented. Hey, Aggie, remember when we gave your parents all fourteen episodes of *The Jewel in the Crown* for Christmas and bought ourselves fourteen hours of freedom? Now, *that* was a great holiday."

"But genuine conversation among friends is one of life's pleasures," Willard said. His eyes were bright blue, hot and glowing like a Bunsen burner flame.

"I take it from that statement that you've never spent an evening with Aggie's parents," Duncan said.

"Honestly, Duncan." Aggie looked annoyed. "Is that any way to talk about two people who were never less than kind to you?"

"Anyway, Aggie's parents aren't here." Willard's voice was reasonable. "Here, we're truly friends who—"

"If you use the word *fellowship*, I'm leaving," Gary said.

The planet paused its rotation briefly: Jane and Gary felt the exact same way.

"What's wrong with that word?" Freida asked.

"It's just a word he dislikes," Aggie said. "I think he associates it with a very severe case of food poisoning he got from a church picnic."

"Well, then, we'll just avoid it." Willard made it sound as though Gary were a normal person making a sensible request. "But the point is that I would like to get to know you all better. Now, Freida, I wonder if you're aware that Beatrice Mooney is offering piano lessons out of her own home."

Freida set her knife and fork down with a *click*. "I would put nothing past that woman—nothing," she said, her nostrils flaring slightly. "She's been trying to corner my share of the piano lesson market for years."

"I saw she'd put a sign up at Glen's," Willard said. "It was just an index card on the bulletin board. It seemed awfully unprofessional."

"Beatrice is the embodiment of unprofessionalism," Freida said vigorously. "Do you know that she has never trained professionally on the piano? She plays the organ well enough, I guess, but the piano requires a different set of manual dexterity and music theory skills—"

"Well, now," Willard interrupted, "if you don't mind me sticking my nose in this business, I think what you ought to do is have a recital and get the paper to write it up."

"I have a recital for all my students in the spring every year," Freida said.

"That's why I'm thinking you should have one now, in the fall, when it will really stand out," Willard said. "Nothing fancy, just you and maybe one student? A duet? Jimmy has nothing but praise for your rendition of 'Early Morning Rain.'"

Freida's eyes had a faraway look. "Maybe me on mandolin and Stevie Campbell on the piano," she said, obviously thinking aloud. "If I simplify the chords, and we get through it without his voice cracking . . . You really think the paper would write about it?"

"Absolutely," Willard said. "A newspaper article with a picture of a pretty lady like yourself and a mention of your esteemed musical background—" He shrugged and held a hand out, palm up, as though gesturing at an invisible army of potential piano students. "You'd run old Beatrice right out of business."

Freida was pink with pleasure. "What a wonderful idea, Willard," she said. She picked her knife and fork up again.

"And I have a question for you, Aggie," Willard said. "I have been staying at the City Motel and—"

"The City Motel!" Aggie snorted. "That's a terrible place! We stayed there once, and the sheets had such a low thread count that Gary broke out all over in boils and hasn't been the same since."

"Really?" Jimmy looked intrigued. "What was he like before?"

"Yes, I share your views on the City Motel," Willard said

smoothly. "I was wondering if you knew someone with a guest room, someone who would welcome a boarder for a few weeks? My job at the mountain doesn't start until mid-November."

"Why, certainly, I do," Aggie answered. "Gladys and Andy Parkins have a guest room with a private bath. I'll speak to them immediately."

"They might have a guest bedroom," Duncan said, "but they don't have a guest bed in it. I know because it's a four-poster that needs refinishing. It's been down at my workshop for a few months now."

"Oh!" Jimmy spoke so suddenly that Jane jumped. "Gladys has been calling and asking about that, but I clean forgot to tell you, Duncan."

Duncan gave a small shrug. "She'll survive."

"Oh, really, Duncan," Aggie said in an aggrieved voice. "Gladys is going to need that bed soon. You know as well as I do that her brother comes up every Christmas."

"Not anymore," Duncan said. "He and Gladys had a falling out over whether Call of Duty is historically accurate, and they're no longer on speaking terms."

"I didn't know that." Aggie sounded like she didn't believe it, either.

"Well, it's true. Gladys told me last April."

"But Gladys didn't mention it to *me*," Aggie said.

"Look, I know it's hard to believe that something happened in Boyne City that somebody *else* didn't know about," Duncan said, "but apparently it did."

"Back to my rooming situation," Willard said, his voice respectful. "I did see an advertisement for a room to rent. A man named Roy Newton—"

"Roy Newton!" Aggie sniffed. "That man is a complete scoundrel. Do you know that he called the police a few years ago and complained that Gary and I were having a big party and disturbing the peace? Absolutely ridiculous. Everyone knows that Gary doesn't like loud noises or having people over. Even the police know that. They called and said—"

"Who is Roy Newton?" Gary said, and everyone went quiet because they tended to forget for long periods that he was present.

"He's our neighbor, Gary," Aggie said. "The one who lives in the yellow house. Anyway, Willard, you just leave it to me. The Schroders have a granny flat over their garage. Mark Schroder's mother passed away recently, and it's just sitting empty."

"I knew you would be the perfect person to ask," Willard said. "Now, Duncan, perhaps you can tell me the difference between a breakfront and a hutch?"

And so it went. Jane knew what Willard was doing—it was a version of Star of the Day. He was giving everyone a moment in the spotlight, a chance to honor their achievements, an opportunity to shine. Jane did it all the time in the classroom, but she had never thought to do it at a dinner party. But maybe that was because Taco Tuesday had never seemed like a dinner party before.

What was most amazing of all—even more so than the fact that Willard asked Gary if he had any coworkers over at State Farm, and Gary answered in a reasonably lucid way, saying that he worked with a lady named Claire and a man named Aaron who had shorted out the toaster oven making grilled cheese sandwiches—was Jimmy during all of this. He was alert, and he watched the face of each speaker, smiling a smile that was different from his usual unselfconscious grin—it was a more confident smile somehow. When he laughed, he sounded more genuinely amused than Jane had ever heard him. (Jimmy didn't laugh very often—Jane wondered if it was because he was afraid he was the butt of the joke.) When he spoke—"Willard and I will clean up"—the note of happy pride in his voice was tangible, a live thing, like a bluebird that had flown in and perched on a chairback, rosy-breasted and silver-songed. For the first time in all the years that she'd known him, Jimmy was animated. No, more than that: Jimmy was *alive*.

MRS. ROBICHEAUX came to class that week, arriving in the morning with Mr. Robicheaux. She was petite and curly-haired, with purple-framed eyeglasses and a slightly formal way of speaking. She was really quite pretty in a subdued sort of way and seemed genuinely sweet. She was much better than Mr. Robicheaux deserved, in Jane's opinion, and if her presentation lacked some dynamism, perhaps that was understandable, given the subject matter.

Mrs. Robicheaux began by passing out blue pencils with the accounting firm's name engraved in gold letters. Then she told the class about the differences between the 1040, the 1040-A, and the 1040-EZ, and the inadvisability of doing one's own taxes.

"Even if you are very, very good at math," Mrs. Robicheaux said. "The tax system is positively *filled* with hidden dangers."

Jane sighed. She was sitting on the floor with the children for the dual purpose of gently tilting Brandon Hicks's head toward the front of the room so it would at least look as if he was listening and also of preventing Dylan McMahon and Kyle Bradshaw from poking each other with the sharp ends of their new pencils.

"Now, you children have no idea what a lifesaver it was when window envelopes came along," Mrs. Robicheaux was saying. "Because at the accounting firm, we lived in fear of sending a tax return to the wrong person. That happened once, a long time ago. We accidentally sent a gentleman here in town *another* gentleman's income tax return, and it so happened that the first gentleman owed the second gentleman over five hundred dollars for, I believe it was, roof repairs. And when the second gentleman saw how much the first gentleman's income was, he called the first gentleman and said, 'I'm

holding the most *enlightening* piece of mail here in my hand and—'
Yes, dear, do you have a question?"

Morgan Cruse had raised her hand. "Is it true you're married to
Mr. Robicheaux?"

"Yes, it is," Mrs. Robicheaux said, smiling.

Morgan frowned. "Why?"

"I think she means, what do you love about him most?" Jane
interposed hastily.

"I didn't mean that," Morgan said to Jane.

But Mrs. Robicheaux seemed not to hear. "So many, many
things!" she said, misting up behind her eyeglasses. "Roland actually dated my older sister first, and one evening, she pulled me aside
and said, 'I can't bear another night of hearing him clear his throat
through a whole movie. You go on down there and tell him all nice-
like that I have a headache.' So I went downstairs, and Roland was
there waiting, and I told him my sister was indisposed, and he said,
'Well, why don't *you* come to the movies with me instead?' Now, my
father was very old-fashioned, and he thought it was *highly* inappropriate for a twenty-year-old man to take a fourteen-year-old girl
out, and he said under no circumstances could I go. But I was so
woebegone, and after my sister shouted down the stairs that Roland
was pretty harmless, my father decided we could sit on the porch
together and have iced tea and cake. But we had to leave the front
door slightly ajar because my father said he didn't trust Roland any
further than he could throw him. So Roland and I had tea and cake
and the nicest, sweetest, most wonderful conversation imaginable!
Then every weekend after that, Roland would show up at our house,
and he and I would sit on the front porch and have iced tea and cake.
This went on for almost two years! We had to sit out there even in
the wintertime because my father refused to let Roland in the house.
And finally, on my sixteenth birthday, I said, 'Daddy, I have gained
nearly ten pounds from all this cake, and besides, Roland and I are

in love.' My father said if I had my heart set on marrying a degenerate, there wasn't much—"

"Georgina, please!" Mr. Robicheaux was looking alarmed. "Nobody wants to hear all this."

Speak for yourself! Jane thought this was possibly the most interesting class discussion ever.

"Was it applesauce cake?" Joshua Curry asked. "The cake you ate?"

"Sometimes it was applesauce cake," Mrs. Robicheaux said pleasantly. "Sometimes it was poppy seed, sometimes it was spice cake."

Jane had the impression that Mrs. Robicheaux would truthfully answer any question put to her, and it was tempting to ask some of her own. What was it like to marry a man everyone disapproved of? Was he a better husband than he appeared? Was marriage everything Mrs. Robicheaux had hoped it would be? Did she still love Mr. Robicheaux enough to sit on a freezing-cold porch with him, or was that not the kind of love that withstood matrimony? What kind of love *did* withstand matrimony? Was it the kind of love Jane had? She really needed to know.

THE VOLUNTEER FIREFIGHTER was supposed to come to class the next day, but he called Jane early that morning to say he was needed at a grease fire in Walloon Village.

"I can send my brother to speak to your class, though," he said.

"Is your brother a firefighter?" Jane asked.

"No, he's an accountant."

"Well, thank you, but we had one of those already," Jane said politely. "Good luck with the grease fire."

She decided to have Duncan and Jimmy as speakers instead, and said they could bring Willard for good measure. But Jimmy said Willard had driven over to Mio to go to the cheese shop there, so it was just Duncan and Jimmy with a whole bunch of wooden wedges, which Duncan said the children could sand and take home as doorstops.

"Okay, everyone," Jane said, as Duncan took a seat in the chair at the front of the room. Jimmy was setting out wood pieces and sandpaper along the back counter. "This is Mr. Ryfield, and he's a woodworker."

"A woodworker is someone who works with wood to build cabinets and furniture and even boats and musical instruments," Duncan said to the class. "It's one of the oldest and most well-respected professions—"

Logan Miles had been picking fluff off the carpet, but now he looked up. "I think you fixed my little sister's crib."

"Please remember to raise your hand, Logan," Jane said.

Logan raised his hand. "I think you fixed my little sister's crib."

"Is that so?" Duncan looked thoughtful. "Probably what I actually did was *refinish* the crib, because I—"

"My mother says you had the crib so long my sister grew out of it," Logan said.

"Oh, well, now—"

"She said my sister was two years old and had got used to sleeping in a regular bed by the time we got it back," Logan continued. "My sister didn't want anything to do with that crib by then."

"Well, no two-year-old should be sleeping in a crib anyway," Duncan said. "So you can look at it like I did your whole family a favor, kind of. Now, who else has a question?"

Kelsey Angula raised her hand. "Aren't you also Ms. Wilkes's boyfriend?"

Jane flushed. Had she mentioned Duncan so much already, this early in the year? Yes, she supposed she had. It was so easy to do, and it felt so good. *I'll have my boyfriend come fix the playground gate this weekend,* and *Mr. Ryfield will know how to get that ham sandwich off the PA speaker.*

"Oh, yes," Duncan said easily. "Couple of years now."

"Years?" Matthew Harvey asked, startled. "Did you get held back?"

Duncan looked puzzled. "Held back?"

"Like flunking," Matthew said.

Jane clapped her hands together. "I think Mr. Jellico is ready for everyone now."

Jimmy threw up his hands in a startled way. "Wait! I'm still counting out sandpaper!" But the children scrambled up and surged toward the back of the classroom.

Jane went to look out the window, biting her lip. The playground was ugly and gray—an apocalyptic playground.

She had always assumed that her relationship with Duncan was getting stronger and more permanent the longer it went on. But maybe that wasn't the case. Maybe Matthew was right, and they had flunked the relationship test by failing to move on to the next level. Maybe they had stopped working and just didn't realize it yet.

Duncan came up behind her and hooked a friendly arm around her shoulders. He rested his chin on the top of her head. "It's nice to be here with you," he said simply.

She leaned back against him, his strong shoulder that was just the right height.

Taylor Beck got a splinter underneath his thumbnail, and Duncan told the children an inappropriate joke about why squirrels swim on their backs—"To keep their nuts dry"—and Jimmy drank two of the little cartons of milk that were keeping cool in a crate at the back of the room because he thought they were free. And that was Thursday, more or less.

DR. HAVEN came to school early on the day of his guest-speaker visit, arriving while Jane and Mr. Robicheaux were still in the teachers' lounge, drinking coffee. He was a stocky, dark-haired, bearded man, and he always wore casual clothes instead of a white coat over a shirt and tie. (Almost every Halloween, some student in Jane's class would dress as a doctor by wearing jeans and a plaid flannel shirt.) He was kind and understanding and wise, the very definition of a small-town doctor. Jane liked him a lot. But—had he ever heard of HIPAA? Because the very first thing he did was ask Mr. Robicheaux about the state of his bowels.

"Now, Roland, when is the last time you ate any roughage?" Dr. Haven asked.

Mr. Robicheaux's face took on a fearful, hunted sort of expression. "Last night," he said unconvincingly.

"And what was that?" Dr. Haven challenged.

"A, um, baked potato."

"That's okay, I guess," Dr. Haven said in a grudging tone, "but what I was really hoping you'd say was a salad. Leafy greens, cabbage, carrots, some nuts and seeds. A good crunchy salad can clean your colon just like a scrub brush. Are you producing stool every day?"

"Oh, hey, I have *never* been a once-a-day man," Mr. Robicheaux protested.

"That's because you don't set yourself a schedule," Dr. Haven said. "Every day you should make an opportunity to sit on the toilet, even if you don't feel the need to go. The same time every day, so your body learns a routine. And I don't mean you should just sit there smoking a cigarette or reading *The Wall Street Journal*—"

"Well, I subscribe to the *Free Press*, anyway," Mr. Robicheaux said.

Dr. Haven was starting to look heated. "You listen to me, Roland! I made my peace with your smoking years ago, but I'll be damned if I'm going to let colon disease carry you off to an early grave and leave a nice lady like Georgina to fend for herself."

Jane, who was enjoying this conversation immensely—and thanking God that she herself was not a patient of Dr. Haven's—finally interrupted. "We better get to class. The students will be arriving any minute."

Once again, Jane and Mr. Robicheaux pushed back the classroom divider, and the children sat in a semicircle around the chair at the front of the classroom.

"This is Dr. Haven," Jane said. "He's here to talk to us about what it's like to be a doctor."

Ryan Andre raised his hand. "Do we have to get shots?"

"Oh, no." Dr. Haven looked thoughtful. "At least, not if your vaccinations are up to date."

"Which all of yours are," Jane said firmly, as several students began to lick their lips nervously. "Every single one of you. No one is getting a shot today. No one. *No one*. Now, I think Dr. Haven has some supplies to hand out."

"I certainly have," Dr. Haven said. He had brought a shopping bag with him in addition to his medical bag, and he now divided the children into pairs and had Jane and Mr. Robicheaux hand out wooden tongue depressors and surgical masks and latex gloves.

"Examine your partners," Dr. Haven said as he walked around the room. "Treat them as patients. Take their pulse, look into their mouths, ask them how they feel. Say 'Now, what brings you here today? Any pain or fever?'"

The children giggled, and Dr. Haven chuckled into his beard. "Say 'How's your heartburn?' and 'Are you getting enough sleep?'"

He moved from pair to pair, allowing each child to use his stethoscope, otoscope, and reflex hammer. Samantha Truitt said she was pretty sure she could see something growing in Madison Lockett's ear, and Kyle Bradshaw kicked Dylan McMahon in the jaw in what was almost certainly *not* a reflex reaction, but otherwise all went smoothly, and the examinations carried them right through to morning recess. Mr. Robicheaux hurried out to the playground to supervise the children with unprecedented speed and enthusiasm—obviously, he didn't want to risk having another conversation about his intestines—but Jane lingered while Dr. Haven packed up.

"Thank you so much for coming," she said.

"It was my pleasure, Jane," Dr. Haven said. "How's Jimmy doing on Lipitor? Is he taking it every day?"

"Oh, yes." Jane nodded. "Duncan gives it to him at lunchtime."

"Good, good." Dr. Haven zipped his medical bag closed. "That reminds me, I saw Jimmy in Grayling earlier this week."

"Grayling?" Jane frowned. "Jimmy didn't go there."

Dr. Haven shook his head. "I saw him there Monday afternoon. My wife and I were driving to her brother's house, and I saw Jimmy and that friend of his, right on Main Street."

"I'll ask him about it," Jane said doubtfully.

"I think it's best if he stays here in town unless you or Duncan is with him." Dr. Haven picked up his medical bag. "Here in town everyone looks out for him, everyone knows him and can help him if he needs it. I don't like to think of Jimmy out dealing with strangers. Oh, and one more thing. You might want to have Olivia Ness's and Sydney Swan's mothers give me a little call. Looks to me like they both have the beginnings of conjunctivitis."

THE MAYOR was unable to come to school because he was having his wisdom teeth removed, so he sent the assistant health inspector, a man named Kelvin Dunn. Jane already knew Kelvin because he ran a roofing business on the side and had replaced the gutters on her house three years earlier.

Kelvin entered the classroom dragging three enormous cellophane bags. He asked Jane and Mr. Robicheaux to wheel in the television from the AV room so he could show a short film, and while they did that, Kelvin gave each child a straw boater with a red-white-and-blue hatband, a patriotic plastic pinwheel, a flowered plastic lei, and a bright red woven-nylon shopping bag. He'd obviously stepped into City Hall's storeroom and helped himself to leftover Fourth of July bounty. Jane was pleased, even though the classroom now sounded like a grove of palm trees in a strong wind, due to all the rustling plastic. The boaters were too big and slipped down on the children's foreheads, and they peered out from under the brims, beady-eyed.

Kelvin gave a short talk about the importance of health inspections, and then Joshua Curry, apparently still thinking Kelvin was the mayor, asked how many people would have to die in the line of succession before Kelvin became president.

"Oh, gosh, I don't know," Kelvin said. "Most of civilization, I guess."

Still, it all went very well until they lowered the lights and started the videotape, which was called *FDA Standards: What You Should Know*. Jane saw the title and felt a flicker of unease. The film didn't start out that badly—it was mainly short clips of peanut-butter factories and tuna canneries and an unseen male narrator talking about food-preparation guidelines. But then the television screen filled with a close-up of a glass bowl full of brown powder, and the narrator proclaimed solemnly, "For every fifty grams of cinnamon, the FDA allows up to ten rodent hairs and four hundred insect fragments," and a girl from Mr. Robicheaux's class named Jasmine Bigelow cried out, "I had cinnamon toast for breakfast!" and burst into traumatized tears.

Kelvin stopped the film, and Jane turned on the lights, but Jasmine couldn't calm down. Mr. Robicheaux had to escort her to the nurse's office, and they could all hear Jasmine's cries as she went down the hall, her voice nearly breaking on the second word. "Cinnamon *toast!* Cinnamon *toast!* Cinnamon *toast!*"

Jane shut the door to the hallway.

"I sure am sorry about that, Jane," Kelvin said.

"Oh, now, I'm certain Jasmine will be just fine," she said, although she was pretty sure Jasmine would never eat cinnamon toast again. She might never eat *breakfast* again, period.

"Can we watch the rest of the movie?" Nicholas King asked, and the other children squinted at her from under their boater brims.

"No," Jane said. "It's almost time for recess."

"No, it's not," said Christopher Goodman. "Recess is at ten fifteen. It says so on the schedule." (Those early readers could be problematic.)

"This is a special recess," Jane told him. "So special it's not even on the schedule."

"Oh," Christopher said. Jane regretted having used that excuse so early in the year. It generally only worked once.

"Everyone, please thank Mr. Dunn for coming," she said. "And then you may all put on your coats."

The children clapped, and Joshua asked to shake Kelvin's hand on the off chance that he did become president someday, and then they all ran over to the line of coat hooks against the outer walls of both classrooms.

"Thank you so much for coming," Jane said to Kelvin. "The Fourth of July stuff was a big hit."

"Oh, that was no problem." Kelvin was shrugging into his own bright blue windbreaker. "But I wanted to ask you: Who's that fella living with Jimmy?"

"That's Willard Williams," Jane said. "But he doesn't live at Jimmy's. He lives in the Schroders' granny flat."

"Nobody's living in the Schroders' granny flat except their granny."

Jane frowned. "I thought she died."

"Nope, that was Mark's mother-*in-law* over in Kalkaska." Kelvin zipped up his windbreaker. "Mark's mother still lives there. I know because I was over there on Sunday, cleaning their ground-level traps, and Mark was outside talking to me when Aggie Polnichik comes driving up and says, 'Mark, I have the perfect tenant for your garage apartment,' and Mark sort of hollers up at the granny flat, 'Ma, how would you like a roommate?' You know how he likes to joke around—"

"Willard's probably still at the City Motel in that case," Jane said.

Kelvin shook his head. "Oh, no, I saw him going into Jimmy's with two big suitcases. And Marie Henderson at Glen's told me that Jimmy bought family packs of cereal and potato chips and told her he was eating for two, and she figured that was Jimmy's way of saying he had a roommate."

Yes, it probably was. Jane was fluent in Jimmy's language, too.

JANE USED HER KEY to let herself into Jimmy's house.

"Willard?" she called. "Willard?" But that was just a formality. She knew from the dry, dusty silence of the house that no one was home. Jimmy would be at work, and Willard must be off somewhere. She closed the door behind her and went upstairs.

Mrs. Jellico's bedroom was so dim and depressing that it wouldn't have surprised Jane to find Mrs. Jellico's body still lying in state there. The room was crowded with bulky furniture laminated in a tortoiseshell finish, and yellowed lace doilies covered the tabletops. The bedspread was fringed pink chenille, and the bedside lamp bases were white porcelain festooned with large pink porcelain roses. Jane could hardly believe Willard had chosen to sleep here, even when faced with the City Motel, but he clearly had: a suitcase lay open on the floor, its contents untidily stirred, and a men's leather toiletry case rested on top of the dresser.

Jane paused for a moment, her hand resting nervously on her throat, where she could feel her pulse beating. She glanced over her shoulder even though she knew the hall behind her was empty. Then she crossed the room and knelt by Willard's suitcase. She lifted the clothes carefully with one hand while she ran the other along the bottom of the suitcase. Her fingers felt only the soft suitcase lining—no papers or envelopes or boxes or whatever she was looking for. She wasn't even sure. She looked at the clothes themselves. She recognized several of the big, loose button-down shirts Willard favored, and the shabby corduroys and khakis. The usual jumble of boxers and pajamas and undershirts, all faded and worn. Only one item of clothing looked new, and Jane pulled it out carefully and shook it open. A long-sleeved black shirt with BOYNE MOUNTAIN STAFF embroidered on the left breast pocket. She refolded it and tucked it back into the suitcase.

Jane went downstairs and stood for a moment in the front hall, her hand on the door handle, her feet in the pie wedges of afternoon sunshine that shone through the fanlight above the front door. She turned and hurried into the kitchen. She took down the Humpty Dumpty cookie jar and removed the worn envelope from inside. She had put forty dollars in there just three days ago. She opened the envelope flap and ran her thumb across the greenish-white edges of the bills inside. Then she pulled the bills out slightly so she could see the denominations. Seven twenties. One hundred and forty dollars.

"Thought I should chip in now that I'm living here," Willard said from behind her, and Jane's hands clenched so violently, she nearly tore the money in half.

"Goodness! You scared me to death," she said. "I didn't hear you come in."

Willard didn't reply.

"I was just seeing if Jimmy needed any more money for groceries this week." Jane's voice sounded false and tinny, even to her.

"I think we're okay," Willard said.

"Of course you are." Jane swallowed. "Of course."

She returned the envelope to the cookie jar with trembling fingers while Willard watched in silence. She said good-bye and hurried out to her car, shame puddling at her heels like a shadow.

THEY DECIDED TO CANCEL Taco Tuesday that week because Gary had chipped an incisor opening a bottle of hot sauce with his teeth and Freida had strained her voice by trying to reach top C during choir practice. Jane was relieved—she didn't want to see Willard again so soon.

Besides, she liked to have nights alone with Duncan. She picked up Chinese food for their dinner on her way home from school. Her neighbor, Clifford Graves, was out in his yard blowing leaves when she got home. He was a ranger at Young State Park, and he looked like an overgrown Boy Scout in his khaki uniform. He was an angular blond man in his late twenties, and though Jane found him somewhat hyper and excitable—watching him use a leaf blower right now was like watching a man fend off an attack of invisible bees—she liked him a lot.

"Hiya, Jane!" Clifford turned off the leaf blower and hailed her with it when she got out of her car. "How are you?"

"I'm all right," she called back. The wind undid her ponytail and her hair rippled in the breeze. "How are you?"

"I'm good!" he called. "You ought to bring your class out to the nature center. We got a new tarantula for the terrarium, and we let people hold her. She hasn't bitten anyone yet, so we don't think she's going to."

The thought of Clifford handling a tarantula was so alarming that Jane missed the next thing he said. "What?" she called.

"I said, did Jimmy find his friend?" Clifford shouted.

Jane went to the bottom of her driveway so she could hear him better. "What friend?"

"That friend who lives with him," Clifford said. "Willard. I saw Jimmy in the hardware store, and he was asking the cashier if she's seen him."

Jane looked at him, frowning. "Why would Jimmy be looking for Willard in the hardware store?"

"That's what the cashier said," Clifford answered. "She said, 'How would I know? This here is the hardware store, not missing persons.' And Jimmy said—"

A car drove down the street then, and both Jane and Clifford backed up. By the time the car had passed, Clifford had started up his leaf blower again and conversation was impossible. Jane could feel the cartons of Chinese food cooling in her hands, so she waved good-bye and hurried into the house.

WHEN THE PRINCIPAL'S SECRETARY, Ms. Lowry, interrupted Literacy Workshop the next day to tell Jane that the sheriff was waiting to speak to her in the main office, Jane's first thought was that she'd forgotten to put the sheriff on the guest-speaker calendar. That's how caught up in the Community Unit she was.

But Ms. Lowry's face was tense and watchful. "You go ahead, Jane," she said. "I'll take over class."

Jane had never known Ms. Lowry to do this. She looked at the children worriedly. It was a bad day for substitutions, a bad day for disruption—the wind had been blowing hard since morning, making the dead leaves whip around the schoolyard like a thousand scampering chipmunks. Windy days were hard teaching days; it made the children glittery-eyed and impulsive. Maybe it was the low barometric pressure, or maybe it was something more instinctual, more primitive.

"Okay," Jane said slowly. "We were just doing fill-in-the-blank worksheets for sight words." She handed Ms. Lowry her own paper. "If you read aloud, they can follow along."

She left the classroom and walked down the hall to the office, her pulse beating in her temples. A car accident, she thought. It must be a car accident. The other half of whatever terrible event she had put in motion on the night Jimmy's mother was killed.

The sheriff, his brown uniform with gold braid vivid against the drab surroundings, was standing next to Ms. Lowry's empty desk with his arms crossed, talking to the principal, Mr. Hawthorn. Jane knew the sheriff slightly—his wife ran a catering company, and Jane had booked them for her wedding reception, for the wedding to Luke that hadn't happened.

"Here she is now," Mr. Hawthorn said. "Jane, please feel free to use my office."

Another first. Entrance to Mr. Hawthorn's office was normally more restricted than the first-class lounge at an airport.

"Hello, Sheriff," Jane said. "Has there been an accident?"

"No, no." The sheriff shook his head. "Everyone's okay. Let's go in here, shall we?" He held the door of Mr. Hawthorn's office for her. He creaked when he moved, the leather of his duty belt rubbing against his handgun holster, radio pouch, and baton holder. It was a harsh, rasping sound.

"Now," the sheriff said as soon as he had shut the door. "First off, I want you to know that Duncan is with Jimmy, and they are both perfectly fine."

"Duncan?" Jane asked.

The sheriff took her arm gently and led her to the small green sofa near the window. She sat down and he sat next to her, leather squeaking again.

The sheriff's voice was calm, unhurried—the voice of someone who is used to relaying information to people who might not be listening carefully. "Now, what happened is that Jimmy didn't show up for work today, and when he wasn't there by midmorning, Duncan called him," he said. "Jimmy takes his job very seriously. Duncan said he'd never missed work before without calling."

"No, he would never do that," Jane said worriedly. "Has anyone checked his house? Maybe he's ill."

"When Jimmy didn't answer the phone, Duncan went over to the house and rang the doorbell," the sheriff continued. "After ten minutes of knocking and hollering and looking through the windows, he gave up and began looking for Jimmy around town, at Glen's and the library and places like that. And eventually he found him, more or less by coincidence, over on Ray Street. Apparently, Jimmy had been up since daybreak, going house to house on foot, asking if anyone had seen his friend Willard."

Jane rubbed her forehead. "Yes, someone told me he was asking around."

"Jimmy was very worked up, almost hysterical," the sheriff said. His voice was still deliberate. "Duncan got him to get in the van and calmed him down a little. You know how good Duncan is with Jimmy, Jane. Anyway, they went back to Jimmy's house—Duncan thought Jimmy probably hadn't eaten in hours and had the idea that breakfast might calm him down. But Jimmy was too upset to eat and couldn't stop saying they needed to find his friend. Finally, Duncan said if it would make Jimmy feel better, he'd call the police and see if there'd been an accident, and Jimmy said, 'No, no, you can't call the police because they'll ask me for the money.'"

"Money?" Jane asked. "This is about money?"

"Yes, these things usually are," the sheriff said bitterly. "Duncan got the whole story out of Jimmy, eventually, but it was fairly garbled, and it took Duncan a while to make sense of it. Apparently, Jimmy's friend, this Willard Williams, convinced Jimmy to take out a personal loan from a bank in Grayling, using Jimmy's house as collateral. Duncan said Willard had evidently been pressuring Jimmy for weeks, promising that he would double the money on the stock market, and Jimmy believed him because—"

"Because Jimmy believes everything," Jane finished softly.

"Yes, it seems that he does," the sheriff said. He shifted creakily. "At any rate, the bank approved the loan, and Willard had them deposit the money in an account in both his and Jimmy's names. Now, if they'd tried to do that at a bank here in town, the bank manager would've called you, or even me. Tim Kelly at Citizen State or Frank Bradley at Huntington, both of them good men, friends of mine . . ." The sheriff shrugged sadly. "Well, I guess Willard knew better than to try it here. Anyway, this was ten days ago, and since then Willard has been driving all over the state, draining the account by writing different cashier's checks to himself. He would do this while Jimmy was at work and then be home in the evening, so Jimmy didn't suspect anything. And then two days ago, he up and disappeared."

Jane swallowed. "How much was the loan?"

The sheriff grimaced. "Eighty thousand dollars."

Jane felt dizzy. It seemed as though eighty thousand moths had swarmed in front of her, blocking her vision. She blinked rapidly. "A bank lent *Jimmy* eighty thousand dollars?"

"Well, you know what the economy's like," the sheriff said. "Banks are practically begging people to borrow."

Good for the economy, Jane thought. Good for the banks. But what about Jimmy?

"Now, I've got people out looking for Willard," the sheriff said.

"But that's not his real name, and Boyne Mountain doesn't have anyone fitting his description on their books."

But he had a Boyne Mountain staff shirt, Jane thought, and then winced at her own naïveté. It would be so easy to steal a shirt like that. They even sold them at the thrift store sometimes—no one knew that better than Jane.

The sheriff was still talking. "That Buick Willard was driving was unregistered, bought just six weeks ago. It looks like he was planning this for a long time, and I'm sure it's not the first time he's done it, but I'm hoping he let something slip while he was here, some personal detail that can help us find him. Jimmy's not in good enough shape to remember much at all, and Duncan says Willard was pretty tight-lipped about his past. Can you remember anything about him? Anything he might have said about his personal life or background that would help us?"

Jane frowned, concentrating. "He said once he had a brother who was—who was like Jimmy. But that his brother was dead."

The sheriff looked at her, patient and encouraging.

Her eyes strayed to the bookshelves, where Mr. Hawthorn kept his twenty-four volume *Encyclopaedia Britannica* set. He had told Jane once that they had been given to him for his high school graduation in 1967 and were his proudest possession. Dusty red hardcover books with no mention of moon landings or pocket calculators. What sort of life did you lead if this was your proudest possession? Jane's mind felt like a box of Skittles dropped on the floor, thoughts scattering and rolling everywhere.

She looked at the sheriff helplessly. "That's it. That's all I can remember. No, wait, he told Freida he played the harmonica."

"Think about it. Maybe more will come to you," the sheriff said. "Little things that didn't seem important at the time."

But Jane was remembering the Taco Tuesday when Willard had played his version of Star of the Week. How he'd gotten them all to talk about themselves, steering the conversation as expertly as a captain steering a riverboat. Freida, Aggie, Duncan, even Gary. But now she realized that Willard had only asked questions, not answered them. About himself, he had not said a word.

MR. HAWTHORN offered to take Jane's class for the rest of the day, but Jane said, "Oh, no, I'll be fine. It's less than an hour."

Why did she say that? She had no idea.

"If you're sure," Mr. Hawthorn said. "And Duncan called and said he'd pick you up after school."

"Okay," Jane said.

She left the principal's office and walked back toward her classroom, trailing one hand against the wall. It was a strange, dreamlike walk. But that made sense because surely she must be dreaming? The carpet was hilly and uneven, the walls bulged inward like warped boards, the floor threatened to rush up to meet her several times. She reached her classroom and put her hand on the doorknob. Brushed steel—cold, almost greasy. It felt real. She wasn't dreaming.

She opened the door and went in. She saw that the children were journaling—that fallback plan of substitute teachers everywhere—and that they had just about reached the outer limits of their compliance. Their cheeks were all chapped, as though they had been out in the wind instead of just listening to it, and the room was filled with the sound of their fingers flipping the edges of their journal notebooks. Ms. Lowry was walking up and down the aisles, her eyes scanning from side to side, as though restlessness were a spider she could track down and stamp out.

"Thank you, Ms. Lowry," Jane said. Her voice was calm, clear. "Children, you may put away your journals."

Her students looked startled; she never called them "children."

Ms. Lowry flashed Jane a grateful smile and slipped out the door, back to the office to fight the good fight against unanswered phone calls and excessive tardiness or whatever it was she did all day. It was beyond Jane's comprehension, now that the world had changed. Now that she knew what people were capable of.

Twenty-two pairs of eyes looked at her.

"Class, it's time for the next subject," Jane said. She never called them "class" either. She seemed to have forgotten how to be herself. Or perhaps she had left her real self back in the principal's office, and now she was just a shadow person, a wraith.

"It's time for Science," Christopher Goodman said. "It says that on the schedule."

Jane swung her head, which seemed ponderously heavy, and looked at the schedule written on the whiteboard. "So it does," she said. "But I've—I've—" What had she done? "I've changed my mind. We'll have Story Time instead."

"On a *Wednesday*?" Kayla Norton asked doubtfully.

"Yes," Jane said. "Kayla, why don't you pick a book, and we'll all go to the Library Corner?"

The Library Corner was in the back of the room, with a rocking chair for Jane and the Peter Rabbit rug for the children to sit on. Blond wood bookshelves held all the children's books Jane had owned as a child and all she'd collected as an adult. Good books, all of them, dog-eared, oversized, begging to be read.

Jane sat in the rocking chair, and Kayla handed her *The Spider and the Fly*. Jane opened it and began to read. Her voice was so clear and steady, so startlingly calm. Strengthened by years of careful, measured classroom speaking, it did not fail her. She read aloud, rocking slowly. She turned a page.

Said the cunning spider to the fly, "Dear friend, what shall I do,
To prove the warm affection I've always felt for you?

I have within my pantry good store of all that's nice;
I'm sure you're very welcome; will you please to take a slice?"

Jane paused. She couldn't see the words on the page anymore. They had pixelated and begun to shimmer. She waited for her vision to clear but it didn't.

She closed the book. "I know what," she said. "Let's do mindful breathing. Remember when Miss Heather from the yoga studio came and taught us that?"

"I don't like this day," Olivia Ness said fretfully. "Everything's changing. We're not following the schedule."

"This is the last change, I promise," Jane said. "Now, everyone, spread out a little bit and lie down. I'll lie down, too, right here next to the chair."

She didn't feel able to stand up, so she leaned forward and climbed out of the chair instead, like a dog climbing down from a hatchback. She lay down carefully and stared up at the ceiling. She listened to the rustling sounds of the children getting into position, and when they grew quiet, she knew everyone had found a place.

"All right," she said, and then fell silent. For a moment, she thought no words would come, that she would not be able to approximate what Miss Heather had said. They would all have to get up and do Independent Reading, and Olivia would probably cry, and Jane would, too. But suddenly Miss Heather's words came to her, swiftly and completely, like a flower blooming in time-lapse photography. "Find a relaxed, comfortable position." Jane spaced her words evenly. "Rest your hands at your sides. Close your eyes. Put your tongue on the roof of your mouth."

Brandon Hicks began making a confused choking sound, so Jane said quickly, "Never mind about your tongue—just relax your body." She slowed her voice again. "Imagine yourself sinking into the floor. Breathe. Breathe. Focus on the natural rhythm of your breath." The spaces between her words grew longer. "In. Out. In. Out. Feel your chest rise and then fall. Enjoy the flow of your breathing. Quiet the buzzing of your mind. Think only of your breathing. Quiet the buzzing of your mind."

"You already said that," Kyle Bradshaw whispered loudly.

"What happens to Science?" Christopher asked, turning his head. "Are we going to do it tomorrow?"

"Breathe, Christopher." Jane stared at the celling. "Breathe. Do not let earthly problems interfere. Let go of cares about material things. Let go of cares about material things. Let them go." She sighed. "Let them go."

JANE HAD DRIVEN HER CAR to school, so there was no real reason for Duncan to pick her up, but she felt a surge of relief when she saw his white van in the parking lot, glowing in the late-afternoon shadows like a rusty rectangular ghost.

She opened the passenger door, and the map light shone on Duncan for a moment. Jane had never seen him so serious. It changed his looks somehow, made them artificial. He looked like a poorly lit actor in a soap opera, handsome but fading. She climbed in and shut the door. The light went out. Duncan turned the key in the ignition but didn't put the van in gear.

"Where's Jimmy?" Jane asked.

"He's at Aggie's," he said, his voice slower and deeper than normal. "I told her we'd pick him up later. I want him to stay with us tonight. I don't imagine Willard will ever come back here, but he does have keys to the house, and I don't want Jim there." He cleared his throat. "I know his name's not Willard, but we've got to call him something."

"Of course Jimmy should stay with us." Jane touched his shoulder gently. "How's he holding up?"

"Jim—Jim's—" Duncan face contorted slightly. "Ah, you know, I don't believe I can talk about that right now," he said in a strangely conversational tone. "Not unless I want to lose my mind. Jim thought Willard was his *friend*."

Jane's vision was blurring again. "I know."

"I never wanted to kill someone until today," Duncan said. "Not even Tony Nowicki that time in high school."

Jane didn't ask who Tony Nowicki was. "How long?" she asked instead. "How long until the first payment is due?"

"Five days," Duncan said. He peered out the windshield, but Jane knew he wasn't looking at the dead leaves and candy wrappers that the wind blew through the parking lot. "Aggie's going to list the house immediately. Maybe we can sell it before he's more than thirty days in default."

Aggie, always Aggie. Even in crisis, Jane could not have Duncan to herself.

"Maybe the sheriff will find Willard before then," she said. "And we can get the money back."

"No," Duncan said. "I don't believe so."

Jane didn't believe so either.

"Maybe—maybe we don't have to sell the house," she said. "Maybe there's another way."

"I've been thinking about it all day." Duncan's voice was slow, morose. "There isn't another way."

"Surely we can make the bank understand." Jane could hear the desperation in her own voice. "We can explain that it was fraud, and renegotiate the loan, and get smaller payments. I could pay a hundred a month, and—"

"No." Duncan shook his head. "You don't make enough money, and you have a mortgage on your own house. I don't make enough either. Eighty thousand dollars? The house is gone, or will be shortly."

"But what will happen to Jimmy?" Jane asked despairingly. "Where will he live? Can he—do you think he could get some sort of state assistance? Maybe a rent-subsidized apartment?"

Duncan let out his breath, a long sigh like the wind outside. "Jim can't live by himself," he said. "I think we've known that all along."

"Well, then what's left?" Jane said. "A halfway house? A group home? We could never do that to Jimmy."

"*Never.*" Duncan turned to look at her. His eyes blazed oddly. Then he looked back out at the parking lot. "That's why I wanted to pick you up."

He took a deep breath.

"I've looked at this from every angle today, and all I can think of is that you and I get married. We get married, and we buy a bigger house, and we make a stable home for Jim."

Jane's voice failed her, finally. They sat in silence except for the rumble of the engine and clicking of Duncan's keyring as it swung in the ignition switch. Jane had the queer experience of a memory forming even as it happened: she knew she would always remember this moment. The cold air seeping in around the doorframe. The smell of varnish and stale coffee. The hollowness of Duncan's voice. But mostly the feeling of her heart turning over sullenly in her chest. This was her proposal, and now it could never be anything else.

The wind slapped a pink plastic plate against the windshield—a plate decorated with glitter and pompons and trailing strings of craft feathers. Jane recognized it as a dreamcatcher made by one of the kindergartners. It stayed on the windshield for a moment while the wind caught its breath, and then it blew away, twirling cheerfully, into the gloom.

2011

I T SEEMED TO JANE that marriages were spreading across the whole land, just like the yawns in that Dr. Seuss book. First Jane and Duncan, then Marla Copeland and Bryant Campbell, Jody Walsh and Willie Roberts, Banjo and his longtime girlfriend, Kelvin Dunn and his short-time girlfriend, Grandpa Pendergrass and his home healthcare worker, and now Freida and Mr. Hutchinson.

Mr. Hutchinson taught biology at the high school. He was a tall, thin man with a blond moustache and a florid complexion. Jane thought he looked like an extra in a Western, or maybe a cardboard cutout of an extra in a Western, because he so seldom spoke. But Freida had fallen in love with him, or rather, they'd fallen in love with each other, and now they were going to get married just as soon as Mr. Hutchinson learned to play the recorder. (Freida told Jane that she wanted to marry a musician, and the recorder was the quickest, easiest instrument to learn.) Actually, they'd already set a wedding date for November, and Mr. Hutchinson had doubled down on his recorder lessons in order to be ready. Mr. Hutchinson had a first name—John—but everyone in town simply referred to them as Mr. Hutchinson and Freida, like a lesser-known Captain and Tennille.

All this marrying was like some sort of fever that had swept over Boyne City, and it made Jane feel like her own marriage was less meaningful, just another flu symptom. A persistent cough. A mild delirium. Everyone had it.

"Aggie and Gary could renew their vows," Duncan said to Jane over dinner as they discussed this. "I doubt Gary remembers the first time."

"What do you mean?" Jimmy asked, because of course Jimmy was there. Jimmy was always there. He lived with them, and sometimes Jane thought that spontaneous adult conversation had fled her life forever.

DINNER WAS EARLY because they were going to the evening concert at the gazebo in Old City Park afterward. As soon as Jimmy had helped Jane clear the table, all three of them climbed into Jane's station wagon. She had traded in her Honda—a family of three adults needed a bigger car.

Their house was bigger, too. They lived on the outskirts of town now, in a brown shingle-sided house with oddly shaped rooms and so much pine paneling in the kitchen that it felt like an Ikea showplace. Aggie had found it for them, of course. She had been like an avenging angel of real estate in the weeks following the loss of Jimmy's house. She'd sold Jimmy's house to a couple from downstate in only ten days—Jane suspected Aggie had shown the couple only inferior and unsuitable properties and then rushed them through the sale before they had a chance to look further—and she had been tireless in her search for a new house for Jane and Duncan and Jimmy. She'd taken them to see at least two dozen houses, and God knew how many more she'd looked at on her own. They'd chosen this house, and Aggie had lowered her angel sword and forced the owners to agree to an immediate move and the shortest possible escrow. Then she sold Jane's house to a man from Kalkaska who had been driving through Boyne City—Jane had never found out how this was accomplished; perhaps Aggie was flagging people down on the highway—and waived her commission on all three sales. All that had been wonderful, lifesaving, heroic, but dear God, it had involved a lot of Aggie.

Their new house was not perfect, but Duncan had liked the back deck, and Jane had liked the "bonus room" with the attached bathroom on the first floor. Aggie had said it would make a beautiful second family room, but Jane had decided instantly that it would be Jimmy's bedroom. Jane could withstand an awful lot of life's slings and arrows, but climbing the stairs to bed with Jimmy every night was not one of them. Jimmy would sleep down here. She had painted the room a rich cream color and furnished it with a sturdy varnished wood dresser and nightstand from the thrift store and the single bed from Duncan's workshop apartment. Jane had bought a new mattress for the bed and made it up with soft flannel sheets and a dove-in-the-window quilt she'd found in a trunk in Mrs. Jellico's attic. Ironic that a bed that had launched a thousand women's orgasms—possibly *tens* of thousands—had come to rest in the room of a man who'd never had a girlfriend, but Jimmy seemed unaware of that. He said he'd never slept better. Jane suspected it was less the bed than the knowledge that he was not alone in the house that made Jimmy sleep so well. How scared he must have been alone in his mother's house, scared for years. It made Jane clench her jaw in shame just to think about it. But Jimmy had caught up on that missing sleep, and his color had improved, and he'd lost weight now that he no longer ate pizza all the time. He looked better, healthier, but lines had etched themselves on his face—the skin between his eyebrows looked like invisible fingers were pinching it—and he'd lost that sweet, glad expression that used to make him seem so young.

On the way to the concert, they drove past the turnoff to Jimmy's old house. Every time they drove by this turnoff, Jane promised herself that they would act as though nothing had happened, and every time, conversation faltered and they fell silent. The couple who bought Jimmy's house had said that Jimmy could visit anytime, that they wanted to know him and the house's history, and he would be welcome, but Jimmy had never gone.

A block later, conversation picked back up, as it always did, with Duncan saying that he hoped Mona Wilbank wouldn't be at the concert because she might ask when her grandma's drop leaf table would be ready, and Jimmy asking if they had time to stop at Kilwins.

They found a parking space and walked to the park. It was late May and the evening held on to a chill stubbornly, the way a dog holds on to a bone. Yet the people sitting on the benches and on blankets around the gazebo wore summer clothing—shorts and T-shirts, sundresses and the thinnest of cardigans—in pastel colors. If Jane squinted, they looked like scoops of every possible ice cream flavor. It seemed as though people thought they could force warmer weather by dressing for it.

Duncan spread an old but clean moving pad on the grass while Jane looked around for familiar faces. Some of her students were here with their families, and the students turned excitedly to point her out: *There she is! My teacher!* Jane smiled and waved. Freida and Mr. Hutchinson were on a blanket closer to the front—Freida always wanted to be near the musicians—and Aggie and Gary were seated on a blue quilt with a picnic basket open between them.

"Hello, Duncan!" Aggie called. "Hi, Jane! Jimmy, would you like to come sit with us? I made fresh cinnamon doughnuts."

"I sure love those doughnuts," Jimmy said, trotting off toward them happily.

Jane sat down next to Duncan. The only thing she wanted more than a fresh cinnamon doughnut was time alone with Duncan. They had so little of it. Sometimes Jane thought her marriage was less like the divine union of two souls and more like when Mr. Gaska and Mr. Bagley combined the feedstore and the pet-supply shop into one business so they could lower operating costs. Really, wasn't that what she and Duncan had done? They had knocked down the wall dividing their lives and converted them into one bigger life so they could care for Jimmy. They would not be married now except for Jimmy, and no one knew that better than Jane. It was a practical arrangement, only faintly tinged with romance. Oh, there were exceptions, of course. Like the day of their wedding, when Jane had stepped out of the car in front of the courthouse wearing a marmalade-colored crochet dress from the thrift store and her hair pulled into a topknot circled with daisies, and Duncan had looked at her in a way that made her feel as if she were floating. Or once when she'd come upon him unexpectedly in the checkout lane at Glen's, and he'd said to the cashier, "Wait, I want to get some crois-sants for my wife," and his voice was so pleased and proud. Or when he woke her in the small hours—even on a school night!—to make love, saying, "You looked so beautiful sleeping there. I can't wait until morning."

But an enormous part of their lives—the bulk of it, Jane felt sometimes—was shared with Jimmy or given over to the care of him. They had breakfast together, and then Duncan and Jimmy left for the workshop and Jane left for school. At least Jane had the escape of teaching—Duncan worked with Jimmy all day long. Jane wondered how he could stand it, but Duncan remained as mild and cheerful as always. They all arrived home at the same time in the evening, and had dinner together, and watched television together, and shopped together, and went to the beach together and to restau-rants, and—well, Jane supposed it was what other couples did, only she and Duncan and Jimmy did it as a threesome. Always, Jimmy was there, asking questions like "Where's the orange juice? Where's the butter? I think we're out." (Jimmy seemed incapable of remem-bering the refrigerator had a door.) Or, "I'm pretty sure I locked the workshop, but would anything terrible happen if I maybe forgot?" (And Duncan would reach for his car keys.) Or Jimmy would be using the computer and call out, "Is it okay to click YES on this box that just popped up?" ("No!" Jane would leap to her feet. "Remember last time!") At least they no longer had Taco Tuesdays, but it was a hollow victory. Meaningless. Every night was Taco Tuesday now.

But here she was, alone with Duncan at least for a little while. She leaned against his shoulder. He put his arm around her and tugged at the ends of her hair.

"I've been thinking," he said, and Jane knew by his tone that he was going to propose some home improvement. Probably he wanted to add some extra shelves to the pantry. She'd seen him in there earlier, trying to retrieve a jar of applesauce without causing ten other jars and cans to tumble to the floor.

But what Duncan actually said was: "I think we should have a baby."

Truly, it was more shocking than if Mr. Gaska had said that to Mr. Bagley.

THEY TALKED about it late that night in bed, the moonlight filtering in through the window and seeming to fill the room with pale blue smoke.

"I just thought, you know, I wouldn't mind the occasional child," Duncan said softly. Jane wore a silky lavender nightgown, and Duncan's hands roamed over her body, not in a sex-initiating way, but the way someone would touch the velvet nap of a favorite chair.

"That's the thing about children, though," Jane said. "They're not really occasional. They're pretty full-time."

"Well, I guess I meant just one child," he said.

"Are you sure you don't have one or two children already?" Jane asked. "Statistically, it seems like you should."

"Oh, no," Duncan said calmly. "No woman has ever thought I

was a good bet to have a baby with. They were all pretty outspoken on that subject, and downright fanatical about birth control."

It's true: you can't help who you fall in love with. That doesn't always make it easier, though.

"So what do you say?" Duncan asked. In the moonlight, his face was all angles and shadows.

Jane had a theory that people spent too long deliberating small decisions and not enough time considering big, important ones. How many days—surely it added up to days—had she agonized over whether to cut bangs? How many hours had she spent debating the merits of wood versus laminate flooring? How many minutes of her life had she given over to working out the number of calories in a salad? How many times had she visited the thrift store, looking for the perfect black cashmere sweater? (The answer: a lot. Cashmere isn't often donated.) And yet, people got pregnant all the time just because one person was too lazy to get out of bed and hunt up a condom, people bought houses after a single viewing, people chose colleges based on whether the cafeteria served caffeinated beverages, people sent their mothers to drive other people's mothers home without thinking about it at all.

So she decided not to overthink this.

"Okay," she said to Duncan. "Okay."

That was in May. By June, Jane was pregnant.

ALMOST IMMEDIATELY, Jane's pregnancy began making itself known in all sorts of ways. First there was the nausea. Endless rolling nausea without vomiting, nausea that spun out before Jane like a curving country lane meandering through a hilly green landscape, the end always just out of sight. And when she did eat, it was only rice and pasta. Well, also popcorn and Skittles and Fritos and milkshakes. Vegetables had acquired a strange metallic taste. And meat was revolting, how could people not see that? Bleeding red *muscle*, that's all beef was. And goose-pimpled chicken with congealed yellow fat. Sausages that looked like intestines. Ham the color of sunburnt flesh. Jane moaned just thinking about it.

And the fatigue was like nothing Jane had known before. Had she really, at other points in her life, thought she was *tired*? That was ridiculous, laughable. Embarrassing, really. Only pregnant women—possibly only Jane—knew true exhaustion. Weariness that made it feel as though she were wading through knee-high molasses, as though her eyes were hot stones in dry creek beds, as though her head were so heavy it might roll off her shoulders onto the floor. During morning recess, she sat on a bench in the playground with her sunglasses on and napped upright. During lunch, she went out and slept in her car. During videos, she put her head down on the desk and slept until she woke up with drool dampening her cheek, the whiteboard showing nothing but the home screen of her laptop. She came home after school and slept on the couch until dinner.

Her breasts were sexily swollen, making her previously unremarkable blouses and cardigans suddenly home to cleavage that rivaled Aggie's. Jane thought she no longer looked like a teacher; she looked like a teacher in a porn film. She was also constipated, and she had waves of dizziness that made it seem as if the horizon were tilting, the world collapsing.

Her sense of smell was amplified, improved, sharpened—it was like a superpower now. She could smell coffee on Duncan's breath from the next room, the neighbors' marinated flank steak from next door, hair spray from the salon on the next block, even fresh blacktop being laid in the next county. One night, watching an episode of *Forensic Files* about a tracking dog who located a young girl's sweater in more than five square miles of wooded hillside, Jane thought, without irony: *I could do that.*

Worst of all were the mood swings. Although, actually, could it be considered a *mood swing* if it only swung one direction? Maybe it was more like a *mood acceleration*. Like the needle on a speedometer that whipped straight from ZERO to ANNOYED and stayed there. Because it seemed like the world was in an unkindly conspiracy to irritate Jane. Duncan drove her crazy by fondling her new breasts at every opportunity, Jimmy told rambling stories that made no sense, Aggie remarked that Jane looked so much *prettier* now that her face was fuller, Gary spent an entire evening with a little wad of mashed potato in the corner of his mouth, and Freida called Mr. Hutchinson "sweet pea." Mr. Robicheaux looked so startled—so *witless*—when Jane asked him if he had any extra blue construction paper that Jane honestly thought she might murder him and end up on a *Forensic Files* episode of her very own.

In the classroom, she was still patient and relatively serene. Her voice was still soft and pleasant, her hands still gentle and kind on students' shoulders, her smile still sweet and loving. Well, maybe not the smile so much. Sometimes students looked at her, and Jane could see in their expressions that her face did not match her warm voice.

In fact, it was Jane's mood acceleration in the checkout line at Glen's that led them to first tell people about the baby. She and Duncan were doing the normal grocery shopping on Saturday morning, and Marie Henderson rang up their groceries without subtracting Jane's coupon for yogurt, and Jane snapped, "Come on!"

"You'll have to excuse Jane, Marie," Duncan said. "It's hormones. She's pregnant."

"What?" Marie pressed the cash register release so abruptly the drawer flew out and hit her in the hip. "On purpose?"

"Yes, ma'am," Duncan said. "Due in February."

"Well." Marie looked uncertain. "Congratulations."

"In fact, we're thinking of naming the baby Glen," Duncan said in an expansive voice, "seeing how we fell in love the second time right over there in frozen foods."

"What if it's a girl?" Marie asked.

"Glen works for a girl," Duncan said. "If it's twins, we'll call them Glen and Glen."

Jane rolled her eyes. "It's not twins."

They paid for their groceries and wheeled the shopping cart out to the parking lot. As soon as they were outside, Jane said, "I can't believe you told Marie Henderson!"

"I like Marie." Duncan was unperturbed. "Besides, everyone's going to know pretty soon."

"I like Marie, too," Jane said. "I just didn't want her to be the first person we told."

"Who did you want the first person to be?"

"Well, I don't know," Jane said. "My mother, I guess."

"Here you go." Duncan handed her his cell phone. Reception had improved in Boyne City, and he had a cell phone now. She did, too, but hers was at home.

"Call your mother right now, and it'll be almost like we told her first. I'll put the groceries in back."

Jane climbed into the passenger seat and dialed her mother's number. "Hello, Mom."

"Why, hello, Jane," her mother said. *Clunk!* went the sound of her recliner going back. "I'm just sitting here watching the news about the space shuttle launch."

"I have some news, too," Jane said. "That's why I'm calling." Duncan slammed the hatchback shut and got in on the driver's side. "I'm—I'm going to have a baby."

"Well, that certainly is news," Jane's mother said. The words were right, but the intonation was wrong, Jane felt. Not like other mothers. Her mother sounded as though Jane's news was less impressive than NASA's news. "When are you due?"

"February twentieth."

"How is the pregnancy so far?"

"Everything is going well," Jane said. "I'm just tired all the time, and I have terrible heartburn."

"That means the baby's going to be born with a full head of hair," her mother said.

"I've heard that, too—"

"I hope it's not born with *fur*," her mother said in a thoughtful tone. "When I had you, there was another baby born at the hospital with hair all over its body. I think the hair fell out later on, but still, it must have been hard on the parents."

"Mom, that's called lanugo," Jane said, her voice rising. "And—"

"I feel for Duncan, of course," her mother interrupted calmly.

Jane frowned. "What does that mean, you feel for him?"

"Well, no man wants to become a father after fifty," her mother said. "I know you probably felt your biological clock ticking, but—"

"Duncan wants to be a father!" Jane said, nearly shouting. "The baby was his idea!"

"Jane, I do hope you're not having a child just to please him," her mother replied. "Because that's no recipe for happiness—"

"I have to go now, Mom," Jane said. "We're about to go through a tunnel."

She pressed the END button and handed Duncan's phone back to him. He slipped it into his shirt pocket and switched on the ignition. "No tunnels in Boyne City that I know of," he said.

Jane was breathing heavily. "I'm *glad* we told Marie first. *Glad*."

"Only tunnel I know of is the Detroit-Windsor one," Duncan continued thoughtfully. "You want to go to Canada?"

"No, of course not," Jane said. "Let's go home and tell Jimmy."

She didn't mean they should tell Jimmy the *second* they got home, but that's what they did. Jimmy came out of the house, squinting in the sunshine, to help them unload the groceries. Duncan opened the hatchback and Jimmy scooped up some rolls of paper towels. Duncan clapped him on the shoulder and said, "Good news, Jim! We're going to have a baby."

Jimmy froze. "Seriously?"

"You bet."

Jimmy looked at Jane doubtfully, and Jane did her best to look pregnant, motherly.

"You're not teasing?" Always Jimmy seemed to worry that people were teasing him, a worry that could only come from a lifetime of having been teased and tricked and lied to. Honestly, people were such assholes. It made Jane want to wring humanity's neck.

"No teasing, Jimmy," she said. "I really am going to have a baby. In a few months, you'll be able to feel him or her kick."

Jimmy looked from her face to Duncan's and back. "Will the baby be related to me?"

Jane wasn't prepared for that, although it made sense. Jimmy was alone in the world now; he wanted some family. She didn't know how to answer, but Duncan said easily, "Of course the baby will be related to you. Our family will be a little bigger, that's all. The baby will know you and love you just like we do."

"Hurray!" Jimmy shouted so suddenly that Jane jumped a little. He looked like he might throw the paper towels in the air. "Hurray for us!"

Sometimes he said just the right thing.

THE WORST THING about Jane's obstetrician was not that his office was all the way on the far side of Petoskey. That was, in fact, partly why Jane chose him. She didn't want to go to an obstetrician in

Boyne City, where she might have taught one of the doctor's children and Duncan would almost certainly have slept with a number of the doctor's patients. The worst part was not that her obstetrician was named Dr. Skyberger and that Duncan immediately began calling him "Dr. Skywalker" and doing things like pointing to Jane's stomach and saying, "*I* am your father!" in a Darth Vader voice, which made Jimmy laugh and slap his knee. (It was right about then that Jane began actively hoping the baby was a girl.) It wasn't even that Dr. Skywalker had the flowing beard and hot eyes of an insane revivalist preacher (though that took some getting used to), or that his receptionist turned out to be the sister of a former girlfriend of Duncan's, or even that Duncan looked fondly nostalgic and said, "How is Denise? She still driving that old Mustang?"

The worst thing was the other people in the waiting room. Very young girls accompanied by grim-faced mothers. Couples who wore sweatshirts reading HUBBY and WIFEY. A man who talked loudly on his cell phone the whole time: "Ask Doug. No, ask Arnie. Wait, didn't we tell them Thursday? I should be back by one, one thirty at the latest. Put it on my desk." What line of work was he in? How was it possible that Jane had to listen to him talk for a solid thirty minutes and still didn't know? Another woman was accompanied by a man with the most unfortunate facial hair Jane had ever seen—a moustache no thicker than dental floss that started under his nose and continued down either side of his mouth to meet on his chin. It looked like someone had circled an area on his face with a marker and said, "This here is where your moustache and beard should go." A heavily pregnant woman who settled herself into a chair and then stared at the wall in a fixed way that Jane found disturbing. A man and a woman, both dressed like corporate bankers, who proudly disdained speaking to each other. A red-eyed, puffy-faced woman who seemed to be crying her way through an entire pregnancy. A man with a military-short haircut who said to his wife,

"I'm telling you right now, you better not go into labor on Super Bowl Sunday."

And then there were the couples whom Jane thought of as mutual-desperation couples. The couples you looked at and thought, *Well, she's homely but he's nerdy* or *He's bald but she's so bossy* or *Her eyes are way too close together but he has that weak chin*. It wasn't nice to think these things but Jane couldn't seem to help it. And of course, maybe it wasn't even true. Maybe these men and women looked beyond the superficial to appreciate the depths of their partners' kindness and decency, their humor and authenticity. (Jane didn't believe that for a moment.) And what did people think when they saw her and Duncan? *He's so handsome but she scowls all the time* or *She's pretty enough but he doesn't look like the faithful type* or *She's probably trying to trap him with this baby—*

It all reminded Jane that having a baby was not that miraculous. Any two fools could do it.

WHO PLAYED THE ORGAN at Freida's wedding? Trick question! Freida played the organ at her own wedding, pounding out Bach's Arioso, while peering nervously over the wooden rail of the organ loft at Trinity Missionary Church.

Jane was the maid of honor, and she smiled up at Freida as she walked sedately down the aisle to where Mr. Hutchinson and the minister waited. Jane was too pregnant now for any of her regular clothes, but it seemed she was not quite pregnant enough for maternity dresses. She wore an emerald-green maternity dress, and it hung so loosely in the front that Jane thought she looked like a choir member.

The last notes of the organ died away, followed by the muffled taps of Freida's heels on the carpeted stairs before she burst through the swinging doors and dashed to her place at the altar, her cheeks Crayola-pink and her veil slightly askew. She was wearing a '50s-style white satin wedding dress, and her bosom heaved slightly against the bodice seams, while the crinolines holding her skirt out rustled like static. But Mr. Hutchinson looked in awe of her as he took her hand.

Jane glanced over to where Duncan sat, hoping to exchange an amused smile with him, but he was watching Freida with the same awestruck expression as Mr. Hutchinson. Jimmy sat next to him, wearing an ill-fitting blue suit that made him look like a convict on work release from prison. Jane glanced away from them, feeling suddenly disloyal.

The reception took place in a wooden lodge just outside town. The main room was spacious and inviting, wood-paneled, with an enormous gas fireplace in the middle, and clusters of soft leather armchairs and padded benches surrounding it.

"Are you sure you don't mind sort of directing everyone?" Freida asked Jane for the third time as they hung up their coats in the cloakroom. They had a shared dislike of wedding coordinators.

Jane squeezed Freida's arm. "Not at all. You go enjoy yourself."

From then on, Jane stopped being the maid of honor and became a sort of point person or liaison officer. In fact, she not only stopped being the maid of honor, she nearly stopped being human and became just a helpdesk in a giant green dress. She had to tell the caterers to start serving and direct the florist on where to put the arrangements and the staff which table to designate for gifts. Everyone had so many questions! What time could the florist pick up the vases? Should the cake be refrigerated? Where could the waitstaff unpack and change? Where should they park the van? When should they pour the champagne? How many guests were staying overnight? Where should they put the gifts? Where had Freida registered? Did they need drinks tickets? Was there going to be music? Why was Freida wearing such pointy shoes?

That last question was from Gary.

"Oh, well, the shoes match her dress," Jane said slowly. "It's all kind of retro."

Gary looked doubtful. "Do they hurt her feet?"

"They probably do." Jane wished that Aggie would come retrieve Gary, but Aggie was across the room, talking to Freida.

"Is Freida going to change her last name to Hutchinson?" Gary asked.

"No, she's going to stay Freida Fitzgerald."

"That's inconvenient," Gary said sternly. "Two names to remember."

"Well, you only ever call Freida by her first name," Jane said. "So I don't think all that much will change."

"What if I write them a letter, though? Two names to put on the envelope."

"Yes," Jane said. "I suppose."

"What if their names don't even fit on the envelope—"

"Gary, if you'll excuse me, I need to manage the guestbook," Jane said. She may have agreed to be an ad hoc wedding coordinator, but she wasn't going to be Gary's personal minder.

Because Freida and Mr. Hutchinson were both teachers, many of the guests were also teachers, and Freida had also invited her whole roster of private music pupils, so many of the guests were students and their families. (One student, Robbie Gentry, played the old upright piano in the corner, an endless loop of three Beatles songs.) The teachers could not resist flexing their authority muscles and addressing the students by their full names: "Timothy Hubbard, don't leave your glass there," and "Maddie Copeland, please hang up your coat." The students looked morose; there could be no anonymous bad behavior tonight. But Jane thought the children were getting their unknown revenge because none of the teachers dared get drunk in front of so many parents. The waitstaff circled endlessly with trays of red and white wine, but most people had only one or two drinks. Mr. Sutton, the high school principal, was sitting in a corner staring into a glass of club soda as though it contained all the world's sorrows.

Those lucky enough not to be students or teachers—or pregnant, Jane thought—were gathered in a merry group closest to the fire. Kelvin Dunn and his wife were there, and Terry Howard, who did Jane's taxes, and Helen Swanson from Jane's book club, and the Millers and the Andres and the Thornhills. Duncan was there, too, sitting between Jimmy and Aggie. Aggie kept throwing back her head with laughter and saying, "Oh, certainly! Certainly!"

Jane tried to circle close enough to hear what they were talking about, but just then Marjorie Graves touched her arm and asked if she could find someone to pick up old Mr. Merriweather because his family seemed to have left him back at the church.

Jane said she could send the Millers' nephew, and then someone asked her what the alcohol percentage in champagne was, and someone else asked her if any of the hors d'oeuvres were gluten-free, and Marie Henderson asked what the difference between an hors d'oeuvre and an appetizer was anyway. Patiently, Jane answered all their questions. She replaced the pen by the guestbook, and restacked the wedding gifts, and at the prearranged moment, she retrieved Freida's mandolin from the back room and handed it to her.

Then, finally, Jane got to sit down on the arm of Duncan's chair. Freida sat in her own chair a few feet away and played "Jerusalem's Ridge" and "Can the Circle Be Unbroken?" and "Bringing Mary Home."

Then she said, "This one is for my *husband!*" her voice cracking on the word *husband* like a scientist who had discovered a new and exciting species.

Jane knew Freida had been debating between "Love of My Life" or "Grow Old With Me," and she waited to hear which song she had decided on. But Freida played a song Jane had never heard before.

"This song is called 'True Love Will Find You in the End,'" Freida said, and everyone murmured appreciatively. Of course Freida would know the perfect song to play! The mandolin notes rose and fell in soft, rapid arcs while Freida sang.

> *This is a promise with a catch,*
> *Only if you're looking can it find you.*

People began exchanging looks—what sort of wedding song was this? Who sang about promises with catches on their wedding day? But to Jane it made perfect sense. Freida was forty-eight, and Mr. Hutchinson was not only her first husband, he was her first serious boyfriend. Freida was singing not to Mr. Hutchinson, but to herself, promising herself that she would not stop looking, not stop loving, not take anything for granted. On the last verse, Freida's voice increased, not in volume but in intensity. Her voice and the mandolin's voice braided together and floated toward the ceiling like the smoke from the sweetest possible fire. Mr. Hutchinson brushed away a tear, and Jane didn't blame him one bit.

A little pause followed as the last mandolin note seemed to linger in the air, then Aggie leaned forward and said, "Jane, I believe there's too much thyme in the stuffed mushrooms."

Jane sighed.

Freida and Mr. Hutchinson cut the wedding cake—vanilla with raspberry filling and white-chocolate ganache frosting—and Jane helped serve it, toddling around in her smock-like green dress. She brought Duncan a small slice and shared it with him. Duncan had reached the state of drunkenness where he patted her approvingly after every sentence.

"How's it going, Janey?" Pat.

"Aggie, send Gary to the bar, will you?" Pat.

"Jim, you go over and tell Mrs. Moeller that I'll have her coffee table done by Christmas. Valentine's Day at the very latest." Pat.

Jane excused herself and went into the kitchen. Plates with more slices of cake were lined up on the counter, and she took two of these and went into the little storage room at the back and sat on a folding chair. She ate the cake in large satisfying bites, feeling the sweetness of the frosting fizzing against the roof of her mouth. Now that she was sitting down, she could feel the baby fluttering and kicking. She cupped her stomach with her hands: *Hello, you.* Through the window, she could see the cars in the parking lot all waiting patiently for their owners like horses tied outside a saloon, the wintry pinkish sky cold and unpromising.

The reception continued until Freida took on the wide-eyed, tilted-head look of a shell-shocked soldier, and then Jane gathered everyone to see the married couple off. Freida clasped both of Jane's hands, whispering, "You are the best friend! Oh, wasn't it a perfect day!"

She pressed her cheek against Jane's, and Jane felt that startled surprise you feel when a bride touches you and you remember that there's a person under all the bridal trappings. She helped Freida into her red wool coat. Mr. Hutchinson offered Freida his arm, and they went out into the parking lot with all the guests calling farewell and throwing rice, although they hardly needed to, since the snow had started and provided its own cold confetti.

The guests departed in large groups, then in small groups, and then one by one. The caterers began clearing up the dishes and packing up the kitchen. Duncan and Jimmy loaded the wedding gifts into the car while Jane retrieved the toasting flutes and the guestbook, and boxed up the rest of the cake. She said good-bye to the staff, and gave the caterers a small envelope of cash.

Duncan came in to help Jane put on her coat, and then escorted her out to the car, although she would be the one to drive home. Duncan smelled so strongly of alcohol that Jane wondered if he had put the gifts in the right car.

"That was a fine wedding," he said to Jane. His eyes, shiny with wine, looked over his scarf at her with no more intelligence than the eyes of a stuffed deer head. "A fine, *fine* wedding."

"Yes," Jane said. "Yes, it was."

She wanted two things only: a hot shower and her softest pajamas. There's a limit to how good a time you can have at a wedding reception without alcohol. There really is.

OBVIOUSLY, they weren't going to name the baby Glen, but what would they name it? Boys' names were difficult because Jane felt there were really only about five decent boys' names in all the world—Lachlan, Magnus, Oscar, Beau, and Macon—and Duncan didn't like any of them. Girls' names were even more problematic because Jane didn't want to give the baby the name of any of Duncan's old girlfriends, which meant they couldn't choose Ann, Annabel, Angela, Barbara, Brandy, Candy, Mandy, Mindy, Lindy, Cindy, Trudy, Judy, Jody, Jill, Jessica, Julie, Jennifer, Gina, Christina, Irina, Regina, Sabrina, Susan, Suzanne, Susannah, Sherry, Barrie, Carrie, Kerry, Mary, Michelle, Isabelle, Noelle, Gabrielle, Janelle, Danielle, Debbie, Denise, Darlene, Darcy, Marcy, or Vicki. And those were only the names he could remember! Lynn, Linda, Leslie, Lori, Laura, Leah, and Lana were also out because Duncan had had a weeklong affair in 1996 with a woman whose name he never learned but whose initials were believed to be LTR based on the monogrammed towel she'd left behind. It was a nice towel. Jane liked it.

Another problem was that Jane didn't want to pick a name that would remind her of a particular student—and she had taught so many students. How could she name the baby Cody when that made her think of Cody Matthews and his constant runny nose? Or Magda, when that made her think of Magda Rutherford and her mean, narrow eyes? Or Dylan McMahon and his spitballs? Or Selena Cantrell with her endless, mindless chatter? Or Merrill Yarbrough, who scribbled on all the pages of his schoolbooks? Or Thalia Tompkins, who pinched the other children so hard she left bruises? Or Augustus Ervin, whose pink-framed glasses and scared expression had always made Jane feel like crying? Or Dalton Dupree, who always smelled so strongly of pickled cabbage? (Dalton was a current student, and Jane's heightened sense of smell made it unbearable to be in close quarters with him—it was possible that he would leave the second grade unable to group numbers because she couldn't stand to go over his math worksheets with him.) And then there were the names of students that were so overused that Jane couldn't remember how many had passed through her classroom: Jacob, Emily, Michael, Olivia, William, Max, Alexander, and Sophia. Those names were holograms to her, little more than blurred outlines.

Duncan said he'd like to name the baby Harriet, after his mother, if it was a girl, and Jane was, as always, startled anew by the fact that Duncan had a mother. She had never been able to imagine him as a child or a teenager. It seemed he had always been as he was now: lean, handsome, confident, slightly worn. When they were first dating, Duncan had so seldom spoken of his mother that Jane had assumed she was dead! It was only after a year that she realized his mother was actually alive and living in Escanaba.

Jane had met her shortly after she and Duncan had gotten married. Harriet was in her seventies, but the years seemed to have only polished her, sculpting her cheekbones and thinning her skin to flawlessness. She had short ash-blond hair with long bangs and a raspy smoker's voice.

"I'm so sorry, but I'm afraid Duncan is just like his father," she'd said to Jane. (Unlike his mother, Duncan's father actually was dead, had been for twenty years.) "His father was charming as the devil and had those same sexy brown eyes, but I'm afraid he was awfully flighty and a dreadful flirt. Kindhearted and loving, yes, but so selfish and irresponsible, really, and terribly vain."

But Jane couldn't help noticing when they all went out to dinner that Harriet touched the waiter's arm when placing her order and tilted her wineglass in a silent toast with a man at another table, that she ordered the most expensive entrée on the menu and didn't reach for the check, and that she smiled at her reflection in the mirror wall next to the table at least twice. No, Jane didn't think it was his *father* Duncan took after.

Yet Jane liked Harriet a lot. "Look at you, prettier every time I see you!" she always said. "And you're always so sweet-natured, too, with such a lovely smile. I wish I could be more like you, more patient." When they'd told her about the baby, she'd said, "Jane, I absolutely know you're going to be the most wonderful mother. I always feared Duncan would have a child with Aggie. Can you imagine? The poor baby would probably be afraid to cry for fear Aggie would say how disappointed she was. The baby would probably never learn to roll over for fear of wrinkling the sheets." (Harriet had great disdain for Aggie; it was possibly the best thing about her.) "But now Duncan has you and you're going to have a baby and I just know for a certainty that you're all going to be happy, happy, happy."

How could you not like such a person? The name Harriet suited Jane just fine.

THEY DECIDED to spend Christmas with Jane's mother in Grand Rapids, mainly so her mother wouldn't decide to spend it with them in Boyne City. Who knew how long she might stay?

"You'll be very welcome," her mother said when Jane called to tell her. "Will you be bringing Jimmy with you?"

"Of course we're bringing Jimmy," Jane answered irritably. "I would never leave him alone on Christmas."

"I'm just asking, dear!" her mother protested. "No need to fly off the handle. I thought maybe he had other plans."

"Well, he doesn't," Jane said grimly. Of course he didn't. Who would he have plans with? He had no other family. Jane's mother was responsible for that.

They got to her mother's house midafternoon on Christmas Eve. Jane knew that the house was exactly the same size it had been last time she visited, but it seemed smaller. It seemed smaller every time. One day she'd come here and there'd be no house at all.

Duncan brought his toolbox along with his suitcase as they walked up the path. "Saves me a trip out to the car," he said.

Jane's mother opened the door looking festive in black pants and a green-and-red striped sweater. "Merry Christmas!" she caroled. "Come on in!"

As soon as Duncan helped Jane out of her coat, her mother looked at her stomach and said, "Mercy, but you've gotten large."

"Mom—"

"Are you sure you're not having twins?"

"It's just that Jane's so slender," Duncan said smoothly. "The baby bump is more obvious."

"Mmmm." Jane's mother sounded noncommittal. "Now, Jane, you show Jimmy to his room and, Duncan, I wondered if you'd mind shoveling my walk and driveway? I hire a neighbor boy, but he doesn't do a very thorough job. He doesn't chip away at the base layer and I don't feel safe unless I'm walking on dry ground."

"We just got here!" Jane protested. "And it's twenty degrees out."

"I don't mind," Duncan said quickly. Jane knew he probably didn't—besides, her mother would be unlikely to follow him outdoors to supervise.

So Duncan put his coat back on and went outside armed with Jane's mother's old and warped snow shovel, while Jane took Jimmy upstairs and showed him the foldout bed in her mother's sewing room. When they came back down, her mother said, "Jane, I'd like you to finish decorating the tree—"

"You don't have the tree done?" Jane asked, surprised. Her mother was usually so organized.

"No need to sound so *judgmental*, dear," her mother said. "I just didn't get around to it. Now, while you do that, I'm hoping Jimmy will help me frost some sugar cookies."

"I'd like that," Jimmy said shyly. "Sugar cookies are my favorite part of Christmas, almost."

"Mine, too," Jane's mother agreed. "You come on into the kitchen."

Jane went into the family room and saw that her mother's artificial tree was up and had lights on it. Boxes of Christmas ornaments were scattered around the room, some opened, some not. It seemed clear to Jane that her mother had begun decorating the tree but either lost interest or felt overwhelmed. Since she'd retired from Dr. Wimberly's, her mother seemed to have lost some of her vitality. A wave of sadness made the room seem blue to Jane for a moment.

She shook it off and began poking through the boxes, locating her favorite ornaments in their paper cradles: the fruit-shaped ornaments she had disliked as a child—couldn't they have snowflake ornaments like everyone else?—and the round gold ones with worn-off glittered stripes, the colored-glass ones she and her mother had made one year from a kit, now sadly tiny-looking.

In the kitchen, she could hear her mother talking to Jimmy. "Now, we start with white for the snowmen, and obviously we'll do green for the trees, but what color should we do the reindeer?"

"Yellow," Jimmy said. "It's the closest to brown."

Jane's mood was improving as she hung the ornaments. It was soothing to handle these time travelers from her childhood, to feel the roughness of the snowball ornaments against her fingers. She unpacked the bright orange-and-gold flowered tree topper that must have been garish even when her mother purchased it in the seventies.

"You must be very excited about the baby, Jimmy," her mother's voice carried from the kitchen. "Won't be long now."

"I sure am," Jimmy said. "We can already feel it kick." He paused, and his voice grew deeper with concern. "But I'm worried, too. I don't know anything about babies."

"Neither does Jane," her mother said promptly. In the family room, Jane rolled her eyes. "You can learn together."

"But I'll be afraid to even hold the baby," Jimmy said. "You know how clumsy I am. What if I drop it?"

Jane's cheeks flushed with shame. This thought had occurred to her, too.

"Oh, you don't need to worry." Jane's mother's tone was certain, authoritative. "Anytime you want to hold the baby, Jane will set you up on the sofa with pillows propped all around you and put the baby in your arms. You won't possibly be able to drop the baby because of all the pillows, you see. Lots of people hold babies that way. I'll bet you'll be a great help to Jane."

"But I won't know what to do if it cries," Jimmy said. "I won't be able to change it or give it a bath. I'd be scared to death."

"You don't have to change the baby or bathe it to help Jane."

"I don't?"

"No, of course not," Jane's mother answered. "There are lots of ways to help, and you'll figure some of them out."

"It would help if you could just tell me what they are," Jimmy said glumly. "I'm not very good at figuring things out."

"Okay." Her mother sounded undaunted. She paused for a moment as though gathering her thoughts. "Here's what I think will happen. Not too long after they come home from the hospital, there'll come a time when Jane will feed the baby, and burp it, and then the baby will get very sleepy—they always do when their stomachs are full. And then Jane will say, 'Jimmy, can you hold the baby while I take a nap? Even just ten minutes would be wonderful,' because new mothers are tired all the time. You'll sit on the sofa with the pillows, and Jane will give the baby to you and go off to take a nap, and the baby will go right to sleep in your arms. And I'll tell you a secret about babies, Jimmy—if you hold them right next to your chest so they can feel your heart beating, they'll sleep much longer than they do in a crib. And the baby will sleep for an hour, maybe even an hour and a half, and Jane will feel so good when she wakes up from her nap. Just unbelievably good. She'll say, 'The baby slept so long! How did you do it?'"

"And what will I say?" Jimmy asked. "Do I tell her about the baby sleeping because of my heartbeat?"

"No, indeed," Jane's mother said. "You just say, 'Aw, I'm good with babies! Nothing to it! Anytime you want a nap, you just give the baby to me!' and Jane will say, 'Oh, Jimmy, I would be lost without you.'"

"I sure would like that." Jimmy sounded wistful. "Do you really think it will happen?"

"Without a doubt," Jane's mother said.

In the family room, Jane nodded in agreement. She would make certain of it.

———

IN LATE JANUARY, Duncan had to go to Kalamazoo to deliver some lady's bamboo Victorian side tables because he'd taken so long refinishing them that she'd moved out of town. But the lady was a jolly, forgiving type—she'd spoken to Jane on the phone and said, "Everything takes longer than you think it will. Once, I set all the clocks in my house ahead two hours and I was still late picking the children up from school!" She'd also hired Duncan to restore her antique patina-rusted French credenza thingy (Jane had a tendency to let furniture details wash over her) while he was down there.

Now the side tables were wrapped in many layers of quilts and moving blankets and secured in the back of Duncan's van. Duncan checked on them one final time and then closed the van's back doors. He turned to Jane, who stood shivering in the driveway.

"Are you sure I should go?" he asked for the third time.

"Yes, of course," Jane said. "It's only four days. I'll be fine."

Anyway, Duncan had to go. They needed the money. They always needed the money. Besides, Jane was actually looking forward to some alone time. Or alone with Jimmy, who would watch three episodes of *The Amazing Race* back to back with her without complaint.

"Well, okay." Duncan pulled her into his arms. "Take care of yourself. I'll miss you."

"Me too," Jane said, but she hopped up and down a little bit. The cold wind was making the hem of her black wool coat ripple like a flag.

Duncan drove away, honking once at the bottom of the driveway, and Jane got into her own car.

The morning sky looked blurry and smudged, and she thought it might snow. She was right. By the time she got to school, the snow was falling in thick, fast flakes. It made Jane dizzy to look up at it.

Her students looked out the window so often and so longingly that morning that Jane finally said, laughing, "Everyone, put down your pencils and stare outside for two minutes. I'll time you."

Her irritability had receded in her third trimester, and once again she could enjoy her students—appreciate their individuality, smile at their antics, marvel at how delightful they were. (Well, most of them.) She had told the class about the baby when she was twenty-four weeks along—none of them had figured it out despite the fact that the baby often kicked hard enough to make Jane's shirt move—and they were mildly interested at best. Did she want a boy or a girl? Did she think Starbuck was a nice name? Could she still do a somersault?

But the children were *very* interested in Mrs. Crenshaw, who was going to teach class while Jane was on maternity leave. The children didn't seem to think Mrs. Crenshaw would be up to the job. Could she peel an apple in one long strip, like Jane could? Did she know all the words to "Paul Revere's Ride"? Would she know about the Attendance Messenger? What about the Kindness Tree? The Reward Jar? The Line-Up Song? Super Sequencing? Yes, Jane told them, Mrs. Crenshaw knew all that.

Mrs. Crenshaw was a retired teacher from Charlevoix, a quiet woman in her sixties with a soft voice and calm manner. Jane had had Mrs. Crenshaw visit the class twice already, and the children seemed mainly focused on the fact that Mrs. Crenshaw had worn the same gray cardigan both times. Did she wear it every single day? Didn't she have any other sweaters? Did she really like gray? Was gray her favorite color? What kind of person picked gray as a favorite color?

"She's really sort of a gray *person,*" Trent Bauer had said, and Jane feared he might be right.

She had, of course, prepared endless lesson plans for Mrs. Crenshaw, along with notes about field trips and class rules and hamster care. (The hamster, Cuthbert III, was getting along in years.) And now, after the two minutes were up, and Jane had asked everyone to get back to their worksheets, she wrote more personal notes in her teacher's binder.

Please don't put rice cakes in the Community Snack Box.

Austin needs to sit in the front row at all times.

Samuel never brings milk money; I pay for his milk.

If you read aloud from Mind's Eye, *please don't read the chapter about the Bunyip. It scares everybody, especially Toby.*

Nicole works best with Elizabeth or Chloe as a partner.

Haley and Grace B. should not sit next to each other, or stand together in line.

Cameron will talk to whomever he sits next to, so changing the seating plan will not make him quieter.

Tyler must never, ever be allowed to hold the hamster.

Students are only allowed to go to the bathroom in pairs.

This applies to Rory in particular.

Jane looked up and allowed her eyes to linger on Rory, who was staring out the window at the falling snow. (So were the rest of the children; the two-minute thing hadn't helped at all.) Rory was a pale, thin boy with no-color hair and eyes as dark and troubled as shadows. He seemed to have great difficulty finding the bathroom, even though Jane had kept him after school to practice the route.

"See?" she'd said. "Just come out of the classroom and turn left and walk down this hall and then turn right."

"That's what I do," Rory said. "And sometimes the bathroom's there, and sometimes it's not."

"It's always there," Jane said gently. Did he think it was the Brigadoon of bathrooms? "Maybe sometimes you take a wrong turn. Let's practice again."

"That's okay," Rory assured her. "If it's there, I go. If it's not, I hold it."

So Jane had made a new rule that students could only go to the bathroom in pairs, and this had caused great consternation and suspicion throughout the class. Why pairs? Why pairs *all of a sudden*? Did Jane think they were babies? What had happened? Had someone gotten lost? Was it a first grader?

"It's just a rule I made," Jane had said. "Like when I made the rule that Thursday was Cookie Day."

The children had quieted right down. Cookie Day had fallen into their laps like a luscious golden ball from the heavens. They knew nothing of the cravings of pregnant women—nothing of the Thursday when Jane felt she could not make it past the bakery without stopping—but they were wise enough to realize that favors granted can be favors withdrawn. So the children went to the bathroom in pairs now, and Jane could rest easy knowing that if Rory had to go to the bathroom, he would get there. Privately, she thought that Rory's attitude was a sensible one. The world was a shifting, dangerous, unpredictable place. Better to learn that early.

IT WAS STILL SNOWING when Jane trudged through the parking lot that afternoon, and snow sifted in over the tops of her boots to wet her socks and chill her feet. She drove home carefully, the car cresting through small snowdrifts. The snowplows were out on the streets, but they were already falling behind the storm.

When she got home, Jimmy was clearing the driveway with the snowblower. He worked so hard to be responsible when Duncan was away. He looked like an arctic explorer: the colors of his hat and coat subdued by a covering of white dust, snow caked on his eyebrows, and ice crystals clinging to his red cheeks and nose. She parked her car on the cleared side of the driveway and got out, waving to him. He waved back, and she crossed carefully to the porch and let herself into the house.

She kicked off her boots and peeled off her wet socks. She curled up on the couch and turned on the Weather Channel. WINTER STORM WARNING: 8–12 INCHES OF SNOW EXPECTED. Well, good. No school tomorrow. She pulled the afghan over her.

She must have fallen asleep because the next thing she knew, it was after six and Jimmy was sitting on the sofa next to her, flipping through the channels.

"Is the baby kicking?" he asked Jane. He loved to feel the baby kick.

"Yes," she said, smiling. She sat up and took his hand and held it against her stomach. The baby kicked obediently.

"How about that!" Jimmy said, as he always did. "Isn't that something?"

"Yes, it is." Jane yawned. "I'm just going to take a shower."

She went upstairs, undressed, and padded naked into the bathroom. She reached behind the curtain and turned on the shower, and at that exact moment, her water broke.

For a moment, she was terribly confused. She couldn't separate the two water sources. She turned off the shower. There, good. Problem solved. But, no, water was still dripping from between her legs. She stared at the puddle on the floor, which was already dampening the edge of the pale green bathmat.

She grabbed a towel and pressed it between her thighs while she shuffled to the bedside phone and called Duncan.

"Hey, Janey," he said happily. "It took forever to get here. The roads are terrible—"

"I think my water just broke," Jane said.

A slight pause. "You think or you know?"

"I know."

"Okay," Duncan said, and his voice was as calm and relaxed as ever. It was only when he began repeating himself that Jane realized he was thinking furiously. "Okay. Okay. You're thirty-six weeks, that's not too early. Not too early. Not too early at all. You're at home, right? You're at home. Good. Good. You call Dr. Skywalker and I'll call Freida and have her drive you to the hospital."

"All right," Jane said. Something was lodged in her throat, making it difficult to speak. Panic. She swallowed, forcing it back down.

She called Dr. Skywalker's office, and his answering service said he'd call her back in five minutes. She pulled on fresh underwear and black stretch pants and a cable-knit sweater that her belly pushed out like a hoopskirt.

The phone rang. She answered before the first ring was half-over.

"Hello, Jane!" Dr. Skywalker's voice boomed down the line at her. "I hear your water broke."

"Yes," Jane said. "I was getting into the—"

"How much water?"

Jane tried to picture the Pyrex measuring cup in the kitchen. "Maybe a pint?"

Dr. Skywalker grunted. "Okay, you'd better go to the hospital.

Hold on." Jane could tell he'd put his hand over the receiver, and heard him shout, "Lois! When did you put the chicken in the oven?"

"Not five minutes ago," a woman's voice called in the background.

"How long does it take?" Dr. Skywalker asked.

"At least an hour," Lois said. "It will get terribly dry if I turn up the oven."

"Don't do *that*," Dr. Skywalker said. "It'll be raw in the middle, and we'll both get salmonella."

"Do you want roast potatoes or scalloped potatoes?" Lois asked.

"I'm on the phone," Dr. Skywalker said impatiently. "But scalloped, I guess."

Jane thought she might start screaming. Couldn't he eat a sandwich like a normal person?

"Hello, Jane?" Dr. Skywalker said.

"Yes?"

"You go straight to the hospital, and I'll meet you there in two hours."

An hour to wait for the chicken and another hour to savor his meal. Jane sighed. "Okay."

She hung up and pulled her suitcase—packed only a few days ago—from the closet.

The phone rang again. It was Duncan.

"Freida and Mr. Hutchinson are having dinner in Harbor Springs," he said. Dinner! Why was everyone worried about dinner in Jane's hour of need? "They're going to meet you at the hospital. I called Aggie, and she and Gary are going to pick you up in ten minutes."

"I don't want Aggie to drive me!" Jane nearly wailed.

"Aggie's a good, fast driver," Duncan said. "And she's already on the way."

"Does Gary have to come, too?"

"You know as well as I do that Gary doesn't like to be alone after dark," Duncan said. "He says the toilet whispers. Now, I'm going to start driving up, but I want you to know that I'm going to drive slowly and carefully." How well he knew her, how well he understood her fears of another car accident. "If it gets bad, I'll pull over and stop. Don't you worry about me. You just get yourself to the hospital. Is Dr. Skywalker meeting you there?"

"Yes," Jane said, her voice shaking a little.

"Good." Duncan paused. If he said *May the Force be with you!* Jane would divorce him. It really was that simple. But he only said, "Jane, I know you can do this. I know it."

They said good-bye, and Jane picked up her suitcase. At the top of the stairs, she felt a pain in her lower abdomen; a tugging, as though someone was pulling a string attached to her insides. She waited for the pain to subside, and then she walked down the stairs, holding the banister.

Jimmy was still watching TV. He looked up and saw her standing there with her suitcase, one hand gripping the newel post of the staircase.

Jane nodded. "It's time."

Jimmy swallowed and said, "Yikes." He spoke for both of them, really.

JANE STOOD by the front door and peered out the narrow sidelight, watching for Aggie. She held her cell phone in her hand in case Duncan called.

"Is she here yet?" Jimmy asked, coming up behind her.

"No," Jane said, "but—"

She stopped speaking when she turned and saw Jimmy standing there with his own bag, a terrible orange-and-yellow flowered nylon suitcase that must have belonged to his mother. She had not meant for Jimmy to come with her. She didn't want to have to worry about him or explain things to him. She wanted him to stay here. She would call him when the baby was born. She would promise that he would be absolutely the first call she made—

"Here she is!" Jimmy said, as headlights lit up the window and then Aggie's SUV rolled into the driveway. "Now, you just hang on to my arm and don't slip."

How could she tell him to stay home? And as they stepped outside and down the snow-coated steps, she was glad to have someone helping her. Anyway, Aggie could easily bring him home again.

Aggie was driving and Gary sat in the passenger seat, so Jane pulled open the rear door, and a wave of heat and car smells puffed out. She felt she could pick out the individual components of that odor: upholstery, lemon air freshener, coffee, very faint aftershave. Aggie's car was her office, and she was devoted to maintaining it.

"I've spread a beach towel back there, Jane," she said. "Make sure you sit on it."

Jimmy helped Jane in and put their bags in back and then climbed into the seat next to her. Aggie pulled out carefully, the SUV's wheels crunching on the snow. It was clear that Aggie had been forced to leave her house without prepping Gary because he was full of questions.

"How long is this going to take?" he asked Aggie.

"I don't know," Aggie said, leaning forward to peer through the blowing whiteness. "It will take as long as it takes."

"Will we be home in time for cocoa?"

"I can't promise you that," Aggie said. "But I can promise you that whenever we get home, I'll make cocoa then."

Jane, frantic for distraction, wanted to hear more about the cocoa ritual. What all did it involve? Was it a euphemism for something more interesting? But then Gary said, "Where's Duncan, anyway?"

"He's in Kalamazoo," Aggie answered. "But he's driving here just as fast as he can."

"Are you sure he's coming?" Gary asked. "He hasn't run off?"

It was a good thing that Jane was sitting behind Aggie and not Gary because otherwise she might have leaned forward and strangled him.

"Duncan will be here," Aggie said firmly, and Jane felt a little better. Aggie almost always got what she wanted; if she decided Duncan should be at the hospital, he would be there.

The tugging pain came again, a little longer this time. The radio was on, and a man with a deep, lugubrious voice began to sing:

> *The engine's running smooth and the moon is overhead.*
> *We got hours before your back will find a bed . . .*

"Could you turn off the radio?" Jane asked, and then she sat back in her seat as another pain came. This pain seemed a little bolder, as though testing Jane: *Can you take this? What about this?*

The windshield wipers slapped back and forth on the fastest setting. The headlights lit up the falling snow in front of them, and the wet black roads with fat white fingers of snowdrifts poking across them. Jane closed her eyes. She could feel each time the SUV hit an icy patch, the small buoyant sensation before the tires regained their grip.

Just outside Petoskey, the tires seemed to lose touch with the road completely. For a brief moment they were all swaying weightlessly, and then there was a lurch and a grinding sound as the SUV struck a snowbank.

Aggie let out a small cry and Jane moaned in spite of herself. Would she have to have the baby in a car by the roadside?

Aggie opened the door and stepped out, instantly becoming little more than a colorful blur in the swirling whiteness. She was back almost at once and slid behind the wheel, snowflakes shaggy on her red wool coat. "We're not stuck. I can just back out."

She put the SUV in reverse, whispering, "Come on, come on," under her breath, and the SUV slid obediently backward, and they were on the road again.

Aggie dropped them off at the hospital's main entrance and went to park the car. "You just go on with Jane and Jimmy," she said to Gary. "I'll be right there."

Jimmy helped Jane out of the car, and Gary carried her suitcase, and Jimmy's. They took the elevator to the maternity ward and went to the nurse's station. An older man wearing scrubs was tapping at a computer keyboard.

"Hello," Jane said. "I'm Jane Wilkes, Dr. Skyberger's patient, and I'm in labor."

"Just a minute." The man didn't look up. He was squinting at the computer screen through his bifocals. He was not the warm, matronly nurse Jane had wanted—she had hoped for a sort of Ma Ingalls with more up-to-date medical knowledge. He typed another minute and then pushed back his roller chair to look at the three of them. "Okay," he said. "Tell me your name again."

"Jane Wilkes."

He looked at Jimmy. "Are you the baby's father?"

"No," Jimmy said proudly. "I'm the baby's brother."

Jane's heart twisted; for moment, heartache blotted out labor pain.

The nurse looked at Gary. "Are you—"

"No," Jane said. *"No."*

"Okay." The nurse rattled his keyboard some more, and then said, "Follow me. Your friends can wait here."

He led Jane down the hall to an unrelentingly beige room with a hospital bed and a lot of round-cornered vinyl-cushioned wooden furniture. It was a room that had seen infinite joy and immeasurable tragedy, and yet it retained none of either. On the bed was a folded hospital gown and a pair of orange nonskid socks.

"You can get changed, and your nurse will be right in," the man said. Evidently that meant the nurse would be someone other than him. Good.

Jane changed into the gown in the bathroom and hung her clothes and coat in the closet. Then she sat down on the bed to wait.

A redheaded girl of about twelve came into the room. "Hi, Jane!" she said. "I'm Melody, and I'm a labor and delivery nurse. I'll be your point person from here on."

Wait, she was a nurse? They let preteens become nurses?

"Just lean back and let me examine you," Melody said.

Jane lay back on the bed. Melody moved closer, and Jane could see tiny lines by Melody's mouth and the kind of dense smattering of freckles that could only be accumulated after decades. So maybe Melody was Jane's age, but she had a youthful, perky-cupcake energy that didn't inspire confidence.

Jane sighed. Apparently, Ma Ingalls was busy elsewhere tonight.

JANE HEARD FREIDA out in the hall, saying, "Where is she? We came just as soon as we could!" A moment later, Freida and Mr. Hutchinson burst through the door, with Aggie and Gary and Jimmy behind them.

"Jane!" Freida cried dramatically.

"Hello," Jane said.

"How long have you been in labor?" Freida asked. "I was so scared we'd miss the birth!"

"I don't think there's much danger of that," Jane said. "I'm only four centimeters dilated."

Jane had assumed that once Freida was here, Aggie and Gary would leave, taking Mr. Hutchinson and Jimmy with them, but instead they all draped themselves around the room, some on the vinyl furniture, some leaning against the walls, and took on the postures of travelers whose flights have been delayed and who know they're in for the long haul. Aggie asked Freida what she'd had for dinner, and Freida said that she'd had fettuccine Alfredo and Mr. Hutchinson had had the baked cod because he didn't like pasta. Freida said that it was so unusual, really, for someone not to like pasta—just one of the many, many fascinating details about Mr. Hutchinson. (Honestly, newlyweds talked such rubbish, Jane thought; they should all be put in quarantine for at least the first year of married life.) Aggie said she'd always felt that fettuccine Alfredo was the SPAM of Italian food, and that she personally went out of her way never to order it. Mr. Hutchinson asked Jimmy if he liked to watch basketball. Jimmy somehow interpreted this as Mr. Hutchinson asking what basketball *was* and launched into a rambling explanation. Gary watched the fetal heart monitor in a rapt sort of way.

Nobody was paying much attention to Jane, who sat on the bed with the sheet and blanket over her and wondered where Duncan was. She wanted to check her cell phone, but it was in her coat pocket. She looked out the window. Snowflakes were falling past like fluffy white spiders. The tugging pain came again, stronger.

"Now, you get three points for a basket from behind the three-point line," Jimmy said to Mr. Hutchinson. "And two points from anywhere inside the three-point line. Free throws are worth one point, and the team with the most points at the end wins, unless it goes into overtime . . ."

Jane was just thankful that Freida didn't have her mandolin.

"If only I had my mandolin!" Freida said at that moment. "Then we could at least have some music."

"I have my recorder in the car," Mr. Hutchinson said.

Fortunately, Dr. Skywalker arrived then, his beard wild from the wind outside, and shooed everyone out while he examined Jane. His hand probed and withdrew just as Melody's had done.

"Six centimeters," he announced in his revivalist's voice. "You're doing just fine. You're still determined to do this naturally?"

He looked so fierce that Jane felt timid. "Yes," she said.

"You can always change your mind," Dr. Skywalker said. "Now, do you really want all those people around? You're the one in labor, and that means you get to make the rules. I can tell them to go home."

Jane smiled at him gratefully. "That would be wonderful. I just want Freida to stay."

"Which one is Freida?" Dr. Skywalker asked, and Jane remembered that he was a stranger to them.

"The one—" She paused as the pain came again. She let it have its way. "The one with the curly hair."

Dr. Skywalker went out in the hall, and it turned out he wasn't a complete stranger, because right away Aggie said, "Now, I seem to remember that you and your wife nearly put a bid in on a house way out on Lakeshore Drive a couple years ago."

"Ah, yes," Dr. Skywalker said thoughtfully. "I believe so. Big blue house with white shutters?"

"That's the one." Aggie sounded vigorous. "Your wife acted all interested at the open house, but I could never get a straight answer out of her. I dislike it intensely when buyers drag their feet."

"Oh," Dr. Skywalker said. There was a little pause, as there often was after Aggie spoke to someone. "Well, anyway, Jane's in labor and she's going to need to focus, so if I could ask you folks to get going now, everyone but Flora."

"Freida," Jane called.

"Yes, everyone but Freida," Dr. Skywalker said. "You all should be heading home anyway, on account of the storm."

There was a little murmur of conversation, and then Aggie poked her head into Jane's room. "We're on our way," she said. "I'm driving Mr. Hutchinson so he can leave his car for Freida."

The pain was making it hard for Jane to concentrate. "What about Jimmy?"

"Jimmy went off to look for the cafeteria and hasn't come back," Aggie said. "Good luck! Have Duncan call me with the news."

Wait for Jimmy, Jane wanted to say. *Take him with you.* But the pain came, stronger than ever this time, and literally took her breath away.

AT FIRST the pain was low down in Jane's abdomen, like menstrual cramps. Then it was like severe menstrual cramps. And then it was nothing at all like menstrual cramps, but a hard, gripping pain that wrapped around her pelvis and lower back and squeezed for long, merciless minutes. If only she could have a break and catch her breath. If only they could call off labor for a little while, just until Jane felt stronger.

"Hold my hand," Freida said, and Jane nodded.

With each contraction, she gripped Freida's hand tighter. Freida smoothed Jane's hair back from her forehead with her free hand and sang to her. Only it wasn't singing, exactly; it was closer to humming. A lovely, molten, effortless sound rising and falling, carrying Jane along.

Jane waited for a contraction to finish. "What is that song?"

"It's 'Ode to Joy' by Beethoven."

It was so odd that Jane had never realized how beautiful Freida was. Freida sat in a chair beside the bed, her face level with Jane's, and Jane could see that the irises of Freida's hazel eyes were edged with a darker brown circle, that her eyelashes were thick as toothbrush bristles, that each of her ten thousand ringlets was a different shade of brown, from auburn to bronze to chestnut to mahogany. Freida's hands were beautiful, too, though she had often told Jane that a musician's hands *should* be ugly, proudly ugly—wide and sturdy, thick with muscle. And this was true of Freida's hands, but Jane thought they were beautiful in their usefulness, strong and comforting in their grip.

The pain came again, a savage twisting that went on longer than Jane thought she could stand. When it was over, she looked at Freida. "I want an epidural."

Freida nodded and pressed the button for the nurse. Jane closed her eyes against the pain, and when she opened them, Melody was next to Freida, saying, "Jane, I'm sorry but the anesthesiologist has been called to the ER because of a multiperson car accident. It's going to be a while."

Car accidents, always car accidents. Jane turned her head away, unable to answer.

After that, the pain changed. Pain flooded the room like water and rose until Jane could feel it lapping at her face, like when you put your head back in the bath to shampoo your hair. Then she sank beneath it. She looked up at Dr. Skywalker and Freida and Melody from below the surface of the pain; their faces were wobbly and distorted, their voices muffled. She could no longer hear Freida humming. Dr. Skywalker boomed words down at her, his fierce eyes blazing, but Jane couldn't make out what he was saying.

Sometimes the pain would pause, and Jane would rise to the surface, but never long enough to say anything. What was there to say anyway?

"Jane?" Freida said. "Jane! Why is she gasping like that? Is she getting enough oxygen?"

Dr. Skywalker answered, but Jane couldn't hear him. She had gone under again.

She stayed under a long time. She didn't know how long. Hours? Days? The world was so far away, so muted. She forgot about the storm, about "Ode to Joy," about her breathing. It didn't seem to matter anymore that Duncan was not there, that he was missing this. Nothing mattered except this pain that would not let up. She was losing strength, but the pain was getting stronger, ready to push itself out of her. No baby would be born, only pain was being born here tonight. Pain would leap out of her and leave her lying on the delivery table, split open.

Then Freida's strong arm was under Jane's shoulder, lifting her until her head was above the surface and she could breathe again. Melody was on her other side, supporting her. Jane took a deep, shuddering breath. The two of them would carry her out of the pain, carry her to some shore. All she had to do was rest. But Dr. Skywalker would not allow that.

"Jane, you need to push," he ordered. "Jane, open your eyes! I mean it! Pull her knee back, Freida, just like Melody's doing. Push, Jane, push to ten. One, two, three . . ."

Jane pushed, but it didn't feel like a push—it felt like she was being turned inside out, like her interior flesh was being pulled out along with the baby. She screamed, and then it was over.

"It's a girl!" Dr. Skywalker and Freida and Melody all said at once, but not quite in synch, so to Jane it sounded like an echo. *A girl . . . girl . . . girl . . .*

Dr. Skywalker held the baby up. She was blood-smeared and white-flecked, her hair wet spikes, her froggy arms waving.

"Ten fingers, ten toes," Dr. Skywalker said. "Would you like to hold her?"

Jane tried to say yes, but just then fluid gushed from between her legs like water out of a culvert. The pain came back, only this time she didn't sink beneath it. This time, the pain grabbed Jane by the hair and yanked her under. It pulled her down deep into water that was not green or blue, but an inky black where specks of light floated, drifted, and then blinked out.

A SOFT TAPPING woke Jane. She opened her eyes. "Duncan?"

It was Jimmy, patting the back of her hand. "Jane, wake up, they're going to bring the baby soon!"

His touch was soft, but his voice was urgent. Jane's gaze went past him to the window where snow fell with blurry speed, so fast and thick that it made the window look like a TV screen filled with static. Jane had lived in northern Michigan long enough to recognize a true blizzard. Duncan wouldn't be getting there that day. The hospital had the hushed, insulated feel that comes from a heavy snowfall, and although no sunshine came through the window, the room glowed with creamy yellow light. Jane realized it was a different room from the earlier one, but just as bland and impersonal.

She tried to pull herself into a sitting position, and pain flared through her pelvis like a thin rope of fire. She remembered she was in a hospital bed and groped for the remote. The bed whirred her slowly into a seated position.

Jimmy was still watching her. She licked her lips and tried to think. "Where's Freida?"

"She went to the cafeteria," Jimmy said. "She said she'd bring back breakfast for both of us. She called Duncan, and he said he had to stop just north of Grand Rapids, that's how bad the storm is."

Jane felt something inside her relax. Duncan was safe, and the baby was here. Perhaps Jane would not always be denied the happiness that other people had. She smiled at Jimmy.

"Wait until you see Glen!" he said. "She's the prettiest baby in the world."

"I'll bet she is," Jane said gently. "But her name isn't Glen. It's Harriet."

Jimmy frowned. "Duncan told me you were naming her Glen, like the grocery store."

"That was just a joke."

"Oh." Jimmy's face fell.

"It's hard to tell with Duncan," Jane said.

"Usually Duncan tells me the truth," Jimmy said. "Usually with him, I understand. It's not like with other people where I get so confused—"

"Jimmy, it's okay, really." Jane put her hand on his arm.

"No, it isn't," Jimmy said bitterly. "I screw everything up. I got lost coming back from the cafeteria and missed the birth, and you probably didn't even want me to stay—"

Just then a nurse wearing purple scrubs came into the room wheeling a clear bassinet. Jane could see the baby in the bassinet, wrapped in a white hospital blanket with a blue-and-pink stripe and wearing a tiny white newborn hat.

The nurse was wiry-haired, small-eyed, stern-faced—another reminder that just because you do this magical, mind-blowing thing of giving birth, it doesn't mean the world is suddenly filled with perfect people from Central Casting.

"Well, Mother's finally awake, I see," the nurse said. (Apparently she was also judgmental.) "Now, Mother, if you're ready, I'll bring Baby over and we'll see about feeding her."

Jane held out her hands for the baby, but the nurse said, "First-timers do better with the football grip. Take down the right sleeve of your gown and lift your arm."

Jimmy retreated quickly to the sofa in the corner.

Jane slipped her arm out of the hospital gown. The nurse pressed the baby against Jane's side and then clamped Jane's arm down like someone lowering a lever. "There, hold her just like you're running a touchdown, and support her head with your hand."

Jane was aware for the first time that her breasts were swollen and hard, hot as baked potatoes. "Hello," she said softly to the baby.

"Remember to bring Baby to your breast, not the other way around," the nurse directed. "And point nose to nipple."

The words *breast* and *nipple* felt like darts the nurse was throwing at Jimmy. Jane could almost hear them striking him. *Thwock. Thwock.* She wished he would go out in the hall.

Jane held the baby to her breast, but the baby turned her head away.

"Oh, now, none of that," the nurse said. She wrapped her hand around Jane's breast and steered the baby's face until she began nursing. "There. That's it. Now, Mother, you should watch Baby's mouth to see when her tongue goes down—that means she's ready to latch on to the nipple."

Tongue, latch, nipple. *Thwock. Thwock. Thwock.*

"Use your other hand to support and squeeze your breast," the nurse said. *Thwock. Thwock.*

The nurse was still gripping Jane's breast. It felt more like the nurse was giving the baby a bottle than it did like breastfeeding. The baby nursed for maybe a minute and then dropped her head back, her eyes closed. Finally, the nurse withdrew her hand. "Give her a couple of minutes and then try the other side," she said to Jane. "Tickle her feet to wake her if you need to."

"Thank you." Jane transferred the baby to her other arm and pulled her hospital gown back up.

"I'll be back to check on you," the nurse said, "and they'll be bringing breakfast around soon." She left the room, her shoes squeaking on the floor.

Jane settled the baby more securely into the cradle of her arm and tucked the blanket around her. The baby was sleeping now, her head tilted back, as relaxed as a sprawled teenager or exhausted partier. Jane had no intention of waking her.

Dr. Skywalker had told her once that all newborns look alike. Jane thought that was (a) not a very nice thing to say and (b) untrue.

Completely untrue. This baby—Jane and Duncan's baby—looked like no other baby before. Remarkably unique, uniquely remarkable. Her eyelids were pale peach, her eyelashes perfect tiny spikes. Her skin was the color of malted milk, her cheeks were softly rounded, and one was marked with a perfect shallow dimple. Dark wisps of auburn hair showed from under her newborn hat, and her eyebrows were finer than threads. Her lips were as full, as lush, as any movie star's, and she had Duncan's straight nose. Jane could never have enough of looking at her.

She glanced up at Jimmy. He was sitting on the couch, his chin in his palm, staring determinedly out the window at the whiteness. His hair stuck up in back, and he had heathery brown stubble on his chin and cheeks—something Jane rarely saw, even though she lived in the same house with him. For once, he looked his age—more than his age. He looked old. Worn down and excluded. Excluded, as always.

"Jimmy," she said softly. "Jimmy, come here. I want you to be the very first person to meet Glen."

2016

THEY WERE ALL SITTING around the breakfast table—Jane, Duncan, Jimmy, Glenn, and twenty-month-old Patrice.

"Patrice, she don't like cinnamon toast," Glenn said. She had a formal way of speaking, often saying "I am" or "I did" instead of yes. And she liked to form sentences in a vaguely French way: "Jimmy, he turned on the TV." "Daddy, he went outside."

Glenn's full name was Glenn Freida. Jane had insisted that they put that name on the birth certificate instead of Harriet Antonia. She didn't want her daughter to be one of those girls who raised her hand at the beginning of the school year and said, "I go by Drew," even though it said "Evangeline Constantina" on the attendance sheet. Duncan's mother took the news that they weren't naming the baby after her with her usual aplomb. "I wasn't all that crazy about sharing my name anyway," she said. "And Glenn is a beautiful name! With a name like that, she could be a movie star or a brain surgeon or an ambassador."

Jane's money was on president of the United States. Glenn was as lovely a four-year-old as she'd been a newborn. Her wavy, chin-length hair was pale auburn and her eyes were flawless China blue. Her mouth was still a rosebud, and her face as perfectly round as a peppermint. She carried herself with poise and dignity—since babyhood, she had preferred dresses to pants, skirts to shorts, nightgowns to pajamas. She was vivacious but not attention-seeking, pretty but not vain, smart but not a show-off, popular but not bossy. The world would be good to Glenn. You could already tell.

Then there was their younger daughter, Patrice Marigold, who was nowhere near as sunny as her name. She had the same auburn curls as her sister, but Patrice's hair was shorter and often clinging to her scalp with dampness. Her eyes had darkened immediately to a hot, glowing amber-brown, and her cheeks were perpetually pink and chapped-looking, her lower lip almost constantly pushed out in a pout. She had spurned all of the pretty hand-me-downs from Glenn and would consent to wear only two outfits: a miniature gray terrycloth sweat suit, or striped leggings and a pink fleece hoodie with kitty ears. If neither outfit was available, she cried until mucus covered her upper lip like a banana slug. (The outfits were almost always available.) She seemed to give off a baking heat at all times, even though she rarely ran a temperature. She went through each day with every muscle tensed for either offensive tackle (should, for example, Glenn pick up the coveted lavender hairbrush) or defensive maneuver (should, for example, Jane approach with a warm washcloth). She had tremendous difficulty with any and all transitions. Never mind significant transitions like home-to-daycare or playground-to-car. Sweater-on to sweater-off could send Patrice into a complete meltdown. It was for this very reason that she seldom wore a coat. She was a late walker and an even later talker, although by no means a quiet child. Her tantrums were the stuff of legends already, her screams like those of a howler monkey. (Jane could imagine that, in twenty years, one of the workers at the Duck Duck Goose daycare would say, "Remember that Ryfield kid? She was the worst!" and the other worker would say, "What? I can't hear you!") Scratchy and out of sorts was Patrice's default setting, and stubbornness her dominant personality trait. So why was it that just looking at Patrice made Jane's heart, like the Grinch's, grow three sizes and made the true meaning of motherhood shine through, until Jane felt the loving strength of ten mothers, plus two?

Patrice was wearing the pink hoodie now, and it was getting a bit small for her, making the kitty ears sit too far back on her head. She looked like an annoyed cat who was ready to swipe someone with her claws out. She sat in a high chair between Jane and Duncan, and every few minutes, one of them would put a small number of Cheerios on her tray, or a few banana slices, or a tiny fistful of raisins. If they put too much food on the tray at once, or a piece of food Patrice did not approve of, she would clear the decks with a swipe of her chubby forearm.

"No, Patrice doesn't like cinnamon toast," Jane said. They had learned that the hard way.

"Aggie's here," Jimmy said, and they all looked out the window. Aggie was parking her giant custard-blue SUV in the driveway.

"Agg-ee," Jimmy said to Patrice. "Can you say 'Agg-ee'?"

"Ghee!" Patrice shouted.

"How about that!" Jimmy said. "Isn't that something?"

He said these exact same sentences whenever either Glenn or Patrice did or said anything. Literally anything. After four years, it had begun to wear on Jane's nerves. But Jimmy had proved to be better with babies and toddlers than she had dared hope. He'd lost his fear of dropping them almost immediately and had carried them everywhere—even now he carried them home from the park or playground if they asked—and the strength and endurance in his slight body surprised Jane.

"Ghee!" Patrice shouted, and clenched her fist around a banana slice. "Ghee!"

"How about—" Jimmy said, but the sound of the front door opening interrupted him.

The front door banged shut—Aggie never knocked—and a moment later, Aggie appeared in the kitchen doorway. She was wearing a ruffled white blouse and a full red skirt and should have looked like a waitress in a German restaurant, but instead she looked as she always did: flaxen-haired, creamy-skinned, freshly ironed. Jane was suddenly conscious of her own faded blue bathrobe and unbrushed hair.

Aggie stood in the dining room doorway. "I have the worst news."

"Good morning to you, too," Duncan began. "Come on in and—"

"Rusty Benson died yesterday," Aggie said.

Duncan grew very still. It seemed to Jane that every cell in his body dimmed for a moment. "I'm very sad to hear that," he said at last.

Aggie sighed. "Tiny Abbot told me on Facebook this morning."

Jimmy frowned. "Who's Rusty Benson?"

"More!" Patrice shouted, and Jane absently set some Cheerios on her tray.

"He introduced me and Duncan back in high school," Aggie said. "And now he's passed away. Tiny said he complained of chest pains and told his wife—Duncan, you know he married that girl from Houghton—that he felt more comfortable sitting up and that he'd sleep in his recliner, and she came down the next morning and he was dead of a heart attack."

She sat down abruptly in the only free chair at the table, which was next to Duncan. "I'm just so upset, I don't know what to think. It seems impossible that we'll never see him again, or talk to him, or hear his voice on the phone."

"Oh, well, now, you haven't spoken to Rusty since we got divorced in nineteen ninety-one," Duncan said. He had picked up his fork and sounded like his usual self again. "You said back then that you were sorry you'd ever met him and that you'd never forgive him for introducing us."

"I know," Aggie said. "But I thought he would always be there, waiting to be forgiven."

Duncan took a drink from his coffee cup. "Mighty thoughtless of him to die before you got around to that."

"Don't be awful," Aggie snapped. "You know what I mean."

"How did he introduce you to Duncan?" Jimmy asked.

Aggie looked slightly mollified and settled into her chair a little. "Well, Rusty had asked me to a party, and on the way there, he said he wanted to buy some beer. We were both seventeen, but Rusty said that he knew someone over twenty-one, a man who would buy alcohol for underage kids."

Jane had never heard this story. She wished with all her heart that it surprised her.

"So Rusty took me over to Duncan's apartment," Aggie continued. "And there was Duncan, sitting on a ratty old beanbag chair. He said he couldn't buy beer for us because the folks down at the party store had gotten wise to it and refused to sell to him and now he had to drive clear to Copper Falls for alcohol."

"They banned me from the store entirely," Duncan said in a faintly aggrieved voice. "I tried to reason with them, saying, 'Okay, look, how about I buy a case every other day? Then you'll know it's just for me,' but oh, no, they wouldn't listen."

"Anyway, Duncan said we could stay at his apartment and help him drink what beer there was," Aggie said. "So we did, and Rusty got very drunk and passed out on the couch. Duncan had to drive me home, and we stayed in the car outside my house until my father began flashing the porch light on and off, and the next day we were a couple." She shook her head, evidently at her own foolishness, but she looked faintly nostalgic, too.

"I had to go to senior prom when I was twenty-five years old," Duncan said to Jane. "Felt like a damn fool."

.

"Oh, honestly, can you ever think of anyone but yourself?" Aggie's voice was sharp. "Who cares about prom now that Rusty's dead? His funeral is Friday. His *funeral*."

Her voice broke on the last word, and her eyes grew very shiny.

"Oh, now, Aggie, don't cry," Duncan said, and he put his hand on her arm.

In all the time Jane had been forced to spend with Aggie—years and years of meals and movies and house-hunting and cocktails and picnics and random meetings—Jane had never seen Duncan touch her. He'd never kissed her cheek or shaken her hand or helped her on with her coat, and now here he was touching her bare arm! Jane felt an actual pain in her chest, as though a drop of hot oil from a frying pan had landed there, sizzling.

"It'll be all right," Duncan said. "Is the funeral in Eagle River?"

Aggie blew her nose on a paper napkin. "Yes."

Duncan's hand was still on Aggie's arm. "Then we'll go and pay our respects," he said firmly. "Of course we'll go."

IT SEEMED TO JANE that when Duncan had said *we'll* go to the funeral, he could have meant a lot of things. It could be that Duncan meant he and Jane and Glenn and Patrice and Jimmy and Aggie and Gary would go. But there was no reason Jimmy would go to the funeral of someone he didn't know. The girls wouldn't go because Patrice didn't do well on long car journeys—Eagle River was a six-hour car ride—and Glenn wanted to have a perfect attendance record at preschool, so someone would have to stay home with them. (Someone who wasn't Jimmy.) And anyway, Jane's class had a field trip on Friday, and she never missed a field trip. So it quickly became apparent that only Duncan and Aggie and Gary would go.

"Are you sure you don't mind?" Duncan kept asking Jane.

"No, of course I don't mind if you go to your friend's funeral," Jane said. Which was true. Or sort of true. You know, in theory, it was true. What she minded were all the texts Aggie was sending Duncan.

His phone kept making its double glass-clinking sound, and Duncan would pull it out of his shirt pocket, read the text, grunt noncommittally, and put the phone back in his pocket. Or roll his eyes and turn the phone off completely. Or smile a little and text something back, and then leave it out on the counter where Jane could grab it as soon as he left the room and read the texts herself.

Arvid Ballard is coming.

Clancy Gross will be there if he can get off work.

Misty and Silas McKinny will be there.

Scratch Thompson is inviting people over after the wake.

Nixie Singleton and Skipper Mendez are going to do the readings.

Clove Everett has reserved a block of rooms at the Holiday Inn.

Summer Barnes is arranging for flowers to be sent in everyone's name.

Jane gave a sort of righteous snort. First of all, why did everyone have such idiotic names? Who the fuck names their child *Scratch*? And did Duncan really need to know all this? Or even if he did need to know it, did he need to learn it from Aggie? Did she—

Duncan's phone rang just then. It was Aggie. Jane answered just to remind Aggie who was in charge here.

"Hello, Jane, dear," Aggie said. "I was calling to talk to you, actually."

"Oh," Jane said. (Aggie could cut the legs right out from under you sometimes.)

"It's about the funeral," Aggie continued. "You know Gary's not going—"

"Gary's not going?"

"Oh, no," Aggie said. "He never goes to the Upper Peninsula. It confuses him."

"Why—"

"And then there's his bursitis," Aggie said.

"Gary has bursitis?"

"Yes, quite badly in his hip, and it's acting up lately," Aggie said. "He could never tolerate six hours in the car. He'd be in absolute agony."

"Well, I'm very sorry to hear that." Jane had a sinking feeling.

"What I wanted to talk to you about, Jane"—Aggie lowered her voice—"is that the doctor doesn't want Gary to stay alone."

Wait, slow down. This conversation was going too fast for Jane. What doctor actually said that, and in what context? How recently? Was it a standing order?

"He says Gary might fall over and not be able to get up," Aggie continued. "He might even hit his head and have a brain bleed."

Jane had sudden insight into how Aggie sold so many houses: no tactic was beneath her. Aggie must know that Jane would never take the chance of being responsible for another person's death, no matter how unlikely. Not after Mrs. Jellico.

"Okay, fine," Jane said, sighing. "Gary can stay here."

"Oh, Jane," Aggie said in a sugary voice, "you're an angel. I can see why Duncan married you."

So *we* turned out to mean Aggie and Duncan, just as Jane feared it would.

EVEN THOUGH GARY wasn't due to stay with them until Thursday night, Aggie came over on Wednesday with a picnic basket full of supplies and a sheaf of photocopied instructions on Gary's care and handling.

Jane was in the kitchen, slicing cucumbers for a salad, when Aggie arrived. Duncan was holding Patrice on his hip while he warmed a sippy cup of milk in the microwave for her. Glenn and Jimmy were sitting at the breakfast bar, playing Go Fish.

Aggie set the picnic basket on the counter and began unpacking it. She took a brown paper bag of rolled oats out of the basket. "Now, Jane, for breakfast"—breakfast? Jane had to make Gary's breakfast?—"Gary likes a cup of oats mixed with milk, a pinch of salt, and a dash of ground cinnamon, warmed up on the stove. I usually do something different each morning, like I slice a strawberry on top or sprinkle a few walnuts, but you don't have to do that."

No, indeed, and Jane wouldn't.

"Does he have a special bowl?" Glenn asked. "Patrice, she only likes the Hello Kitty bowl."

"No, Gary's not fussy about dishes," Aggie said. She put just enough emphasis on the word "dishes" to make Jane sure that dishes were the exception that proved the Gary rule.

"Now, he also needs to watch *Jeopardy!* every evening at seven," Aggie said.

Glenn frowned. "That's when Patrice watches *PAW Patrol.*"

"Is it?" Aggie gave Patrice a determined smile. "I'm sure you won't mind sharing TV time with Gary, will you, Patrice?"

Patrice bared her teeth at Aggie in a feral sort of way.

Glenn sighed. "She'll mind."

"Well, I'm sure you all can figure something out," Aggie said. "*Jeopardy!* is how Gary keeps his mind sharp."

"Man," Duncan said, "I hate to think what he'd be like without it."

Aggie made an annoyed clucking sound, but he didn't seem to hear her. He handed Patrice her sippy cup, and she poked the spout of it into her mouth, still glaring at Aggie.

Jane wiped her hands on a dish towel and paged through the

instructions. They were somewhat dog-eared and tattered, leading Jane to believe that there were other Gary-sitters out there. Why couldn't he be left with one of them? There was a long list of foods that Gary didn't eat: eggplant, hummus, pine nuts, peppercorns, artichokes, bowtie pasta, American cheese, capers, paprika, anchovies, anything labeled "artisanal," and every single member of the parsley family, including carrots. And another list of foods he disapproved of and preferred not to have in the house. Jane began reading aloud. "Grainy mustard, bone broth, beer cheese, salmon burgers, chunky peanut butter, frozen yogurt, garlic bread." She looked up. "No garlic bread? That's the most ridiculous thing I've ever heard of."

"Well, I don't know about that," Duncan said. "There's also his aversion to slipcovers."

"But—*garlic bread*," Jane said. This seemed to her, of all Gary's beliefs, the least understandable, the least forgivable.

"Why does Gary get to have all those don't-likes?" Glenn asked. "At school, we're only allowed to have three. That's what the teacher says."

"It's how he remembers himself," Jimmy said unexpectedly.

Glenn looked at him, puzzled. "What do you mean?"

"It's how he remembers who to be," Jimmy said patiently. "Like if he goes to Glen's and buys smooth peanut butter, he knows he's Gary. But if he bought chunky peanut butter, he might forget."

"And then what would happen?" Glenn asked.

"Well," Jimmy said. "He might forget where he lives and go to the Huggleses' house instead of his house because he'll have forgotten he don't like red-colored houses. And he'll park in the garage because he'll forget that garages bother him. And he'll go inside and Linda Huggles will have made meatloaf with mushroom gravy and he'll eat it because he's forgotten he don't like mushrooms. And then Linda Huggles will ask him to stay and watch TV and he will because he'll have forgotten he's married to Aggie."

They all stared at him, and then Aggie said frostily, "Gary happens to be allergic to mushrooms, no matter who serves them to him."

She set a Tupperware box of cookies on the counter so abruptly that Jane blinked.

JANE AND DUNCAN had just made love; the air in the bedroom was heavy with the scent of their bodies. They had rushed the girls through their bedtime routine and abandoned Jimmy to watch *Bakery Boss* on his own in order to make this happen. Jane had the bright, expansive clarity that happens after sex.

"Have you ever thought," she said into the soft semidarkness, "that Jimmy is like some sort of oracle?"

"No, I can't say that I have." Duncan swept a bare foot across the sheet idly. "But I do think Gary would make a good monk."

"I think there's more to being a monk than disapproving of handheld mixers," Jane said. "There's, like, a whole spiritual element."

"But that's what I mean," Duncan said. "I feel like he's simplified his life. He's done away with all the unnecessary stuff, and only left what you need to live. I could learn by his example except I don't want to."

Jane didn't want to, either, and she wasn't even sure she agreed. Yes, of course, you could live without handheld mixers and garlic bread, but could you live *well* without them? Jane didn't think so. To live well, you needed garlic bread. Garlic bread and satin pillowcases. And leather jackets. And salad spinners, and rinse aid, and *People* magazine, and iTunes, and scented candles, and hair detangler, and eye masks, and sex, and love, and everything else Gary disapproved of.

JANE WAS STANDING on the porch the next afternoon, holding Patrice on her hip and saying good-bye to Duncan, when Aggie drove over to drop Gary off.

Aggie parked her SUV and marched Gary up the walk. She was wearing a purple wrap dress that reminded Jane of a plum—that ripe and sweet.

"You still want to take your car?" Duncan asked.

"Absolutely," Aggie said. "The day we got divorced was the last day I agreed to ride in that death-trap van of yours. And the varnish fumes always gave me a headache."

"You said it was me who gave you the headache," Duncan said.

Aggie laughed suddenly. "I guess we'll find out. Are you ready?"

Duncan held up his overnight bag. "Yes, ma'am."

"Good-bye, dear," Aggie said to Gary. "I'll be back soon."

Not soon enough, Jane thought. She blew out a breath.

"Good-bye, sweetie," Duncan said to Jane, kissing her. "And other sweetie." He kissed Patrice.

"No." Patrice was suddenly alert. "No bye."

"Just for a little while," Duncan told her. "I'll be home before you know it."

He walked down the porch steps, and together he and Aggie walked to her SUV. Duncan said something Jane couldn't hear and Aggie laughed again.

Gary was standing at the bottom of the steps with his backpack, as meek as a guppy brought home from the pet store.

"Come on in," Jane said to him, striving for a welcoming tone and falling short. Perhaps very short.

Aggie's SUV pulled away, and Patrice reached one pudgy, star-shaped hand after it. "Back," she said.

Jane sighed. "I know," she said to Patrice. "I know."

THEY MADE IT THROUGH DINNER that night, just barely. Aggie had left a foil-covered casserole dish of her baked ziti along with a note:

> *Jane, dear,*
>   *You will need to bake this at 350 degrees. Bake for 15 minutes with the foil on and then remove the foil and bake for another 30 minutes or until the sauce is bubbly and the center of the ziti is hot. I often serve this with a simple tomato salad with red onion and dill, and peach melba for—*

Jane crumpled up the note and threw it in the trash. Aggie was crazier than Gary.

She reheated the ziti and made a tossed salad as well as a plain grilled cheese sandwich for Patrice while Gary and Jimmy watched the girls in the living room, and then they all sat at the table.

Jimmy told a long, confused story about a lady who'd parked her car half on the sidewalk, Gary examined every bite of his meal suspiciously, Glenn complained that they were out of apple juice, and Patrice threw her spoon at the wall. Jane tried not to despair.

After dinner, she tried to negotiate an armistice to end the *Jeopardy!–PAW Patrol* conflict, but neither Gary nor Patrice seemed willing to engage in conflict resolution or a cease-fire. Patrice liked to lie on the beanbag chair in the living room with a sippy cup of milk while she watched—she would start yelling if she had to watch on Jane's iPad or laptop—and Gary told Jane that he refused to use computers or handheld devices outside of work because of the harmful radiation output. "I'd just as soon eat a Brazil nut," he said, somewhat cryptically. Finally, Jane just set the kitchen clock ahead—Patrice couldn't tell time, but Gary and Jimmy and Glenn could, and Jane didn't trust any of them not to blurt out the truth. At six thirty, she said, "Patrice! *PAW Patrol* is on!" and Patrice watched a *PAW Patrol* DVD while Jane operated the remote from behind her.

Just before *Jeopardy!* started, Jane whisked both girls upstairs. She ran water in the tub, and then prepared for battle with Patrice, who did not care for bath time. Every night she fought Jane fiercely, silently, in the manner of someone who knows her life is on the line and that the time for screaming has passed. Patrice tensed every muscle, one hand gripping her clothing, the other hand wrapped around the chair leg or changing table or whatever she could get ahold of, while Jane gently undressed her, murmuring softly, "The bath is going to feel so good, sweetie. Glenn is in the bath, Patrice! Don't you want to see Glenn? We have bubbles, and the boats, and the water crayons."

Jane carried Patrice into the bathroom, patiently unwrapped Patrice's legs from around her waist and Patrice's hands from around her neck. Patrice made one last effort, assuming the rigid shape of a starfish, but Jane merely turned her sideways and slid her into the tub. As soon as she hit the water, Patrice said, "Ahhhh," in a happy way and slid down until the water reached her chin. This happened every single night.

"Are you okay, honey?" Jane asked Glenn, who was already in the tub, drawing loops and swirls on the tile with the water crayons.

"I am," Glenn said. She pointed to the crayon swirls. "Does this say anything?" She so much wanted to be able to write cursive even though she couldn't read yet.

Jane squinted, considering. "It's mainly just *L*s. But I can see *I'll* and maybe *will*." This was a game Glenn usually played with Duncan, who would claim to see *lilliput* and *willful* and *malleable*. "Careful now, I'm going to do your hair."

She used a plastic cup to pour water over Glenn's hair and added a capful of baby shampoo. She washed Glenn's hair, and then turned to Patrice, who was lying on her back with just her face poking out of the water. Her expression was serene, almost beatific. She reminded Jane of the pre-cogs in *Minority Report*.

"How long is Gary going to be here?" Glenn asked.

"Just tonight, and maybe tomorrow night."

Glenn pushed a toy boat in a circle. "Why don't he sleep at his own house?"

Because he thinks the toilet whispers. Because he thinks a cockroach might crawl into his ear while he's sleeping. Because he's worried the mirror reflection won't match up with his body movements. Because he might fall over and suffer a brain bleed. These were not things you could say to a four-year-old. Not without possible lifelong consequences.

Jane sighed. "I guess he's just lonely without Aggie."

"Gary, he played Patrice's xylophone," Glenn told her sadly. "She yelled and yelled."

"Oh, is that what she was yelling about?" Jane said. "I wondered."

"That was only part of it," Glenn said. "He also sat on Daddy's chair. She only likes Daddy to sit there."

"This I know." Jane smiled and patted the top of Glenn's head. Then she straightened up and pushed her hair back. Her face in the mirror was flushed, rosy. She dried her hands and then stepped out into the hall and took the Tupperware container of Aggie's cookies from the linen closet where she'd hidden them.

"Are you going to eat those?" Glenn asked when she came back in.

"Mmmm-hmmm." Jane sat on the closed toilet seat. "Would you like one?"

"What kind are they?"

Jane lifted the lid. "Chocolate chip and cherry." She handed one to Glenn.

"Can I eat it here in the bath?"

"Sure." There were eight small cookies in the plastic box. Eight undersized cookies for five people. Jane sometimes thought that was part of the secret of Aggie's cooking: she always left you wanting more. She handed a cookie to Glenn and took one for herself.

Glenn took small, dainty bites. "Aggie, she said those cookies were for everyone."

"I decided they would just be for you and me and Patrice."

"Patrice, she won't like them. They have lumps."

"Well, just you and me, then," Jane said.

And she ate the other six before the bathwater had cooled.

AFTER BATH, Jane went back downstairs, the girls following her in fresh pajamas, their hair drying into two-toned waves of red and mahogany.

Jimmy and Gary were sitting idly on the sofa in semidarkness, waiting for whatever came next. Two travelers on the road to eternity. Jane's was a heavy burden, no doubt about it. She had earned those cookies.

"Hey, everyone," she said. "It's time for cocoa."

"Now?" Gary asked.

"What time do you normally have it?" Jane asked.

Gary glanced at the kitchen clock and then lapsed into silence, staring at it and frowning. Eventually, Jane said, "Let's do it now so the girls can have some before bedtime."

Aggie had included the cocoa recipe along with the ingredients. First Jane was supposed to warm half-and-half in a saucepan, then add shaved pieces of Leonidas Belgian chocolate and a cinnamon stick and stir it until the chocolate melted. Then remove the cinnamon stick, add a pinch of salt, and stir in more half-and-half, and then use a blender to whip it all smooth. (Here's what Jane would like to know: How, exactly, did Aggie ever get anything done?)

Still, she followed the directions, and it was, somewhat depressingly, the best cocoa ever. Jane even poured some in a sippy cup for Patrice, who tasted it and said, "Ohhhhh," in a rapturous voice.

Jane smiled at her. "It's good, isn't it?"

"Good," Patrice said.

"She likes cocoa," Jimmy marveled. "How about that?"

They all went to bed at eight thirty, mainly because Jane couldn't face the prospect of staying up any longer. Jimmy went into his room, and Gary followed Jane and the girls upstairs. He was going to sleep on the single bed in Patrice's room, and Patrice would sleep with Jane.

Jane tucked Glenn in and kissed her good night and then stepped out into the hall, carrying Patrice. Gary came out of the bathroom, wearing blue-and-green striped pajamas. Patrice pointed at him and screamed, "Mo! Mo!" and burst into tears.

Gary looked startled, and then alarmed. Jane wanted to explain that Patrice was upset because Gary was wearing the same kind of pajamas Elmo on *Sesame Street* wore and Patrice disliked Elmo. But better just to take Patrice into her room and shut the door. All three of them were probably traumatized enough as it was.

Jane woke up at midnight. The smell of chocolate was strong, undeniable. Oh God, she'd left the burner on.

She slid out of bed quietly so as not to wake Patrice and padded quickly down the stairs to the kitchen. But the burners were all off, the pan and cups soaking in the sink. Puzzled, Jane walked through the main floor, inhaling deeply, but the smell had disappeared.

She turned on the porch light and stepped outside, wondering if the chocolate smell could be coming from some other house. But the outdoors smelled of nothing but spring and nighttime, loam and velvet. Jane stood there until the coolness crept though her nightgown and blew softly against her skin.

She climbed the stairs again and lay down next to Patrice. Suddenly the chocolate smell was back, stronger than ever. Jane sat up on one elbow, frowning. Then she leaned over and sniffed Patrice's hair. Chocolate. Patrice's skin, her breath, her pajamas—pure cocoa. Maybe she had rubbed some cocoa into her hair, or spilled some on her pajama top, but it seemed more organic than that. She lay curled there in the moonlight, a literal sugar baby dreaming sweet dreams.

Jane wrapped her arms around her daughter and was asleep in no time.

EVERYTHING WAS AGAINST JANE the next day. Everything.

Jimmy and Glenn wanted Jane to make them oatmeal, too, not just Gary, and they wanted their oatmeal with raisins. Gary picked all the raisins out of his bowl and left them in sticky lumps on the table. Glenn was uncharacteristically slow and grumpy, claiming she couldn't go to preschool until Jane found her butterfly hair clips. She wanted them, *needed* them, and no, not the daisy hair clips or the green ribbon ones—the butterfly ones! The butterfly ones! Jane, holding a squirming Patrice in her arms, finally found them on a chair in Glenn's room under a pile of clean clothes.

She herded everyone into the car—Gary stood absently by the passenger door until Jimmy opened it for him—and she dropped Jimmy off at Duncan's workshop and Gary off at his office and Glenn at preschool.

Patrice had apparently decided to experiment with passive resistance, and instead of clinging to the car door handle and screaming wildly when Jane tried to drop her off at daycare, she fell to the sidewalk and lay there, glassy-eyed and unmoving. She wouldn't stand up, no matter how much Jane cajoled, coaxed, and ordered, and other children had to step over her on their way inside. Finally,

Jane picked her up. Patrice was limp and unresponsive, her head tilted back on her neck. Jane, suddenly frightened, wondered if Patrice was having some sort of seizure. She carried her inside, where Patrice saw another child using the orange Play-Doh and came instantly to life, bellowing savagely.

Afterward, Jane sat in her car in the daycare parking lot, trying to calm her nerves. She wished she could go home and crawl back into bed. She called Duncan's cell phone, hoping for sympathy.

He answered, sounding distracted. "Hello? Hello?"

"It's me," Jane said.

"Oh, hey, how are you? How are the girls?" His words were bunched together unnaturally.

"Patrice just melted down at drop-off."

"Well, that's her baseline, pretty much," Duncan said. "I'm going to have to go to the funeral here in a minute."

"Oh," Jane said sadly. She wanted to tell him about seeing Gary in his pajamas. Shared misery being joy and all that.

Then, suddenly, in the background, Jane heard Aggie say something.

Duncan spoke but not into the phone. He was not talking to Jane. He was talking to Aggie. "Honey, you look great, let's just go."

Jane felt suddenly as though her heart was cooling, had cooled, was cold.

"Good-bye," Duncan said into the phone. "I'll call you later."

Jane said nothing at all.

SHE DROVE TO SCHOOL in a daze. Duncan called everyone "honey." Waitresses, bartenders, cashiers, nurses, receptionists, babysitters. Sometimes he called Jimmy that. And Freida. Even Jane's mother. But not Aggie.

Honey, you look great.

When Jane got to school, she discovered that two of the four parent chaperones had canceled. (Parents got less reliable as the school year went along; by May, they scattered like cockroaches in the light whenever help was needed.) The two parents who had shown up were Edwin Mueller's mother and Liam Bruggie's father. Jane already knew Mrs. Mueller well because Edwin was a budding sociopath with no impulse control, and Jane had mandated that he couldn't go on any field trips unless accompanied by a parent. Mrs. Mueller looked like a hastily drawn cartoon woman, with her washed-out coloring and long limbs, her round face and blunt-cut hair. Right now, she was panting raggedly around the playground after her son, calling, "Edwin! Yoo-hoo! Come back!" and Jane had no doubt that Mrs. Mueller would be doing that all the day long.

Mr. Bruggie was standing by the school entrance, bouncing on the balls of his feet. He was slender and dark-haired, and he wore khakis with knifelike creases and a red polo shirt. He had his arms crossed and nodded curtly to Jane. Jane had not met him before, but *Mrs.* Bruggie had served as a chaperone on the November field trip to the pumpkin patch, and Jane suspected that afterward Mrs. Bruggie had had to lie down in a darkened room and drink gin straight from the bottle. (It had been rough, that pumpkin patch trip.) Probably Mr. Bruggie had told her not to be ridiculous, and Mrs. Bruggie had wailed, "You have no idea!" And Mr. Bruggie was now here to prove to Mrs. Bruggie how easy it was if she only handled field trips in a more businesslike way. (After a few years of teaching, you got a sense for family dynamics.)

Jane had always taken her classes on the May field trip to a nearby petting zoo, but the week before the zoo had been shut down by the Michigan Department of Agriculture for illegally selling rabbit meat. (The place had not been without drawbacks.) She had been forced to go online and research other options, finally settling on a place called Stick Farm. The website showed beautiful photos of the farm shop and café, and promised visitors could enjoy nature walks, outdoor playgrounds, a livestock encounter program, petting zoo, barn tour, picnic lunch seating area, and a "souvenir" to take home, which Jane sincerely hoped would not turn out to be a live chick. She'd called and booked a guided tour.

It was nearly impossible to take attendance. The children were so excited and chattery that no one could hear anything, and finally Jane had them stand single-file against the classroom walls, and then she walked along the line, writing down names. Then there was a massive scramble while everyone retrieved his or her backpack, and they went outside to wait for the bus.

They could actually hear the bus before they saw it. It was one of the older models, and it rattled and coughed up the street like a laboring dray horse. It turned into the school drive, its yellow paint long faded to a curdled-cream color, its black lettering chipped away. They all waited patiently as it heaved its way over to them and the doors wheezed open.

The driver was a heavyset, deep-voiced woman called Quiche, who wheezed just like the bus.

"Find your seats, people!" she called out in a raspy voice as soon as the doors closed behind the last person. She put the bus in gear so abruptly that everyone swayed alarmingly.

The drive out to the farm took over an hour, during which Julia Sherman threw up and lots of other students looked like they wanted to, Edwin Mueller pulled most of the stuffing out of one seat through a rip in the cover while Mrs. Mueller pleaded ineffectually with him to stop, and Mr. Robicheaux took a nap. And what did Jane do?

Jane thought about Duncan. Duncan and Aggie. She thought

about Aggie's pale prettiness, her corn-silk hair, her creamy-white cleavage. She thought of her own body, her stomach soft and baggy after two children, her hair darkened from caramel blond to dishwater. She remembered glimpsing a woman on Main Street shortly after Patrice's birth and thinking, *That woman wouldn't look so bad if she wore makeup and better clothes,* and realizing abruptly that she was seeing her own reflection in a storefront. And yet, still, Jane hardly ever bothered with makeup and wore jeans and plaid shirts on the weekends, wool pants and blouses to teach. She thought about how handsome Duncan still was, his older cowboy looks a perfect match to Aggie's milkmaid beauty. She remembered him telling her that he and Aggie had still slept together even after she married Gary. "Just once in a while," he had said. "Usually when she sold a house and wanted to celebrate. It was like a treat for her. The other real estate agents used to go to the Sportsman after a sale, but Aggie never was much of a drinker."

But that had all ended long before Jane even moved to Boyne City. What had Duncan said? "Aggie stopped wanting to, and I always felt kind of bad about it, even though I did mow their lawn and clear their snow."

The dirt road that led up to the farm made the bus shake so much Jane feared it might jitter apart like an old toy. Quiche parked the bus in the farm parking lot and turned off the engine. The bus made three alarming clunking sounds and then fell quiet. They all got off and Jane made sure everyone had their backpacks and water bottles. It was hot for a May morning. The sun shone down on them like a laser, flashing off the bus's rusty chrome.

The farm had the air of an uncompleted—perhaps never-to-be-completed—renovation. The building that housed the shop and café was spotless green clapboard with fresh white trim and flower boxes of bright blooms, but the lovely patterned-brick footpath stopped ten feet from the building, as though the owners had run out of funds at that point and the contractor had said, "I'm stopping right here unless you pay up." The footpath changed to plain beaten dirt and curved down into a charmless grass-tufted farmyard with splintery gray wood fences and chicken-wire animal enclosures. A dilapidated barn leaned to one side in the distance.

Quiche struggled off the bus with a green vinyl lawn chair and an ancient bottle of suntan oil and a Big Gulp cup of soda. "I'm gonna do some sunbathing while you all are off on your trip," she said.

"Are you going to put on a swimsuit?" Owen Downing asked.

"Nah, just roll up my sleeves," Quiche said.

Just then, a short, stocky man with a bristly black beard and thick black eyebrows came charging out of the farm shop. He was wearing a checked shirt, denim overalls, and a fierce expression.

"I'm Farmer Kev," he said abruptly. "You the lady who called about the school trip?"

"Yes," Jane said. "I'm Jane Wilkes and this is Mr. Robicheaux and these are our second graders."

"Anybody got questions?" Farmer Kev asked. He said it the way someone would say it after having made a long presentation.

Joseph Burd raised his hand. "What do you grow?"

Farmer Kev frowned. "How do you mean?"

"Do you grow sticks?" Joseph asked. "Is that why it's called Stick Farm?"

"Stick is my last name."

"You just said Kev was your last name."

"No, I said—"

"Perhaps you could tell us all where the bathrooms are," Jane interrupted smoothly. "And then we'd like to start with the playground."

"Edwin's already on the playground," Grace Sellick said, pointing. "See?"

Jane squinted across the dusty open space and could make out the faraway figures of Edwin climbing a fence while Mrs. Mueller loped behind him, her purse and his backpack dangling by their straps from her shoulders and bouncing against her hips.

"You're going to have to keep a better eye on that boy," Farmer Kev said severely. "Won't be my lookout if he gets lost."

"What if he falls and hurts himself?" Nicholas Beslock asked.

"That either."

"What if he gets trampled by cattle?"

Farmer Kev narrowed his eyes. "Don't have cows."

"What if he gets run over by a tractor?" Nicholas said. (He had some anxiety issues.) "What if he falls down a well? What if he eats rat poison?"

"Nicholas, I don't think we have to worry about any of those things," Jane said. "I'm sure this is a lovely, safe place where nothing bad ever happened to anyone."

"Is that true?" Nicholas asked Farmer Kev.

Farmer Kev thought for a moment. "More or less."

"Has anyone—"

"Okay, off to the playground!" Jane announced cheerily. "Farmer Kev, you lead the way."

"I thought we were going to the bathroom," Avery Heller said.

"Okay," Jane said. "Anyone who has to go to the bathroom, go with Mr. Robicheaux and Mr. Bruggie. Everyone else come with me."

She started off across the farmyard with Farmer Kev and most of the children. As they drew closer, Jane could see that the playground was more like an installation art exhibit. Some irrigation pipes had been twisted into interesting squiggles and sunk into the ground, and a huge wooden wire spool was tipped on its side. It was mainly a patch of bark chips surrounded by a rail fence, which any child older than four could easily step over and any child younger than four could just as easily crawl under.

Edwin Mueller was sitting on the fence and shouted out to them, "This place sucks!"

"Critical little bastard," Farmer Kev muttered.

Jane was beginning to think Farmer Kev was new to farming. Perhaps until recently he had labored in some occupation—possibly as a prison guard or customer service representative—where his worst expectations of human behavior had been strongly reaffirmed.

But the beauty of seven-year-olds (excluding Edwin) is that they can play anywhere, and soon, the children were racing around and shouting and getting bark chips in their sandals.

Jane leaned against a tree in the shade and wondered if Duncan and Aggie would stay for Whatsit's after-party. Scratch, that was his name. Duncan would almost certainly want to—Jane had never known him to skip a party. Jane's cell phone was in her pocket, and she traced its outline with her finger. Maybe she should text Duncan and ask him to come home tonight instead of tomorrow. But then she'd seem clingy compared to Aggie's cool reserve. Maybe she could say that one of the girls had spiked a small fever? But then she would look all needy and helpless next to Aggie's poise and independence. Or maybe she could text *Aggie* and say that she was worried about Gary because this morning he had seemed—what? Confused? Mentally altered? (That wouldn't even be a lie!) But then Jane would seem alarmist compared to Aggie's calmer approach. Maybe she should text and *encourage* Duncan to stay for the after-party so he and Aggie could tell how secure Jane was, how confident of Duncan's love, how much she trusted him. Because she did trust him, didn't she?

The bark of the tree seemed imprinted on her shoulder at this point, so she straightened up and walked back toward the playground. Farmer Kev announced that it was time to visit the animal enclosures, and led them over to what Jane had assumed was a pile of scrap metal and spare lumber but turned out to be the pigpen, where two large pigs were lying desultorily in the shade of a slatted wooden roof. One of them struggled to his feet and walked slowly out into the penned area. His body was white and black, but he didn't look like a white pig with black spots; he looked like a white pig with patches of dark fungus growing on him. The pig drew a deep breath and vomited a glut of mustard-colored liquid onto the ground. The children cried out in disgust.

Jane looked at Farmer Kev.

He shrugged. "Heat bothers 'im."

Next was an arched metal frame covered with fabric and surrounded by steel-pipe fencing, which turned out to be where the lambs lived. To Jane's relief, the lambs appeared healthy and sweet. And hungry. Farmer Kev cut open a fresh bag of grain pellets, and even the shyest students cupped their hands for the lambs to eat from. When Farmer Kev told them none of the lambs had names, the children debated the choices endlessly. Woolly? No, Lambert! Cloud? Maybe Cream? No, Snowball! Wait, what about Curly? Fluffy? Daisy?

"Daisy's a stupid name," Farmer Kev said to Kaitlyn MacLeod.

Kaitlyn frowned. "It's my little sister's name."

Jane took her phone out of her pocket—Jane, who made it a point never to check her phone during school hours, much less on a field trip! No message from Duncan. She took some photos, including a beautiful one of Samantha Denny kneeling down in order to be face-to-face with one of the lambs. The lamb and Samantha regarded each other with perfect understanding.

"You probably have anthrax now," Nicholas Beslock told Samantha.

Jane straightened up. "All right, I think we're ready for lunch." She looked around. "Where's Mr. Robicheaux?"

"He went away about fifteen minutes ago," Addison Jacobs said.

"What do you mean, went away?"

"He went in there," Addison said, and pointed to the back entrance of the café, where a sign read FREE WINE TASTINGS.

Jane glanced at Mr. Bruggie, and found him staring harshly back at her. She looked away.

"I'm sure he'll be back momentarily," she said. "Right now it's lunchtime."

It had been deathly still all morning, but the moment they sat down at the picnic tables, a strong wind blew up from nowhere, sending napkins and paper plates and plastic wrappers flying. Even Quiche folded up her lawn chair and went inside the bus, a dim figure slouched behind the wheel.

"Maybe we could move to the café?" Jane asked Farmer Kev.

"Café's for paying customers," he said sternly.

So they sat outside, huddled in small groups like penguins at a winter breeding ground. They ate with one hand clutching their sandwiches and the other holding their water bottles. Owen Downing's potato chip bag took off as if by magic, scattering everyone with crumbs, and Landon Burke remembered belatedly that the ENT doctor had instructed him to wear earplugs in windy weather. The only pleasure Jane had was how miserable Mr. Bruggie looked.

She finished her lunch and sheltered in a corner of the tall cedar fence to check her phone. Still no message. She scrolled through her photos to find the picture of Samantha and the lamb and sent it to Duncan, because it really was very sweet. And it would remind him that, you know, in addition to caring for their two daughters and Jimmy *and* Gary, she was also guiding a class of second graders though a valuable learning experience in the richly educational atmosphere of nature and whatnot.

Just as they gathered up the bits of trash that hadn't blown away and stuffed everything back in their backpacks, and Jane had sent the children to the bathrooms in groups of four, Mr. Robicheaux came stumbling out of the café, squinting in the sunlight.

"Sorry to disappear," he said to Jane. "I had terrible diarrhea."

Oh, for God's sake. Couldn't he just lie like a normal person?

"Maybe you're lactose intolerant," Brody Pfeiffer said. "I get diarrhea if I eat dairy."

"Wait a minute." Jane turned to Brody. "Weren't you eating a cheese sandwich just now?"

"We don't know for sure I'm lactose intolerant," Brody told her. "It's only happened about ten times."

Jane made a mental note to have Brody sit near the front of the bus on the trip home, and then Farmer Kev announced it was time for the barn tour.

He led the way to the swaybacked, gray-shingled building that looked like the straw house in *The Three Little Pigs,* only less stable.

When they got to the barn doors, Farmer Kev gestured and said, "This here is the barn."

Jane thought that might be the tour in its entirety, but they went inside, and she saw that actual farming seemed to be happening here. A dozen goats with slender necks and twitchy ears poked their inquisitive faces over and through the gated doors of their pens. *Hello? Hello? Hello?* Goat pens lined one half of the barn, and the other half was devoted to wooden stanchions and milking stations. A stoned-looking teenage boy was pushing a broom along the concrete floor.

"This is Travis," Farmer Kev said. "And he's going to show you all how we milk the goats."

Travis nodded agreeably and went into one of the pens. He came out leading a black-and-white goat on a sort of leash. She went willingly up the wooden stairs to the platform.

"This is Lady," he told the children, tying the leash to the railing.

Travis showed them how he cleaned Lady's udder with a cloth and then clamped two industrial-looking suction cups onto Lady's teats. Lady kicked her back legs a bit but seemed resigned, more or less. Travis flipped a switch on the platform, and milk began running through tubes to a silver canister on the floor.

"That's all there is to it," Travis said. "But I'm going to stop now because this isn't her regular milking time."

Farmer Kev had been standing by watching all this, but now as Travis unclipped Lady, he turned to the group and said, "Anybody want to try fresh goat's milk?"

The children squealed in dismay and shook their heads.

"Oh, come on, now," Farmer Kev said. "Nothing as fresh and delicious as milk straight from the goat."

Students began shifting nervously, afraid of being singled out, but fortunately, Mrs. Mueller said, "I'll try some."

"Attagirl," Farmer Kev said. "Come on up here and kneel down."

Mrs. Mueller made her way to the front of the group, all long limbs and moon face, and knelt awkwardly but good-naturedly.

"Open up," Farmer Kev said, and Mrs. Mueller obediently opened her mouth. Travis aimed one of Lady's teats and shot a stream of creamy milk in. Mrs. Mueller swallowed, her eyes closed. She opened her mouth, and Travis shot another spurt in.

Jane stared at the floor, blushing. Surely—surely she wasn't the only adult here who'd seen a porn film? The very *end* of a porn film? She glanced up and saw that Farmer Kev was looking at her, his teeth showing in his black beard. No, she wasn't the only one.

"Okay," he said. "Travis, lock Mama away and we'll have the livestock encounter."

Jane thought he was referring to his own mother or even his wife, but he was actually talking about a pretty little fawn-colored goat who had big brown eyes and an arching neck. She also had four adorable baby goats who bleated when Travis stepped over the fence into their pen. Travis and Mama had a brief clash of wills and a momentary struggle, but Travis forced her into a cage at the back of the pen without seeming to exert himself at all. (Jane wondered if she could hire Travis as a classroom assistant.)

Farmer Kev produced an orange crate of baby bottles filled with milk and said the children were allowed to climb right into the pen and hold the baby goats and feed them from the bottles.

"All except 'im," Farmer Kev said, jerking his thumb at Edwin, so Mrs. Mueller took Edwin off to the farm shop.

The girls made delighted cooing noises and the boys made scornful scoffing noises, but every single child climbed in and began petting the goats. Jane watched, amazed, as Mackenzie Krieg, who was too squeamish to touch orange peels, sat down in the dirty straw, and Aubrey Kuhlman, who had significant Sharing Problems, placed a baby goat in Mackenzie's outstretched arms. Jayden Holmes, so often a loner, cradled a baby goat while Sophia Boyle, the most popular girl in the class, held the baby bottle. Hunter Carpenter and Kylie Spillman had treated each other with exaggerated disdain ever since word had gotten out that they'd played in the same paddling pool when they were toddlers, and yet there they were, sitting next to each other, stroking a baby goat's ears. Andrew Wilsie, known for cuffing people in the back of the head to get the lunch line moving, cuddled a baby goat in his lap, his face as serene as a Madonna's. Classroom rivalries, friendship jealousies, playground power dynamics—the baby goats swept all that away. It was hard to tell who enjoyed this more, the children or the goats or Jane. (Probably the goats, who grew heavy-lidded with pleasure.) The only one who didn't enjoy it was Mama, who kicked and thrashed in the cage.

Then it was time to go. They walked back to the bus, and Mr. Robicheaux poked Quiche, who was dozing in her lawn chair again. Jane thanked Farmer Kev for the tour and handed him an envelope of cash, which he peered into suspiciously. He handed out the farm souvenirs to the children: cheap plastic pinwheels that made an annoying buzz when the children blew on them.

Edwin Mueller told Farmer Kev the pinwheels sucked ass. (They sort of did.)

THE BUS RIDE HOME was unspeakable. Or perhaps it was unsmellable. The children smelled more like goats than actual goats did, and their animal stench combined with the hot stale air of the bus and the rancid tang of Quiche's suntan oil to form an odor so potent that it was nearly visible. Everyone opened their windows, and the pinwheels buzzed like angry bees.

Jane sat down in a seat about halfway down the aisle and pulled her phone out of her pocket. There was a text from Duncan. *Cute picture. Decided to stay for the party. See you tomorrow. D xx*

The impulse to write back and say, *Have a good time, HONEY!* was so strong that for a moment Jane's knuckles shone white as she clenched the phone. Instead, she put the phone back in her pocket and stuck her head out the window as the bus rattled back down the lane to the highway. She would never permit a student do this— Nicholas Beslock told her she would probably get an eye poked out—but she felt she might break down completely without fresh air. She spent ten minutes letting the wind press her eyelids closed and push air down her throat, feeling her hair flatten against her scalp. When she finally pulled her head back in, she saw that Mr. Robicheaux was standing at the front of the bus, talking to Quiche.

He made his way jerkily back to the seat in front of Jane and sat down next to Carter Huber.

Jane leaned forward. "What were you saying to Quiche?"

"I just asked if she could drop me off at Hooters," Mr. Robicheaux said.

Mr. Bruggie and Liam were sitting in front of Mr. Robicheaux, and they both turned around.

"I really think you should come back to the school for dismissal," Jane said.

Mr. Robicheaux shook his head. "Oh, now, don't you worry, I'm sure the kids won't mind."

Jane was thinking more about whether the *principal* would mind, but she supposed that was Mr. Robicheaux's problem.

"How will you get home?" she asked.

"My car's still in the parking lot from last weekend."

"Are you going to get a lap dance, Mr. Robicheaux?" Carter asked.

"It's not a strip club," Mr. Robicheaux said. "It's a restaurant. Besides, lap dances are very expensive."

They pulled into the Hooters parking lot, and sure enough, there was Mr. Robicheaux's dusty red Datsun. Hooters wasn't open yet, but Mr. Robicheaux said he didn't mind waiting.

The bus made its clunking sound again as Quiche pulled to a stop. She yanked on the lever and the doors wheezed open. "Anyone else getting off?" she called.

"Just me," Mr. Robicheaux said, walking up the aisle and stepping down the stairs.

"Well, good," Quiche muttered. "Because this ain't Greyhound."

She closed the doors and put the bus in gear. Mr. Bruggie was still staring at Jane, but she refused to meet his eyes. Instead, she looked back as the bus drove away and saw Mr. Robicheaux sitting on the hood of his car, his elbows resting on his knees and the sun glowing softly through his nimbus of white hair.

NORMALLY, Duncan picked Patrice up from daycare at around three in the afternoon, but today Jane didn't get there until nearly five, and Patrice threw herself into Jane's arms, sobbing incoherently.

"She's had a rough day," Ms. Shelton told Jane.

"Rough days are going around," Jane said.

She knew she sounded unsympathetic, but she couldn't seem to help herself. Last year, one of the third-grade teachers had returned to school following her maternity leave and quit for good a month later. "It turns out I can be nice at work or nice at home," the teacher told Jane. "Not both." And that woman didn't even live with Jimmy! But Jane couldn't quit. Her salary kept the whole family afloat.

Jane struggled back out to the car with Patrice clinging to her like a piece of wet spinach. Jane pried her off gently and buckled her into her car seat. Patrice wailed. Jane drove to Glenn's preschool, where Glenn came out, scuffing her feet moodily. "We were watching *Winnie the Pooh*."

"I know," Jane said tiredly. "But we're going home now."

They picked up Jimmy, and then Gary, who was waiting expectantly outside his office. (The temptation to keep driving was nearly insurmountable.) And when they finally got home, Freida and Mr. Hutchinson were sitting on the porch steps because Jane, that idiot, had invited them to dinner.

"Freida!" Glenn cried happily, climbing out of the car. Even Patrice stopped crying and snuffled interestedly.

"Hi, sugar," Freida said. "Come give me a hug."

"Did you bring your mandolin?" Glenn asked. "Will you play 'Sweet Violets'?"

Freida smiled. "Of course I will. I'll play whatever songs you like."

They all went inside, and Freida took her mandolin out of its cotton bag.

Patrice took her thumb out of her mouth and pointed. "Tar."

"It's not a guitar, sweetie, it's a mandolin," Freida said as she tuned it. "A mandolin is actually closer to a violin."

Patrice said, *"Tar,"* in an ominously firm voice and put her thumb back in her mouth.

"As long as it's not a banjo," Gary said critically. "I don't hold with banjos. They're nothing but cigar boxes with string."

Jane could tell it was going to be a long evening.

Freida played "Sweet Violets" and "Soldier, Soldier, Will You Marry Me?" Jane left them singing all nine million verses of "The Wheels on the Bus" and took a quick shower to wash the goat smell from her pores. She couldn't seem to wash away the memory of *Honey, you look great.* That might be permanent.

She got dressed again in jeans and a soft blue T-shirt. She decided they would order pizza for dinner, and anyone who felt the need for fruit and vegetables could have an apple. Gary was sure to tell Aggie, and Aggie would disapprove. But you know what? Fuck Aggie. That was Jane's opinion.

Jane always felt that ordering pizza for any group larger than two was like trying to settle the Great Southwest railroad strike. Patrice would eat nothing but plain pizza, Jimmy liked thin crust, Glenn wanted cheese but no sauce, Freida fancied a veggie combo, and Gary told Jane he didn't approve of that Hawaiian kind. Mr. Hutchinson said he was fine with whatever anyone else wanted, but Freida told Jane privately that he really had a very strong preference for Chicago-style pizza, which only made sense since he'd lived there for five years and was just terribly cosmopolitan, really. (She didn't actually say that last part.) Even four years after their wedding, Freida still blathered on about Mr. Hutchinson like the newest of newlyweds. Jane hardly ever said more than hello to Mr. Hutchinson, but she knew a whole host of interesting (to Freida anyway) things about him: how he had a sentimental fondness for *I Love Lucy* reruns, how he loved the smell of furniture polish, how he thought the British royal family was overrated, how he disapproved of red mulch in landscaping. Jane thought that perhaps because Freida had been unmarried for so long, her honeymoon stage was lasting longer, too. It could mean a rough decade ahead.

It took Jane at least five minutes to order pizza to everyone's specifications, and when the pizzas finally arrived, the plain cheese one for Gary and Patrice turned out to be covered with pepperoni. Patrice screamed at the sight of it, and Gary refused to eat a single slice, even after Jane picked the pepperoni off. Jane had to make two peanut butter sandwiches.

Glenn called into the kitchen, "Remember, Patrice, she don't like crusts."

Probably Gary didn't either. Jane trimmed the sandwiches with hands that trembled.

As they cleared the plates away, Freida said, "I do believe your clock's wrong," and Jane realized that it was almost seven. Patrice would want to watch *PAW Patrol* and Gary would want to watch *Jeopardy!*

Patrice stood in the kitchen and held out her right hand, which was her signal that she wanted a sippy cup of milk to drink while she watched her show. Gary put down his napkin and said, "Seven already?"

"Uh-oh," Glenn said ominously, and Jane agreed. Why had she ever thought it was a good idea to have just one television?

But Freida explained the problem to Mr. Hutchinson, and he offered to take Gary next door to watch *Jeopardy!* with the Wilsons. (They could see into the Wilsons' living room and it appeared they weren't watching anything, so hopefully they wouldn't mind.) Jane had a moment of clarity as to why Freida had married Mr. Hutchinson, of what a kind and marvelous human being he was.

Jane hoped vaguely that Gary would stay next door, but he came back promptly at seven thirty, and Freida got out her mandolin again. Jane sat in an armchair, thinking about the dishes to be done, the children to be bathed, the sleep to be sought; trying *not* to think of Aggie and Duncan, Aggie and Duncan, Aggie and Duncan. Freida played "Tangled Up in Blue," and "Kisses Sweeter Than Wine," and "My Darling Clementine."

"Gain," said Patrice, who was sitting in Duncan's armchair. "Gain." She was running one hand across the nubby green fabric, trancelike. Apparently, she missed Duncan. Jane missed him, too.

So Freida played "Clementine" again. Jane's phone buzzed in her pocket, and she pulled it out. Another text from Duncan. *Hegt.* She could see he was typing again. *Heru.* He tried again. *Hey.*

Duncan typed, *This ids a reakky fin oartu.* Translation: This is a really fun party.

Jane knew that soon he would be too drunk to text at all. What would happen then? Where was Aggie? Anxiety squirmed and rolled under Jane's rib cage, making it hard for her to sit still.

Freida's mood changed, and the mandolin followed suit. She played a sad, gentle song, singing mournfully:

> *It's a tunnel kind of vision, like alcohol's involved,*
> *And I stray like a hound dog, but I come back when she calls . . .*

"Freida," Jane said rudely. "Please play something else. Something more cheerful."

Freida looked surprised, but then merely thoughtful. She strummed idly for a moment, letting the music wander, and then she played faster and began singing in a particularly rollicking voice:

Another business trip,
another reason to stay away!
Coming home on Monday, smelling tangerine!

"Freida, for God's sake!" Jane snapped. "Just stop playing! Stop! I can't stand it!"

Freida stopped midstrum, and everyone stared at Jane.

She stood up, the squirming feeling in her chest now, clawing and scrabbling like a rat. Soon the rat would climb right up her throat. She went blindly from the room, fumbled the sliding glass door open, and stepped out onto the deck.

She stood, breathing harshly for an unknown time, until her pulse slowed and the ratlike gnawing inside her subsided a little. She dropped into a deck chair and tipped her head back. Her face cooled so rapidly, she was surprised it didn't send out billows of steam. She stared at the sky. It was dusk, and although Jane couldn't see the sunset, the sky was metallic orange, a smooth silvery dome above her.

The glass door slid open quietly, and Jimmy poked his head out. "Freida says if you're okay with the girls skipping their bath, she'll put them to bed. Mr. Hutchinson is reading them a story."

Jane swallowed with difficulty. "That would be very nice, Jimmy. Please tell her it's fine for them to skip bath."

The door closed and opened again about a minute later. Jimmy came to sit in a deck chair beside her.

"Gary's doing the dishes," he said.

"That's very kind of him." Jane seemed capable of speaking only in stilted, talk-show-host sentences.

They were quiet for a while. The crickets began to turn up the volume. Jane's breathing slowed even more. Maybe it would stop altogether. A flock of birds flew overhead, black against the sky, reeling and falling in perfect sync, like iron shavings pulled by a magnet.

"I've always been glad I'm not a bird," Jimmy said.

"Really?" Jane squinted upward. "They look very happy, very free."

"But you ever see a bird when it's raining?" Jimmy asked. "When I was little and it was raining and my ma was driving us someplace, I used to look out and see these big birds—I guess maybe they were crows—sitting in the trees with no leaves. They'd be all hunched over, just getting wetter and wetter. They couldn't go indoors because they didn't have a home to go to. It always made me feel happy about going back to our house and being warm and dry."

"Oh, Jimmy." Jane reached over to take his hand. Her own hands were icy, numb. "Thank you for coming out to talk to me."

Jimmy was obviously eager for things to go back to normal. "Want to go inside now?" he asked. "And make that cocoa again?"

"That sounds lovely," Jane said. It didn't sound lovely, or even partially lovely. But when Jimmy rose and went into the house, she somehow found the strength to follow.

DUNCAN DIDN'T TEXT AGAIN that night. Not at one a.m., or at three thirty, or at four fifteen. Not that Jane was awake and checking her phone, you understand.

Finally, a text came at five thirty from Aggie's phone: *On our way. D.*

Aggie's phone. On *our* way.

Jane, she don't like it.

THE GIRLS WOKE JANE before seven. Usually she and Duncan spun out Saturday mornings with cartoons and Mickey Mouse–shaped pancakes and wooden-block tower building, but today she fed both girls right away and got them dressed. Actually, Patrice didn't need to get dressed—she'd slept in her leggings and cat hoodie—and Glenn dressed herself in a white shirt and purple corduroy jumper.

Jane pulled on the same clothes from last night and left a note for Jimmy to make Gary and himself some cinnamon toast. She felt certain that Gary would object to cinnamon toast, but guess what, Gary? It's a rough old world.

She packed a canvas beach bag with an enormous number of sweaters and towels and diapers, filled a foam cooler with picnic supplies, loaded the girls into their car seats, and drove to the North Point Nature Preserve in Charlevoix.

"Oh, this place," Glenn said happily as Jane parked the car. "Are we going to walk to the beach?"

"We certainly are," Jane said.

She carried the beach bag, the cooler, and Patrice through the first part of the trail, a small winding path through the trees. Rust-colored pine needles were thick on the ground, and coins of sunshine shone through branches. This was one of Jane's favorite places.

They reached the dunes, and Jane set Patrice down.

"Ohhhh," Patrice said as her bare feet sank into the sand. She picked up a fistful and let it run through her fingers. "Dis?"

"It's sand," Glenn told her. She looked at Jane. "How can she forget what sand is? We went to the beach a million times last summer."

"Last summer was a long time ago to her, I guess," Jane said. "Here, put your sandals in the bag."

They walked through the dunes, Patrice exclaiming over everything like some sort of space alien. When they crested the last dune and saw the lake, her eyes got very round.

"Dat?" she asked, pointing.

"That is Lake Michigan," Jane said. It spread out before them like a lazy blue beast stretching itself in the morning sun, sending small waves forth to crash on the shore.

The sun was shining, but the beach was cool and windy. Jane gave Glenn a sweater and helped her pull on leggings under her purple dress. Patrice narrowed her eyes when Jane approached her with a sweater, so Jane gave up and pulled on her own sweatshirt. She piled beach toys in the sand for the girls to play with, and constructed a makeshift deck chair for herself out of towels and the beach bag. She wrapped another towel around her shoulders and slumped down to think.

Hers were not pleasant thoughts. She thought about funerals and how funerals led to sex, with people wanting to be life-affirming and stuff. High school reunions were just as bad—all that fondly remembered adolescent passion. And Duncan and Aggie were at a combined funeral and high school reunion! She thought of Aggie treating herself to sex with Duncan, of Duncan letting himself be Aggie's treat. She remembered Duncan saying that Aggie had stopped wanting to, but had Duncan stopped wanting to? Had Duncan ever, in his whole life, stopped wanting to have sex, with anyone? Jane didn't think so. Women had broken up with him or moved away or gotten married, but if they came back looking for him (and a large number had), Jane guessed he was always right where they'd left him, in his workshop apartment, usually with an erection, or about-to-be erection. But all that was before he married Jane. Right? Or was Jane the only one who believed that? Why, oh, why had she ever been such a fool as to marry someone so untrustworthy? Why hadn't she listened to everyone?

The girls ambled up and down the beach, but Jane's thoughts ranged further still, out across the lake to the horizon where the water met the sky in a hazy blue line, and even beyond that, to the unknown mists on the other side.

————

THE WALK BACK to the car seemed endless. Patrice had hit some sort of exhaustion wall, and Jane had to carry her as well as the beach bag, Jane's feet slipping on the sand with every step, her shoes filling with sand. She had never made this trip without Duncan or Jimmy, and she missed their strong shoulders and how they let Patrice ride up there as though she weighed nothing at all. Glenn trudged along behind, carrying the foam cooler.

When they reached the parking lot, Patrice had a temper tantrum so severe that it might have qualified as a psychotic break.

"No car!" she yelled, kicking and thrashing so hard that Jane almost dropped her. "No car! No! No! No!"

Jane set her down. "It's okay, sweetie—"

"No car!" Patrice screamed so loudly her voice cracked. "No! No! Want Mama!"

Was Patrice hallucinating? "I'm right here," Jane said gently. She was glad there were no other cars in the small parking lot. People would think Patrice was being kidnapped.

"Want Mama!" Patrice hollered. "No car! No you! Want Mama!"

Glenn tried to hug her but Patrice staved her off with flailing fists. "No! No! No!"

Jane sighed and set the beach bag down. She could pick Patrice up and stuff her into her car seat, but that would involve a physical wrestling match that she didn't feel capable of right now.

She reached for patience the way she might reach an arm behind the sofa to retrieve a dropped television remote. She groped for a moment, felt patience fumble from her fingertips, and then got a grip on it and pulled it out.

"You stay right here with her," she said to Glenn.

She walked across the parking lot to the car, unlocked it, and opened the glove compartment. She shoved aside the usual clutter of car documents and maps and Kleenex packs. *Please be here.*

Please be here. Yes! The bag of pink marshmallows that she remembered tucking in here at some point in the past.

She crossed the parking lot again. Patrice's face was red and dripping. "No car! No! No! No!"

"Patrice, look," she said, holding up the bag. The marshmallows were stale and stuck together, but Patrice wouldn't mind.

Patrice tipped back her head and wailed like a small wolf, but Jane persisted. "Look, baby, just look. Don't you want a marshmallow?"

Patrice drew several long, shuddering breaths. She wiped her nose with the back of her hand, smearing her fingers with mucus.

"I know how much you like marshmallows," Jane coaxed. She opened the bag and pried off a sticky pink lump. "Here you go. Marshmallow for Patrice. Marshmallow for Patrice."

She held the marshmallow out. After a long, long moment, Patrice took it and popped it in her mouth. Glenn let out a breath of relief.

Jane waited for Patrice to finish chewing. Then she took a step backward and held out another marshmallow. "Marshmallow for Patrice." Patrice stepped forward and took it.

"Glenn," Jane said softly, never taking her eyes off Patrice, "can you go open the car door on Patrice's side?"

"I can," Glenn said. Jane could hear her footsteps tapping away.

Jane took another step back. "Marshmallow for Patrice," she said, and held out another one. Patrice stepped forward and took it. Jane waited while she chewed it.

Step back. Marshmallow for Patrice. Step back. Marshmallow for Patrice. In this manner they crossed the parking lot and Jane climbed slowly into the car. Marshmallow for Patrice. Jane was sitting between the car seats now. Jane held a marshmallow out, and Patrice climbed in the car and sat down in her car seat. Jane gave her the marshmallow and then quickly buckled the straps.

Then she backed out the other side of the car and let Glenn get in. She retrieved the foam cooler and beach bag and handed Patrice a sippy cup of milk.

Patrice took a sip and yelled, "Kalt!" (Apparently, she had returned from psychosis speaking German.) She threw the sippy cup, and it hit Jane in the forehead.

Jane winced and picked the sippy cup up. "You need to drink something," she said. Patrice wouldn't fall asleep in the car unless she had a sippy cup. "I know it's cold, but it's all we have."

Patrice took the sippy cup and regarded it suspiciously, but eventually she popped the spout into her mouth and began drinking.

Jane climbed into the driver's seat and glanced at her forehead in the mirror. The sippy cup had left a light red mark above her eyebrow. She used a Kleenex to wipe the moisture from her face.

She backed the car out and drove slowly up the street. Patrice was asleep before they had gone three blocks.

"Okay, Glenn," Jane said, pulling into an empty church parking lot. "Time for you and me to have lunch."

She parked in a shady spot and let Glenn climb into the front seat. They ate peanut butter sandwiches and potato chips and Oreos, and played the Baby Animal Game. What's a baby cow called? What's a baby horse called? What's a baby duck called? What's a baby swan called?

"I can never remember that one!" Glenn said. "Tell me again."

"Cygnet," Jane said.

"Cyg-net," Glenn repeated. "Ask me another."

No day would ever be as long as this one. It just wasn't possible.

"These cookies aren't as good as the ones Aggie makes," Glenn said.

"No, they're not."

Jane wondered if this would be her life from now on: fatigue, and loneliness, and store-bought cookies.

JIMMY CAME OUT of the house almost as soon as Jane pulled into the driveway. Jane held a finger to her lips while she parked the car and rolled down the windows.

Jane looked in the back. Glenn was awake, drawing with the Magna Doodle. Patrice was still asleep, her head tilted back so that Jane could see the line of grit on her neck. All of Patrice looked gritty, actually; gritty, grubby, sticky, sandy. Her cat ears were crooked.

Jane got out and then helped Glenn out, closing both doors softly.

Jimmy was waiting on the porch. "How are my girls?"

Jane swallowed hard. That was what Duncan always said.

"We're good," she said. "Patrice is asleep. Is Gary still here?"

"Sure is." Jimmy sounded cheerful. "He's playing with the train table. Do you want me to carry Patrice up to her room?"

Jane shook her head. "She might wake up and see Gary." Patrice did not like non-family members to touch the Brio. "Let's just—let's just let her sleep here. I'll stay outside and keep an eye on her."

"Okay," Jimmy said. "You want me to keep you company?"

"Sure," she said. "But first, do you think you could bring me a beer from the fridge?"

Only the very best mothers drank alcohol at one in the afternoon while their children napped in cars. She had to remember that.

"You bet," Jimmy said.

"Can I stay out here, too?" Glenn asked.

"Uh-huh."

Jane dumped the sand out of her sandals and used the garden hose to rinse off her feet and let Glenn do the same. Then she sat on the porch steps while Glenn filled the watering can and began to water all the flowers.

The screen door squeaked open and slapped closed, and Jimmy sat down beside her. He carried two cans of beer and handed one to her. The beer was Duncan's favorite, Bell's Two-Hearted Ale. It was stronger than what Jane usually drank and stronger than what she liked Jimmy to drink, but surely whoever had coined that phrase about desperate times calling for desperate measures had had Jane in mind. Jane on this particular day.

She popped the tab on her can and clinked it against Jimmy's. "Cheers."

"Cheers," Jimmy said.

Jane took a long drink of her beer and waited for it to work its magic. But maybe not even alcohol could bring her back from the dark edge where she now resided.

She was taking another drink when Aggie's SUV turned onto the street, as sinister as a custard-blue shark fin slicing through water. Aggie was behind the wheel, leaning forward like the aggressive driver she was. Her wide face was highly visible and highly annoyed: her eyes narrowed, her brows drawn together, her mouth a grim line. It was amazing how she could project anger at a hundred yards.

"Whoa," Jimmy said in a startled voice, so Jane knew he had seen it, too.

The SUV pulled into the driveway behind Jane's car, and Aggie got out. She had the tarnished look of someone who has gotten ready in a hotel bathroom and then driven for many hours. Her cotton dress was as blue as a hydrangea blossom, but the fresh color only made Aggie look more shopworn. The dress was wrinkled and one bra strap showed at the neckline. Her hair was crookedly parted and her skin was slightly blotchy.

Duncan emerged from the car more slowly. *He* had the exceedingly rough, haggard look of someone who had perhaps *slept* in a hotel bathroom—and not a very clean bathroom in not a very nice hotel. His denim shirt was covered with stains in various stages of drying—he'd clearly wiped his hands on it at some point. Maybe several points. His khaki pants were grass-stained and his hair was stiff and spiky. Worst of all was his face: unshaven, gaunt and yet oddly bloated, one eyelid so puffy that his eyes looked as though they were two different sizes. Jane had not known it was possible for someone to be so hungover and not be hooked up to dialysis somewhere.

"Daddy!" Glenn cried. She dropped the watering can and ran to him.

"Hello, darlin'," Duncan said. His voice was deep and ragged but happy-sounding. He swung Glenn up and kissed her cheek.

Patrice let out a bellow from the back seat, and Jane started to get up. Duncan was quicker, though. He set Glenn down and leaned in through the car window to unclip Patrice and pluck her out of her car seat. "Upsy-daisy," he said, settling her on his hip. "How's my baby?"

Patrice squinted at him, confused. Then she sighed and rested her head against his shoulder. Sometimes Patrice's tantrums could be averted, like a toppling wineglass grabbed in the nick of time. Her bad mood sloshed around but didn't spill out.

"Hello, Janey," Duncan said. "Hi, Jim."

Patrice stuck out one of her feet and pointed to it. "Gar."

Duncan frowned. "Sugar?"

"She means sand," Jane said. "We went to the beach."

"Cello," Patrice said.

"And you listened to cello music?" Duncan guessed.

"No, I think she's talking about marshmallows," Jane said.

Duncan frowned. "Why is she talking in code?"

"It's a long story—"

"Jane," Aggie interrupted loudly. Her voice was sharp, probing, like a finger poked at Jane's chest. "Could you please tell Gary I'm here?"

Jane paused. Something was going on here, and no way was Jane going to miss it. "Glenn, sweetie," she said, "would you go tell Gary that Aggie is ready to go?"

"Okay," Glenn said. She walked up the porch steps, squeezing between Jane and Jimmy, and let herself into the house.

"So, how was your trip, Aggie?" Jimmy asked, smiling.

"Thank you for inquiring, Jimmy," Aggie said, biting off the end of each word. Jimmy flinched a little bit. "My trip was just dreadful."

"Oh," Jimmy said uncertainly. "I'm sorry to hear that."

"We went to the funeral and the wake yesterday," Aggie continued. "And I wanted to drive home, but, no, Duncan had to go to Scratch Thompson's after-party."

Jane and Jimmy looked at Duncan, but he just went on holding Patrice, who was sucking her thumb.

"Right away, Duncan begins acting in the most immature, selfish way imaginable," Aggie said. "Drinking can after can of Genesee Cream Ale. Sitting on the sofa with Scratch and making stupid jokes, telling stories that weren't even funny in high school—"

"They were pretty funny in high school," Duncan said mildly.

Aggie ignored him. "And then at midnight, Duncan and Scratch go wandering off into the woods behind the house, and no one hears from them again! Scratch's wife was beside herself because Scratch hadn't taken his blood pressure medicine. I'd never, ever met the woman before, mind you, and there I am, patting her arm and assuring her Scratch won't have a stroke! And people are outside, shining flashlights and calling for Duncan and Scratch, and not one peep out of either of them."

"We got a little turned around," Duncan said. "And I lost my phone somewhere out there. Scratch said he knew the perfect place to watch the sunrise—"

"Sunrise!" Aggie cried indignantly. "When sunrise came, you and Scratch were passed out in a neighbors' yard ten blocks away! Scratch's poor wife called me at five this morning and said, 'The

Fergusons just phoned and said we have ten minutes to get them off their lawn before they call the police.'"

"Now, that was pure overreaction," Duncan said. "We weren't—"

"So I have to go *fetch* him." Aggie's voice was as bitter as chicory. "Then he sleeps all the way home, except when I wake him to check the map, and then he's so hungover he reads the map wrong! We circled Munsining for nearly forty minutes!"

Aggie didn't believe in GPS or Google Maps. She said they were for lazy folks, for people who were not civic-minded.

"I'm sorry about that," Duncan said. He kissed the top of Patrice's head, but not before Jane saw that he was smiling. She knew suddenly that he had read the map wrong on purpose. He had wanted to annoy Aggie, and it had been worth it to him—even with a monstrous hangover—to drive around pointlessly for forty minutes in order to do so. These were not two people who had taken pleasure from each other in the last forty-eight hours. Jane drank the last of her beer, feeling suddenly as though she were swinging in a soft hammock with a warm breeze blowing, although of course she was just there on the hard porch steps.

The screen door wheezed open behind Jane, and Gary stepped out onto the porch, carrying his backpack. He looked at Aggie and said, "I haven't had my lunch."

"Oh, for God's sake," Aggie said. "Well, get in the car, and we'll go home for your lunch. I want to get out of here."

Gary walked slowly around the passenger side of the SUV while Aggie said stiffly, "Jane, thank you for your hospitality."

"Bye, Aggie," Duncan said. "And thanks for a fun weekend."

Aggie gave him a look so withering that it seemed possible it might leave a brown patch on the grass. She got into her SUV and slammed the door shut. She gunned the engine and backed to the end of the driveway and stayed there, waiting for traffic to clear. She kept her face turned away from them.

"Aggie sure is mad at you, Duncan," Jimmy said.

"Aggie is a pain in the ass," Duncan said, so sincerely that to Jane it sounded like *I will love Jane and Jane alone for all my life*.

Patrice took her thumb of out her mouth. "Ass."

"How about that?" Jimmy said. "Isn't that—"

"Come on, madam." Duncan shifted Patrice higher up on his hip. "We're going to go inside and play a game called Everyone Is Real Quiet for About Two Hours."

Jimmy and Jane stood up. Duncan climbed the porch steps, still holding Patrice, and kissed Jane on the lips. He tasted like a beer-soaked breath mint. It was not unpleasant.

Duncan and Jimmy went inside, but Jane lingered on the porch for a moment.

The traffic had finally cleared, and Aggie was driving away. She had been in such a hurry that she'd slammed the car door on a corner of the full skirt of her dress, and it fluttered forlornly, like a handkerchief waved from a departing train. Their street was old and humped slightly in the middle, so that even Aggie's perfectly maintained SUV looked a little lopsided, a little tired. Although that was ridiculous—a car was just a car. Still, Jane couldn't shake the feeling that the SUV wanted to stay at her house, even if the people here made cocoa from Nesquik, and swore in front of toddlers, and passed out on people's lawns. This was a house where love and desire and tenderness dwelt. Imagine having to leave that and go make Gary's lunch. Just imagine.

She watched until the SUV paused at the stop sign on the corner and then limped out of sight.

2019

I T WAS SUCH A SURPRISE, Jimmy falling in love.

Jane didn't even hear about it until hours after it happened because it was a Monday and by the time she and the girls got home from tumbling class, it was almost seven thirty. By then Patrice was near tears, as she almost always was at the end of tumbling.

Patrice was every bit as challenging a five-year-old as she had been a toddler. (Once, Jane had searched her emails for a notice about sales at Challenge Mountain Resale Store and as soon as she'd typed *c-h-a-l-l-e-n-g* into the search bar, nearly sixty emails from Patrice's preschool had popped up: *It's been a challenge to get Patrice to follow instructions . . . Patrice finds it challenging to listen when others are talking . . . Patience is a challenge . . .*) More often than not, the preschool teacher, Miss Meredith, would be waiting with Patrice at afternoon pickup in order to have a word with Jane or Duncan about the day's upset. Either Patrice had refused to get off the swing after the allotted time at recess, or Patrice had let out a scream when she saw her lunch contained one cookie instead of two, or Patrice had had a tantrum when another child used the red crayons. Jane found these conversations unbearable, but Duncan seemed to take them in stride, so now he always picked up Patrice. "We're working on that," he would tell Miss Meredith. Or "Thanks for letting us know." Or "Let me think about that and get back to you." Jane supposed it was all those years of deflecting commitment; he knew how to shut a conversation down quickly. *I'll call you. I'd love to but I have to work. That sounds great—I'll let you know if I can make it.* It made Jane wonder if you could get through life with only a certain number of stock phrases.

Next year, Patrice would start kindergarten, and God knew how that would go with Jane just down the hall, well within hearing range of Patrice's screams. Perhaps Jane could pretend not to know Patrice. Glenn would be in second grade, and Jane was pretty sure Glenn would pretend not to know either one of them. School policy dictated that Glenn be placed in the other second-grade class. Jane would have defied this policy if Mr. Robicheaux was still teaching, but he had retired a year ago. (Jane had seen him once since then, at the dollar store, and he'd told her that his Hooters membership had been upgraded to VIP status.) The other second-grade class was now taught by an overly serious man who made Jane feel young and lighthearted by comparison.

Now school was out for the summer, and Jane and Duncan had reversed roles: Jane was the one who took the girls to tumbling, and Duncan waited at home with cookies and alcohol and sympathy at the ready. (Jimmy went to the Summer Sounds concerts with Freida and Mr. Hutchinson on Monday nights.) Tumbling was challenging for Patrice because she couldn't do a cartwheel. The cartwheel switch had not flipped yet. That was how Jane remembered it from her own childhood—you couldn't and you couldn't and then one day the switch flipped and you just could, much like turning a pancake or reading a map or putting on a condom. Patrice had a fair amount of upper-body strength and coordination, and she had mastered the forward and backward roll, the handstand, the handstand-to-bridge, and the balance beam, but the cartwheel eluded her. She lacked the timing—or maybe it was the courage—and she always clapped her legs together in the middle and fell over sideways. Glenn could do cartwheels, a dozen in a row, each perfectly timed and identical. It made Jane think of those paper dolls cut out so they were holding hands. And Patrice wanted—always—to do what Glenn did.

Glenn seemed like the most delicate of swan girls in her pearly pink, long-sleeved leotard, her auburn hair smoothed back into a low ponytail, her skin glowing softly from exercise.

"I know you can do it," she said sweetly to Patrice, "when you're older. You're just too little now."

When had Glenn learned to be passive-aggressive?

Patrice pushed out her lower lip and began to breathe heavily. She wore a dark purple bodysuit with an uneven taffeta skirt. With her round face and stocky build, she looked like a very small Russian peasant woman, and right now, like a Russian peasant woman who'd just gotten the news about the Mongol invasion.

"Maybe when you're seven—" Glenn began.

Jane reached out to intercept Patrice's striking fist, possibly before Patrice herself was even aware she intended to retaliate. "Bedtime, girls," she said firmly.

Duncan rumpled Patrice's hair. "Let's get you up for bath," he said, "and then you can have milk and cookies."

As often happened on tumbling class nights, Jane and Duncan became a sort of pit crew, but instead of changing tires and refueling a car in ten seconds, they washed and changed two children, distributed a snack, supervised tooth-brushing, read them a story, and sang the shortest lullaby they knew, "I See the Moon." If pressed, they could do it all in twenty minutes. Patrice, worn out physically and emotionally, fell asleep with her eyes open, and Jane waited a few seconds until they fluttered shut. She and Duncan tiptoed downstairs to the kitchen.

Duncan took two beers from the refrigerator and handed her one. She took it gratefully. "How was your day?" she asked softly.

"I've been waiting to tell you," Duncan said. "Big news: Jimmy's in love."

Jane's fatigue fell away from her like corn silk drifting to the kitchen floor. "Seriously?"

Duncan nodded.

"I'm so happy for him!" Jane said. "When did this happen? Can we meet her? What's her name? What's she like? I want to know everything."

"He says her first name is Raelynne," Duncan said, "and all he knows is that she's the new assistant manager at Kilwins."

"Oh," Jane said.

"Yes," Duncan agreed, watching her. "It's that kind of in love."

SO NATURALLY JANE CALLED AGGIE. It had turned out that the only thing worse than being friends with Aggie was not being friends with her. After Duncan and Aggie had returned from their trip to the Upper Peninsula, a cool frost had lain between the couples for months. Duncan had mowed Aggie and Gary's lawn as usual, but he refused to apologize. ("Apologize for what?" he'd said to Jane. "Getting drunk at a party? What business is it of hers how drunk I get? No, ma'am. My days of apologizing to Aggie are over.") He had a point. And hadn't Jane longed all these years to be free of socializing with Aggie, let alone Gary? But still—still—there were others to consider. Aggie no longer saved empty canning jars for Glenn's sand collection, she no longer called when she made double-butter cookies (Patrice's absolute favorite), and she and Gary no longer took Jimmy with them when they went out for pie.

That last part seemed particularly cruel, although Jimmy had been mystified rather than hurt, saying only, "It's weird how we never see Aggie and Gary."

"Aggie, she don't like us no more," Glenn had said sadly.

Jane had sighed. Were they really at a point in their lives where they could be jettisoning people, even if (as in Gary's case) the people in question barely qualified as people? She didn't think so.

And Duncan was not the only one who could be charming. Jane sent Aggie a text one evening and said that she'd made beef Wellington (a lie) and that it hadn't turned out very well. Almost immediately, Aggie had texted back to say she just bet Jane's beef Wellington had turned out with the beef too well-done and the pastry soggy. Jane had written back and said those were exactly her problems. Aggie wrote back and said that the secret was to dust the beef with flour and fry it in oil until browned and then slow-cook it in red wine before she even *started* the pastry. Jane said she'd had no idea. Aggie said she felt beef Wellington was an awfully ambitious dish and really only more experienced cooks should attempt it, but that she had a recipe for Moroccan lamb meatballs that even someone as hopeless as Jane could master (Jane was paraphrasing here) and she would be happy to teach Jane how to make it.

So Jane had invited Aggie and Gary and the recipe over for dinner the next night. She fed Glenn and Patrice early and turned on the fairy lights strung around the back deck. Jimmy agreed to keep the girls occupied playing croquet, and even the weather seemed bent on pleasing Aggie—the air was as soft and warm as cotton. Jane had made an extra-large pitcher of sangria, and they all had drinks on the back deck.

She had found an old *Jeopardy!* board game in the thrift store and had stacked the question cards in a pretty cut-glass pickle dish. She shuffled them slightly and began asking Gary questions while Duncan talked to Aggie.

"This is the world's largest bird," Jane said.

"Wait," Gary said. "What's the category?"

"Science."

"Not birds?"

"No, it says science."

"Okay," Gary said. "What is the ostrich?"

Duncan said to Aggie, "I see you sold that house on Beardsley Street."

Aggie sniffed. "I could have sold that house in my sleep."

"This is the largest ocean in the world," Jane said to Gary.

"You have to tell me—"

"The category is Science."

"Shouldn't I be choosing the category?"

"We're not actually playing *Jeopardy!*" Jane said. "We're just doing the questions."

"What for?"

"For . . . fun, I guess."

"Okay. What is the Pacific Ocean?"

It took Jane a moment to realize he was answering. "Yes, correct."

"Now, maybe you've already heard this," Duncan said to Aggie, "but the Alfords are planning to build a swing bed."

Aggie frowned. "On their porch or in their bedroom?"

"Their bedroom."

"They're liable to pull the ceiling right down on top of themselves," Aggie said indignantly. "You need to go over and help them find the ceiling studs." Then she paused and bit her lip, perhaps realizing that she'd been drawn into two of her favorite subjects: other people's ineptitude, and things she wanted Duncan to do.

"Travel Hawaii," Jane said to Gary. "This tower in downtown Honolulu was built to say welcome to tourists arriving in the nineteen twenties and thirties."

"What is Pearl Harbor?"

"No, Aloha Tower."

Gary frowned.

"Travel Hawaii," Jane said. "This royal palace completed by

King David Kalakaua in eighteen eighty-two had electricity installed before the White House."

"What is Pearl Harbor?"

"They're not all Pearl Harbor, Gary."

"Some of them will be."

Duncan stretched his legs out and said, "Remember when the Kerns put striped carpeting on their stairs? And then kept falling down them because they couldn't tell where the edges were?"

Aggie laughed, and glancing up, Jane saw her shake her head just slightly and give a nearly imperceptible shrug. Apparently, Aggie had decided—as so many women had before her—that being angry with Duncan was just not worth the effort.

The rest of the evening was less awkward. Gary watched *Sponge-Bob SquarePants* with Jimmy and the girls. (It was a Saturday, so *Jeopardy!* wasn't on.) Jane made another pitcher of sangria, and Duncan drank so much of it that she wondered if he might end up sleeping in the hammock. Aggie taught Jane to make Moroccan lamb meatballs and said bad things about people who use dried ginger and that sangria was really a lower-class sort of drink, and it was just like old times.

Well, almost like old times. Except now, Jane was the one Aggie contacted, not Duncan. Jane was the one Aggie texted when she had surplus tomatoes or homemade jam. Jane was the one Aggie asked for help when her washing machine went berserk and shimmied its way half out of her laundry room, although in that case, all Jane did was dispatch Duncan. Jane was the one Aggie asked for advice on her bathroom tiles, and then rejected the color Jane chose. ("She does that," Duncan said. "She asks you your opinion when she already has her mind made up. Drives me crazy.") Jane was the one Aggie called when Gary began having dizzy spells and blurred vision and Aggie thought he might be having a stroke, although it turned out that he was just wearing the wrong eyeglasses, having accidentally picked up someone else's at the office. Jane was the one with whom Aggie chose to share a few of her treasured recipes. (Perhaps, after Gary's health scare, Aggie was feeling Death at her own shoulder.) She told Jane that you should never make a dish exactly the same way twice, that you should vary it slightly each time to keep it fresh. "Now, *that* drove me fucking nuts," Duncan said. "She used to tell me we were having eggs Benedict and I'd look forward to it all day, and come to find out, she'd swapped the Canadian bacon for chorizo. Or she'd up and decide to put pineapple in the coleslaw. Who puts pineapple in coleslaw? Or toffee chips in Toll House cookies? Set me on edge, and I think that was her intention. It was the opposite of comfort food—it was *dis*comfort food. I'm glad you're friends with her now instead of me."

"Aggie and I aren't friends!" Jane protested.

They weren't, were they? Although Aggie was the first person Jane told about Jimmy being in love, and Aggie said, "If you know Raelynne's last name, I can pull her rental agreement and see what she's all about," and it was really very comforting in an odd sort of way.

TACO TUESDAY had started up again. Jane wasn't sure how. It wasn't something that she'd voted on, or even had a say in, although it took place in her house. It was like some larger, vaguely official declaration. Like National Pancake Day, only not national and not about pancakes. It wasn't even about tacos anymore—they had moved on to other foods. Jane didn't mind Taco Tuesday. She even sort of liked it. First of all, Aggie did the cooking, and that was always a positive. Second, Jane considered these new Taco Tuesdays as a way to atone for all the Taco Tuesdays when Jimmy had lived alone. Each successful Taco Tuesday was a layer she could put over the old ones, like putting a coat of lacquer on a table until the top was glossy and smooth, the original surface obscured.

Glenn and Patrice loved Taco Tuesday. They got to stay up late, and drink milk out of wineglasses, and sit on barstools at the table because there weren't enough chairs. Children were the opposite of adults; adults hate novelty, especially when it comes to uncomfortable chairs. And they got to play *Life*. Glenn had asked for a *Life* game, and Jane, charmed by the old-fashioned request, had given it to her. But Jane found playing it stupefyingly boring. (She imagined it had been created by middle-aged bankers in three-piece suits, sitting around and saying, "You know what would be great? A board game about mortgages and savings!") Luckily, Jimmy and Patrice liked to play, although Patrice needed someone to read the cards for her.

So now on Tuesdays, while Jane and Duncan had cocktails with Aggie and Freida and Mr. Hutchinson, the girls and Jimmy and Gary played *Life*. Neither Jimmy nor Patrice managed money very well—Patrice cared only about landing on the child-acquiring squares, filling the little plastic car with blue and pink pegs until it overflowed and peg children lay scattered along the roadside. Glenn played like the mini-mogul she was, accumulating degrees and salaries and insurance and stocks. Gary played suspiciously, squinting at the board and hesitating before spinning the wheel. If the square he landed on read *Volunteer at Charity Sports Event*, Gary would say, "But I don't like sports." If the square read *Win Nobel Prize, Collect $100,000*, Gary would ask, "What did I win it for? Was it physics?" If the square read *Get Married*, Gary would say, "But I'm already married." This made Jimmy and the girls laugh uncontrollably, and they always begged Gary to play. "It's so funny when he pretends it's real," Glenn said. Jane was not so sure he was pretending, but it did make Taco Tuesday easier.

That Tuesday, everyone wanted to go to Kilwins to see Raelynne.

"We can't all go together!" Jimmy said in dismay. "She'll think I never had a girlfriend before!"

Jimmy never *had* had a girlfriend before; it would indeed drive that point home if they all went there together in a big excited group. They debated it for a while and decided that Jane and Duncan and Aggie would go. Jimmy and Gary and the girls would play *Life* while Freida played the mandolin and Mr. Hutchinson kept an eye on dinner.

"We won't be but thirty minutes," Aggie said to him. "All you need to do is stir the gravy continuously, nice sort of medium-hard strokes."

That showed Jane how momentous this was, that Aggie was willing to relinquish gravy control. She and Aggie and Duncan drove to town in Jane's station wagon and parked just outside Kilwins.

"Freida wants us to bring back a pint of Chocolate Caramel Cashew," Jane said. "It's Mr. Hutchinson's favorite."

"I thought Mr. Hutchinson's favorite was Rum Raisin," Duncan said, "seeing as how he has such a sophisticated palate and all."

"Well, whatever flavor, we have to get it to go," Aggie said. "I don't want you all ruining your appetites."

Into Kilwins they went. It was crowded, as usual, with the ice cream line doubling back on itself, and the air so heavy with the smell of sugar that it seemed to shimmer. They got in line, but it was a few minutes until they got close enough to see the scoopers behind the counter and read the nametags they wore.

Jane had pictured the girl that Jimmy liked as just that—a girl. A girl would be perfect for Jimmy, even though he was fifty-four. Maybe one of the college kids Kilwins hired in the summer, a girl with long blond hair and a shy smile, maybe plump with dimples. But the woman whose nametag read RAELYNNE turned out to be whippet-thin and in her forties. She had russet-colored ringlets pulled back in a ponytail, and her facial features—enormous eyes, high cheekbones, full mouth, arched brows—were as voluptuous as ripe strawberries, as exaggerated as a clown's. She wasn't at all pretty, or wait—was she extremely pretty? Jane couldn't decide. Raelynne seemed to be one of those women who flip between beautiful and ugly like a coin falling through the air, flashing heads and tails. It all depended on the angle.

But what most surprised Jane was Raelynne's, well, roughness. Her hair was coarse and unruly, her eyes were sharp, her arms corded with muscle. This was what Jimmy longed for? Jane supposed she would feel the same blend of surprise and disapproval fifteen years from now when Glenn brought home a long-haired biker or a married college professor.

She and Duncan and Aggie stared at Raelynne from their place in the line. Aggie clutched Jane's elbow, and Jane knew why. As always, when meeting an unfamiliar woman, the crucial question arose: Had Duncan slept with her?

Duncan looked at Raelynne and stroked his moustache thoughtfully. "She's not from around here," he said at last.

Jane and Aggie exchanged glances. That didn't mean he hadn't slept with her, only that he didn't recognize her. (If he'd slept with her—if he'd *known* he'd slept with her—he would have said, "Well, dang.")

When they got up to the counter and Raelynne asked him what he'd like, Duncan said craftily, "What flavor do *you* think I like?" And Raelynne said, her voice raspy but not unfriendly, "I don't give a rat's butt what flavor you like, but you better order because there are folks behind you," which was sort of shocking but did seem to indicate that she didn't recognize him either.

Raelynne was cheerfully, almost brutally efficient, assembling their order while barking at someone in the back room to bring more sugar cones and calling over to the candy counter that she needed more rainbow sprinkles *now*. She rung them up at the cash register and counted back the change with a machine-gun sort of rapidity.

"Thank you and have a good night," she said, already turning to the next customer.

Almost before they knew it, they were back out on the sidewalk in the sultry night air with a paper bag full of outrageously expensive cartons of ice cream. Duncan said that Raelynne looked like the type who would respond well to flowers you bought at the farmers' market but said you picked yourself, and Aggie said that Jimmy should order an ice cream soda next time to make him seem like a more discerning customer, and Jane said nothing at all because her chest was too constricted with hope for Jimmy.

THAT WAS ON TUESDAY, and on Wednesday, Jane and Aggie and Freida had a three-way conference call to pool their knowledge about Raelynne. It reminded Jane of when her class had a group meeting to discuss what they wanted to learn about land mammals.

Freida and Mr. Hutchinson had been to Kilwins earlier in the day for a Raelynne viewing, and Freida said Raelynne made her think of "The Maid with the Bonny Brown Hair," but something in her voice made Jane suspect that Freida had been surprised by Raelynne, too. Freida had also called Kilwins using an unnecessary French accent and asked who the new assistant manager was, so they knew Raelynne's last name was Collins. Aggie had pulled Raelynne's rental agreement, so they knew that she lived in a mobile home in Lakeview Village. Gary had actually stirred himself over at State Farm to look up Raelynne's credit rating, so they knew she was forty-seven and had a Sam's Club membership (a store Gary disapproved of).

All this, they decided, was good, even the Sam's Club thing. But how could they know for sure that Raelynne didn't have a boyfriend?

"We need to stake out her house and see who comes and goes," Freida said. "But I have back-to-back piano lessons tomorrow."

"Jane and I will go," Aggie said. "I don't have any morning appointments."

She didn't ask whether Jane had any morning plans, but Jane didn't protest. Sometimes with Aggie it was easier not to resist.

Aggie picked Jane and the girls up at nine the next morning.

"This is so exciting," Glenn said, bouncing slightly in her seat. "Like a movie."

"Where are we going again?" Patrice asked. (It took her a while to wake up in the morning.)

"To see Jimmy's girlfriend, stupid," Glenn said.

"Mommy!"

"No names, Glenn," Jane said, while Aggie took a corner so fast that it felt like the car was on two wheels. In no time at all, they were parked just down the street from Raelynne's mobile home—a neat little beige house with brown trim. A battered blue Dodge hatchback was parked in front.

"I'm hungry," Patrice said.

Aggie looked concerned. "I do hope you girls aren't getting crumbs back there."

"We're not eating anything," Patrice said. "That's why I'm hungry."

Aggie took a paper cup of coffee from the cup holder, removed the lid, and blew on it while she told Jane how much Raelynne paid in rent and that garbage pickup was included and that there was a summer cookout on Resident Appreciation Day.

"Now I'm *starving*," Patrice said.

Aggie frowned at her in the rearview mirror. "What did you have for breakfast?"

"I don't remember."

"You don't remember?" Glenn scoffed. "That was like half an hour ago."

"So what did I have?" Patrice asked her.

"A blueberry Pop-Tart, same as me."

"Was it good?" Patrice sounded intrigued. "Did I like it?"

"Jane, dear," Aggie started. "You must see to it that the girls get better nutrition—"

Just then, Raelynne came out of her house, wearing pink sweatpants cut off at the knees and a turquoise tank top. She wore not a single speck of makeup, and yet Jane could still see her eyelashes from the car. She was carrying two bags of trash, and her biceps stood out like halves of tennis balls. She plunked the bags down at the curb and went back in her house.

Aggie started the car. "I guess she's single, all right. Only women living alone take out the trash themselves."

Such unstable beliefs they clung to.

SO NOW all Jimmy had to do was call Raelynne and ask her out. They knew Raelynne's phone number from the rental agreement.

"I can't do that," Jimmy said, sitting at the breakfast bar with Duncan that evening while Jane made meatloaf for dinner. The girls were playing croquet in the backyard. They were squabbling, but below the parental-interference threshold.

"Sure you can," Duncan said. "If she asks where you got her number, just say you have a friend at the phone company."

"No, I mean, I really can't do it," Jimmy said. "I know I'd get a pain in my throat like I'd swallowed a chicken bone, and I wouldn't be able to talk, and she'd say hello a bunch of times and then hang up, and I *still* wouldn't have said anything, and for a long time afterward, I'd think about it and kind of moan, even if I was all alone."

Oh, to know yourself as well as Jimmy did! And people said he was slow learning.

"We'll practice," Duncan said. "Jane, go out on the porch and pretend to be Raelynne. We'll call you shortly."

"It's no good to practice." Jimmy sighed morosely. "I just can't do it. I'm not you, Duncan. I can't go around asking all and sundry out on a date."

"The secret is to cast a wide net," Duncan said, "and then you don't take rejection so personally."

Jane sighed as she shaped the meatloaf. Duncan had indeed cast a wide net, and she had swum willingly—eagerly—into it, and now she remained caught there with Aggie and pretty much every other female resident of Boyne City.

Jimmy shook his head. "I only want Raelynne."

"Well, okay, how about this," Duncan said. "How about you go into Kilwins late, just before closing, and offer to help her clean up? Then you'll have stuff to talk about, like where to put the chairs and the extra gallons of ice cream, and at the end you ask her to go see a movie or something."

"Aw, Kilwins is always busy," Jimmy said. "The only way I could ever, ever ask her out was if we was all alone and no one else could hear and it was dark so she couldn't see my face."

"Okay," Duncan said. "Then we'll make that happen."

NATURALLY, it was Aggie who thought of the solution. During dinner that night—were they all going to have to eat together every other night until Jimmy asked Raelynne out? Jane thought it might be possible—she said, "It's no problem at all. I'll have a dinner party and invite her and Jimmy will be my spare man."

"What's a spare man?" Jimmy asked.

"When you have a dinner party where you don't have an even number of men and women attending," Aggie told him, "the hostess invites a spare man, a male friend who happens to be handsome, charming, and sophisticated."

Jimmy looked overwhelmed. "I think you'd better invite someone else."

"Nonsense," Aggie said. "You'll do absolutely fine. And my house isn't far from Raelynne's, so afterward, you can walk her home."

"How are you going to invite her, though?" Duncan asked. "Just go to Kilwins and say, 'I'll have the mocha chip, please, and come on over to my house on Saturday'?"

Gary looked up from his plate, agitated. "I don't like ice cream with chips in it."

Aggie ignored him. "No, Duncan," she said coolly. "I'm going to call Kilwins and say that I want to hand out miniature tubs of ice cream at an open house. I'll schedule an appointment to come in and discuss pricing, and I'll get to know Raelynne then and invite her."

"Are you?" Gary asked.

Aggie frowned. "Am I what?"

"Giving away ice creams at your open house."

"Oh, no," Aggie said. "I'm not even having an open house."

"Well, who's going to eat all the ice creams?"

"No one. I'll say I've decided against it."

"Can you make sure none of the ice creams have chips?"

"Gary, there aren't going to be any ice creams."

"Also, no pie flavors," Gary said. "I find that bewildering. Is it pie or is it ice cream?"

"I still don't see how you're just going to invite Raelynne out of the blue," Duncan said.

Aggie lifted her chin a little. "You just leave it to me."

And she called Jane the very next day to say it was all set.

THEY HAD NEVER PLANNED anything so carefully. Aggie debated menus endlessly with Jane and finally called her on Thursday to say she had narrowed the main course down to three options: charred chicken with sweet potatoes and oranges, seared scallops with brown butter, or pork chops with fig and grape agrodolce.

"The scallops sound delicious," Jane said.

Immediately, Aggie said, "I believe I'll do the pork chops. Also, I forgot to say anything to Raelynne about the dress code, so I think some of us should dress up and some of us should dress down so she doesn't feel out of place."

"Okay," Jane said.

"Now, obviously it's most important that Jimmy looks his best," Aggie said. "So please see to it that he wears clean khakis, and I believe Duncan has a very nice linen shirt with a Cuban collar—perhaps he would lend that to Jimmy."

"I'm sure he would," Jane said.

"I think Duncan should wear dress pants and a plain white button-down shirt," Aggie continued. "I dislike it so when he wears cargo pants. And now you, Jane—don't you have a very sweet denim dress?"

"Well, chambray, yes," Jane said.

"Please wear that," Aggie said, "so that if Raelynne wears denim, she won't feel she's the only working-class person present. She should realize that not all of us are glamorous and sophisticated."

This was what Jane got for being friends with Aggie.

"I have to go," she said. "I have something in the oven."

She hung up, and Glenn glanced up from the kitchen table, where she and Patrice were coloring with crayons. "You don't have anything in the oven," Glenn said. "You were lying."

Patrice looked at Jane worriedly.

"I wasn't really lying," Jane said. "I'm about to bake a cake, and if I don't put it in the oven now, it won't be ready before you guys have to go to bed, so that's why I sort of exaggerated and told Aggie it was already baking."

"Oh," Glenn said.

Jane thought that Glenn was on the verge of being able to see through explanations like that, and though it would make life more difficult, Jane was secretly pleased. (Patrice would probably go on believing everything Jane said until age thirty.) Jane knew it was irrational, but sometimes she worried that she and Duncan would be unable to raise anyone past the intellectual age of seven. They hadn't done very well with Jimmy.

"What kind of cake?" Patrice asked.

"What kind of cake would you like?" Jane asked, resigned now to baking.

"Strawberry," Patrice said.

So Jane made a strawberry layer cake, and she let Patrice and Glenn frost it, and they all had some for dessert. The girls took their cake out to sit on the porch swing while Jimmy and Duncan sat with Jane at the table.

Jimmy was nervous, licking his finger and picking crumbs off the table. "What if Raelynne doesn't want me to walk her home?"

"Oh, I'm sure she will," Jane said. "Aggie will say something like, 'Jimmy, please walk Raelynne home,' and Raelynne will say, 'That would be very nice, if you're sure it's no trouble.'"

"And then what do I say?"

"You say 'It's no trouble at all.'"

"Say, 'It would be my pleasure,'" Duncan suggested.

Jimmy looked unconvinced. "But what do I say when we get to her house?"

"Just say 'I'd like to see you again,' or 'Maybe we could watch a movie sometime,'" Duncan said. "Be polite and respectful, just like you are at work."

Jimmy shook his head. "At work I never say anything but that you're not there and I don't know when you're coming back."

"On the phone, yes, maybe so," Duncan conceded. "But I've heard you be mighty polite to customers. You always say hello and compliment people's choice of furniture and thank them for stopping by. Just pretend Raelynne's a customer and say, 'It's been a pleasure meeting you,' and 'I've enjoyed talking to you,' and 'Maybe we can have coffee and discuss this.'"

"Like you said to that one lady?" Jimmy asked.

"What lady?"

"That one pretty lady with the fiddleback chairs," Jimmy said. "She had six of them and a dining table, too, and you said, 'Maybe we should have coffee and discuss this.'"

Duncan looked at Jane. "That was a long time ago."

She looked back at him silently.

"A very long time ago," Duncan said. "So long ago I forgot all about it, but yes, Jim, that's the kind of thing you say. Just, you know, 'I'd love to get together and talk some more.'"

"But what if we haven't even *been* talking?" Jimmy asked. "What if we walk the whole way to her house and I can't think of a single thing to say?"

"Just ask her how she likes working at Kilwins," Jane said, "and what she thinks of Boyne City."

"What else?" Jimmy asked.

"Doesn't matter. Women love to talk about themselves," said Duncan, who had once dominated an entire evening talking about the smell of spar varnish. "Once she gets started, you just act like it's the most interesting thing you ever heard and ask lots of questions."

"Aw, you know I'm not good at remembering stuff," Jimmy said.

"You don't have to remember it," Duncan said. "If you forget something and she asks why, just say, 'You looked so pretty tonight, I can't remember anything.' But if you do say that, then don't give her another compliment for at least a week, so she'll start wondering what was up with the first one. Pretty soon she'll wonder if she imagined the first one, or she'll wonder if maybe she somehow offended you by not acting pleased enough—"

How sad was it that Duncan was the man Jane loved? How sad was it that he believed what he was saying? How sad was it that Jane believed it, too?

IT HAD BEEN SO LONG since Jane had gone to a dinner party that she'd forgotten how awful they were. Well, maybe not awful, but certainly exhausting. You book a sitter and feed the children early and get dressed up and figure out who's going to be the designated driver and go over to someone's house and by the time you've finished your first and only glass of wine, you've already listened to another guest tell you about their gluten allergy and you realize that it's hours before you can go to bed. But tonight was for Jimmy, so it would be different. Maybe.

When Jane and Duncan and Jimmy arrived at Aggie's house, Aggie was busy in the kitchen, so they were greeted by Gary. He was wearing corduroy pants and a stiff new-looking plaid button-down shirt.

"You look nice, Gary," Jane said. He didn't look especially nice, but she felt she had to say something.

Gary pulled at his collar and grimaced. "Aggie told me to wear this, but it's not very comfortable. I don't like it when she dresses me."

"I feel you, brother," Duncan said with more sincerity than Jane had ever heard him use when speaking to Gary. "Now, how about you get us some drinks?"

While Gary was getting the drinks, Freida and Mr. Hutchinson arrived.

"I brought my mandolin," Freida said to Jimmy, quite unnecessarily since the mandolin bag was hanging from her shoulder. "You can tell a lot about a person by their taste in music. Personally, I've never trusted anyone who dislikes Lester Flatt."

Raelynne was the last to arrive. She wore a short denim skirt and a ruffled pink blouse with a drawstring neckline. She had pulled her hair back and wore pink tasseled earrings, and she looked attractively disheveled, the way she had at Kilwins.

Aggie came bustling out of the kitchen and made introductions. Gary poured her a glass of wine, and they all sat down in Aggie's living room. Raelynne perched on the edge of the sofa next to Aggie, holding her wineglass with both hands. She glanced around, smiling nervously.

And then it was like a black hole opened in the middle of the room and sucked all the conversation down into it. No one said a word. Jane realized that none of them had thought past the moment Raelynne would arrive for the dinner party. She flipped desperately through her mental files, trying to remember what they usually talked about, but all they'd talked about recently was Raelynne. Finally, Gary asked Raelynne if she still shopped at Sam's Club. The rest of them glared at him, but Raelynne didn't seem to wonder how he knew. "Not since I moved here," she said. "I don't think I'll renew my membership."

"Where did you move from?" Freida asked.

"Muskegon," Raelynne answered. She took a big drink from her glass.

"Muskegon?" Duncan leaned forward, his eyes sharp with interest. "Did you know the Trimble sisters?"

"No, I don't believe so."

Duncan sat back. "Good."

Everyone let out a breath of relief. Duncan had slept with two or perhaps all three of the Trimble sisters. He said they were all so close in age and looked so much alike, he'd never been sure who he was with. Mr. Trimble had threatened to shoot Duncan with his duck-hunting gun if he ever showed up at their house again.

Aggie touched Raelynne's arm. "Now, what made you decide to move to Boyne City?"

"I wanted to get away from my ex-husband," Raelynne said promptly.

They all glanced at each other. Ex-husband? Was that good or bad? Good, Jane decided. It would make Jimmy seem all the more kind and loving in comparison.

"Was your first husband . . . stalking you?" Freida asked delicately.

"He's my second husband," Raelynne said, sitting back on the couch, "but he wasn't stalkin' me. Him? He's too lazy to stalk anyone. No, he was just calling me all the time." Abruptly, her voice grew deep and somehow whiny. "'Raelynne, the toilet's backed up again and I don't know what to do. Raelynne, I used Dawn in the dishwasher and now the whole house is full of suds. Raelynne, I tried to clean the shower with malt vinegar and the tile turned brown.' I mean, imagine gettin' that type of call ten times a day. And then he would show up at the bar where I worked wearin' some sorry-ass shirt he'd shrunk in the dryer."

Nobody knew quite how to respond to this, but finally Jane said, "You worked in a bar?"

Raelynne turned to face her and flipped from ugly to beautiful in the process. "Yes, I was a bartender. That's where I met both my husbands, and finally, I thought to myself, 'Raelynne, maybe the problem is not just the men but also where you're meetin' them. Maybe you'd better try your luck in some other establishment.' So here I am."

Aggie looked concerned. "Did your first husband have a drinking problem?"

"Oh, no," Raelynne said easily. She seemed to have relaxed. She crossed her legs and swung one pink-sandaled foot. "Me and him got divorced over chicken pillows."

"What's a chicken pillow?" Jimmy asked.

"It's an awful dish his mother raised him on," Raelynne said. "It has like ten ingredients—crescent rolls and cream cheese and saltine crackers and cream of chicken soup and a whole bunch of others I can't even remember."

"Goodness," Aggie said weakly. She always said any dish with canned soup in it made her feel faint and dizzy.

"Came out of the oven lookin' less like a chicken's pillow than some chicken's upchuck," Raelynne said cheerfully. "I made it once a week for that first year—you know how newlyweds are, so eager to please. And then I made it less and less and finally not at all. Chester kept askin' for it and I made up excuses, but finally I said, 'Listen, mister, if you want chicken pillows so bad, you can make them yourself.' Chester said I was disrespectin' his mother. I said, no, I was disrespectin' chicken pillows and doin' the world a favor while I was at it." She shook her head. "It seems like such a little thing, but it led to a big argument, and I moved my stuff out that very night."

They were all so absorbed by this that when the kitchen timer went off, everyone jumped a little. Aggie leapt out of her chair, crying, "My pork chops!" and rushed from the room.

The pork chops were fine, nowhere close to overdone, and they all sat down to eat them at the table covered with a white cloth and laid with Aggie's fussy floral-patterned china. Aggie had put out name cards, too, and seated Jimmy and Raelynne next to each other. Everyone else immediately engaged their nearest seat partner in a low, intense conversation so that Jimmy and Raelynne would be forced to talk to each other.

Jane turned obediently to Mr. Hutchinson, and he asked her softly if she had heard rumors that the city water supply was contaminated with wild boar excrement, and she said, "No, not a word," and Mr. Hutchinson said he'd heard it from someone at Glen's, and Jane murmured, "It's certainly something to think about."

Across the table, Raelynne said "Now, where do you work, Jimmy?"

Jimmy swallowed audibly. "I work with Duncan at his woodworking shop."

"Is that so?" Raelynne said. "Maybe you can come over and build me a little porch overhang. I hate to stand there in the rain, searchin' for my keys."

Jane and Mr. Hutchinson beamed at each other. Things were going so well! (Although under no circumstances should Jimmy be allowed to build a porch overhang.)

Jimmy asked Raelynne how she liked working at Kilwins, and Raelynne said it was a sure sight better than being hassled by drunk folks all the time, although the tips were not as good. Gary said that he was perplexed by Superman ice cream. Was it supposed to taste *like* Superman, or only like ice cream Superman would like? Everyone frowned at him—Jimmy was supposed to be the one talking to Raelynne!—but Raelynne said that she thought it was because Superman ice cream was red and blue and yellow, like the colors of Superman's costume. And then they did an around-the-table analysis of everyone's favorite flavors that carried them all the way through dinner.

After dessert—raspberry panna cotta—Duncan said, as planned, "Well, we'd better be going."

Everyone else made noises of agreement, and Raelynne said, "Oh, yes, this has been so nice, but I have to work tomorrow."

They all pushed back their chairs and started making that strange rustling sound people make when they're getting ready to depart, even when they have nothing—no newspapers or windbreakers—that actually rustles.

Aggie cleared her throat. "Jimmy, could I ask you to walk Raelynne home?"

"Oh, that's not necessary," Raelynne said.

"I insist," Aggie said. "I wouldn't think of sending a young woman home alone after dark."

Raelynne glanced out the window, confused. "It's eight thirty."

"Well, but still, you can't be too careful," Aggie said.

"I'll be fine, seriously."

"I'd like to walk with you," Jimmy said shyly, surprising them all. "If it wouldn't bother you."

"Well, okay." Raelynne shrugged. "Maybe you can give me an estimate on that overhang."

Everyone thanked Aggie and Gary for dinner and walked outside, but since they had no intention of leaving, they just stood around awkwardly until Jimmy and Raelynne walked away together on the sidewalk, Raelynne with her purse slung over her shoulder and her hand resting on it like a farmer toting a rifle. Jimmy and Raelynne turned the corner, and Jane and the others dropped into Aggie's front porch chairs.

"Heavens." Aggie fanned herself with her shirt collar. "I'm completely wrung out."

"Wasn't it terrible when she didn't want to be walked home?" Freida asked. "I thought she was going to keep arguing and say she knew self-defense."

"The worst was when Jim volunteered," Duncan said. "I was holding my breath."

Freida took out her mandolin. "We need a little music to relax us."

"You'll have to play quietly," Aggie said. "The Bullards next door have a ten-month-old and her bedroom is right there."

So Freida played softly. She played only love songs, saying perhaps they would bring Jimmy luck. "Sally in Our Alley," "Lark in the Morning," "Drink to Me Only with Thine Eyes," and "Can't Help Falling in Love."

The music was soothing and ripplelike. Jane, exhausted from the tension, felt herself drifting away on it. Twilight was turning the sky to sapphire, and a crescent moon was already out, looking down his long chin at them.

Suddenly Jimmy was standing there in front of them. No one had seen him arrive because he'd come from the other direction.

"I got a little turned around," he said. "I started up Meadow Lane and thought 'This doesn't look right' and—"

"Never mind that!" Aggie cried out. "Tell us what happened!"

Jimmy smiled and ducked his head. He rubbed a little circle in the grass with the toe of his shoe. "I asked her if I could help her close up at Kilwins sometime, and she said she'd like that a lot."

They cheered so loudly they woke the Bullards' baby, and Mr. Bullard snapped up a window shade and shook his head at them in disapproval.

JANE KNEW that most things that are too good to be true are, indeed, not true, like that idea about Nutella being a healthy food. (Or else they're *true* but not really that *good*, like *Avatar*.) Raelynne seemed too good to be true, and, yet, amazingly, she was. She appeared to be genuinely interested in Jimmy and to honestly enjoy his company. Jimmy began riding his bike to Kilwins around ten most nights to help her close up, and before long he was filled with information about her—literally filled, as though he were an empty container into which she poured all her views.

Raelynne was a Gemini, and a night person. Her favorite drink was a strawberry margarita and her favorite perfume was straight vanilla extract. She preferred Coke to Pepsi and jeans to chinos.

Also, French fries to potato chips and candles to air freshener. And being early to being late, TV to books, McDonald's to Burger King. And Facebook to Twitter, the beach to the woods, country to city, summer to winter, cats to dogs, carpets to floors. And pizza to burgers, plain M&Ms to peanut, earbuds to headphones, Netflix to YouTube, phone call to text, cake to pie, laundry to dishes, couch to recliner, pancakes to waffles, coffee to tea, soup to sandwich, ketchup to mustard, steak to chicken, the dentist to the gynecologist, caffeine to sugar, and naps to yoga. She preferred baths to showers, but not bubble baths because the bubble stuff bothered her skin. Her favorite movie star used to be Mel Gibson, but now that he'd had such an obvious midlife crisis, it was Matthew McConaughey, and she felt too much loyalty to *ER* to even start on *Grey's Anatomy*. If she were a Crayola crayon, she'd be Blue Bell, and if she were a kind of weather, she'd be the rain when it spits. She couldn't even remember her natural hair color, and she twirled spaghetti, not cut it, and if she knew the world was ending tomorrow, she would go out and eat a whole pecan pie and not care if it gave her a migraine.

Jane didn't know if Raelynne preferred her men shy and inexperienced, but she hoped so. They all hoped so. If only Raelynne could see past Jimmy's deficits to the deeply kind and honorable man who dwelt inside.

Jimmy didn't go to Kilwins every night, because Duncan had told him to skip nights here and there, so Raelynne would wonder where he was. But Jimmy should be careful not to pick the same days every time, Duncan warned, or Raelynne would think he had another girlfriend, a girlfriend who had book club on Sunday nights, for example. (Jane gave him another look; *her* book club met on Sundays, and always had.) Jimmy worked out a whole schedule and consulted Jane—did it look random enough? Raelynne wouldn't think he had a girlfriend, would she?—before he carefully circled the dates on the kitchen calendar.

After Jimmy helped Raelynne close the store, they would put his bicycle in the backseat of her car and drive to her house. Jimmy said she had fixed up the mobile home so nicely you'd never guess it wasn't a real house, with rainbow-colored wall hangings and braided rugs, embroidered furniture with fringed pillows, colorful velvet footstools and scented candles everywhere. (Aggie told Jane it sounded like a fire hazard and was almost certainly in violation of HUD standards.) Jimmy said that as soon as they got to Raelynne's house, she smoked a cigarette—Jimmy said he worried no end about her smoking but that she had cut down to two a day—and changed from her Kilwins uniform into jeans and a sweatshirt. (Jane and Freida hoped Raelynne would change into something sexier, but so far she hadn't.) And then she'd make a cup of coffee with a quarter-stick of butter melted into it and a tablespoon of protein powder sprinkled on the top—she told Jimmy this made up for having skipped dinner—and they'd watch a movie. Raelynne watched more movies than anyone Jane had ever met. *Titanic, Dirty Dancing, 10 Things I Hate About You, The Breakfast Club, When Harry Met Sally, Groundhog Day, The Wedding Singer, Notting Hill, That Awkward Moment, The Perks of Being a Wallflower, Tangled.* One after the other. Surely it was a good thing she liked romantic comedies so much? Didn't it show she hungered for love?

When the movie was over, Jimmy would bike home. (After an enormous amount of debate, everyone had decided that Jimmy should tell Raelynne he was saving up for a car, rather than tell her outright that he didn't have a license. Freida was a holdout, insisting that Jimmy should say he bicycled to reduce his carbon footprint. But it didn't matter in the end because Jimmy said that Raelynne never asked.)

But—but—what happened between the movie ending and Jimmy getting on his bicycle? This was what they were all dying to know. Jimmy had reported that he and Raelynne hugged when he got to

Kilwins, and hugged again when he left her house. He said he was getting better at hugging, which made Jane feel as though someone were pinching her insides. He said they watched TV sitting side by side on a loveseat covered with an Indian-print throw blanket, and the loveseat had broken-down springs so they sort of naturally sank toward each other, and once Raelynne had fallen asleep with her head on his shoulder and her hair had smelled like Strawberry Chunk ice cream and now that was his favorite flavor. But they hadn't kissed yet, and everyone agreed privately that Raelynne should be the one to initiate that. And surely she would. No woman had a man over for so many movies and hugs without *some* romantic intent.

"I think you should have a talk with Jimmy," Jane said to Duncan one afternoon as they weeded the flower bed. The girls and Jimmy were inside watching *Finding Nemo* for at least the seven-hundredth time, and Patrice was brushing Glenn's hair. Patrice loved anything that had to do with grooming Glenn—brushing her hair, putting calamine lotion on her mosquito bites, massaging her cuticles. Jane thought Patrice would make a very good gorilla. But then Jane would make a good gorilla, too, or maybe a wolf: she could scent the air of any room and tell which family member had passed through most recently. She could smell not just their shampoo and soap, but the personal odors they seemed to emit—Duncan's trace of hickory smoke, Glenn's tang of peppermint, Patrice's hint of bitter lemon. They all had a very faint smell of pencil shavings.

Duncan threw some weeds in the old white bin they used for yard debris. "What sort of talk?"

"About sex," Jane said. "I'm sure he doesn't know the first thing about it."

Duncan didn't say anything for a long moment. When he spoke, his voice sounded tight. "Jim knows about sex. A little, anyhow."

Jane stopped weeding and looked at him. He looked very serious, very solemn—sober in the nonalcoholic sense. "What do you mean?" she asked softly.

Duncan sighed and leaned over to turn on the spigot. He picked up the hose and fiddled with the nozzle setting. "A long time ago when he worked at the feedstore, the cashier there—a girl named Chantilly—took Jim home with her after work. She wanted to make her husband jealous, though she didn't tell Jim that. She got him to drink most of a bottle of rosé and then led him into the bedroom and they got into bed together and they had sex."

"Actual sex?" Jane asked. "Honest-to-God sex?"

Duncan nodded. "Her husband was out playing poker and she wanted him to come home and find her in bed with someone else." He began to water the flowers. "Chantilly—Chantilly—from what I heard later, she wanted to be on top so that when her husband got home, he'd see she was doing it willingly, that he wouldn't think she was being raped and shoot Jim. Nice girl, huh? Nice of her to look out for Jim. So anyway, her husband comes home and sees them, and he didn't shoot Jim but he roughed him up quite a bit, blackened one of his eyes."

Jane's hand rose to her mouth. "That's terrible."

"Chantilly's husband threw Jim out in the yard and threw his clothes after him," Duncan said. "Jim had to go to a neighbor's and call his mother to come get him. Word was all over town by the next morning."

Jane couldn't speak. She could only stare at the faint rainbow that had appeared where Duncan was spraying water. Odd how rainbows could go on appearing when there was so much evil in the world that Jane could barely comprehend it.

She left Duncan standing with the hose and dragged the waste bin out to the curb, her mind spinning. The air seemed to flicker in front of her.

This was almost certainly why Duncan hated rosé, had hated it since before she met him. Jane sighed and wiped the moisture from her face with the back of her hand. But maybe—maybe what had happened before was actually a good sign, in a cosmic sort of way? It couldn't be that Jimmy would go all his life having terrible things happen to him, could it? Not someone as kind and loving as Jimmy. The universe would not allow it, and neither would Jane.

JANE'S MOTHER visited every year on the last weekend in June. She said the rest of the summer was too hot for her liking, and the winters were too brutal, and she'd never cared all that much for the autumn. So every year, Duncan drove the three hours to Grand Rapids and picked her up, and then drove all the way back to Boyne City. The official reason for Duncan doing this instead of Jane was that Jane got carsick if she drove for that long, but the actual reason was that Jane dreaded her mother's visits so much that she probably would have turned the car around before she got to Cadillac. Jane didn't know how Duncan could make the drive so willingly. He was such a good husband, so much better than most people realized.

"You're so nice to do this," she said now, leaning down to kiss him as he sat in his armchair in the living room.

"I don't mind when your mother visits." Duncan pulled her onto his lap. "Because it means you and I have a lot of sex."

Jane frowned. "What are you talking about?"

"What are *you* talking about?" Duncan said. "It's always been this way. You have a lot of sex with me before she gets here and for however long she stays. I think it's your way of softening me up."

A silent film clip ran through Jane's mind then, an odd flickering vision of college boyfriends and later lovers who had always seemed to look forward to her mother's visits with puzzling eagerness. Well, everything in life had a price, she supposed, and you were constantly paying it.

Duncan left the next morning and returned with Jane's mother in the midafternoon. Jane and the girls came out to the driveway to greet them.

Jane's mother struggled out of the van, hitching her purse strap up on her shoulder. She was in her mid-eighties now. Her hair was whiter and more finely spun, her face had taken on the texture of wrinkled paper, she had broken capillaries and liver spots, and she moved more stiffly—but her personality, her essential self, remained the same (unfortunately).

"Hi, Grandma," Glenn said.

"Hello, Glenn," Jane's mother said. "Hi, Patty."

Patrice began chuffing softly, like an animal getting ready to charge.

"She really, really prefers to be called Patrice," Jane said.

"Well, she needs to learn the art of compromise." Jane's mother slammed the van door shut. "The world doesn't always work the way you want it to. You have to be flexible."

Duncan was getting Jane's mother's suitcase out of the back of his van, and he smiled sardonically at Jane when her mother said that.

"Did you bring us presents?" Glenn asked. "Grandma Harriet brings us presents."

"Goodness, no," Jane's mother said. "It seems to me that you girls have more than enough possessions already."

Some people speak to children like they're adults and it's charming and respectful, and then there was Jane's mother.

Glenn paused delicately. "It's just that we really like presents."

"Well, you can't always have your heart's desire," Jane's mother said.

Duncan tossed his keys from one hand to the other. "I'd better go to the shop and see how Jimmy's getting along."

Jane knew that Jimmy was undoubtedly playing solitaire at the shop, and Duncan would either join him or take a nap in the back room, but she was so grateful to him for driving her mother up that she just smiled.

She and the girls led her mother inside and helped her settle into Jimmy's room. (Jane's mother could no longer climb stairs easily and said it would be a fine mess if she fell down the stairs and broke her hip and had to stay three months while she recovered. She could be oddly persuasive.) Jimmy was going to sleep on the couch.

Jane was touched by how excited the girls were to have her mother visit, although she suspected Glenn was still hoping for presents. If only more people brought presents with them! The world would be a better place. But Jane's mother did seem to be making an effort and agreed to play *Life* with the girls while Jane did the lunch dishes.

Jane's mother played much like Gary. "Recycle trash!" she said, squinting at the board. "What if I don't believe in recycling?" And "Adopt twins! I would never sign on for twins. Don't I have any say in it?"

The girls giggled, and Jane's mother seemed to be enjoying herself. Maybe, Jane thought, you could only like playing *Life* when you didn't actually have much of one.

"Car crash, pay fifteen thousand dollars if not insured," Jane's mother read. "Goodness, it must have been serious."

It seemed to Jane that the sunny kitchen cooled for a moment, chilling her. The accident that killed Jimmy's mother could never be left behind. It followed her everywhere.

"Grandma, do you want to go to Kilwins and see Jimmy's girl-friend?" Glenn asked.

"Heavens, Jimmy has a girlfriend?" Jane's mother sounded startled.

"Yes, she works at Kilwins," Glenn said. "And she has the most beautiful peacock-feather earrings." The girls thought Raelynne was gorgeous and exotic and had the dream job.

"Of course, I'd love to meet her," Jane's mother said. "Let's go on down and have a look-see."

Jane dried her hands on a dish towel and came out to the living room. "You can't say anything to her, though, Mom."

"Like what?"

"Like anything."

"How'm I going to order a cone?" her mother asked in a jolly voice. "Sign language?"

"You can order a cone," Jane said patiently, "but you can't say anything about Jimmy."

"Oh, honestly, dear, why are you always so sure I'll embarrass you?"

Because she always did. But Jane didn't say that. Instead she loaded everyone in the car and drove to Kilwins. Maybe coming to look at Raelynne would be a thing she did with visitors now, instead of going to the South Pier Lighthouse in Charlevoix.

Kilwins was busy, as always. Raelynne was working in the candy section, but she saw them and came over to the counter when it was time for them to order.

"Hi, Jane!" she said. "Hey, girls." She was wearing the same khaki shorts and magenta polo shirt as the other employees, but on her the colors seemed lusher, richer. Her blue eyes were enormous and her lips were like plump pink pillows. "What can I get you all?"

"Now, let me see," Jane's mother said. "I'm in the mood for something sweet, but not bland. What do you recommend?"

"Oh, for heaven's sake." Jane gave her a hard look. "Just get Peppermint Stick like you always do."

"I'm looking to expand my horizons." Jane's mother was using that jolly voice again. "Can I try the Butter Pecan?"

Raelynne was helpful as always, handing Jane's mother various tiny tastes and remembering that Patrice wanted the kiddie scoop but would start yelling if anyone actually *called* it a kiddie scoop.

Jane's mother decided she would have Peppermint Stick after all. Raelynne flipped from beautiful to ugly and back again twice while ringing up their purchases. It was very disconcerting.

As soon as they were outside, Jane's mother said, "Her facial features are too large. She looks like a marionette."

"Mom, honestly—"

"Also, she didn't strike me as terribly bright."

"You exchanged five sentences with her!"

They began walking back to the car. Her mother continued in a reflective tone. "I suppose the lack of intellect wouldn't be a drawback as far as Jimmy's concerned. I imagine you'd love for him to get married and move out."

"Jimmy's not going to marry Raelynne," Jane said irritably. In the past she had occasionally imagined Jimmy getting married and moving away, had imagined a life with just her and Duncan and the girls, but it had been years since she'd thought about that and it annoyed her now to be reminded. Anyway, marriage was not the goal here; she just wanted Jimmy to know love, to have love reciprocated.

"No, I suppose he'll live with you forever," Jane's mother said cheerfully. "It was bound to happen anyway."

"What do you mean?"

"Well, his mother was old and in poor health long before the accident, wasn't she?"

Jane frowned. "I can't really remember." She wondered if that was how her mother justified things to herself—that Mrs. Jellico had been hovering on the brink of death anyway, so what was the harm, really?

"It seems to me she was," Jane's mother said. "And after she was gone, someone would have had to take Jimmy in eventually."

Jane stopped walking so abruptly that Glenn stepped on her heels.

"Keep walking, Mom," Glenn said. "And Patrice is getting chocolate all over herself."

"I am not!" Patrice cried, furious. "Just on my shorts and shirt and shoes."

Jane scarcely heard them. She had never realized before that Jimmy's mother would have gone on to die of natural causes. She had thought—however unrealistically—that but for the accident, Mrs. Jellico would still be living in the dingy green house, making Jimmy's lunch in the ancient yellow kitchen. How had she never thought of this before? Would Jimmy have eventually come to live with her and Duncan anyway? Was it possible that Jane's whole life *didn't* lead back to that one event?

"I myself believe I've lived so long due to my lifelong avoidance of alcohol," Jane's mother said. "That, and I always vote for whichever presidential candidate seems most likely to win. It has saved me untold disappointment."

AFTER DINNER THAT NIGHT, Jane put the girls to bed and took a shower while Duncan and her mother sat out on the back deck. She was still awake and reading when Duncan came up to the bedroom. He dropped onto the bed and leaned back, not even bothering to take off his shoes. His head hit the pillow heavily.

"Your mother is getting scarily candid," he said, staring at the ceiling.

Jane put down her book. "Please don't tell me things I can never un-hear."

Duncan ignored her. He continued staring at the ceiling in a dazed way. "She told me menopause was the best thing that ever happened to her, and that it would be for you, too. Said it was positively liberating to be free from the mood swings and the bloating."

Jane stroked the hair back from Duncan's forehead. "I'm so, so sorry."

"She told me in later years her 'flow' got very heavy," Duncan said, still in that soft, almost marveling voice. "Her 'flow,' that's what she actually said."

"Oh, sweetie."

"She said it wasn't the blood itself she minded so much, it was the *smell*," Duncan continued. He had the bewildered air of a natural-disaster survivor. "I honestly think I may never be the same again, and the back deck is ruined for me now."

It seemed to Jane that Duncan *was* different—diminished some-how, weakened. She doubted it was permanent, but she understood how the world (especially in the form of her mother) caught up to you sometimes, and left you frail and defenseless.

She got out of bed and eased Duncan's shoes off his feet. She turned off the lights and helped him undress, and then she made love to him, softly, gently, in silence. Partly to remind him that he was resilient and loved and essential to all their lives, and partly because, you know, her mother was visiting.

JANE'S MOTHER went home two days later, on Sunday. Duncan drove her and although he seemed to be his usual cheerful self, Jane noticed that he left right as the Tigers game began and told her mother that he wanted to listen to it without interruption all the way to Grand Rapids.

Jane and the girls began their summer in earnest. And in the three weeks that followed, they did all the usual summer things—beaches and playgrounds and parks and McDonald's—and other, more unique outings, too.

Raelynne had suggested they go to the Kilwins Chocolate Factory

Tour in Petoskey, where Patrice turned out to be the ten-thousandth visitor. A little sort of siren went off when she handed in her tour ticket, and at the end of the tour, the factory owner presented her with a special gift basket of chocolates and a teddy bear. Channel Nine was there to film it. The teddy bear turned out to be blue—a *boy's* color—and Patrice had a meltdown on local television. (The chocolates sure were good, though.)

They went to Avalanche Bay waterpark on a rainy day, and Jane chased doggedly after the girls—splashing through tepid water, sweating profusely in the tropical atmosphere, head aching from the sound of rushing water—amazed, as always, that she actually paid money to do so. This year was the first year Glenn was tall enough to ride the Vertigo Cannonbowl, which she did while Jane watched, cheering proudly, and Patrice watched, pouting jealously.

They went to tumbling class, where Glenn graduated to Level Two, and on the way home, Patrice let out a wail from the backseat and cried out, "I'm trying to be happy for Glenn, but I just can't do it!"

They drove to Williamsburg to visit the Butterfly Garden and an orange sulphur butterfly fluttered down to land on Patrice's outstretched hand. The butterfly was the same bright hot amber color as Patrice's eyes, and its wings beat slowly, almost in time with Patrice's blinks. After a long moment, it flew away and Patrice called softly, "Good-bye, beauty!"

Some occasions were magical, like that, and some occasions were the opposite of magical, whatever that is. Real, Jane supposed. (Life with small children is often real in a visceral, corporeal sense that people without children know nothing about.) This was like every summer, with times Jane thought she was the luckiest woman alive to be able to spend the summers with her children, and times she wished school were in session year-round.

But mainly she was happy to devote her days to summer pursuits, happy to see Duncan when he came home in the late afternoons, happy to have leisurely mornings when she didn't have to flog the girls over the getting-ready-for-school hurdles. She enjoyed the mornings so much that she began rising earlier than usual to make complicated breakfasts for her family in the bright, pine-paneled kitchen. But before she went to the kitchen, the first thing Jane did every morning was creep quietly to Jimmy's room and peek through the door to see if his bed was occupied. It always was, and Jane always felt a pang of disappointment. She supposed it was the opposite of what she would feel when Glenn and Patrice were teenagers; then she would want nothing more than to know they had returned in the night.

Only once did she find Jimmy's bed empty. Her heart rose briefly, but when she looked outside for his bicycle, she saw that Jimmy was asleep on the porch swing. She opened the door and stepped out quietly. Jimmy stirred and looked up at her. His hair was spiky as a hedgehog's spines.

"What are you doing out here?" Jane asked gently.

"I forgot my key," he said, sitting up and stretching. "I didn't want to ring the doorbell and wake everyone."

Jane sat beside him in her bathrobe. "Did you have a good time at Raelynne's last night?"

Jimmy smiled shyly. "She called me her *guy*," he said. "The manager, Mr. Vickery, stopped by as we were closing up and looked at me and said to Raelynne, 'Who's that?' and Raelynne said, 'Why, that's my guy,' and Mr. Vickery said to me, 'Aren't you Jimmy Jellico? It seems to me you did some yardwork at my house years ago,' and I said, 'Yes, sir, but you all let me go after I knocked your birdbath over with the lawn mower—'"

There was more, but Jane didn't listen. My guy! What a lovely phrase! How well it summed up Jimmy, how well it summed up his relationship to Raelynne. She couldn't wait to tell Freida and Aggie.

Eventually, Jimmy sort of ran out of steam and stopped talking, but Jane didn't mind. It was enough just to sit with him on the porch, looking at the dew sparkling on the grass and the sun shooting biblical-looking rays of light through the pine trees. She should sit out here more often early in the morning. She and Duncan could have coffee here, start their day with calm and beauty. But she knew it was one of those things—like Sunday afternoon drives and mother-daughter yoga class and vacuuming the refrigerator coils—that she would think about but never actually do again, and that made it all the sweeter.

IT WAS NOT FOR NOTHING that Jane taught second grade. On the August evening Jimmy came home from Kilwins early, she knew just from the way he was walking, pushing his bike slowly—just from the way he had his free hand crammed in his pocket—that something bad had happened. She was off the porch swing and across the lawn before Duncan had even set down his beer.

"What is it, Jimmy?" she asked, putting her hand on his arm.

"Nothing," Jimmy said, and then as though two seconds were all the dishonesty he was capable of, he added, "Except that Raelynne has a boyfriend."

Jane heard Duncan come up behind her and felt his arm around her waist.

"His name is Mason," Jimmy said. "And Raelynne said she wanted to introduce me special. She said, 'Mason, this is Jimmy, the friend I was telling you about. And Jimmy, this is Mason.'"

"Maybe Mason's just a friend, Jim," Duncan said.

Jimmy shook his head. "I could tell from the way she said it. Just his name, nothing after it."

Oh, Jane knew all about men who were so superior, you didn't add the identifying phrase. Men you loved so much it would only diminish them to refer to them by those common terms—*boyfriend, lover*—that other people used. Jimmy was right.

"And he looks good in a cowboy hat and he works in construction and he only went to Kilwins once in his whole life!" Jimmy's eyes were damp and his voice shook. "And the worst part is she asked me to come home and watch a movie with them. With *both* of them."

Jane's heart cramped. Your heart was a muscle, right? Hers had a charley horse.

"Why don't you come on and sit on the porch, Jim?" Duncan said softly.

"No," Jimmy said heavily. "I think I just want to go to bed."

"Have a beer with us," Duncan urged. "Or we could all do something, drive over to the lake, maybe."

"Yes," Jane said unsteadily. "Stay with us."

Jimmy shook his head. "I just want to go to sleep."

"Well." Duncan's voice was thick. "See you in the morning, I guess."

They watched him go into the house. He pulled open the screen door as though it were a boulder he had to roll out of the way, and his footsteps made heavy thudding sounds on the floor inside.

Jane and Duncan looked at each other helplessly.

If only Jane could tell Jimmy it was Opposite Day, or promise him a Popcorn Party, or tell him he could skip the spelling homework and have him feel better instantly. Second grade didn't prepare you for heartbreak, she thought bitterly. Nothing prepared you for heartbreak, although high school probably came the closest.

JANE WAS SO UPSET that night that after the girls and Jimmy were in bed, she and Duncan called the Wilcox's youngest daughter over to babysit and went to the Sportsman. Jane ordered vodka-and-cranberry-juice spritzers, something that usually cheered her right up. But not tonight—occasional tears ran down Jane's cheeks and plopped onto the scarred wooden bartop.

Banjo was bartending, and obviously seeing Jane cry made him uncomfortable. He set their drinks on the bar gingerly with his arm extended fully, like someone setting down a grenade, and then he busied himself washing glassware as noisily as possible. Otherwise the place was empty, except for a young couple poring over their selections on the jukebox.

One of the very nice things about Duncan was that women's tears did not make him want to leave the room. (Although maybe that was because he'd caused so many women to cry.)

"Honey, it'll be okay," he said, squeezing Jane's shoulder.

Jane shook her head and blew her nose on a cocktail napkin. "I just wanted this so badly for him."

"I know."

"He deserves to be happy, and I don't think he ever will be."

Duncan thought for a moment. "Maybe he *is* happy, though. Maybe Raelynne would have made him *happier,* but he still has us, his family."

A tear splashed into Jane's drink, and she shook her head again. You needed romantic love to be happy—it was right up there with garlic bread.

Duncan pulled his barstool closer to hers and put his arm around her. "You'll see," he said. "I'll give Jim a promotion, and we'll go walleye fishing, just him and me, and he'll be good as new."

Good as new? Was Duncan crazy? Jimmy would never be new, never be the same. How could Duncan not realize that every time you fell in love and it didn't work out, it scraped out a little piece of you, like scooping out a piece of cantaloupe with a melon baller, and there were only so many times that could happen before the scoop marks started to show? That in really no time at all, your heart could become a cold, pockmarked stone?

The jukebox clunked, and Jane heard the sound of a record dropping. The young couple returned to their table. The song that came on was a strange combination of boisterous music and slow female vocals. Jane leaned her head against Duncan's shoulder and listened. At first, she thought it was a love song, but slowly she realized it was something more profound, and that it could have been written for her. Her and Jimmy.

> *If things are going wrong for you,*
> *You know it hurts me too.*

The last note of the song played and then hung there in the stale, beery air, fading softly until finally until there was nothing left but the faint hiss of static.

BUT ODDLY ENOUGH, Duncan was right. Jimmy was moody and withdrawn for a day or two, and he stopped going to Kilwins completely, but after a while he did seem as good as new, or at least as good as he was before. Well, except sometimes, Jane caught Jimmy with a faraway, melancholy look, as though contemplating a desolate and lonely future. Though it's possible she was just projecting her own heartbreak, her own devastation.

Jane's world had not gone cold and gray; quite the opposite. The world had become too brightly colored, garish almost. Reds were now bloody, greens were turquoise, all yellows were yolk-colored, pink and lavender had failed to exist, and even the blue of the lake was harsh and squint-making. Sounds were too loud, and smells as strong as they'd been during her pregnancies. It seemed as though some outer protective layer had been peeled off, and now Jane's entire self was like the raw skin under a scab.

No one else seemed to understand the depth of Raelynne's betrayal, or to show anything beyond the most superficial sympathy. When Jane told Aggie about Raelynne's boyfriend, Aggie said, "Oh, poor Jimmy! I'm going to make some apple fritters and bring them over right away." Apple fritters? This kind of hurt went beyond apple fritters! But Jane supposed anyone who was married to Gary wouldn't understand that. Even Freida seemed lacking in sympathy. "That is the worst," she said to Jane. "Once, I waited nearly a week for a man to call me back, and when the phone finally rang, it was a man who'd found my purse at the library. I thought I'd never get over it. But Jimmy will find someone worthy of him. I just know it." They were all as bad as Duncan.

Only Patrice seemed to understand. When Jane told her gently that Jimmy wasn't friends with Raelynne anymore, Patrice threw herself on her bed with a wail of anguish and refused to be comforted.

"She's just overtired, I think," Jane said to Duncan in the kitchen.

"*I am not overtired!*" Patrice shrieked from upstairs.

"She really is," Jane said, and then had to stop and tilt her head, listening. Who had just spoken? Was it Jane's own mother, throwing her voice from Grand Rapids? Patrice was upset; let Patrice be the judge of why. At least she understood the seriousness of the situation.

And yet—and yet—no one could stop summer from continuing. Duncan took Jimmy to work, and Jane took the girls on outings. They drove all the way back from Sleeping Bear Dunes with Patrice saying, "Glenn is touching me again! She's touching me!" every ten seconds. They had Taco Tuesday. Gary tried pasta with white sauce for the very first time and liked it. ("How about that?" Jimmy said. "Isn't that something?") Aggie sold the old Hemple house to a man who raised ferrets and reported that the man himself looked so much like a ferret that she half expected him to hold the pen with both hands at the closing. Freida had a small dustup with a mandolin student who refused to learn the Compton grip. Mr. Hutchinson took a glass of tap water to the Health Department to have it tested, but the results came back negative for wild boar fecal material.

Only Jane seemed to realize that happiness had fled their lives along with Raelynne. Every night when she did the dishes, she thought of a particularly sorrowful song Freida had played once:

She clears the table and she scrapes the plates,
And sends the children off to bed!

Sometimes Jane wished Freida had never learned to play the mandolin. Those lines summed up the rest of Jane's life, the dreariness and repetition and futility. She would stand for long minutes at the sink, staring at her reflection in the kitchen window until her eyes were dry enough for her to turn around and face her family. She was doing exactly that one night when Duncan said, "It's beautiful out. We should go to—to the beach."

Jane knew he'd been about to say they should go to Kilwins. But the girls clamored excitedly about the beach and Jimmy seemed agreeable as always, so off they went.

They drove to a little public beach on Lower Lake Drive that Glenn had said once was like a doll's beach, everything was so small. One parking space, one picnic table, one tree. Only twenty yards of shoreline, but it was all the beach they needed. Glenn and Patrice had already been swimming earlier in the day, so they were content to wade in the water while Jane and Duncan and Jimmy sat on the table and watched the sunset.

The sunset had turned the sky a hostile orange, or perhaps that was just Jane's new vision. The sun seemed like an angry, pulsing ball, shooting lines of harsh vermillion light through the clouds.

The lake was a bright, hurtful blue, and the sun glinted off it, tossing sun dazzles as sharp as Chinese throwing stars.

Jane got up from the table to wander the beach. Jimmy followed her, picking up stones. She felt a sort of cellular-level sorrow and wondered if she loved more deeply than other people. Or was everyone else just more mature, more rational? More realistic? Maybe everyone else was right, and Jane was wrong. Maybe—

Glenn's excited voice interrupted her thoughts. "She's doing it! She's doing it!"

Jane looked up and saw Patrice turn a cartwheel. It was a wobbly, uneven cartwheel—if it had been an actual wheel on a cart, the ride would be exceedingly bumpy—but it was a still cartwheel, a genuine cartwheel.

"Oh, Patrice!" Jane whispered.

"Congratulations, sweetie," Duncan called, standing up from the table. "Do another one!"

Patrice turned another cartwheel, this one not so wobbly. And another. And another. The switch had flipped.

Glenn was hopping up and down and clapping, sibling rivalry momentarily forgotten. Duncan stood with his arms crossed, his body casting long, lean shadows on the sand, his look full of loving pride.

Patrice turned another cartwheel, her round face flushed, her hair a glinting auburn tangle.

"Did you see, Mommy?" she yelled. "Did you see me?"

"Yes!" Jane answered. "I saw you!"

Patrice shaded her eyes. "Did *you* see, Jimmy?"

"I sure did!" Jimmy called from behind Jane, and Jane turned to look at him.

He was smiling proudly, his face as sweet and open as a sugar cookie. He was so happy for Patrice, so happy for all of them, so delighted by their accomplishments. Could anyone else, ever, be so devoted and selfless? Maybe Jane *was* wrong; maybe she had been wrong all these years. She'd spent so much time either feeling responsible for Jimmy or feeling sorry for him that she'd forgotten to love him.

"Patrice can do a cartwheel, Jane!" Jimmy said. "She really can!"

Jane gave him a small smile. "How about that?" she said. "Isn't that something?"

Jimmy looked confused for a second, and then he laughed— the strong, easy laugh he so seldom used. Without thinking, Jane reached out and hugged him.

"Oh, hey, now." Jimmy's arms went around her, and he patted her shoulder awkwardly.

Jane closed her eyes and inhaled. He had his own smell, too— pine, and also, very faint, pencil shavings. Jimmy smelled like family. Why had Jane never realized that before?

Jane's chin didn't fit neatly into the dip of Jimmy's shoulder like it did on Duncan's—she had to turn her head sideways—but Jane kept hugging him anyway. She felt sure that if she could just stay like this for a moment longer, the harshness would fade. When she opened her eyes, the alien sun would be gone, the beach would be as softly colored as chalk dust. All she had to do was stay here and let Jimmy hold her. Just let him hold her until the world slowly righted itself, and she could go on.

Acknowledgments

THANK YOU

To Kim Witherspoon, for being the best agent ever. Period. To Felicity Rubinstein, for giving me courage when I had none. To Maria Whelan, for always having my back.

To my editor, Jennifer Jackson, for her unbelievable wisdom, encouragement, diligence, and kindness. (And, at times over the past year, for single-handedly restoring my belief that humans still do possess those qualities.) To Helen Garnons-Williams, for believing right from the start. To Maris Dyer for hand-holding beyond measure. I am forever in their debt.

To Patrick Walczy and Jennifer Close, for reading early drafts so willingly and so wisely, and for talking me off the writing-insecurity ledge so many times. I can never thank them enough.

To James Ohlson, Gary L. Aschenbach, Stephanie Agnew Kornoely, and Sean Ryan, for advising me on everything from law enforcement to folk songs. To Dede Roberts, especially, for her expertise on all things second grade.

To Jesse Woods, Big Harp, and First Aid Kit for generously lending their song lyrics to this book. I could not have written the novel I wanted to write without their music or their inspiration.

Acknowledgments

To my brother, Christopher Heiny, for being such an endless (and endlessly patient) source of helpful plot ideas. To my sons, Angus and Hector, for (literally when they were toddlers, metaphorically all the time) filling my life with song. And most of all, to my husband, Ian McCredie, for letting me take all the credit.

A NOTE ON THE TYPE

This book was set in a typeface named Bulmer. This distinguished letter is a replica of a type long famous in the history of English printing that was designed and cut by William Martin in about 1790 for William Bulmer of the Shakespeare Press.

Typeset by Scribe, Philadelphia, Pennsylvania

Designed by Anna B. Knighton